Ads for God

Also by Tony Vanderwarker
Writing With The Master
Sleeping Dogs

Forthcoming
Say Something Funny

Ads for God

A Novel by
Tony Vanderwarker

Jefferson Madison
Regional Library
Charlottesville, Virginia

Cedar Creek Publishing
Virginia, USA

This is a work of fiction. While some of the locations, celebrity and merchandising product names are real, the characters, circumstances, and dialogue are the product of the author's imagination. Any resemblance of fictional characters to persons living or dead is entirely coincidental.

All rights reserved. Outside of preview chapters in their packaged form, no portion of this book may be reproduced, stored in a retrieval system, or transmitted in any form or by any means–electronic, mechanical, photocopy, recording, scanning, blogging or other–except for brief quotations in critical reviews, blogs or articles, without the prior written permission of the publishers.

Copyright © 2015 by Tony Vanderwarker

Collaboratively published by:

(EBOOK)
AuthorsPress Publishing, LLC
Virginia, USA

(PRINT)
Cedar Creek Publishing
Virginia, USA
www.cedarcreekauthors.com
Facebook.com/CedarCreekPublishing
Twitter @VirginiaBooks
Pinterest.com/ccpublishing

Printed in the United States of America

ISBN 978-1-942882-00-8
Library of Congress Catalog Number 2015931096

For Matthew Weiner and the writers and cast of *Mad Men* who legitimatized advertising as a dramatic subject and paved the way for my novel.

1

My name is Dinsmore P. Rein, and this is the way I see it.

Either I'm dead or I've been in the advertising business too long.

So I sit on my doctor's examining table and look out at the angry lake, waiting for Dr. Poesemon to give me the verdict.

I make the appointment for my annual physical in February. That way, if Poesemon tells me I have liver cancer or lymphoma, I won't feel so bad about dying. In my mind, dying and spending February in Chicago aren't that far apart.

"Dinny, how are you?" Poesemon says, sliding through the pocket door into the examining room. Short, belly bulging between the buttons of his white doctor coat, Poesemon looks like a mole. With pink skin, squinty eyes and an elongated face, I've always thought Lester Poesemon M.D. would find his true calling five inches under Grant Park, quietly chewing on a crocus tuber with his little eyes clenched shut.

"Okay, Lester... I guess," guessing because I don't know any longer. I used to be a big deal at the agency. I used to be married. I used to be well respected. I used to be fairly affluent. Now I live in a walkup apartment in Wrigleyville, pay alimony to a wife with a trust fund as large as the Northern's, have a job that makes me feel like I have a noose around my neck, get called "Noodles" instead of by my proper name, and have an internist whose cold fingers are right now probing my neck for tumors.

"Everything feels fine here," Poesemon says, patting me on the shoulder. His pink nose twitches.

I'm vaguely disappointed. I can imagine Lester saying, "Oh dear, Dinny, I think we're going to have to send you over to Northwestern, I don't like the way this feels at all." If he said that, everything would be resolved. I would have a biopsy, then listen as the thirty-five-year-old oncologist who looks like a young Dick Cavett and wears Timberlands and a bright plaid tie from the Gap tells me the odds.

But my life isn't like that. Poesemon gives me a slap on my doughy belly, says, "Looks like there's a couple more good years in the old carcass yet," and adjusts his glasses and widens his eyes so he looks like a mole coming out of the ground, seeing light for the first time in weeks. "There's a couple more good years in the old carcass yet," he says again. Poesemon blinks and snorts. Thinks his joke is funny. Says it every year.

Used to be this, used to be that and there's a couple more good years in the old carcass left. See what I mean? Not a lot of evidence that I'm actually alive.

I snort back. Poesemon snorts again. His nostril hairs fluff out as the air pushes past them. We're trading snorts. The way I was brought up, trading snorts with your internist is not a positive indicator of life.

I say thank you to the pert nurse at the front desk who takes my check and I walk the old carcass back to the office. The wind whips pieces of newspapers up in front of the Tribune building and spirals them down the slope of Michigan Avenue. I lean into the wind and shake off a piece of newspaper hugging my ankle. The office is four blocks up Michigan. The sky is a cold gray. A cannon shot of blistering cold air fires down the avenue. The newspaper scraps run and hide.

Inside my topcoat, or inside my belly, something is going on. I have two choices: my cell phone is ringing or I have severe indigestion. I reach down into the pocket of my suitcoat and feel for the phone. I don't have indigestion. "Hello," I say, fumbling with the antenna, "hello?"

"Good morning," the voice says. *It's him again.* I stop, plant my feet firmly on the sidewalk, and yell into the phone. "Look, don't call me again."

"I'd like to talk with you, when you have a minute."

"Send your tape to me, and stop calling, good-bye!" I say and push the rubber button on the face of the phone. *Damn voice-overs are so pushy, call you at any time of the day or night. Heard you can make a hundred grand a year saying a few catchy phrases about antacids or tomato juice. Big baritone, with a swirl of Yiddish laced through, whistling around the vowels. Probably grew up in the Bronx, busted his ass on Broadway for forty years and now's trying to break into voice-overs. Figures he'll prey on the suckers in Chicago.*

Put the phone back in my suitcoat. Hate carrying it. Nobody has ever called me on my cell to tell me good news. "Your apartment was robbed," my secretary says over my cellular, or "The client hates the new rotini commercial," or I hear "You have to present to the sales force in Wichita tomorrow at seven." I'll probably get fired on the damn thing.

I dodge a bunch of tourists, pudgy in parkas, staring up at the crisscrosses on the John Hancock building, and barking away at each other in German. The wind makes my face feel like it's on fire.

In front of the building, the Polish super is Brassoing the company nameplate. His name's Woogie. I can never remember his last name—only that it has fourteen consonants in it, and he looks like Guy Lombardo. He's not wearing a coat. Won't even put one on until the wind/chill sign on the Playboy building goes below zero. "BFP&G Advertising" gleams. Woogie Brassos the nameplate so much, the granite around it is turning black.

"Morning, Mister," he says. He calls all the VP's "Mister."

"Morning, Woogie," I say, sissy-stepping to keep my heels from being eaten by the revolving door.

He's polished the nameplate by the elevator also. In the old days, the plaque used to spell out, "Boston, Frank, Pogue, and Gersenweser Advertising." For one month, it was going to read, "Boston, Frank, Rein, and Gersenweser Advertising." I have the layout somewhere in a drawer back at my apartment. The pictures of the founders line the walls of the elevator. Glass covering the photographs, their thin black frames securely screwed into the dark cherry paneling. The elevator feels like a London men's club—that's Benny for you.

Benny Boston was the art director, Frank Frank was his writer, and Gus Gersenweser was their account man.

Benny knew the three partners with their paunches, perpetual five o'clock shadows, and shiny suits looked more like a Catskill lounge act than advertising executives, so Benny did the first makeover in the history of the advertising business, renting outfits and taking the three of them on location for a week. I always wondered whether Ralph Lauren, who I heard had a cousin living on Michigan somewhere, got the inspiration for his Polo line from riding in this elevator.

Anyway, there's Frank, Benny, and Gus in their jodhpurs and hunting coats sitting on rented horses in Grant Park, looking to all the world like Virginia foxhunters. There they are at center court at Forest Hills in their tennis whites, standing in front of the Yale Bowl in raccoon coats toasting each other with silver flasks, and bundled in fur, big as bears, curling on a Wisconsin pond. If you'd asked Gus Gersenweser what curling was, he would have told you curling is what happens to hundreds when you leave a rubber band wrapped around them too long.

In the corner of the elevator, past the picture of the three partners posing with President Truman on the fantail of the Sequoia, are the pictures of Corny Pogue. Gersenweser created Cornelius Batters Pogue so they'd have their token Wasp, back when that mattered. Gus bought pictures of a fresh-faced Wasp chap at a second-hand shop, had them duplicated, framed, and mounted in the conference rooms, elevator, and dining room so the three founders could stand in front of the pictures and sigh to their Wasp clients about what a great guy Pogue was before he succumbed to the freezing waters of the North Atlantic after rescuing four members of his sub crew.

"We might be peddling noodles and dog food, kid," Benny used to tell me. "But you always gotta remember," he'd say, shaking his index finger which was always burnt umber or cerulean from the oil pastels he drew with, "you gotta remember—this is a glamour business."

Frank, Benny, and Gus built a successful agency off the pictures of their concocted pasts, their combined talents, and two accounts: a family-owned noodle business and the first semi-moist dog food. They were going to make me a partner, going to slip my name in where Pogue's was, make it "Boston, Frank, Rein, and Gersenweser Advertising," until the other deal came along. Now they're in Florida, and I'm stuck handling the Sirini and Woof!Burger accounts while the rest of the agency goes on without me.

"Noodles!" someone screams as the elevator door opens. It's a cocktail party at ten-thirty in the morning. Lobby packed with people. Noise comes at me like a hot wind. A short girl in ruby Spandex wearing a Roy Rogers belt and holster and holding two Bloody Marys steps out of the swarm. "Noodles, have a drink," she says, pushing a plastic glass toward me. Her name is Rosemary. She's an art director, and her skirt is split up to her waist. She wears fat black horn-rims like Woody Allen, and her hair looks like she stuck her finger in a socket. I take the drink. A slice of pink lace flashes behind her holster. Rosemary is wearing neon-pink lace panties and packing a toy gun.

"Hot visual, huh, Noodles?" Rosemary asks, catching me looking at her panties, sliding back the holster to give me the total effect. Her legs are muscled like the statue in Lincoln Park of the guy holding the world on his back.

"Hot, Rosemary," I say, admiring the wedge of leg she's showing me. Art directors are like that. Everything is a "visual." Those aren't her neon-pink panties framed by her hardbody little legs I'm looking at, that's a "visual."

Rosemary winks, draws her Roy Rogers pistol and shoots me. The pistol clicks, she giggles, drops the flap of her skirt and I squeeze into the crowd, smiling back at Rosemary of course—always have to stay popular in the advertising business.

A computer-generated sign hangs on the back wall. "We're high on American Distillers," it reads. Agency people think in slogans and talk in one-liners, though you've probably figured that out already. I look around. Twenty minutes ago, I was sitting on a cold metal table in my underpants, now I'm carrying a drink walking around what looks like a cast party from a Fellini movie and a Peat Marwick summer outing combined. Circus freaks and certified public accountants. Brooks Bros. pin stripes and Levi's with more rips than fabric. Young female account executives in pale wool suits and Pappagallos looking like they stepped out of *Town & Country* talking to ponytailed copywriters wearing second hand denim coveralls over bare skin, ready to take off for the Dead concert at the Rosemont Horizon as soon as work is over.

Someone's got a joint going, I can smell it. The lobby sounds like Soldier Field before a Packers game. A Busby Berkeley girl from the Land Beyond O'Hare wearing her hair in tight chrome curls slinks up with a tray of drinks. Velvet bodice, milk-white skin, fishnet hose and a short skirt shooting out horizontally from her hips, five ounces of eyeliner loaded on her lids, a printed sign on the tray reading: "Thunder Bay Gin turns a gimlet into a ginlet."

"Try a ginlet?" she coos. I put the Bloody Mary down on her tray, take a ginlet, and ask, "You work here?" I see Rosemary over by the elevator showing her underpants to a tall Account Director whose name I can never remember, except I know he works on Steigerlager beer and looks like a young William F. Buckley.

"No, I'm with the caterer," the Busby Berklette answers, flashing her fat and webby lashes at me. "But I'm getting my book together. You in Creative?" She moves the tray around to her hip so she can come closer.

"Isn't everyone?" I say.

"When I get my book together, will you look at it?" she asks, winking and squeezing her arms against her body so the white slopes of skin well up in her bodice.

"Sure," I say, starting to walk away. I can't take women with hip-high skirts and homogenized skin coming on to me with their books that early in the morning. "Noodles! It's Noodles!" my name bounces around the fringe of the crowd assembled in the lobby.

"That your name—Noodles?" she calls to me.

"That'll do," I shout back over my shoulder. People don't usually call me "Noodles" to my face unless they are drunk. Which everyone is. Even Sinkle is drinking. I catch him over on the edge of the crowd. He calls and waves me over. People slap me on the back and "Noodle" me as I shoulder and excuse myself through the lobby, smiling like I'm running for office, walking gingerly, trying to keep my ginlet from sloshing out of the wide glass.

I'm a curiosity around BFP&G, a holdover from the old days of the company, a war-baby relic who can remember iceboxes, Eisenhower and listening to Jack Benny on the radio, a genuine antique, since everyone in the ad biz these days seems to be healthy-haired, tight-bodied and twenty-nine or under. I'm fifty-five, with white temples, shoulder slump, and a jelly-donut belly.

Ester is beside Sinkle. Three buttons of her blouse are unbuttoned, and her arm is draped over his shoulders. She's hanging off him, her mouth open in a big laugh. She's the only one in the agency who can have a dog in the office, a little gray drop-kick dog that toddles along after her on a red leather leash. Dog's name is Mort, go figure. Mort's got a chip on his shoulder, snarls at everyone and pisses all over the place. I wave lamely at the terrible threesome. Ester hee-haws, Mort snarls, Sinkle chortles. Sinkle's smile is wider than usual. *Oh boy, ten o'clock in the morning and the entire agency is on its ass.*

"Dinny, did you hear? We got American Distillers, twenty-eight million bucks. I just called the boys in Florida," Sinkle says as I walk up to him. "They're down there enjoying a Bloody Mary with us even as we speak."

I bet they are. Benny, Frank, and Gus, sitting on their cabin cruiser at the dock in Delray, drinking Bloody Marys with their wives, counting up the additional dinero Sinkle is going to be sending down to them in exchange for another wad of BFP&G stock.

"Congratulations, Steve," I say, trying not to grimace. Ester looks away and rolls her eyes. If I could see her dog's eyes, I bet they'd be rolling also, but they're buried under so much hair, it's a wonder the mutt doesn't walk into walls. Ester's seen my movie before, and it bores her. Ester's hair is mussed. She is swinging off Sinkle and stumbling around like she's reached her ginlet quotient. Ester Platt is the Creative Director. She's an eyeful. Looks like Sigourney Weaver after breast augmentation. Ester has wanted to change the creative on my accounts ever since she arrived at the agency. But she can't because the clients are wedded to them. So instead, Ester wants my head.

"Steve, let's find someone to talk to," Ester says, looking at me like I'm a clerk at the Motor Vehicle Bureau. "There's Panky, let's go talk to him." She drags the President and Chief Executive Officer away to talk to the Director of Strategic Planning, and I'm left standing against the wall with my gimlet, or ginlet, I guess it is.

The drink lady in the fishnets is squeezing her breasts together trying to get someone else to look at her book. Sinkle, Ester, and Panky are laughing. Mort is licking his crotch. My mouth is puckering so much from the ginlet it feels like it's going to turn inside out. Ester leans over and howls. Her ginlet slurps over her wrist. Her blouse flops open, and Sinkle's eyes bug out. She straightens up slowly, adjusts her blouse and smiles at Sinkle. Ester is a master at using her tits tactically.

Panky Durnberg is not interested in Ester's chest since he's grooving to the reggae that's constantly running through his head. Bob Marley and the Wailers play Panky's skull twenty-four hours a day. The music's had a definite effect on his posture over the years for his head rides like it's on hydraulic dampers, his backbone seems like it's made of aspic, and his shoulders and hips bob independently, like logs floating on active water. When Panky Durnberg walks by, you can almost hear the Wailers.

Panky is the chief planner, the agency strategist, and the developer of proprietary software that can accurately analyze and evaluate any piece of advertising and predict its effect on sales. He is Steve Sinkle's right hand man, brain trust, and a growing legend in the advertising business because of his predictor system. Panky's the main reason Sinkle got the chance to buy the agency from the founders. In the ad biz, Panky Durnberg is one hot commodity. All the other agencies are scrambling to develop competing software and "Durnberg it," has become the new watchword of BFP&G's clients.

Steve Sinkle boasts that one lobe of Panky's brain is equivalent to the aggregate brainpower of the entire ad business. Whether Panky's a true intellectual is an open question. He's more of an academic operator. The previous research director called him a "power nerd," before Panky pushed him out, but in the advertising business, he's Einstein. Panky plays the game by flaunting his doctorate from UC Berkeley and occasionally quoting Sanskrit in client meetings, alluding to his reading knowledge of the language.

People say Panky looks like Bill Gates except for the Gorbachev mark that slid down his forehead at birth, enveloping his left eye, making him look like he has half a hangover. His eyes are buggy and are surrounded by too-big glasses, and his hair's never combed, it's all bent over like a field of tall grass that's recently been rained on. He's skinny with sallow skin and wears black suits, tan desert boots, and a lime-green tie all the time. Studied scruffiness on a major power trip, for Panky's got at least six of the outfits, all the same.

Although it's hard to hate someone who looks like he's held together with string and gelatin, I hate Panky Durnberg, I really do.

Actually, I hate them all, I think, as I head back to my office carrying what's left of my ginlet in the pink-stemmed plastic glass—Sinkle, Platt, Durnberg, *I hate Murray the CFO, Bobby Plevis, the Office Manager—I hate the whole stinking bunch of them.* They hate me too. In the advertising business, that's what's called status quo.

"Hi, Bobby," I say as I pass Plevis in the corridor, carrying his pink plastic glass. Plevis is tottering mildly and has a stupid smile on his face from too many ginlets. Plevis is sixty-five and counts paper clips for a living. Could pass for Tweedledum if he had the right suit.

"Twenty-eight million bucks, how'd you like that, Reinny baby? That's no small change, huh?" He's toasting me as he waddles past.

"You got that right, Bobby," I say, turning into my office. Plevis is from before, like me, but Sinkle's turned him into a Stepford wife. Those who wouldn't sign up for a Sinklebotomy, Sinkle fired—except for me. Because I'm the keeper of the holy grail, the only one left who can write the ads for Sirini and Woof!Burger. The campaigns the clients love more than the agency, certainly more than me and more than Ester. Another reason why Ester wants my head.

Not that the Woof! or Sirini campaigns are great or even notable advertising, you've probably never heard of them. *Woof! is The Only Food Dogs Ask For,* and *Nobody Makes A Noodle Like Sirini?* See, I was right. They're what's known as regional brands and, unless you live in certain areas, they're as unknown as the name of the local telephone company that services Stergus, West Virginia, which is where I grew up.

Ads for God

I hear Plevis slam into the drywall as he stumbles around the corner. Dull thud and then I hear him say "Shit" as his ginlet slops all over the place. I pick up my lacrosse stick and push the buttons for my voicemail. The first is from Patti asking me if I want to have dinner at the new Greek place down by the train station. I check my watch, wondering if she's finished work. I'm about to call her when I hear the second message.

"Rein, get your butt over here quick. We got problems with the radio," Margaret's voice barks over the speakerphone. Margaret Sirini is a fifty-something Wharton MBA with a huge chip on her shoulder. She's the marketing director for Sirini Pasta and has me sharply aligned in the sights of her corporate bazooka. When her siblings start paying attention to her, I'll get wasted. I don't lose sleep over it since the three Sirini brothers have ignored their sister for years, regularly calling her "Smartypants" and, when she gets nasty, "Sourpuss."

The third and fourth messages are also from Sourpuss. Her voice makes me wince. I speed dial her number, "Margaret, how are you?" I say, putting on my best "Isn't the world a beautiful place?" expression, hoping it seeps into my voice.

"I'd be fine if it weren't for your fucking advertising," she says.

"But it's the Chicago Symphony," I protest, wondering what problem the Sirinis could have with the Chicago Symphony playing the Sirini jingle. *Nobody Makes A Noodle* is Frank Frank's jingle, cleverly designed with a memory hook so it springs into people's minds at the oddest times.

The singers on the soundtrack keep repeating the last two syllables, "rini, rini, rini, rini, rini." Though Frank won't admit it, I know he had the seventeen-year locust in mind, the bug that burrows out of the ground on its own schedule and invades the air with swirling black hordes? For the jingle leaps into your head out of nowhere and runs around willy-nilly, permanently embedding the name of one pasta product into your brain cells, and incurring a minor amount of hostility in certain parts of the country. People have been known to take hammers to their radios, and even run their cars into trees, to get rid of the music. I can sympathize with them when I'm awakened at four in the morning with "rini, rini, rini, rini," honking like a horn through my head.

"I don't care if you hired Beethoven, the advertising's history," Margaret snarls, "and you'd better get your ass over here and tell us how you're going to replace it."

"Be there in twenty minutes," I say.

"What? You going to walk over here backwards?" she asks, referring to the fact that Sirini is seven blocks from our office.

"I've got a couple of things to clean up first. See you at eleven-thirty, Margaret."

"We'll be waiting for you," she says in a voice that Sitting Bull very well might have used before Custer rode off into the Little Big Horn.

I take my lacrosse stick, pick up a ball off my desk, drop it in the pocket, and hold my stick up, cradling the ball the same way the Plains Indians did three hundred years ago, shuttling the stick back and forth so the ball swings loosely in the webbing. I started playing lacrosse thirty-five odd years ago for Waverly, a small college just over the line in Pennsylvania. Crease attack.

My body was in post-adolescence and used to hiccup, one part rapidly moving away from the other, my hips shooting out or my torso hitching left, so it would inadvertently throw the defenseman off. My hips would stay put, but my legs juked like they were going to move. Or my shoulders would shift quickly as if I was going to run in toward the crease, and the D would go with it and milliseconds later would be out of position while I stayed in place and took the pass. Score. The net in the crease fluffs out as the ball bangs into it. Another goal for Dinny Rein, star crease attackman. I didn't know how to control the moves, they just happened, and I scored forty-eight goals my senior season.

I peek out my door down the hall. Coast is clear. I sprint down the hall and do a head fake to the corner, spin around it with my arms cradling like mad, my elbows knocking against the walls. Even with my jelly doughnut belly, I have a lanky body and arms so long the sleeves of my suitcoats, even if they are 44 long, make me look like I'm in seventh grade. I bang my back against the men's room door and roll inside. The action around the crease is like around the bar of a busy cocktail party. Head fake here, take him this way and come back quick. Fake a shot, back off, then come back quick again. Shoot and score. Moves. Moves. Moves. I had moves back then just like I had moves in advertising.

At thirty-two, I was one of the most successful creative directors in Chicago. Gave clients what they wanted, but my ads had moves. Although they looked standard, they won awards. I pulled in business for Benny, Frank, and Gus and made them rich enough to retire. They were going to make me...*I told you that already.*

Anyway, the change began around the time I turned forty-five. I started realizing my mouth was hanging open at times. The way a movie gangster stares down at his revolver when he realizes he's out of bullets. Like I was stunned by something but I had no idea what. I'd be in a new business meeting and Gus or Benny would turn to me and say, "Dinny, stand up and spitball a couple of ad campaigns for the LawnAid folks, would you?" I used to—*see, there I go again, I used to, I used to.*

Back when I had the moves, I'd stand up and act out five or six ad campaigns right off the top of my head. I'd give them a slice-of-life. I'd do a celebrity presenter for them, do George Burns talking about the merits of the LawnAid system—complete with the cigar. I'd whistle out a jingle and sing a new slogan for them. I'd come up with Rodney Dangerfield dressed in a brown grass suit saying "I don't get no respect" until LawnAid turned Rodney green again. I'd do twenty minutes on my feet stunning them with my imagination.

Then my mouth started dropping open. Benny would turn to me in a new business meeting and say, "Dinny, stand up and give us an idea of what you'd do with this account." My mouth would drop open. I'd stammer, say, "ah, ah, ah," and after four or five more new business meetings, Benny didn't ask any longer. Soon after, Steve Sinkle and his reggae software wizard took over the agency, and I was toast.

Standing in the men's room posing in front of the mirror with my lacrosse stick, I think of going back to Waverly for a thirty-fifth reunion last June and playing for the alumni team, scrimmaging against the varsity. Around the crease, the hiccups didn't happen any longer. I stood there with my defenseman stuck to me, dancing with him like Lester Lanin was playing for us on the sidelines, the D anticipating every move, staying with me step for step, slamming my stick down when I tried to hold it up for a pass, bending into me when I bent into him. I tried to cock my hips, shift my shoulders, but the nineteen year-old D with blond hair curling out of the back of his helmet and blue eyes, his shirt cut short so his stomach muscles showed, that kid was on me worse than glue.

I look in the mirror. Set the lacrosse stick on the floor. Pull the skin of my cheek down. Sagging, soft, but my eyes are sparkling. My face looks fine for fifty-five, it's my life that's a mess. All I have left is two accounts, and an ex-wife who hates my ass.

I take a piss looking over my shoulder. Looking at the closed doors of the three stalls, evenly spaced down the wall of the men's room. Three defensemen I have to get by. I poke myself back into my pants and zip up my fly. Pick up my stick. Check the scoreboard. The game is tied, seventeen seconds left. I drop one hand and move the stick behind my shoulder, the ball hanging easily in the pocket. I have to score. Spin and juke the first cubicle door, sliding my shoulder inside as it opens, pivoting inside, I bang into the far wall and come out of the stall spinning, loosely cradling my stick, turning into the next, kicking open the door, twirling along the wall, my loafers scraping over the tiles, Barishnykov in the bathroom.

I swirl out of the stall and duck in front of the mirror, slamming my foot back against the third door, flinging it open, quickly backing into the toilet, whipping back my stick and firing hard, streaking the ball by the goalie's right knee. His eyes drop, widen and watch the ball sail into the net before he can even lift his stick off the grass. The ball splashes into the toilet. The crowd bellows. Water drops sail back at me in slow motion.

My right foot shoots out and kicks the handle. I should have stopped right there because the toilet spits and gurgles like it's choking then suddenly upchucks the lacrosse ball in a cascade of water, shooting the ball up out of the stall over my head and sending it crashing into the mirror over the sink and it shatters and glass is clinking down all over the place. I'm standing halfway out of the toilet stall holding my lax stick with the pants of my light gray suit drenched like I've been swimming just as Steve Sinkle comes in carrying a ginlet and sees me and says "Having fun, Dinny?" like I've lost my mind.

And that, as I see it, is what my life in the ad business is like.

2

Ten minutes later, snowflakes are drifting down between the buildings, and I'm jumping slush and dodging cars, waving for a cab going the other way as I sprint across Michigan trying to get to my eleven-thirty at Sirini, dancing in and out of grooves cut in the slush by the passing cars, gobs of mush spitting up and clinging to my topcoat and pant legs. I figure I can hide my legs under the clients' conference table—at least my suitcoat is dry.

The cab pulls over to the curb to wait. The cabby takes a closer look at me and steps on it. No stinking slush on the fine vinyl of his backseat, he's thinking as he takes off up Michigan, his wheels spinning back gray slime. With what little cabbies make, it's a wonder they can be so picky. I flick a freezing dab off my cheek and decide to walk.

"Daddy," a voice says as I step onto the curb. She is always smiling, every time I see my daughter, Addy, she is smiling.

"How are you?" she asks and throws her arms around me. I hitch my hips out so she doesn't get slush all over her sunflower yellow coat and feel her warm hair against my cheek. She kisses me hard and takes my arm. Snowflakes glisten on her shoulders. I look at her. Addy has my height and thick, easy-going hair, and a face with the laugh lines already etched in so the smiles come easily.

Addy freely admits that she took the best from her mother and father and tossed the rest in the trash. "Didn't leave me much to work with, but somehow I made out okay," she jokes everytime I bring it up, spanking my hand and sparkling her eyes at me. She's shattered the glass ceiling at the bank and is scorching the career paths to the higher levels. Somebody who's seen her in action says she has a chance to be chairman someday. Fancy that. Girl whose mother floated around in a cloud of marijuana most of her life, vague as fog (Reavis is fifty-four now and still says "groovy"), and whose father used to...*never mind, you've heard enough of that already.*

"Where are you going?" she asks, looking at me like I've made her so happy. Then, looking down at my sodden loafers and my wet pants wrapped like spats around my ankles, she asks, "What happened, Daddy?"

"Oh, you know." I wave at my surroundings, blaming with one minor arm motion the entire Greater Metropolitan area, winter, the Midwest in general, cold winds, snow, and life.

"I keep thinking if I can just get through February..." she says, not scowling like most Chicagoans, but smiling. *Damn, the girl's always smiling. How'd she get that way? Must have been me, I must have been happy back then—it certainly wasn't her mother.*

"Walk with me, will you? I'm rushing over to Sirini," I say. Only thing about Addy is—despite her smiles—I worry that the girl doesn't have any fun. Works until nine, then goes to the gym, gets up at five, and, for fun on the weekends, runs a marathon or two with a bunch of other scrawny people.

Only hobby she has is cultivating wax begonias. Windowsills are a parade of primary colors, orange, yellow, red, blooms as big as dinner rolls, looks like Times Square with all the neon lights on fire. When she goes away on a business trip, I take care of her begonias for her. Water, feed, and play Mozart for them. They perk right up and positively start to glow when you put on that Mozart.

She used to have fun, Addy did, used to go out for quite a while with a guy named Carlos, Spanish racecar driver, sweet man and dead ringer for Jose Iglesias, killed in a big accident at Monte Carlo four years back. Everyone thought they'd get married. She watched his car lose it on a hairpin, crash through a barricade, flip over the crowd, and tumble down a hill into the harbor. She went to the funeral and never said another thing about him. I don't ask about her social life any longer. Last time I did she got quiet, her eyes went misty, and she waved the conversation away, shooing at the side of her head with her hand like she was brushing away cobwebs.

"A little ways at least," Addy says to me, slipping her arm further into mine. Not like we're going to be walking west toward Cabrini Green in the middle of a Chicago winter, but as if we're setting off together on a great adventure. *How about this daughter of mine, always making me feel like a million bucks? At least God isn't totally treating me like trash.*

"How'd you get so wet?" she asks, her eyes coming up from examining my spats again.

I put on my big smile and say, "I was playing lacrosse in the men's room and I scored big time on the toilet and it got pissed and drenched me, if you really want to know."

Addy shakes her head and snorts, pecks me on the cheek, I guess out of sympathy. It's one of the things I do, play the goofball for Addy so she doesn't think I'm so pathetic—I worry about that a lot. Has to be hard to see your daddy slip-sliding toward sixty with his career heading for the dumper, living in a drafty walkup with a leaky ceiling, cracked china, ratty rugs, and rumpsprung furniture, not even a junky car to his name any more.

"So how're things at the bank?" I ask.

"Good," she says, and I can tell she's toying with me again. *At least someone in the family's a success.*

"C'mon, let's have the truth."

"I think I'm getting promoted," Addy says, blushing. She has my green eyes and it's the damnedest thing looking at her close-up because I can see myself in her eyes. I can sweep away all that rosy tourist-poster Irishness my wife Reavis gave her and see in her Crayola-green eyes what little good there is left in Dinsmore P. Rein, the half-dead ad man.

"Promoted again?"

Addy nods her head and goes into a Class Five blush, which means her skin goes all the way to tomato and then comes back to flush again, even through the pads of makeup. It's her mother's Irish skin, but I don't mind because I'm so damn proud of her.

"Yup, first vice-president—brand-new job. I'll tell you about it sometime." I squeeze her to me and don't say anything because I can't. I'm getting a thick lump in my throat and a tear is swelling up to tidal wave size in the corner of my right eye. Addy catches it with a knuckle as it tumbles out and slides down my cheek. *She must be making over a hundred grand now, the girl will be chairman some day if she doesn't run herself ragged first.*

"I'm proud of you, girl," I say, squeezing her again. She says, "Thanks, Daddy. Now stop the tears before you soak your jacket too," taking a big wad of my cheek between her thumb and forefinger and giving it a healthy tug. We stop for a light and she kisses me, "I've got to go this way," she says, pointing down Ontario. "I'll call you. We'll have dinner, okay?" she says.

"Way to go—with the promotion," I say. She smiles over her shoulder. I wave good-bye and watch my daughter Addy disappear into the Michigan Avenue crowd. Sometime, I have to introduce her to Patti, my girlfriend who runs the show over at the Starlight Drive-In Clean Car Experience. Maybe they'd like each other.

Sirini is a couple blocks from Cabrini Green in a rundown area that used to be an Italian neighborhood before the projects went in. The Sirini building is two-stories high, a city block of yellow brick with glazed tiles on the facade illustrating the variety of pasta shapes made inside. Fusilli, rotini, macaroni, vermicelli, farfalle, penne, twenty-eight shapes in all. Many of the tiles are still left. All the doors are brown metal with small, chicken-wired windows to keep the gangbangers from breaking in.

I bang on the door, and Sidney, the Ukrainian security guard who looks like Lenin, peers out through the chicken wire. He nods and lets me in. Sidney wears quilted brown coveralls and a moth-eaten tan fedora. He lumbers back over to his card table, walking so slowly he looks like he could be pulling a barge, sits down at his Parcheesi board, and says, "Morning, Mr. Rein," in his world-weary, heavily-accented voice, the same way he has for eighteen years.

The place always smells like wet flour. The pistachio green paint on the walls is peeling. The machinery in the plant rumbles through the masonry. My footsteps bang on the aluminum stair treads as I take the stairs in twos.

When I get to the top, I give Myrtle a breezy, "Hiya, Myrtle baby, how's tricks?" Drop my slush-soaked topcoat on a hook in the coat closet and head down the hall to the conference room of the Sirini Pasta Company.

Ads for God

"Better for me than they're going to be for you," Myrtle mutters, barely looking up over the top of her magenta reading glasses. I can hear the Chicago Symphony blasting out of the conference room. The volume's up so loud it's drowning out the noise of the stampers and extruders in the back.

Stories about the Sirinis' weird and bizarre behavior have been circulating around the advertising community for years. A lot of it is talk—agency people love to gossip.

But I have to admit the Sirinis can be unpredictable. For instance, agencies normally hover over each other's accounts like vultures and love to get a foot in the door to see if they can win the business. But no agency has gone near Sirini Pasta since a small agency from out of town—Omaha, as I remember—made a cold call on Sirini ten years ago. The Sirinis had them thrown in the Cook County Jail for trespassing. The new business team, two women and two men, spent a frightening seven hours in the slammer until their lawyers could get them out. One of them even wrote an article about it.

Many family-held companies have reputations of being difficult to work with. Gallo and Wrigley come to mind. Fiercely proud of their company and distrustful of outsiders, the families focus on their wine, gum, or noodles and keep the rest of the world at arm's length.

The Sirinis, for instance, hardly ever go out. Their whole life is noodles. They spend their time worrying about the depth of the flounce on their lasagna and the evenness of the grooves on the fusilli, so it's no wonder they are a touch eccentric. Remember though, they built a two-hundred million dollar-a-year business out of mixing flour and water, squirting it through metal slits, and boxing it in cardboard, so they aren't that crazy.

You have to know how to handle them and can't take their comments too seriously, the way I see it. Sinkle, for instance, won't even come over to Sirini anymore, not even for their Christmas party, just because one day Forbes called him "a lousy gangster fop." Forbes wasn't far off.

I peek in the door. The four of them are sitting on one side of the conference table like they're posing for The Last Supper. This is not a stylish bunch. Pongi, Siggy, and Forbes Sirini buy their suits at an outlet up in Racine. Blue or dark gray, plain, no pattern. They have Sidney take them up in the company van once a year for the three-for-one sale. The material used to make their suits doesn't look as stiff as canvas but their collars stand out from their necks like they're starched and the wrinkles in their sleeves look like they've been sewn in.

Aside from a feature or two, the Sirini brothers could be Ross Perot's younger brothers, except for Forbes who, with his wet-look long hair and pearl earrings, looks like Salvador Dali dressed in a cheap suit. Today Pongi and Siggy remind me of retired Marine Corps lieutenant colonels, all crew-cut and sitting up stiffly in their chairs, scowling like they're itching to court martial someone.

I walk in. *Nobody Makes A Noodle* is still playing. I avoid walking to the beat. Margaret taps a pencil on the table. Even though her outfit is out-of-season for February, Margaret's looking smart today. Where she finds her clothes, nobody knows.

Her outfit isn't easy to describe, but I'll try because it's a beaut. The closest I can come is Baltic cruisewear. Silver-braided epaulets on the shoulders of a light cotton, short-sleeved utility suit in midnight blue with fat chrome snaps down the placket and on the pockets—almost the kind our super, Woogie, wears in the summertime. Pinned over her breast pocket are four medals the size of English muffins. They have a lot of shiny spikes and colorful enamel, they're gaudy, like something you'd have seen on some Generalissimo.

Margaret's even sporting a cotton baseball cap with an omelet of silver on the brim that's set jauntily on the back of her red beehive hairdo. Nothing high fashion about Margaret Sirini, but don't get me wrong, if you knew how she often dressed, you'd agree with me that on this Tuesday, the 17th of February, Margaret is looking pretty snappy.

"Stand there," Margaret says, pointing her pencil at a space in front of the conference table. Margaret's face never sees the sun. It's so white it looks like the surface of a Dunkin' Donut dusted with confectioner's sugar. I walk up to the spot she's pointing at and take my place in front of the four Sirinis. Look up at them and smile. The four of them remind me of the Parole Board from a '50s prison movie.

Ads for God

You can guess what part Dinny Rein's playing. The Sirinis look like they want to send me back to the Big House for another forty years. All for a crummy radio track.

I button my suitcoat. Forbes is shaking his head. I know they can see my wet pants. No place to hide. Margaret's mouth winds up into a wide sneer. When she first sees me, Margaret scowls, like she's sorry I didn't get hit by a cab on my way over. "Morning," she says, checking her watch. "Or maybe I should say good afternoon?"

"Good afternoon, Margaret," I say cheerily, and nodding at her outfit, "Nice suit."

"Fuck off, Rein," she says. Now it's remarks like that from a client that can throw an advertising person off. I've learned just to ignore them, shrug my shoulders, and smile. You end up doing a lot of smiling in the advertising business.

I can see Pongi wincing as the singers on the radio commercial finish the jingle. *"Macaroni, orzo, capelli, and fettucine, nobody, nobody, nobody makes a noodle like Sir-ini, rini, rini, rini, rini..."*

"Ugh," Pongi snorts. He points at the speakers where the jingle came from. "You do this?" he asks.

"Yes, sir," I answer.

"It's dog shit," Pongi says.

"What happened to your pants?" Forbes asks, pointing at my spats. Pongi and Siggy glare at him. Forbes has a habit of sidetracking the conversation.

"Slush, sir," I say, trying to shake out the fabric so it doesn't stick to my legs.

"Pretty disrespectful, coming in here looking like that."

"It is February, Forbes, and this is Chicago," I explain. Forbes isn't the well one. He's terribly moody, has a short attention span, and a disturbing habit of sticking a sharpened pencil into a fold in his cheek. At least three times in the past fifteen years, the pencil has poked through the skin, and they've had to call the paramedics.

I watch as he slips the lead of the pencil under the flap of his jowl, wondering if this could be another bloody day.

"With what we pay you, you'd think you could afford another suit. Ever get up to Racine?"

"Not often, Forbes."

"Too bad," he says, slowly twisting the pencil into his cheek.

"Okay, about this radio commercial," Margaret says, shaking the empty plastic cassette box. "For one thing, it's off-strategy."

"C'mon, Smartypants, knock off the marketing talk, the music sucks," Siggy purses his lips into a circle and jerks his head up and down. "Know what I mean, sucks?"

"Siggy's right. This track sucks, Dinny," Pongi whines. "It really sucks. Nothing you've brought us has ever sucked as bad as this track."

"And do you know what sucks about it?" Siggy says, getting up and coming around the end of the conference table toward me. "Sit down, Margaret," he barks at her before she has even begun to get up. Siggy motions to Pongi to follow him, jerking his hand behind him like his brother Pongi is on the end of an imaginary leash.

This is the point where I have to keep my cool. Other agency people would probably be tempted to take a swing at Siggy. Or his brother. Or walk out, or something like that. But with only two accounts left, I'm not in that position. Watch what happens.

"The orchestration?" I suggest, as the brothers storm up to me, circling and jutting out their chins.

"No," Siggy shouts in my face. I can tell he had pasta for breakfast.

"The arrangement, maybe?"

Now it's Pongi's turn to do his Manchurian Candidate act on me. "No!" he screams. Pongi had breakfast with his brother. There's a lot of pasta left between his teeth. Fusilli, I think. My cell rings.

"What's that?" Pongi snaps. The phone rings again.

"My phone, I'll turn it off." I slip the phone out of my suitcoat pocket.

"No, answer it. It could be important."

I nod at Pongi and slide up the antenna. "Hello?" The four Sirinis are staring at me. I hear the voice again. "No, and stop calling," I say, turning off the phone, punching the antenna down with my palm, and sliding it back into my pocket. "Wrong number," I say to the Sirinis. "Happens all the time. I'm going to have to call the cellular company. Now where were we? Oh, yes, maybe it was the tempo you didn't like?" I offer.

Margaret grunts, "Uh, uh," and shakes her head. Siggy whirls around and yells at her, "You stay out of this!" She looks down and fusses with her papers. The way the veins stand out on the brothers' temples is quite remarkable. Looks like mole burrows in the grass in front of my apartment building. Fat and wide, swelling—Pongi's almost get purple.

I look over at Forbes as Siggy corrects me again. Forbes' eyes are shut and his head is bowed. I think he's trembling. Only half of the pencil is visible.

"The instrumentation?" I ask. I have to play this game with them, guessing what's wrong with my advertising, getting sprayed with spit and noodle bits, until they decide to tell me. Then I tell them I'll fix the problem. They'll threaten to fire us if I don't. I'll thank them for their comments and go back to the agency.

They never fire us. They run the advertising and pay us promptly every month. I even saw the four of them walking down Michigan Avenue last Christmas, singing the jingle out loud like it was their favorite carol.

"No, stupid, not the instrumentation—it's the first cellist!"

"The first cellist?" I ask.

"Yes, the first cellist! We make prepared pasta! Right?"

"Yes, sir," I say. Siggy is up on the balls of his feet yelling at me. I can see tomato sauce stains on his suitcoat.

"The first cellist only eats fresh pasta! Ask him! So, what's he doing on our track?"

Margaret is shaking her head like I've committed the original sin. Forbes' head is still down. Only the last two inches of the pencil are visible.

"Mistake, sir. Sorry about that. I'll fix it as soon as I can rebook the Symphony." I'm wondering how they could have discovered the Chicago Symphony Orchestra's first cellist's preference in pasta.

"Oh, no you don't. Here's what you're going to do," Siggy says, clasping his hands behind his back and stalking back around the conference table like Field Marshall Montgomery. "You're going to have every musician in the Chicago Symphony sign an affidavit that they regularly eat Sirini pasta."

"Sir, I don't think I could get everyone in the symphony to sign. I'll try but…"

"Then get another symphony. Get Milwaukee, or Eau Claire, or Moline, if Chicago won't sign. Otherwise you're fired." Siggy and Pongi sit down beside their sister and fold their hands on the table in front of them, acting like I'm not there.

I'm thinking of the hours I'll have to spend on the phone, driving out into the flat hinterlands of the Midwest having affidavits signed, recording screechy small-town symphonies in drafty little studios with antiquated electronics—when two things happen simultaneously.

"Aaaargh," Forbes shouts and jumps up out of his seat with the eraser end of the pencil dangling from his jowl like someone plugged him in the cheek with a crossbow bolt.

And my phone rings again, going *cheep, cheep, cheep,* out of my suitcoat like it's a starving baby bird. Forbes is screaming bloody murder, his mouth open so wide that I can see the point of the pencil inside his mouth, the lead tapdancing around on the surface of his tongue.

The other three Sirinis sit quietly, staring down at the table top, shaking their heads, acting as if they ignore their wounded brother, maybe he'll go away. My phone is ringing and Forbes is screeching like Janet Leigh in the shower. High, piercing shrieks as the pencil wags up and down in his cheek. His wound reminds me of Christ on the cross in the paintings in Italian churches, blood neatly welled up around the nails sticking out from his wrists and ankles.

My phone keeps on ringing. I take it out. Whip up the antenna and push the SEND button.

Even though I've had lots of crazy things happen to me in the ad biz, Forbes' screaming is getting to me or I'm so fed up with this guy pestering me on the phone that I find my hand reaching out, grabbing Forbes' pencil, whipping it out of the wound, and now I'm walking around the conference room swearing at the guy on the other end of the line, jabbing at the air with the bloody pencil as my clients stare at me with their mouths open, "You call me again and I'll have you sued for invasion of privacy. I've had it up to here with your damn calls. Now stop it!"

Forbes is pressing his hand to his wounded cheek, looking at me like he's upset I stole his pencil, and whimpering quietly. "I'll call the cops, the FCC, the FBI. I'll bring a suit against you that'll make your socks roll up and down. I'll make sure you never get a job in this town!" I punch the END button so hard I get a blood blister and turn around to face my clients.

They're sitting like they're in church, eyes down, hands folded except for Forbes who's sobbing and cradling his cheek in his hands.

"Sorry," I say. "I lost it, I guess." Forbes daubs at his wound with a finger and stares at the blood on his hand. Margaret is looking at me like she's trying to gut me with her stare. "I'm sorry. Here's your pencil, Forbes," I put the sticky pencil down on the table in front of him. Forbes shakes his head and turns away from the pencil.

"I'll have the track re-recorded and the affidavits to you in a week."

"You'd better," Margaret says. "Or you know what'll happen."

I turn toward the door, "Thanks for your comments, I'll get back to you soon with an exact timetable." You always say that in the advertising business, "Thanks for your comments." Even if they've just told you they're going to fire you in a week, you say, "Thanks for your comments."

"Don't mention it," Margaret says to me, sneering of course.

"And next time," Forbes manages to say, using his free hand to point down at my ankles, holding his hand over his cheek with the other, and speaking like he's had a major Novocain injection, "wear some better pants."

"Right," I say, closing the door to the conference room.

I think to myself as I say good-bye to Sidney the security guard and step out into the blowy cold Chicago afternoon, *for this I get sixty-seven-five a year and the nagging feeling that I'm not alive anymore.*

3

Chicagoans call the winter wind "The Hawk." As I turn the corner onto Michigan, The Hawk takes the tip of my nose in its beak and bites down hard. I jam my hands deep into my pockets to try and keep them warm. My ankles are so cold they're burning.

Walking back up the sloping sidewalk, my phone rings again. I can feel my blood pressure inching up. *If it's that voiceover creep again,* I say to myself as I extend the antenna. I'd leave the phone at the office if it wasn't for Sinkle's edict that we carry the phones at all times. Every VP and up at BFP&G has a cellular phone. "We're in the communications business, so we have to communicate," is a standard Sinkleism.

"Hello!"

"Jeez, doesn't sound like you're having too good a day," Patti Shaw says. I can hear the sprayers going in the background.

"Sorry," I say. "I thought you were someone else." Patti reminds me that she called to invite me to dinner. We talk about where we should meet. She gets off at six.

Patti works the cashier cage at the Starlite Drive-Thru Clean Car Experience, the Las Vegas version of a car wash over on Elston Avenue. She's part-owner and takes down over sixty-grand a year out of it. On the outside, the place shimmers all over with a million silver disks, has a tower you can see from the expressway, and, if you're driving by and the sun strikes the place, you better have a seeing eye dog at your side.

Inside, Louie (he's the other owner) has digital surround sound and strobe lights going full blast. He sprinkles sparkle dust in one of his pre-washes as the music from *Top Gun* turns on to full volume, and you feel like you're in a starship going through a meteor shower in a far-out galaxy somewhere.

I met Patti Shaw when I did some freelancing for the guy about three years ago. The Clean Car Experience was my concept. Made a couple grand on that job and Patti was bowled over by my marketing smarts, also thinks I'm cute. We've been an item for a couple years now.

Patti's the first thing you see when you drive into the Starlite and let me tell you, she's a sight you don't easily forget. Big blonde hair and a body that would make a French curve covetous, Patti's perched on a revolving, glittered stool in a glass box wearing metallic hot pants, big metal belt, a silver tube top, chrome go-go boots, and a helmet right out of Star Trek crowning her beehive.

Don't let the bimbo outfit mislead you. Even though Patti never got through high school, she's one brainy lady. When she's not at work, she goes to the Chicago Public Library and reads. Everything from Grisham to Thucydides, she can quote people you've never even heard of. I love talking with her, learn something new every day. Convinced her into taking a course down at UIC, Introduction to Modern Civilization, I think it's called. A mind is a terrible thing to waste, as they say, particularly when it's in a body like Patti Shaw's.

"I've got to run, we've got cars stacked up around the corner," she says.

"See you at six at Greek Isles, okay?" I say.

"Bye, Mr. Big Ad Guy," she says. She's always joking about my job, part of the reason we get along so well. Patti Shaw doesn't take anything too seriously, except cleaning cars and she's dead serious about that.

I'm about to bring my palm down on the antenna when the phone rings again.

"You're walking past the Marriott and it's cold out. Come on in and let me buy you a cup of coffee," the voice says. "Five minutes and I promise I'll never bother you again."

As I pause in front of the Marriott, a burly doorman in a maroon wool coat slaps the revolving door and starts it spinning for me. He's got a maroon fez-like thing on his head with a gold silk tassel and his hat and the braid on his uniform make him look like he's auditioning for a Gilbert and Sullivan production.

Five minutes—I'm thinking I can get rid of my mystery phone caller forever. "Okay, five minutes," I say, stepping into the revolving door. Maurice slows down the door so it doesn't sweep me into the lobby. *Maurice*—that's the name embroidered on his doorman's uniform.

"How will I recognize you?" I ask the caller.

"You won't. Sit down anywhere. I'll find you."

The lobby of the Marriott makes the hotel look like it belongs in Vegas. They've chromed everything. What they couldn't chrome, they gilded and what they couldn't gild, they painted purple and put a lot of potted plants around. Visually, the place makes me sick. A sunken area the size of a hockey rink is ringed with banquettes covered in vermilion plush.

I walk past a group of little old ladies eating small sandwiches with the crusts cut off. *Remind me when I get older never to order sandwiches with the crusts cut off. Cut-off crusts are a sure sign you're nearing death.*

I sit down in an empty section. I look around for a guy with a cellular phone. *Where the hell is he?*

The voice startles me, "Good afternoon, Mr. Rein." I leap up off the banquette. A second ago, I could have sworn there was no one there. Now a thin old man who looks like Joseph Cotten's father is sitting next to me, not a foot away, holding out his hand and smiling at me like we're old friends.

"Nice to meet you. I appreciate you taking the time," he says, in the same deep baritone Broadway voice I've heard over my cellular for the past two weeks.

"Sit down, sit down," he says, patting the plush of the banquette with his bony, veined hand. He doesn't look like his voice. I'm surprised Maurice let him in. He's wearing an old overcoat buttoned to the neck. I can see his legs are bare and white with a few dark wispy hairs. On his feet he's wearing two-toned plastic flip-flops. His toenails are yellow and curled.

He sees me looking at his legs. "I just came up from Florida. I had to borrow the coat," he explains, opening his coat to show me his blue and yellow madras swimsuit.

"You just came up from Florida?" I ask. "When?"

"A couple of minutes ago. When you were passing the hotel, I thought it would be a nice place to meet." He tilts his head slowly, gives me a beatific smile and says, "So?"

He says "So?" like I'm supposed to know what we're going to talk about. "So?" like I'm supposed to accept that he instantly flew up from Florida. "So?" like it's okay he's sitting around the lobby of the Marriott Hotel in the middle of winter in a herringbone topcoat with a madras swimsuit underneath.

And before I can get up and get the hell out of there, he puts his hand on my sleeve and says, "So—you're in advertising?"

I nod.

"Good, that's good. I need some advertising."

I look at my watch, siting back down. Two minutes and I'm out of here. "You do?" I ask.

"Yes," he says, "and some solid strategic thinking—that's why I picked you."

The phrase "strategic thinking" stops me. Normal people don't talk like that. Bunch of years ago, a guy made the rounds of Chicago agencies with a contraption that brewed fresh coffee quickly and easily. Every agency in Chicago thought he was a quack and showed Mr. Coffee and his fifty-million dollars worth of advertising the door.

Is this guy some Howard Hughes-type? Some reclusive old billionaire who has a crazy cause he wants to champion?

"I used to own the category. The other guys were nothing. Now I've got competition, big competition. They're eating into my market share. How about some coffee?"

I shake my head. "Who is?" I ask.

"The other guys," he says. "Sure you don't want coffee?"

"The other guys?" I ask.

"Mohammed, mainly."

"Mo-hamm-ed?" I say slowly, trying to make sure I've heard him correctly.

"You betcha—and Buddha too," he adds.

"You're crazy," I say, getting up off the banquette and heading for the revolving door, knowing I have better things to do than listen to some daffy old man wearing flip-flops in the middle of February.

I hear him say, "So?" in his loud, booming baritone as Maurice starts to spin the revolving door for me. I look back at him over my shoulder as I push through the door. His arms are held up imploringly, like he's a prophet in some biblical epic.

"So?" he says again. His coat sags open so I can see his madras swimsuit.

Jesus, I think. *I hope I don't act nuts like that when I get old.*

4

Whoever said people are out of touch these days doesn't have voicemail. In the time it took me to walk back from Sirini, Margaret called twice. First telling me to audition the Springfield Symphony and then to check out the Moline Philharmonic.

Bernie, the voiceover for Woof!Burgers, called to try out a bark for the new commercial. He starts to yap and arf over the speakerphone. I turn down the volume so no one will think I'm keeping animals in my office. Ester's the only one who's allowed to keep an animal, if you call that Mort thing an animal. Bernie does a Lhasa apso, Shih-Tzu and a fox terrier. None of them are right.

It's Sophie from Accounting next, then my landlord who wants the rent check, Reavis wants her support payment, my broker from Merrill Lynch wants me to buy a hot new issue (which is a joke since I have to scrape my bus fare out of the couch cushions), and the cleaners are calling to tell me my other suit is ready.

I start with Sophie from Accounting.

"Are you there?" she asks. Sophie always sounds like she has nasal congestion, but it's because she's from the Bronx. Two minutes later, Sophie, the assistant to Murray the CFO, is standing in my office doorway waving a sheet of paper at me. Sophie's sixty but isn't giving up easily. Looks like a skinny Penny Marshall. Wears bright, short dresses, black stockings, and spends a lot of money on makeup. Today she's wearing chartreuse. Her makeup matches.

"You know anything about this?" She flaps the paper in the air like she's trying to get the ink to dry.

"What?"

"A deposit slip. The bank faxed it over. Our new business account."

She skids the paper in front of me. "It has your name on it so I figured you might know something."

Sophie is a refugee from the ad business in New York. She puts her lipstick on so there's no mistaking she wears lipstick—fortunately it isn't chartreuse—and constantly complains that there's no decent yogurt in Chicago. "I tell you," is her favorite expression. When people point out that the same brands of yogurt are sold in Chicago as in New York, Sophie shakes her head. "They're not the same here," she explains. "Yogurt's got cultures and shipping kills cultures—I tell you." I must have heard that fifty times. Every time she tells the yogurt story, I see cultures in their little waxy cups screaming bloody murder in the back of a Jewel truck heading to Chicago.

I pick up the fax off my desk. The copy of the deposit slip has a bunch of computer type on it. "Deposit to the account of BFP&G the sum of $10,000,000," the slip reads. My name is typed on the bottom.

"What about it?"

"Dinny, c'mon, it's ten million bucks. It's a couple thousand bucks a day in interest alone—you got to tell me what's going on! Is something fishy here?"

"What do you mean?" I ask, studying the fax, wondering how my name could have gotten on it.

Sophie closes the door and pulls a chair up in front of my desk. She hikes her skirt and tucks her leg up on the chair. Her slip is chartreuse too. She has class for an Assistant CFO. Also nice legs. When she wants something, she shows them off.

She looks around like she doesn't want to be overheard, leans into me, and whispers, "We're not laundering money, are we?"

"What?"

She leans closer and looks around. "Drug money—are we laundering money for someone? Like in a Danielle Steele book? I mean ten million bucks just doesn't drop out of the sky—I tell you... You didn't expect this money?"

Ads for God

Still looking at me for an answer, "If I knew where the money's from, what am I doing down here? I come down four floors for my health?" Sophie tightens her lips and exhales between them, making the sound of compressed air escaping. "Dinny Rein, I tell you."

I shrug. "Sorry I can't help, Sophie," I say.

"Your name's on it, and the bank says that means you're supposed to know about it. You sure it didn't come from Sirini or Woof!?"

"If we'd gotten ten million from the Sirinis, you don't think I'd know about it? And the people at Woof!—the only time they've seen ten million is in the movies."

Sophie shakes her head. "Murray's in New York. I guess I'll have to see Sinkle about this by myself—I tell you." No one in the agency likes to see Steve Sinkle by themselves.

Sophie picks the fax up off my desk and leaves, turning back to kiss the air behind her. I think to myself: *Ten years ago, the agency wasn't even billing ten million—now it drops through the cracks.*

I leave messages for Margaret, Bernie, my landlord, Reavis, and my broker while I look out at the churning brown water of the lake and I'm dialing information to get the number of the symphony in Springfield when I see Steve Sinkle appear in my doorway. Sophie's fax in his hand. Sinkle's smiling. Not a good sign. A lot of people get fooled but not me. I've learned the hard way. A smile means Sinkle's laid a trap for you somewhere, and pretty soon you'll step in it.

"Dinny, my man, you didn't tell me you were going after a new piece of business. What a surprise!" he says, coming into my office and shutting the door behind him. Which really means, "What are you trying to do, schmuck, steal stock from me?"

With Sinkle, every encounter is a third down. He doesn't live life rolling with the punches and taking it the way it comes. He's always looking for an opening up the middle so he can pick up five yards and the first.

Sinkle sits on the corner of my desk and hitches up his pant leg to show off his shoes. Must have cost five hundred bucks. So buffed and burnished, they look like he stole them off the statue of Prince Philip at the Wax Museum. I stick my feet further under my desk to hide my salt-stained loafers.

Sinkle's low-life Indiana upbringing and the tattoo on his shoulder he got one boozed-up night in the Marine Corps (saw his arm art at a company outing at Oak Street beach, reads 'Born To Sell', and has his B-school logo emblazoned beneath it in four colors) is buried under a couple thousand dollars worth of Polo, maybe more.

"Tell me about it—what's it going to bill?" he says, holding up the fax, meaning "How much stock will you try to get out of Benny, Frank, and Gus?"

"I don't know anything about a new piece of business," I say.

Sinkle gives me one of his extra-wide smiles, which means "You better come clean, Buster, or I'll kill you with my bare hands." A lot of people are disarmed by Sinkle, and it's not simply his smile. He looks like he stepped out of a Polo ad in the *New York Times Sunday Magazine*. Which is not surprising once you learn that all his clothes are from the shop on Michigan: shirts, suits, socks, handkerchiefs, tee-shirts, even his underwear.

Every three months, the shop sends a selection of custom-tailored suits, shirts, slacks, sportcoats, hacking jackets, raincoats, belts, vests, storm coats, and boots directly to his home in Barrington. The bills go to the office. And every time Sinkle cleans out his closet, the Thrift Shop in Barrington ends up looking like the Polo Outlet, and for two days, you can't get near the place.

Sinkle smiles at me, saying nothing. He specializes in silence. Smiling silence, like he knows something I don't.

I can feel the sweat begin to break out along the back of my neck. He smiles wider, like I told him a joke. I wonder if he's going to fire me on the spot. I've talked to people who've been fired by Sinkle. One guy thought he was going to get a bonus. Freddy Hoops was sure he was being moved to a corner office. Sinkle smiled Freddy right onto the elevator, pushed the LOBBY button, and told Freddy he was fired and never to set his foot in the office again, or he'd sue his ass off. The receptionist said Sinkle was still smiling when he got off the elevator, letting the doors squeeze shut on a stunned and speechless Freddy Hoops.

"Steve, if you're talking about the ten million Sophie found—I don't know anything, honest," I find myself saying.

Sinkle wears his thick sandy hair long so he's constantly raking it back from his forehead with his fingers. The raking motion would look girlish if anyone else did it. When Sinkle pulls his fingers through his hair, it's ominous.

"Okay, I believe you," he says, which I know means "I'm going to watch you like a hawk."

"Just wanted to check," he says, which means "I'm going to nail you on this." He slides his hip off my desk and stands up. Some people say Sinkle looks like that Australian movie star with the big knife—what's his name? Anyway, I don't see it. Okay, he's got the cheekbones, blue eyes, and narrow face, but to me, he's another corn-fed Indiana farm boy with a quick mind. The kind that goes into politics or advertising. He's big too, six-three and solid. Played slotback or something at Purdue and must have majored in intimidation.

Sinkle stands there looking at me. Wondering if he can go off tackle for ten. Before Steve Sinkle got to BFP&G, I was in the advertising business. Now I'm wandering around a Big Ten football field with a game going on, without pads and a helmet, wondering from which side I'm going to get hit next.

I don't know what to do so I try a smile. Sinkle turns and walks out of my office like he forgot something. Maybe I shouldn't have smiled.

I wait, wondering if he's coming back. With Sinkle, the other shoe often drops.

He reappears in the doorway. Leans against the jamb. Gives me another smile and runs his fingers through his hair. His teeth are perfect except for one incisor that got busted off by a Notre Dame nose tackle. Looks out at the lake. The busted tooth is short and ragged and leaves a black hole in his smile. Makes him look felonious, which is probably why he never got it fixed.

"Funny the slip would have your name on it," he says. He walks into my office again.

"Yes, it's odd," I say. "I can't figure it out."

Sinkle turns around, leans against the window and looks at me. He wears two-toned shirts. The cuffs and collars are always white, the shirt blue, pink, striped or checked. Today it's blue but the cuffs and collar are always white. Very spiffy, dressed to kill.

"Funny," he says. I know he's staring at me. I hate it when he looks at me. Makes me feel like I'm five and I've been bad.

"Funny," I say, quickly looking up at him. A strange sound comes out of my throat, half-gurgle, half-choke. He pushes himself away from the window and walks out of my office without looking back.

I don't move. I feel like he's just gone up my middle for a big ten yards. *Why do I always feel like I've been had after a talk with Sinkle?*

I wait a minute. No other shoe. I check my watch, 4:30, put my feet up on the window sill, and lean back in my chair. The surface of Lake Michigan looks like mocha frosting, the kind my mother used to spread on angel food cakes in waves and swirls. She'd spatula the frosting up into peaks, tiny mountains that would lean helter-skelter in all directions so the top of the cake looked like it was alive.

"Don't worry about it," I say out loud. My voice sounds deeper, like something's stuck in my throat. I clear my throat, cough again. "You'll be fine with me," my voice says. I stop. I can hear the heat whooshing in through the ceiling vent. There's something wrong. I sit up in my chair. Look around my office, out at the lake. If it wasn't brown, it would look ferocious.

I know I said: "Don't worry about it, you'll be fine with me," but I didn't think *it. The thought came from somewhere else.*

"What?" I ask, my mouth hanging open even more than usual. I hop up and shut the door quickly. *Am I talking to myself?*

I hear myself say in that deep voice, the same voice I heard on my cell phone, "You'll be fine. We'll take care of little Stevie Sinkle. He's nothing. Crapped his pants until he was almost ten."

I freeze. Look slowly around my office. *Maybe there's someone hiding in my office.* I open a file drawer. *Maybe there's a tape recorder, maybe Sinkle's trying to drive me nuts.* Peer under the desk. Feel around on top of the credenza, kick back the blinds. Nothing.

Ads for God

I clear my throat again. I pat my chest to make sure I'm here. I feel my forehead. Put my fingers on my pulse. My heart is working overtime. *Sit down. Think. Get a grip, Dinny, get a grip.* I sit at my desk staring at my knuckles. I don't want to say anything. *Maybe I should feel my lips, make sure they're mine.* I feel my lips. *They're mine.*

I get an idea. I punch the RECORD button of my phone. It's a memo thing, a Sinkle innovation he had installed on all of our phones. I sit down, lean back in my chair, and wait for myself to say something again.

"You'll get used to it," I say to myself in the deep voice.

"What?" I ask, checking to make sure that the red RECORD light is blinking. I feel like a ventriloquist, talking out of one side of my mouth and then the other, Edgar Bergen-like, except I don't have Charlie McCarthy on my knee. One side of my mouth is me, Dinny Rein. On the left is the baritone from who-knows-where.

Left, right, left, right, I listen as I carry on this conversation with myself.

"How'd you like the thing with the ten million bucks?" the voice asks.

"Excuse me?" I ask, checking the RECORD light.

"Diverted a wire transfer, easy as pie."

"You what?" I ask.

"They send money flying through the air these days, all I have to do is reach up and snag one like I'm pulling down a line drive in center field, change a number or two, send it back on its way, and bingo!"

"Interesting," I say. I figure I'll chat with myself for another minute and then listen to the recording. That way I'll know if I've gone nuts or not.

Maybe I'm hallucinating or maybe I've died and gone to heaven or something.

"No, I'm in heaven. You're still on earth," the voice says to me. "Except I don't call it heaven, I call it something else—but that's another story."

I quickly reach over and punch the play button on the phone. I hear the voice saying over the speakerphone. "You'll get used to it."

Then, "What?" and "How'd you like the thing with the ten million bucks?"

"Excuse me?"

"Diverted a wire transfer, easy as pie."

"You what?"

"They send money flying through the air these days, all I have to do is reach up and snag it like I'm pulling down a line drive in center field, change a few words here and there, send it back on its way, and bingo!"

I turn off the recorder. *I'm not crazy—it's much worse than that.* "Oh, God," I say.

"Please—don't remind me," the voice says. "Who doesn't like George Burns, okay? But he's the last guy I would have picked to play me. So I'm old—but I don't look that bad! Maybe Redford or Newman or someone. Heck, even Heston, but not some shriveled-up looking coot like George Burns, jeez."

My mouth is open wider than usual. "You're?—" I say, gesturing around at the air in my office.

"You betcha, have been for a long time," he says.

I sit forward in my chair like I'm talking to someone but don't know where to look. I stand up and start walking around.

"And you were the guy in the hotel?" I ask.

"No, that was Abe Moskowitz from Daytona, had to borrow him for a few minutes..."

"But that was you talking?"

"You betcha."

"And that was you on the phone?"

"You betcha."

"And you put the ten million in our new business account?"

"Got to start with something."

"So you're a voice..."

"No, no, no, I'm omni, you know? Omnipresent, omnipotent, omniscient—omni-everything—I'm in the air all over the place and I got a bag of tricks big as life. Except I don't eat or drink which is not so bad except I'd like a beer once in a while. What does beer taste like?"

"It's bitter, fizzy, has a sour taste..."

"Doesn't sound so good."

"It's good when it's real cold."

"I see. So—I guess we'll make some ads together," he says. "But first, you have to go to dinner with Patti, right?"

I check my watch. Five-fifteen, time to leave. *This guy knows everything.* "Right," I say. "So maybe we should make an appointment? Sit down and talk?" I grab my coat.

"How about tomorrow?"

"Tomorrow's fine. Nine sharp?"

"Great."

"Where?"

"Anywhere you want. Just start talking, and I'll be there."

"Okay, see you at nine," I say, pulling up the collar on my coat and picking up my briefcase.

He doesn't answer. *Maybe He's gone.*

I open the door to my office and look down the hall. I start for the elevator. I'm worried that He's going to talk to me again. Someone will see me.

I can't afford to have people start saying Dinny Rein is talking to himself. I make it to the elevator. The cab is empty. The doors start to close, and three secretaries rush up. I pretend that I'm reaching for the STOP button. As the doors close on them, I shrug my shoulders like I couldn't help it.

I get out on the ground floor. Woogie is squeegeeing the lobby. Against its ochre walls, Woogie bent over in his blue suit looks like an Edward Hopper painting. I wait until his back is turned and dash past him out the door onto Michigan. I step into the crowd of commuters heading up Michigan toward Wacker.

Good, I made it.

If He starts talking to me again, no one will pay any attention since my chin is tucked deep into the collar of my topcoat, and my shoulders are hunched up against the wind. Even if someone were to see me talking, I wouldn't look any different than the bond traders muttering into their overcoats about the recent turn in interest rates, or the lady who must be a commercial real estate broker striding past me cursing her boss for not letting her have the new listing in the IBM building.

"Don't be so worried, I won't talk to you when there are other people around," I hear Him say in a quiet voice.

"I'd appreciate that," I whisper.

"People would think you were crazy."

"That's what I mean, I'm on the edge as it is."

"I might whisper, but I'll be discreet."

"Discreet is good."

"You betcha."

The temperature dropped twenty degrees when the sun went down so the streets and sidewalks are glistening black mirrors. Every couple of minutes, a commuter flies up in the air out of the crowd and thumps to the ground, briefcase skittering over the ice. The surrounding commuters briefly stopping to help the slippee up, dust off the snow and frozen slush, gather in his briefcase, and get him going again.

"Am I crazy?" I ask out of one side of my mouth.

"No," I say out of the other. "Just temporarily possessed." I'm wondering what that means when I find myself asking: "Why me?"

"Why not? You're smart, a strategic thinker, you've got style, and you did the best on the questionnaire." I step gingerly across a patch of black ice, carefully setting my loafers down and twisting a purchase into the slick surface, wondering, *What questionnaire?*

Then He says, "You wouldn't remember, I gave it to you when you were asleep."

"Jeez," I say. "you can do that?"

"You betcha. I do trick stuff like part seas... I do earthquakes, avalanches, all your natural phenomena. I can make it rain in Abu Dhabi or snow in the upper reaches of the Amazon. There's only two things I don't do so good. One is, I got a problem relating to people, especially large groups—that's why I got you."

"What's the other thing?"

"Don't be so curious."

"So what do I do about Sinkle?"

"Let me worry about him. You make the ads. I'll run interference for you."

God, that's all I've wanted to do for the last ten years—make the ads.

"I know," He says.

I see the Greek restaurant on the next corner. When I get to the door, I stop and wave good-bye, quickly putting my hand down when I realize how stupid I look waving to no one. As I open the door to the restaurant, I look back out into the empty space under the El. A cab whizzes by. Slush flies. The stop light casts a long scarlet shine across the pavement.

I think to myself, *For the first time in a long time, I don't feel dead anymore.*

And He says, sotto voce, "You aren't dead. You've just been in advertising too long."

5

Plastic grapes hang from the ceiling and bouzouki music twangs through the place. Empty wine bottles crowd the windowsills. I expect to see Anthony Quinn come dancing out from between the drapes. The restaurant is warm and smells slightly sour, maybe from the feta. My Timex says I'm twenty minutes late.

I look around for Patti. The maitre d's wearing what looks like a bad toreador suit. He's carrying an armful of wooden menus. I see Patti at the bar, mink carefully folded on the barstool next to her. She's wearing a taffeta cocktail dress with a diving neckline and matching shoes, in some light green color, guess you'd call it seafoam.

If that sounds cheesy to you, that's your problem—me, I love every minute of it. I hold two fingers up as I point to Patti. The maitre d' nods and steps out of the way. He's wearing little silk slippers.

Patti gets up off the bar stool. "How's tricks in the ad biz, Dinny?" Patti Shaw is short so she always throws her hands around my neck and boosts herself up to give me a big kiss on the lips. She's drinking Greek beer. I have to wipe a little off my lip.

"You couldn't guess what happened to me today."

"I bet," she says. Patti can't believe the crap that happens at BFP&G. She calls Sinkle "Gordon Gekko," calls Ester the "Dragon Lady," and keeps tearing job prospects out of the paper for me. She's had a jaded impression of advertising ever since she found out that Woof!Burgers are 28% ground-up chicken feathers and have enough red dye #3 in them to turn the Chicago River ruby-red for the entire summer.

Ads for God

The bartender is stuck cleaning the same glass. He's staring at Patti Shaw the way a lot of guys do, because Patti is a dame. It's the only word that fits her. I guess I should be telling you how old she is but I don't actually know myself. "For me to know and you to guess, Dinny Rein" is what Patti always says when I ask her. Could be thirty-five, could be forty-five.

But age doesn't really enter into it, not when you're dealing with dames. And Patti's a big time dame, more of a dame than somebody like Dolly Parton. Not only because of her figure. Patti's a real head-turner, a throwback to the days when women showed cleavage, wore rouge and eye shadow, bleached their hair until it was almost white then teased it into monumental swirls and waves, wore slit skirts and garters, and blew smoke rings with their Chesterfields.

Patti also has Jane Russell moves. Old-time movie star moves like bending over. Leaning down so the cleavage between her breasts widens and you stare and she looks up at you and smiles. Or she'll reach with one hand and pull down her skirt. She'll make sure you're watching and then she lifts the hem up a bit, slips it up so you see a flash of her upper thigh and a glimpse of garter before she stretches it back down. Then she looks at you and smiles. Smiling like if you're real good, you might get to see more, and so I'm always real good.

I love everything Patti Shaw does because she makes me feel like a hot-cheeked kid again. Don't get the idea that Patti hasn't heard of women's lib, you ought to see what happens when someone crosses the line at the car wash. She's just a woman who makes me feel like a man, and I like that.

"You look peachy, Dinny, just peachy. Sit down," Patti says, moving her mink and patting the barstool beside her. She uses words like "peachy," calls me "Big Boy," and has been known to faint when she wants attention. "How about an Athenian beer?" she asks, holding up the bottle and turning it to me. I nod.

"Give my big boy a bottle of Taverna, please?" Patti pronounces the Greek word perfectly, or it sounds perfect to me.

"So what happened today?" she asks as she holds up a Chesterfield for me. I take a pack of matches off the bar and strike one. She leans over for me to light it. I look down the front of her dress as I hold the flame to the end of her cigarette. Her dress is so low-cut that in the shadows between her breasts I can see almost to where the dark of her nipples starts.

She inhales, looks up at me, winks, says, "I thought you were hungry," and blows a big blue smoke ring.

"I was," I say, and she puts out her cigarette and stands up with her back to me so I can put on her mink. I throw down a five and follow her out the door.

See what I mean about Patti Shaw? One little look, and we're off and running. Big improvement over my ex-wife. Reavis regarded sex as currency and made sure I ended up with the small change.

In the back of the cab, I'm all over her like I just got back from four years in the Arctic Circle. My hand's up her skirt, and my tongue is halfway down her throat, and she's saying, "Whoa, boy, whoa, boy!" but she's giggling like she loves it and she has me in her hand, working my fly down with her wrist, and when we get to my place I throw a ten, or maybe it's a twenty, over into the front seat and I open the door and we race up the stairs laughing loud enough to make Rodriguez, the disabled former El conductor who rents the upstairs apartment, bang his crutch on the floor so hard it sounds like an angry judge gaveling for attention in a crowded courtroom.

I open the door to the apartment, and she pins me up against the wall, kissing me all over the neck and face while she flicks open my belt, unbuttons my pants and shoves everything to my ankles so I'm naked from the waist down. Then Patti Shaw goes to work.

I forget about Sinkle and the Sirinis and God and the ten million bucks until Patti Shaw stops and takes me by the hand down the hall to the bedroom. I'm shuffling along with my pants wadded down around my ankles with my erection wandering around like the prow of a ship pitching on a big sea and Patti lies me down on the bed and only faintly in the dim light of the streetlight fading though the curtains can I see her taking off her clothes and she starts whistling the theme song from *The Bridge Over The River Kwai* (don't ask me why she does that, I've asked her a couple times and she doesn't even know). I think she is slipping off her bra, now her panties, but I can't tell for sure and now she's whistling the song in two parts (Patti's some whistler) and from the little bit of light sneaking through the curtain I can tell she is naked so I open the covers for her to get in. She trills the finale to *River Kwai* (dah dah dah, dah dah dah, da duh, tweet, tweet) and slides in on top of me.

Patti Shaw is always warm. She's noisy too, and this causes Rodriguez to get busy again with his crutch. Patti yips when she's coming, high, short little sounds from the back of her throat that increase in intensity until she sounds like a Jordan-crazed Lovabull during a close playoff game. Next door, Mrs. Doherty's blind Dalmatian wakes up and joins in and we have Patty yipping, me thrusting up and up into her like I'm seventeen, Rodriguez keeping time with his crutch, bang, bang, bang, bang, and Mrs. Doherty's blind Dalmatian howling in harmony until Patti yelps one last, long, plaintive wail and collapses on top of me and we lay there for a while, panting and sighing and kissing each other while we listen to the traffic outside, the whimpering of Mrs. Doherty's dog, and the sound of the Honeymooners arguing with each other on Rodriguez's TV.

When Patti turns the light on to get a cigarette, she holds the covers tight around her. She smokes as she strokes the inside of my thigh and I get to thinking about my new client again.

"Patti, can I ask you something?"

"Sure," she says, looking up at the two smoke rings floating in the air above my bed.

"Do you believe in God?" I sit up on an elbow and wait for her response.

"Huh?"

"God—do you believe in him?"

"I guess." The smoke rings shy away from a draft coming from the window. They drift over the bed, twisting and stretching in the slight breeze. I pull up the covers, look at Patti.

"I think I might have met Him today."

Patti squeezes a fleck of tobacco off her tongue with her fingertips. "Who?"

"Him—God."

She sits up in bed quickly. "Where?" The covers fall off her chest, she pulls them back up and tucks them into her armpits.

"At the Marriott, then at the agency. We had a meeting. We even walked over to the restaurant together. He wants me to handle his advertising."

She puts her cigarette in the open beak of the pelican ashtray on the night stand and turns to me. "You need a back rub, turn over," she says, making a rolling motion with her hand.

I turn over on my stomach. Patti starts kneading my shoulders.

"He deposited ten million dollars in our new business account."

I wonder about that money, was it just floating around up there? Like some astronaut's space garbage? And He just snagged it? With his celestial boathook or something? Or did He really rip-off a wire transfer? But that would be stealing, and God, I mean God wouldn't go around stealing money from people, would He? He is God, after all. You do have to keep that in mind, don't you?

"It'll be all right," I hear her say.

"You think?"

"Just relax." Her hands are small but strong. She's working hard. I can tell she's trying to knead the craziness out of me.

"But you know the weirdest thing?"

"What's that?" I can tell she's taking a drag on her cigarette. One hand's still working my neck. I smell the smoke.

"He speaks through me."

She goes back to work on me. "Your shoulders are very tense. Relax your shoulders."

"Want to see?" I turn over. She's let the covers sag, and for a second, I can see her right breast. She covers it quickly.

"What?" she asks.

I sit up. "Want to see God speak through me?" Patti turns her head so she's looking at me slanted. She pulls up the covers, looks away from me, and shrugs like she isn't sure.

"He probably isn't there now..." I lean forward and look into a corner of the bedroom. "Say God, do that voice thing you did with me this afternoon."

Patti looks at me. Her eyes are narrowing, creases appear alongside her eyebrows.

"I swear, he talks out of one side of my mouth. I sound like Charlton Heston. Watch." Nothing happens. "Maybe he's sleeping," I say.

Ads for God

Suddenly the baritone booms out of my mouth, "Remember, it may be dark in Chicago, but in Auckland, it's another day."

I shake Patti's shoulder and point at my mouth.

"It's Him, see? He's talking."

"Nice to meet you Patti," He says in His deep voice. "I've been through your carwash a couple of times."

Patti leaps out of bed, tripping over the covers, bangs over the light on the night table, and throws herself against the wall.

"Love the way you make the water sparkle in the car wash," He says. "I really appreciate tricks like that." The light lies on the floor pointing up at Patti so her face goes Halloween. She's naked and leans back against the wall and starts to scream, staring at me with her eyes so wide they're more white than brown, screaming louder than Forbes Sirini did when he had the pencil stuck in his cheek. I'm afraid she's going to faint.

Mrs. Doherty's Dalmatian starts to bark again. Patti's backed up against the wall with her palms splayed out over the plaster like she wants it to absorb her, looking at me like I'm Frankenstein. The screaming gets to Rodriguez. His crutch sounds like a machine gun. I get up and try to hug her. Patti holds her head away from me, trying to cover her breasts with her forearms and her crotch with one hand.

"Patti, it's okay. It's okay." The sound of my normal voice seems to calm her. She turns and looks at me. I can tell she's looking deep into my eyes, trying to see if the demon that had possessed me is still there. I forgot Patti was brought up in the hills of Arkansas. Ghosts are a big thing to her.

"That's so spooky. Don't do that anymore, okay?"

"Okay," I say.

She's shivering. "It was like a horror movie, your head turned to the side, your lips all—that voice coming out."

"I'm sorry. I won't do it again."

"Whew," she says, shaking her head. "Promise?"

"Promise."

She puts her arms around my neck and pulls me to her, gives me the big googly eyes, then stands back so I can see her naked body and flicks her hips at me so her breasts do a shimmy thing and her body is so abundant with glorious curves and soft-looking things that I pull her to me quickly and put God and his ten million bucks out of my mind. I don't give a damn if this particular night causes Rodriguez to break his crutch or if Mrs. Doherty's dog barks himself so hoarse he won't arf or yip or even growl again for another five days. So there.

6

I wake up with a start, eyes clicking open to stare at the ceiling. I'm thinking—*thinking I should be somewhere*. Rust stains following the ceiling cracks, spider veins running across the plaster. Must be Rodriguez leaking water upstairs. Have to talk with the landlord before the ceiling falls on my face.

My Timex tells me 7:48. *That's it—I have a nine o'clock with you-know-who. My new client.* Slap, slap. Pat the covers for Patti Shaw. No Patti. Must have snuck out early to take care of her clients who roll through the Starlite early on their way in from the suburbs. Road salt on the interstates is money in the bank to the Starlite Drive-In.

I roll over and hang my legs off the bed. The floor feels like ice. My eyes find Patti's green lace panties draped on the bathroom doorknob, left like a calling card, emerald and shiny silk, like warm water on my fingers. *Thank the Lord for Patti Shaw. That girl keeps whatever's left in me alive*, I think to myself as I stand in the doorway in my shorts, staring into my skinny bathroom, shivering and scratching my stomach hairs. The light comes through the shade hard and blue, it's ten degrees outside if it's anything. The corner of the window shade slumps down off the pole. At least twice a week, Patti points out that the shade is only hanging by three staples.

I lean over the sink and look at myself in the mirror. *Yipes! It's not me. It's someone else.* Quickly look back over my shoulder to see who's standing behind me. *Whoops! Nobody's there.* Slowly turn and look back into the mirror. Squeeze my eyes shut, real hard. Count to three. *One, two, three.* Open them again. *It's still not me. Oh boy, standby Houston.* Blink a couple of times. Shake my head hard, stare at myself. *I look like I just went for a trip in a time machine.* The bags under my eyes have disappeared, my crow's-feet have been ironed flat, my hair's golden-brown and bushy, the gray is gone, and the furrows on my forehead where the sweat wells up are smooth.

I look like some movie star—what's his name? Patti saw a picture of me when I was younger, said I looked like him, what's his name? *Keith, no, not Keith. Kevin! Yes, Kevin...Kevin Something, oh dear, I can't remember, I'll have to ask Patti.*

My hand flies up to my face. Feel my skin. Tight, hard. I poke my cheek with my finger, and the skin pops back fast. My cheeks used to look like I was carting bags of instant frosting around. Now they're contoured, pulling in under my cheekbones, taut under my chin. *Damn, I look thirty-five, thirty-eight maybe.* I turn my head, profile reminds me of my picture in the Waverly yearbook. *Jeez, He's taking me back to the time when my career was soaring, and I was the talk of the agency, running all the big accounts and heading for a partnership.*

"You betcha," He says. "No old farts working on my account." Queasy feeling starts in my stomach when I see my mouth moving.

"Wait a minute, say something else," I ask.

"I know, I know. I'm working on it," He says. Now I see why Patti Shaw was so freaked last night. Though His voice is deep and baritoney, I turn into Lenny Lobotomy when He talks, my lips reaching out for the words like the tip of an elephant's trunk searching for peanuts, all pink and glistening, then going limp and floppy between the words.

Oh boy, if ever there was a good news-bad news joke—He's made me look like I'm thirty-five, but when He talks I look like a duck-billed platypus.

"Do you have to make my mouth move like that?"

"Pretty low-tech, I know," He says.

"I'll say, we have to figure something else out." I can see myself in a meeting at the agency, getting God's opinion on a strategy or something, and I'm looking like the lead geek in a small circus sideshow, "Man With The Latex Lips."

"You'll get used to it. We can always chat on the phone if we have to. I can usually get to a phone. So, how do you like the face lift?"

"Nice, very nice."

"Actually I did a rhytidectiomy, blepharoplasty, a little brow lift, and some liposuction here and there. Oh, and some abdominoplasty on that duffel bag you call a stomach."

I look down. Feel for my gut, stomach's thin and flat now, the stomach I had when I was playing crease attack at Waverly, the abdominal muscles bumping down my belly where my paunch used to be. "So what do you want in return?"

"Ads."

"Ads?"

"Yes, like a campaign, an ad campaign."

"An umbrella campaign?" I ask, cranking on the taps, water spurting into the bowl.

"A what?"

"Umbrella campaign, advertising covering all the religions?"

"No, no, no, just my division."

"There's more than one of you?"

"Used to be just one, now there are so many I can't even keep track. Things aren't like they used to be, I'll tell you that." The hot water on my face makes me realize how cold the bathroom is. I swing back the shade and stuff the towel further down into the crevice between the window and the sill. Dinny Rein's patented wind stop.

As I let the shade flop back against the window, the staples decide to let go and *whang bang!* the shade comes crashing down over the toilet, booming and rattling like a piece of escaping sheet metal then sliding off the seat onto the floor.

"Nice place you got here," He says.

I set my razor by the side of the sink and plump up a fat pile of Barbasol on my palm. "After alimony and taxes, it's all I can afford," I say, patting the foam over my face. "So what's your problem?"

"My comparables—been down four quarters in a row."

"Comparables?"

"Attendance, church attendance. I've been up nice each year for the past ten, but that Mohammed's been off the charts, double digits with practically no marketing. Guy makes me look like I'm standing still."

"Any reason?"

"That's why I'm here."

Jeez, do I look good, I think as I glide the razor down my cheek, *will you look at that skin, glows like a little kid's!* Flicking a glob of shaving cream off the razor, I watch it spin around in the bowl. "You know, just off the top of my head, I'd say it's a high awareness/low usage kind-of-thing in your core target with the need for increased penetration among the fringe."

"See? You are one smart cookie."

"Everyone's heard of God, but not enough people are going to church, right?"

"You got it. I'm a household word that never gets spoken."

"You're Arm & Hammer."

"I'm what?"

"Arm & Hammer baking soda. Everyone had it for recipes, but it seldom got used—classic marketing story."

"That's what I need—marketing."

I stroke the razor over the new lines of my jaw, cleaning up under my chin, swishing the razor around in the water. "There are a million examples, Tabasco sauce, Bisquik, products everyone has in their cupboards but the usage interval is so long..."

"Like between Christmas and Easter, you mean."

"That's it, so the products either go bad and get thrown away...."

"Or they get ignored. Pushed to the back of the shelf with the pickles Granny canned ten years ago. That's me, God, out-of-sight and out-of-mind until little Jimmy gets run over by a car, Sis gets diagnosed with leukemia, or a tornado up-ends a trailer park, and everyone starts praying to beat the band."

"You got it."

"So what do we do?"

"Piece of cake," I say, toweling off and heading back into the bedroom. "High awareness/low usage situations are right up my alley. How much you got to spend?"

"Sky's the limit."

"Are we talking twenty million? It'll take at least twenty."

Slide the closet door open and feel my jaw dropping. Six suit bags from Bigsby & Carruthers. *You shouldn't have,* I think, looking up at the rust streaks in the ceiling.

"What?" He says. "I'm going to let my ad guy go to work wearing one of those feed sacks you call a suit? That's all the latest stuff, Armani, Abboud, Perry Ellis, take your pick. All the shirts and ties are with them, all color-coordinated, you can't go wrong."

I unzip one of the bags and slide out the suit. Shirt and tie are under the suitcoat, take off the jacket, and toss it on the bed. I haven't felt fabric like this in years. I slide a leg into the trousers, skipping over to look at myself in the mirror. Pull up the pants and stuff my arms into the shirt. *Shirt must have cost a hundred-and-a-half, sleek cotton, tiny blue stripes on white.* I slip on the jacket, 44 long, the thing fits me perfectly, even the sleeves are right. *The suit must be custom,* I think as I shoot my cuffs out so they show a quarter-inch past the sleeve. I align the ends of the tie and flip the long end over, up and through the loop. The tie is silk like Patti's panties, smooth and soft, small white stars sprinkled on navy.

"I told you—the sky's the limit. I don't care if we spend twenty, forty, sixty—whatever it takes. I've got money coming out of my ears."

Did you hear that? He's got money coming out of his ears! He must have his own mint up there. I step back and look at myself in the mirror in my new Armani, check out my new face. You should see me. The new Dinny Rein. I look like a power-broker, a Wall Street investment banker, no, no, a Hollywood agent—yes, young Hollywood agent, all I need is a tan, and I'll look like a guy who's ten years out of the William Morris mailroom and about to walk away with Demi Moore as his newest client.

Talk about makeovers, just wait until Steve Sinkle sees my new act. I'll walk into BFP&G Advertising and I bet the place will go up for grabs.

"So if I told you it will cost a hundred million bucks to get people piling into churches, that would be okay?"

"You betcha. Now I got to go, see you later."

"Wait a minute," I ask, rooting around in the junk at the bottom of the closet, old baseball mitt, couple pairs of old Nikes, some sandals. "How about some shoes?"

Wait a minute, will you look at these! A four-foot high stack of Cole-Haan shoe boxes.

I flip open the top box, gleaming black tasseled loafers, major league power shoes. *I feel like Cinderella did when she got her glass slippers.* I tuck them back in the box and push my feet into my old L. L. Bean's, stick the shoe box under my arm, grab my topcoat off the rack, and check my watch, 8:35. Stop in front of the mirror by the door.

You ought to see me—Dinsmore P. Rein—the once down-and-out ad man now fresh and crisp in an Armani suit, silk tie, and hundred-and-some-dollar shirt, with the face I had when I was thirty-five. *Just wait until they see me at the agency.* I pull the door shut behind me and squeak, squeak, squeak down the iron stairs, my Bean boots squealing on the metal treads as I juggle my box of shoes and shrug on my topcoat.

The Coca-Cola thermometer Rodriguez glued to the door pane reads thirteen above. Bang open the vestibule door and step outside.

The wind chill makes the air feel like I'm wading into freezing water, the cold rock-hard on my face and hands. A salt truck lumbers by, spinning ice-blue granules over the street. They bounce around on the frozen slush like hailstones. When the salt bounces that high, I can tell the temperature's going below ten.

The 309 bus crunches down the street hanging its exhaust out behind in a tight line. Stops in front of me. Door doesn't open. I can hear the driver shouting. He's telling me the door's frozen shut. "Door's froze shut," he yells again. I nod, stomp my feet, wave at him like it's okay. *I've got to find a better way to get to work.*

Look down the street. The next bus comes up with the door frozen open. The driver's moustache and eyebrows are loaded with frost, like someone sprayed aerosol snow on his face. I clink my coins into the change box and sit down away from the doors. The passengers are perched rigidly in their seats, occasionally blowing thought balloons of breath into the air and grimacing like they're headed to prison. I see why. When the bus gets going, the wind whistles in so hard through the open doors, we might as well be ice boating in Eau Claire.

The time/temp sign on the bank says its 8:45 and twelve degrees. Patti's just finishing up with the morning crush of commuters, blowing smoke rings in her booth and waiting for Louie to replenish the sparkle dust. *When Patti sees my new face, she'll probably faint.*

Hear the woman next to me grumbling. Look around at her. She's staring at me, her eyes are as big as golfballs. *Oh no, I sat down next to a crazoid.* Woman's got hair combed out into a fright wig like one of the Three Stooges. She's wide as a house. "Pretty fancy suit, mistah," she says, sneering at me. *Woman hasn't bathed in a week, smells like an open dumpster.* I smile at her and say, "Thank you."

"I mean, for this here bus, it's a pretty fancy suit," she says, eyeing me up and down. "You tryin' to lord it over us, wearing a suit like that on this bus?" *Maybe if I just look down at the floor she'll shut up. Not only did I pick a bus with no doors, I had to sit down next to a full-fledged fruitcake.* "I mean you got some nerve comin' on our bus lookin' like that!" Her voice starts out booming, then goes into a high screech. "Wearin' a suit like that, whatcha doin' on our bus, you honky motherfucka?" She leaps out of her seat and stands over me.

I try to smile at her, give her my widest and most genuine ad man smile. "I be saying to you, honky motherfucka, whatchoo doin' on our bus?" My smile isn't working.

She's got a rolled up copy of the *Sun-Times* in her hand. She raises it over her head. I look around at the other passengers. They're sleeping or hiding behind their newspapers. "Get offa our bus, you rich white motherfuckin' honky, this be a poor peoples' bus and you getcha ass offa it or I be whackin' you silly, you hear me, you motherfuckin' honky?"

She threatens me with the paper, curling her lip at me and shaking the paper in her hand. *That's the only problem with living in the city, never know when someone's going to go bonkers on you. They ought to lock this one up though, she's really out there.*

I'm trying to duck down in my seat in case she tries to take a swack at me.

"I be tellin' you, git off our bus, you rich honky motherfucka. Git your fancy ass offa our bus! Motherfuckaaaa!" She flails the paper down at me, once, twice, whap! Whap! The blows land on my head. I get my hands up to shield myself, slide out of the seat, and work myself toward the door trying to avoid the flailing paper. *That damn paper's hard.* Whack! Whack!

I grab for the cord, pull it. "Go buyin' yourself one of them rich people's cars, one of them Range Rovers there, and keep your motherfuckin' rich ass offa our bus, you hear?" I stumble down the steps clutching my box of Cole-Haans as the bus lurches to a stop. The woman's newspaper slams me on the back, whack! My boots crunch on the icy sidewalk.

I turn around and watch the bus pull away with the crazy woman standing at the bottom of the stairs, cackling loudly and pointing at me like I'm the funniest thing she's ever seen, howling wildly over the accelerating bus, leaning out of the door shaking her rolled-up *Sun-Times* at me.

I look around. I'm somewhere on Clark, I look for a cross street. I remember there are a bunch of car dealers up and down this part of Clark Street. Nothing open this early in the morning. My breath is frosty. *Damn, it's cold. Here I have a multimillion dollar account and an expensive new suit and I'm standing out on some godforsaken street like a homeless bum.*

I look around for a cab. Start to walk. Crunch, crunch, crunch. I hear my name, "Mr. Rein." An English accent. "Mr. Rein, your car is ready."

I turn around. A man in a sportcoat and ascot holds a glass door open. He's smiling like he knows me. I look up. It's a car showroom. "Please come in, we've been expecting you," he says All kinds of gleaming new cars in the window: Range Rover, Mercedes, Porsche. *I remember this place. I used to walk by here when I had an apartment in Lincoln Park, stop and ogle all the expensive cars. Dream about someday owning a Porsche. Fat chance.*

"Excuse me?" I ask. *He's been expecting me, how could he be expecting me?*

Ads for God

"Your car is ready," he says. I'm still standing on the sidewalk. *What car? I haven't had a car in ten years.*

"Oh, sure," I say, walking up to the door. *What in the hell is he talking about?*

"We've had it ready for an hour, thought you'd be in here a bit earlier."

Maybe he's got me mixed up with someone else?

"I got hung up on the phone unexpectedly," I say, stepping into the showroom. The carpet is thick and gray. Muzak is playing in the background. I can smell coffee.

"My name's Delbert Peabody," he says, and we shake hands. *Delbert Peabody? Jeez, sometimes those English go too far.* Delbert's got a foulard ascot tucked into a Norfolk jacket. He's wearing corduroys and suede O.J. shoes. Delbert needs to go back and get his rug fitted. It's the wrong color and looks like someone laid it on his head with a spatula and forgot to glue it down.

"Rein," he says, motioning me to sit down in front of a desk, "That's an interesting name, am I pronouncing it correctly, Mr. Rein?" He's shuffling through a pile of papers on his desk. Pulls one out and runs a pen down it.

"Rain in Spain, you got it," I say, giving him my standard pronunciation guide to my surname, someone's always trying to be cute with it. I look around the showroom.

There's a green metallic Porsche 911. I can see a huge Mercedes 600, a roadster, more Mercedes, some Range Rovers on the far side.

"The reason I ask is that in the UK, we might pronounce it 'Rhine', you never quite know." He swings a piece of paper around so it faces me and holds out a pen. "Yes, well it certainly has been a pleasure to do business with you, Mr. Rein, now if you'll just sign here to acknowledge receipt of the vehicle."

What business? What vehicle? He's giving me a free car? Wait a minute, did God go and buy me a new car?

I sign the paper where he's pointing. I try to read the handwriting to figure out what kind of car it is but he quickly pulls the paper back across the desk and stands up.

"And here are the keys," he says, pulling a set out of his desk drawer and coming around the desk, the keys jingle in his hand. "Let's go find your car."

My car! I'm actually getting a new car! I try to see what kind of keys they are. He's walking too fast. I follow him through the showroom, around the Porsche. *Is it the Porsche? God, I'd love a Porsche.*

We walk past the green Porsche, swing around a yellow convertible. *No, I guess it's not a Porsche. Okay, they're not very practical in the city, too low, the potholes would bust the bottom out inside of a week.*

He's heading toward the Mercedes. *I wouldn't mind a Mercedes. There's a beautiful dark blue one. I can see myself in that baby.* Catch the price on the sticker, $79,500. *Seventy-nine-five, hot damn! Oh, boy, I'd love that car. Can you imagine me picking up Patti in a dark blue Mercedes 500?* He goes past the blue Mercedes.

He pauses in front of a dark green 450 SL. *A 450SL, I don't believe it! I've dreamed of driving a 450SL ever since they first came out.*

He looks back at me and smiles. "Nasty weather out there, isn't it?" he says and turns, heading past the 450. I nod.

Okay so I don't get the 450. It would be cold in the winter, I guess. He's heading into the Range Rovers. Okay, Dinny, God got you a Range Rover—a Range Rover! For years you've dreamed of driving a Range Rover. It's the perfect car for Chicago and you can drive it to Michigan to pick up a Christmas tree with Patti or take her skiing in Wisconsin, go camping in Canada.

He stops in front of a white Range Rover. *White, yes, my favorite!* I catch up with him, and he walks around the white one. *Okay, I'll take the tan one there. I've always liked tan, sort of.*

He's heading for a black Range Rover. *Black! I've always wanted a black car!* It's decked out for a safari with floodlights the size of dinner plates on the roof rack, brush guards around the headlights and tail lights.

"And here's the machine you ordered, Mr. Rein, we just finished putting on all the custom equipment you asked for last night." He pats the Range Rover on the fender, then polishes off his fingerprints with the cuff of his jacket. "Your car phone's all hooked up like you asked, and it's ready to go," he says as he opens the front door. "Your mobile number's right here."

Ads for God

I peer into the car. Smell leather. Dark gray, the interior is stitched and padded, sleek and elegant. He points at a yellow square of paper stuck on the shift. I see the phone number written on it. I climb up into the seat. I settle in. I can imagine myself bumping up a mountain in Nepal, fording a stream in Borneo.

"Here's the sticker," the salesman says, handing me a sheet of paper. "We do appreciate people who understand our one-price policy and don't need to haggle," he says.

I look at the sticker. *55 grand base, another eight grand worth of options, taxes take it up to 65. Who's haggling? Boy, does this car smell neat.*

Delbert Peabody shows me all the features of the car, heated seats, subwoofer on the stereo. *I'm wondering if I should ask Delbert who arranged for the car? But I'd probably sound stupid. Maybe He impersonated me when I was asleep? Maybe that's how He got my suits to fit so well. Who knows and who cares?*

"Enjoy your new Range Rover, Mr. Rein," Delbert says as he shakes my hand again and shuts the door. He walks toward the wall and pushes a red button.

I start the car as the overhead door screeches up, shift into D, and turn on the stereo. It's Beethoven's *Seventh Symphony*, or maybe it's the *Ninth*. Buy a $65,000 car, and they throw in a free CD, not bad.

Delbert waves at me as I pull out of the showroom, adjusting his rug with the other hand. I make a left down Clark and step on it. The Range Rover jumps forward. Beethoven's blasting away, subwoofers thumping out the tympani, and I'm wheeling in and out of traffic, cruising down Clark, sitting high and mighty in my new Range Rover.

People look up at me as I pass, wondering who the guy in the new Rover and snazzy suit is. I hear a buzz, then another. *It's the car phone. Who would be calling me on my car phone? No one even knows the number yet.*

I grab the handset and push the SEND button.

"Hello," I say.

"Yo, honky motherfucka, how you be likin' your new car?"

7

I walk quickly into the lobby. No one's on the open elevator. Hit 10 and do an Inspector Clouseau tuck and turn in the lobby of my floor so the receptionist won't see me, hunching my shoulders down into the collar of my topcoat, and speedwalking toward my cubicle.

Slip into my office and shut the door. Hang up my topcoat and check myself in the mirror on the side of my bookcase to see if I still have my new face. Brightly-painted frame Addy brought me from Mexico, octagonal with pink and yellow dogs barking in the corners.

Yup, still have my movie star look, my slightly hangdog but oh so handsome face. What was that movie star's name anyway?— and watch what happens when I smile. *C'mon Dinny Rein, give us a smile. There, that's it!* My face brightens like the sun's coming out, the smile that used to make the girls sidle up and the clients sign on the dotted line. *Okay, Sinkle, here I come—ready or not.*

Open the door and step out into the corridor. Walking like I strode onto the lacrosse field at Waverly. A trick I had. I kept my spine straight and head up but my right arm bent slightly and my wrist limp. My secretary (when I had a secretary) said I walked like JFK. Remember how he walked bent forward a little bit with his hand in his pocket?

So my body language is saying, "Yeah, I'm the guy who scored thirty-five goals so far this season, but I'm gangly and slight so don't worry about me." The defensemen would step back and play me loose and I'd score one, two, three, four, five goals just like that and before they knew it put the game away for dear old Waverly.

Ads for God

Two receptionists carrying Dr. Peppers and muffins in wax paper bags stand aside for me, deferentially backing against the corridor walls. *They don't even recognize me—must think I'm a client or something.* Walk past a work area, bunches of desks, Xerox machines, secretaries and typists, phones ringing, messengers slouched on an upholstered bench. A secretary looks up as I pass.

"Morning, Darlene," I say. I can see her eyes took a picture of me and her brain's now trying to process the picture. *It's going to be a day of double takes.* "It's Dinny Rein," I hear someone whisper.

"Look, it's Mr. Rein," another secretary says. Much elbowing and pointing. I turn around and give the group a wink and a wave.

An audible chorus of "ooooh's" rises from the area. Pass a glassed-in conference room where Marcus What's-His-Name from Media is giving a presentation. All heads turn to me as I walk past, eyes locked onto the new Dinny Rein like they're soldiers in formation passing a reviewing stand.

"The agency business runs on rumors," Benny Boston said more than once, "and people stand around the water cooler all day going yamma-yamma-yamma." He'd say, "yamma-yamma-yamma," making a noise in his screechy voice like a car's wheel trying to spin it's way out of a snow rut.

Around the agency, rumors used to be called scuttlebutt or gossip but Benny's comment spawned a new expression: "What's the yamma-yamma?" Meaning what are the rumors of accounts won or accounts lost, accounts on the rocks or ready to skyrocket; who's promoted or demoted, who's in, who's out, who got a big offer from the hot new agency in Palo Alto, or who's crashed and burned and is looking for a hideout in Terre Haute.

I had the best yamma-yamma in the office for years. Then everything went south and I had to start slinking out of my office, walking quickly to the elevators so no one would see me and be forced to say, "Sorry to hear you lost snacks, Dinny," making lame attempts at cheering me up by saying, "Who wants all that responsibility anyway?" or cracking dumb cup-of-coffee jokes, "Know what ninety-cents and a vice-presidency will get you?"

My daughter Addy was convinced all the bad yamma-yamma affected my posture. Said I was starting to carry myself like Jimmy Durante.

By the time I get to Sinkle's office, the yamma-yamma has hit the executive floor. People are lining the hallways like it's VJ Day, standing in their doorways waiting to see the new Dinny Rein. Assistant AE's and account executives, account supervisors, account directors, management supervisors (there are more titles in ad agencies than toilets), people are leaning against the doorjambs pretending they're reading reports so they don't seem obvious, standing chatting with their neighbors, one guy's even acting like the door hinges are interesting.

As I pass through the gauntlet of account people, I leave a chatter of conversation in my wake.

"He must have gotten a face-lift."

"I wonder how much it cost him?"

"Must be that new kind of plastic surgery."

"He looks twenty years younger."

"That's what losing thirty pounds will do for you."

"I wonder what he's seeing Sinkle about?"

"I heard he got a big account."

"He sure needs one. I heard he was on his last leg."

"Sure doesn't look like the Noodles I used to know."

The corridor widens and the walls change when you get close to Sinkle Territory. Drywall turns to somber veneer, then the carpet gets thicker, you can feel it with your feet. The lights dim, acoustical panels on the ceiling change to flat white punctuated by pin-spots casting pools of light over the gray pile.

Pass offices with smoke glass windows and dark wood doors. Sinkle's top flunkies (Platt, Plevis, Durnberg, and Murray the CFO) are massed around him like knights around a king, arrayed down the darkened corridors decorated with Currier & Ives prints and covered with dark green felt so the place feels like a men's club (which it is, except for Ester).

Walk past Lorna at the antique desk. She wants to ask "Do you have an appointment, Mr. Rein?" but her eyes are open so wide her mouth is forced out of commission. I head into the inner sanctum, hearing Lorna frantically punching buttons to alert her boss of my arrival.

Ads for God

Stride past the painting of the Pantheon by Gainsborough's protégé into Steve Sinkle's private reception room. The carpet gets even thicker. Mozart is playing on the Muzak. Harpsichord. *Wrong music for an ad agency,* I'm thinking, *should be Spike Jones.*

Vincent, Sinkle's English butler who peels him a navel orange each morning for breakfast, stripping the oranges so clean they look naked, stands with his back against the far wall, guarding the corridor to Sinkle's office. He's all duded-up in his morning coat and would look mildly impressive except Vincent has dense stands of white hairs sticking up from the tops of his ears and his skin is pink and flaky. I wouldn't let him peel my morning orange in a million years.

"You have an appointment, Sir?" he asks, his words arch and reedy from years of talking through his nostrils. He huffs and snorts as I stride past him into the passageway to Sinkle's office.

I used to get the sweats walking into Sinkle's office. He must have told his architect to design it to make people feel inconsequential. The architect does his research and discovers spelunking isn't a popular sport so he designs a long and narrow corridor leading into Sinkle Land. It must be a good twelve feet, shoulder width, with a ceiling so low you feel like you're going to hit your head, so you feel like you need to crouch down and tilt your head to the side.

I used to start sweating halfway through, the perspiration wicking through the front of my shirt, my forehead starting to drip like it was the fourth quarter of a close lacrosse game on a steamy June Saturday. And if the passageway makes you feel small, when you enter his office you feel like a midget climbing out of a small box and standing up under a big Montana sky.

The huge room stupefies people, renders them speechless (which is exactly what Sinkle wants). It's 30x40 easy with a seventeen-foot ceiling. We're talking high Kensington Palace here. Walnut wainscoting, English antiques, and crystal chandeliers that used to shine down on Queen Victoria's state dinners.

The walls have what I call his Family Windsor wallpaper, hairy swirling shapes of green and cream that look like the planaria I used to slice apart in junior high, all turning and swimming against a ball park mustard-colored background.

Sinkle caught a bad case of Anglomania from his two cultural mentors, Benny Boston and Ralph Lauren, so the place is cluttered with British Empire bric-a-brac, Churchillian mementos, even models of castles.

I step into the room and see Sinkle at his Regency desk, feet up, arms behind his head, ignoring me. Normally I'd cough or say "excuse me," but now I'm holding the high cards, no more slinking and sniveling.

Just remember Rein, stay silent like you've got a secret—turn away from him when you talk and always keep your back to the window, play Sinkle's game and one-up him at it—you can do it.

I walk quickly toward the window. Sinkle's got a double-wide window so when he opens the drapes, the light blinds you. He hits the switch on his desk to part the curtains. "Let's have a good look at the new Dinny Rein," he says, like he's already gotten the yamma-yamma on my face-lift.

I walk past him and sit down on the window seat so the light is behind me. Pick up a copy of the English edition of *Town & Country*. Ad for a castle on the back cover. I put a leg up on the window seat so Sinkle can see my new shoes. Sinkle's blinking. They want a million pounds for the castle.

I look up from the magazine slowly. "Morning, Steve," I say and go back to reading about the view of the English countryside from the castle's tallest parapet.

"I need a D & B on that new client of yours," Sinkle says, swinging his feet off the desk and shifting his body so I block the light from the window.

"What makes you think I have a new client?"

"C'mon, Rein," he says, blustering, his lip curling as he taps his Tiffany letter opener on his desk pad. "There's ten million bucks in our new business account. It didn't pop out of thin air."

Don't bet on it, Buddy, I'm thinking. I set the *Town & Country* down on the window seat, start around in front of his desk. I don't even glance at him. Hitch my leg up on the seat of one of his leather-upholstered chairs rimmed with a million round-headed brass tacks running around the edges of the dark green leather, turn, and face him.

"You'll play by my rules on this one, Sinkle, or I'll walk the account down the street to another agency in a flash. Thompson or Burnett would love this one."

We start a stare-off. Stare-offs are another Sinkle specialty. Who's going to flinch first? Like a shoot-out in the old westerns. Keeps drilling you with his eyes, slight smile cracked across his face, until you cave and say something you don't mean to say to fill up the silence.

I read in an airline magazine, inflight wisdom, that people can't stand silence. Makes them skittish, uncomfortable, so they fill up the space with blather. Words they say just for the sake of saying something. Back when Sinkle demoted me, he stared at me for a full three minutes and I got so nervous, you know what I finally blurted out? I said, "I'm sorry, Steve."

Can you believe that, Sinkle demotes me and what do I do? *I apologize.*

Sinkle quickly stands and turns toward the window, his back to me. The stare-off is over. He broke it, but he's not looking at me, so to Sinkle, it's a tie. Steve Sinkle doesn't ever like to lose. "What's the billing?" he asks.

I take the most circuitous route around the office back to the window. Past the bust of Oliver Cromwell sitting on the marble column, past the deep frames rimmed in gold containing personal letters from Winston Churchill to FDR, around the scale model of the Windsors' country retreat, walking right up to Sinkle's shoulder.

I'm looking for a thread, a piece of lint, flake of dandruff. Fortunately there is a ball bearing-sized lint ball on his lapel. I reach for it like I'm a surgeon reaching into the abdomen to excise a tumor. Lift the lint ball off the lapel. Slowly. Sinkle's watching me. Flick the lint ball across the space in front of him. It arcs through the light coming off the lake and bounces on the oriental. I try to toss off the words, in the same tone I'd answer Patti if she asked me what I wanted from the Jewel. "Fifty to start, could go high as a hundred," I tell him, like I'd say to Patti, "Loaf of bread and some Delicious apples."

I dust off Sinkle's lapel and go back to my museum tour, checking out the model castle, tiny trees massed around it that look just like the real thing.

I can hear the Pentium processor embedded in Sinkle's brain running the numbers. Even if he's working with the low figure, the commission's almost eight million. Sinkle knows he can take at least two to the bottom line. Big leg up on his stock buyout. He'll be able to get Benny, Frank, and Gus off his back in less than two years. No more sitting in a deck chair on the back deck of Benny's boat with the stink of sea bass all around, listening to lectures on how to run the agency. He can get rid of Sirini and Woof!, the deadbeat accounts he can't control, and change the plaque downstairs so his name is emblazoned in bronze on Michigan Avenue for the next fifty years.

"What's the product?"

I walk up to the window. The air is still over the lake. The water gray. Wait four beats and then say, "Love, peace, brotherhood, charity, hope, patience, and understanding," slowly and quietly, my voice taking on a bit of a southern preacher cadence.

I hear Sinkle's chair creaking as he bounds up and barks in my ear, "What? You got some crackpot for a client? Some former peace-and-love hippie who's made a billion in real estate and suddenly seen the light?"

I do a wide circle around his office. Stop in the center and look back at him, "You got a ten million dollar advance with at least forty more to come. What do you care? I'll run the business, give you a weekly report—looks like easy money to me, Steve."

"I've got to know where this money's coming from, Rein. I can't put the entire agency at jeopardy by taking ten million from a client I've never even met."

"You'll meet him."

"Super—when?"

"When I'm good and ready."

Sinkle sits down slowly. Swings his feet up on his desk. Taps his desk with his letter opener. A minute goes by before he looks up at me and asks, "Where'd you find this client, Rein?"

I walk up to him, stand in front of his desk. For the first time in my life I'm looking down on Steve Sinkle. I can feel my fist clenching. I want to punch him in the mouth. For taking away my title and corner office, for letting Ester knock my salary down to next to nothing and banishing my secretary to the office pool, and then for taking me to the Mid-America Club one fine day in May, sitting me next to a window a hundred stories up, and dropping a nuclear device on my career.

While the waiter set the hearts of palm with gorgonzola dressing in front of me, Sinkle told me that I was talented but needed direction. I looked over my knee at Michigan Avenue a thousand feet down and heard Sinkle say that he was hiring a new creative director. Over lamb chops with mint jelly, browned new potatoes and French cut string beans, Sinkle told me that Ester Platt was the most talented creative person he'd ever met and how much I'd like working for her. Then as we walked out of the Mid-America Club toward the elevators, he swung his arm over my shoulder and told me that the most amazing thing about Ester Platt was that she'd never spent a day in the advertising business.

I wanted to kill him then. I want to torture him now. So I shake my head.

"What do you mean?" he asks.

"No details on the client, no names, not one piece of information, that's the deal. Take it or leave it."

"You're not going to tell me who the client is or even how you found him? C'mon, Rein, this is ridiculous. I'm president of the damn agency and I've got to know if this whole thing is legit."

"It's legit, believe me. He's somebody who made millions in the market and now he wants to give something back. That's all I can say. He's intent on remaining anonymous. It's part of the deal."

"Nothing doing. Unacceptable."

I reach across his desk and extend my hand. "It's been wonderful, Steve," I say, letting a sardonic grin spread across my face.

This is the way you play the Sinkle game, check your civility at the door and bluster, bully, and bluff until you get what you want.

"Hang on," he says slowly. "Let's see if there's a middle ground here."

I shake my head, "No middle ground, Steve. And there's a few more things you should know about. I want to be Co-Creative Director with Ester. I'm running this business. She can run everything else. I'm not going to have her mucking up my account with a bunch of hip, snide, in-your-face advertising done by her crew of overpaid adolescents."

"She'll quit."

"That's your problem. The creative on this account needs to be handled with restraint and discretion—which is in short supply in her group. So—I run the show, you triple my salary and stay on the sidelines—or..." I flip my thumb toward the passageway.

Sinkle's eyes are flitting left and right. He's looking for a way out, trying to figure out how he can one-up me, slant off-tackle and break into the secondary, shed a few defenders, and take the fifty-million dollar account in for the score. But he knows he's dead before he hits the line.

"I'll double your salary effective today, triple it when your client's spent twenty-five million—that's the deal." *He's giving me the Co-CD job. He'll cave on the rest.*

"Triple it now, and guarantee me you'll stay out of the business." I give him one of those open-arm gestures the pushcart vendors down at Maxwell Street used to give you when you got their best price.

With a hundred and fifty grand a year, I can send Patti Shaw to college full-time, get a decent apartment, rent a vacation place in Michigan—finally get some payback for being pissed on for the past eleven years.

"On the sidelines," he says, "that's what you said before."

He went for the raise. I've got my job back, tripled my salary. I've finally got Steve Sinkle right where I want him.

He stands and buttons his charcoal-gray worsted. Game's over and, in Sinkle's mind, he thinks he's won. He walks around the side of the desk and puts out his hand. We shake. He tries a vise-grip. I jack up the pressure. I didn't hold a lacrosse stick five years for nothing. He slackens his grip, puts his arm around me. For a second, I feel like I'm back in at the Mid-America Club.

Watch it, Rein, you're dealing with the devil here.

"So gimme an idea about your client," Sinkle's foraging for information. "What's his name? Where did he make all his money? C'mon Rein."

He's sniffing the info out like a beagle rummaging around tree roots for a rabbit. To account people, information is power. Give it to them and they're gone, like an attackman getting around a defenseman in lacrosse. The defensemen have to keep the attack guy away, fend him off with their stick, keep whacking him silly, bashing him away with their forearms. For once he gets in close and rolls a shoulder into the D, he'll lickety-split rotate right around them, leaving the D flat-footed and watching with his mouth open as the attackman races in and whips the ball into the goal.

"Can't. I talk and the client walks. It's that simple." Look up at Sinkle. Our faces are ten inches away. I can see the hole where his tooth used to be.

Are we going to go for another stare-off?

Sinkle turns and walks back behind his desk. "Okay, when do we start?" he says.

No, he's going into the locker room and try to come out big in the second half.

"Tomorrow. I'll need three teams."

"I'll talk to Ester."

It's time for my lead balloon, I say to myself, *drop it and get the hell out of there.*

"Do that," I say, and head out the door, without looking back, spelunking straight into the tunnel and out into the reception room, sailing past Vincent who's still sputtering, and past Lorna, who still hasn't got full control of her facial muscles, thinking *I never knew how good it feels to have your boss by the balls.*

8

I take a walk at lunchtime. The air's chilly, but the sun is sliding in and out of the clouds, bringing people outside to enjoy the first sunshine they've seen since September. I pass the good doctor Poesemon doing his penguin walk down Michigan, legs moving like they're tied together at the knees, upper body bopping back and forth, his little eyes squinting even in the slight sunshine. *Will you look at that—my doctor of twenty-two years doesn't even recognize me.*

As I walk by the tall lady in the yellow cloth coat with the marathon runner's body, holding her Starbucks bag and looking right through me, I think, *Hold on. Wait a minute. That's my daughter Addy.*

I turn around and watch her striding down the sidewalk, waiting until she gets ten feet away, then call out, "Hey Addy—how about dinner tonight?" She stops and turns around. Turns away again, pauses, looks back. Her face is a puzzle. All she recognizes is my voice. Faces her body to me.

Her coat has those braid buttons like in *Dr. Zhivago*. Her hand comes up slowly, finger extending as if pointing will help identify me. Her lips separate, jaw keeps dropping, eyes widen, finger straightens. She's almost got it.

"It's me," I say, walking toward her, holding up my arms like I'm Billy Graham. Addy can't talk. I mean she can, her mouth is moving sort of but there are no words coming out.

A businessman bumps me in the back. Starts to mutter as he comes around me. Sees I'm somebody, somebody in a fancy suit, thinks maybe I might know his boss, says, "Oh, sorry," and scrambles on.

"How about having dinner tonight? I want to hear all about your new job." I give her a hug. "And I've got a bunch of good news for you, too." She puts her hand on my face, tentatively, stroking my skin the way she'd pat a strange cat.

"It's you..." she says, like she just came up with the Theory of Relativity.

"Who'd you expect, Harry Truman? So how about dinner?"

She comes closer, bends back my ear and peeks behind it, whispers, "Where are they?"

"Where are what?"

"Scars, I don't see any scars."

"Miracle of the laser," I say, while she's laying back my other ear to make sure.

"And I saw you yesterday..." she says to herself, shaking her head.

"It's amazing what they can do these days, isn't it?"

A smile starts in her eyes and speeds across her face, "You look wonderful, Daddy." She leans in and gives me a big kiss and a hug. She steps back and takes another look at me. "New suit too, huh?" she says, sliding her fingers up and down the lapel.

In her eyes there's a look I haven't seen for a long time, instead of stringing together a bunch of stupid jokes to cover up my slide downhill, Addy can see I'm finally doing something for myself.

"Like my daddy said, no point in washing the car unless you wax it too." Mentioning her grandfather Clarence melts her. Addy used to sit on my dad's knee for hours back in Stergus listening to his stories about hunting skunks and picking blueberries.

Addy gives me a half-laugh. "So, dinner, what time?"

"6:30 sharp."

"Where?"

"Where else?" I say. I love the restaurant but I can never remember the name.

"Scoozi?" she says.

"6:30."

"See you, Daddy," she says. We both do that movie walk-away thing, slow-walking backwards, both facing each other, like we can't figure out how to say good-bye.

"Bye, girl," I say and turn back up Michigan, feeling my daughter Addy's wonderment shining back at me from ten feet away. "You look wonderful," I hear Addy call out. I turn around and wave back at her, "Thanks." Addy blows a kiss at me, turns, and walks off leaving a little wave of her hand behind.

I watch her meld into the hustling commuters, thinking *Even my daughter's looking at me differently.*

The yamma-yamma about my meeting with Sinkle is all over the office by the time I get back upstairs and everyone's all over me with compliments and praise, flattery, and blandishments. Someone finally is standing up to Sinkle. *And it's me, Dinny Rein, doing his Lazarus act, the formerly half-dead ad man back from advertising oblivion.*

"Congratulations, Mr. Rein."

"Hey, Dinny, way to go."

"Now we're really going to take off" people are saying as I walk down the corridor toward my office.

"Dinny, you look great."

"Now we're really going to have some fun around here."

"Nice suit, Mr. Rein."

I get to my office, shut my door, and hook my topcoat on the nail. *I've got to do something about this office.* To show you how far I got pushed down the totem pole in my dark days, Office Services wouldn't even put a hook on the back of my door. "You're no longer at the level authorized to have door-mounted coat hooks," the girl in Office Services said. I had to bring in a nail and hammer from home and pound the sucker in all by myself so I'd have somewhere to hang my coat.

Turn around and head for the phone.

Come to a dead stop when I feel something in my office. I'm not into Zen, but when you've got an office as tiny as mine, it's something you feel right away, bad vibrations, as we used to say back in the Seventies.

Look up and see a hefty guy sitting by the window reading *Car And Driver*, weighs two-fifty at least, maybe more. He's got his legs crossed, blue suede Hush Puppies, and shiny green pants.

Ads for God

Chewing gum, wearing a blue satin baseball warm-up jacket, see the Yankee emblem, bat sticking through a top hat. Orange and blue Chicago Bears stocking cap perched on his head. Looks like he used to be a light heavyweight. Rocky Marciano's second cousin. Nose smushed against his face, puffy ears, raised strips of skin peeking through his eyebrows, needs a shave. I figure he's a messenger and the receptionist let him in. Supposed to pick something up from me maybe?

"Can I help you?" I ask.

He looks up from his magazine. Not a friendly face. "Yeah," he says, like he forgot why he's sitting in my office. "Yeah, you can, as a matter of fact." He puts down the *Car And Driver* and turns to me, resting his forearms on his knees. His head hangs like it's heavy. "As a matter of fact, you can." His neck is the size of a paint can. "You can help."

He gets up like he's got arthritis, twisting his back and grimacing. Comes up to me hands on his hips, shaking one leg and flapping his pants so they unstick from his leg. Clears his throat.

"So you make commercials?" he turns his head to the side and shakes his head. Then bangs it with the flat of his hand twice, like he's got water in his ear.

"Sure, that's what I do, commercials." *What's this character doing in my office? What does he want out of me?*

"Any commercials I'm going to know?" he says.

"How about Woof!Burger dog food? Or Sirini Pasta, you know the commercials for Sirini, the jingle? Nobody makes a noodle like Sirini?" I say, bright and breezy like the typical ad guy.

The man in the Bears stocking cap slides his hand into his baseball jacket. Slowly extracts the largest knife I've ever seen. Fifteen inches long and shiny, something Daniel Boone would have used to gut bear.

Oh shit, now I'm really in trouble.

He looks at me as the knife glides out. "This make you nervous?"

"No, yes, I mean..."

"Manicure, that's all," he says and giggles, a string of high whinnies like you hear from a horse. "I got ingrown nails," holding the knife by the end of the blade and delicately running the point under his thumbnail. His face gets serious again, "Now sing it."

"What?"

"Sing the Sirini thing."

"You want me to sing the jingle?" *Maybe I should call Security.* He stops cleaning his nails and looks up at me. *Maybe I should just sing.* I feel my stomach involuntarily sucking in. He's holding the knife so if he suddenly thrust it forward, he'd turn me into instant shish-kebab.

I'll just sing one verse and hope he goes away. "Okay," I say, starting to sing the jingle:

"Orzo, penne, and linguine,
farfalle, riso, and rotini,
macaroni, capellini, gnocchi, and tor-tell-i-ni,
nobody, nobody, nobody...
makes a noodle like Sir-i-ni!,"

and I do a *sotto voce* ringout at the end, "rini, rini, rini, rini..."

"Yeah, I heard that. Not bad. Noodles are shit, though." He looks up at me to see if I'm going to challenge him.

I give him a shrug. *Time to see if I can get this character out of here.*

"So what can I do to help you? I'm pretty busy here, so if you don't mind."

"No, that's okay, I'll be going. I just wanted to meet you."

Meet me? Why does he want to meet me?

He nods, sticks out his hand, "Name's Ralph."

I shake hands with him, "I'm Dinny Rein."

"I know and I'll be in touch with you," he says as he reaches for the door handle. "As a matter of fact, I'll be in touch *soon*." He sticks the knife back in his jacket and steps into the corridor.

"Can I ask you about what?"

He shakes his head and walks backward down the corridor, eyes leveled at me. Points at me from halfway down the corridor. He's starts to shake his head like I've done something wrong, then disappears around the corner.

Holy shit, what was that all about?

I adjust my tie and step back into my office. Shut the door. Pick up *Car And Driver,* look at it. Set it back down on the sill.

Ads for God

I'm going to give Him a piece of my mind. That's what I'll do.

I lift my head up toward the ceiling so I'm staring at the acoustical tile and the bank of fluorescents. "You up there?" I ask. "If you're up there, I want an answer, okay? Was that you or what? Can you clue me in on what's going on here? Who's that guy and what does he want?" I'm starting to get aggravated. I take out my cell phone, whip up the antenna, and turn it on.

I yell into it, "C'mon, God, where are you? Show up as Abe Moskowitz or the black lady on the bus, I don't care. I need to talk to you. I don't need characters like that coming into my office waving a big pigsticker around like that. If this is your idea of a joke, I've had it," I continue. "C'mon, I'm serious. If he's looking for that ten million you said you snagged, count me out, okay? Take back Your suits and Your shoes *and* Your ten million bucks. Take back the car and make me fifty-five again if you want, I don't care. I'm not going to play if the game's going to be like this. You hear me? C'mon, God, You up there or not?"

I stop, realize I'm almost shouting.

Jeez, maybe I'm talking too loud. Got to watch things like that.

Stop and listen. All I can hear is the low hush of the heat blowing in through the ceiling vents. Put the phone down. *Okay, maybe nobody heard me.* Sit down at my desk. Catch my new face in Addy's Mexican mirror. *Boy, do I look good.* Adjust my tie, straighten my suitcoat. *Okay, maybe that Ralph character showing up in my office was just a one-time thing. But if he shows up again, you can be sure the big guy's going to hear about it.*

Uh, oh, what's that? *Sounds like a growl.* Then I hear knocking on my door. *I wonder if they heard me yelling?* I get up and walk to the door. Listen. More growling. Open the door slowly. Look down and see that hairy little face, snarly muzzle with the lip curling up. Pair of cream high heels right behind the little critter, it's Mort and his master, the one and only Ester Platt, my Co-Creative Director. I open the door wider.

Oh boy, it's her in all her glory. Sigourney Weaver in my doorway, three feet away. We've never been so close, the sight of her hits me like a blast of hot humid air. Heart's going, "ka-thunk, ka-thunk, ka-thunk."

Mort lifts his lip at me and gives me a low snarl as Ester brushes past, wearing something that makes her smell like the daylily greenhouse in Grant Park during the spring flower show, so perfumey-sweet it makes me dizzy.

"I thought you might have been in a meeting," she says, looking around, "I heard someone talking." Mort's casing my office, probably looking for a place to piss. Ester stops in the middle of my office and turns around to face me.

Va-va-va-voom. Tight blouse, six-inch dart in her skirt, hair shading one eye, sly smile. The woman gets me nervous, rattled is a better word. She's a double-barreled shotgun. One barrel's a heavy load of women's lib and the other's a sultry sexpot, skin-tight skirts and blouse buttons working overtime to keep her tits in, legs that go on forever, and an ass I have a hard time keeping my eyes off of.

Ester's got a new twist on gender equality. Her reasoning must go something like this, "We're all equal, but I've got a better body." She uses her body as a weapon, flaunts it around to get you looking, and then beats you silly with it. Admire her cleavage when she bends over and she'll catch you with her eyes and stare you down until you start to blush. Gaze too long when she crosses her legs and she'll call you on it. "Something distracting you, Dinny?" she once said to me in the middle of a meeting, sneering at me as she adjusted the hem of her skirt.

Everyone knew what Ester was talking about. Glances ricocheting around the conference room like bullets. And the yamma-yamma around the office the next day was that Dinny Rein was a lecherous pig. For the next two weeks, Ester made me the featured entree at her male chauvinist pig roast.

I told Sinkle her behavior was Sexual McCarthyism. He said he didn't care as long as she kept the quality of the creative up. "That's why *she's* got the job..." he said, letting his voice trail off and giving me one of his most poisonous smiles.

Ester Platt's eyes walk up and down the new Dinny Rein, checking out my hair, face, the cut of my new suit, stopping at my shoes. You can be sure if I had looked at her that way, I'd have been out of a job in a second. "Congratulations on your new job," she says. "Steve said you need some help."

I nod, sit down at my desk. She sits down in the chair near the window. Makes a three-act play out of crossing her legs and arranging her skirt. My eyes dart back and forth over the show, quick cuts of gleaming polyester and silky legs, skirt dropping in slow motion over her knees, one thigh sliding over the other accompanied by the soft shush of her pantyhose as they slide together.

"Yes, thanks. I'll be needing three or four teams for two or three weeks to get this thing off the ground," I say.

Creative directors are like army generals, the larger their armies of writers and art directors, the more accounts they can handle. More accounts mean more money for the agency and a larger budget for the creative director along with a bigger office and more yamma-yamma. A creative director with a healthy budget can lure creative stars away from other agencies, add to the group's firepower, steal accounts from other creative directors, win new business, strengthen his or her position in the agency, maybe eventually take over the whole shop.

Back in my salad days, I used to have fifteen teams of writer/AD's, came close to getting my name on the door, I used to—*oh boy, there I go again.*

"I'll give you Peavis, Billy, Sondra, and Roscoe for two weeks," Ester offers, holding her hand out to check her nails. She's trying to pass off her marginal people to me, saddling me with her deadwood while she puts her ace teams on my business and takes the account away from me. That's S.O.P. in the ad biz.

Her writer, Peavis, spends more time down in the Flying Schooner than he does at the agency. His AD, Billy, is not bad but he's got a wicked temper. He's threatened people at pencil-point for not liking the color blue. Sondra and Roscoe are both over the hill, fifty-plus year-olds who dress like ad people did in the Seventies. Roscoe still wears a coat and tie and Sondra wears striped shirtwaists and blue high heels, hair clipped in a pageboy like Doris Day. Stars in the Seventies, they haven't done any television in twenty years. Instead they've become the grunts in the creative army (not far from where I was two short days ago), trying to hang on to their jobs: doing odds and ends nobody else wants to do like writing box and coupon copy, shooting package shots, doing Christmas cards for clients, brochures for Plevis on the new dental plan.

"That's not who I had in mind," I say.

"Those are the only people I can free up right now," she says, getting up and heading toward the door. "I don't have anyone else to give you."

Ester stops and leans against the glass block wall of my office, arms and legs crossed, like she's waiting for a bus. She's so cool she should be smoking a cigarette.

I hear the ringing, muffled sound of a cell phone somewhere. "It's for me," she says, patting the pocket of her jacket. She takes the phone out, one of those little Motorolas the size of a makeup compact, opens it up, and turns to the wall.

Ester says, "Hello?" I can tell it's the beer client the way she's talking. "Perry, I'm so glad you called…" Sounds intimate, like she's got something going with him. "Excuse me just a minute…"

She edges out of my office and pulls the door closed behind her so I'm left alone to dog-sit. I look at Mort, the four-legged dust mop. He turns to the closed door and gnarls. Then he starts to skitter across the rug toward me. Mort's got midget legs and his hair's so long you can't see his feet move. He looks like he's a motorized toy from Mattel. The dog stops, looks up at me, and rotates his head to the side, almost like he's going to say something.

"You know, I thought I'd like being a dog, but it sucks." *Wait a minute, who said that?* I look behind me to make sure no one's in my office.

"It's me, Rein, down here. I'm the dog." Mort's mouth is moving. *The dog's talking, God is the damn dog.*

"You're a dog?" I ask.

Is this crazy or what? Here I am in an advertising agency talking to God and He's transmogrified himself into a talking schnauzer!

"You betcha, always wanted to see what it was like to have four legs. But I tell you, after walking around this office all morning, I've had it. You know what four legs means? It means you've got to take all that walking and multiply it by two. By two! Now tell me that's not tired. And you're so low to the ground, you pick up all this lint—now I see why they call it a dog's life."

"Listen, I've got some things I want to talk to you about."

"Yeah, yeah, yeah, but we don't have much time. She'll be back in here any minute. I'm warning you, Rein. You've got to watch this broad. Watch her like a hawk. She's wily like a weasel. She'll do you in before you know it, I tell you. Vicious, she's very vicious, very very vicious, had problems with her father, it's a long story—all that psychology stuff."

"So what do I do?"

"Don't give her an inch, you understand? Not one stinking inch. Otherwise before you know it she'll be having you for lunch... Say, do me a favor?"

"Sure."

"Scratch behind this ear, willya?" I reach down and wiggle my finger behind Mort's ear. "A little to the left," he says. I hear the door opening and look up to see Ester coming back into my office.

"I'm surprised that Mort's letting you do that," Ester says. "Normally, he tries to take a chunk out of anyone who tries to pat him."

"Actually, he asked me to."

Ester gives me a look. I can tell she's thinking, *"Right, buddy, and I'm the Queen of Sheba."*

"Look, Ester," I stop scratching Mort. "I've got a big account here, could be very important to the future of the agency. I'm asking you for some more firepower."

Ester's looking at her foot, sliding it in and out of her shoe, focusing on it as if the way her neatly-sculpted heel slips in and out of the back of her pump was infinitely more interesting than Dinny Rein and his staffing problems.

"Why don't you hire some freelancers?" she says, acting like she's trying to be helpful.

"I don't have the time to get freelancers up to speed. How about giving me Rosemary and a couple of your beer teams."

Ester shakes her head, "Look, I've got fifteen accounts and you've got three, we might be sharing the same job now, but all my accounts are active so I don't have anybody available, okay?" Her voice tells me she's tired of talking to me.

She looks toward the door like she's going to leave, then stops suddenly and asks, "So, who's this new client of yours?" She's looking up at the ceiling tiles like she couldn't care less. "Steve didn't give me much of an idea."

"Wealthy retired guy—he has this idea that advertising can help change the world and he's chosen us to help him."

"I don't know if we can change the world but we can sure make a splash with fifty million. Is he some friend of yours?" Ester says, as if friendship could be the only motivation for someone to bring Dinny Rein an account of this size.

"Business acquaintance," I counter.

Ester sighs. Relationships complicate things. She doesn't want to have to deal with Dinny Rein again. Now she has to. At least, she figures, until she and Sinkle succeed in winning my client over to their side.

"Really?" she says, nodding and shifting into gear. She strides quickly across my office, pulls my other chair over, sets it in front of me, and sits down. Shifts her butt sidewise in the chair, crosses her legs, throws her arm over the back, and extends her index finger so it rests under her chin. Real relaxed posture.

"Let's have a little chat" is the message she's trying to convey with her body. But to me, anyone who swims with Steve Sinkle has at least two rows of teeth and tears flesh for fun.

This is the lady who called me into her office two weeks after her arrival at BFP&G and told me she liked me. Said she really did. "I like you Dinny, and I respect what you've done here." Then she gave me the sucker punch, "but that isn't the reason I'm keeping you on."

She went on to tell me that she respected my talent, thought she could really help me develop it. "Just because you've been in the business twenty years doesn't mean you're over-the-hill. What we're going to do is hone your creativity, Dinny, take you beyond talking dogs and jingles so you can really compete. When I get through with you, Dinny, you're going to be kicking ass and taking names."

Of course, the corollary to Ester's plan was to take away my vice-presidency and lop fifty grand off my salary "to protect me" as she put it. "So you won't be so vulnerable," she explained. "At your salary, with only two accounts, you're a sitting duck for Plevis and his bean counters."

There I was in the middle of my divorce from Reavis, being taken to the cleaners twice a day by her team of lawyers with the long teeth. I didn't have any choice.

She took away my vice-presidency, halved my salary and used the money to hire a new hipster, and then banished my secretary Evelyn to the office pool. And I'm supposed to be grateful that she didn't fire me.

"Why don't the two of us team up on this account, Dinny, ever thought about that?" Ester rearranges herself in my chair. Slides forward and stretches her legs out, spreading them so her skirt snaps taut, caught five inches above her knees, the heels of her shoes driven into my carpet, her legs a flying vee, opening and asking me in.

Venus Flytrap, I'm thinking, remembering the plants along the border of my mother's garden that I used to tease with the stems of leaves. "You run the account side. You be my account partner. You manage the client and we'll take care of the creative for you." I'd tickle the hairy fingers of the Venus Flytrap's mouth, letting the stem slowly slide in until the trap sprung and the green lips slid shut.

"The two of us would make a great team. Dinny, we'd waste them," she turns her head to the side, the placket of her blouse just coincidentally gaping open as she gives me a look out of one eye. "The two of us will leverage this account and—who knows? Someday we just might take over the agency."

This is vintage Ester Platt, I'm thinking, *the way she's driven her wedge deep into the formerly all-male agency with her brains and bravado, her Nineties concoction of cleverness and cleavage, gams and gumption, dealing sensible gender equality from the top and in-your-face Women's Lib rhetoric from the bottom, styling herself so she's halfway between Joan of Arc and Gloria Steinem, part girl-next-door and part Dragon Lady, but in reality a bitch on Big Wheels ready to eat you alive.*

"C'mon, Dinny, what do you say?" her hand comes out toward my knee. She's either going to slap it or squeeze it. I don't give her the chance to do either. I'm up and over to the door, whisking it open and motioning her out.

She's steamrollered me, stripped me of my title and group, sent my secretary to Siberia, and sliced my salary in half. Now she's trying to seduce me into taking over the agency with her. How dumb does she think I am?

"I say we're going to duke it out on this one, Ester. See you in the first meeting—strategy session the day after tomorrow, 9:30 sharp."

Ester gets up from her chair slowly, dusting off her sleeve like it's dirty. "Have it your way, Rein," she says, walking toward me.

"Bye, Ester, nice of you to stop by," I say into her ear as she pivots out my door, Mort clipping along behind. Three steps out, she stops. Turns around. Sort of smiles. Traipses back toward me, sidles up alongside and curls her arm through mine, her voice going low and growly. Hollywood tough girl.

"Come play with the big boys if you want, Rein," she says, giving me a squeeze. Then she narrows her eyes and hisses, "But to beat me, you're going to need a lot more than a face lift."

And she's off down the corridor with a "humph" and a haughty head toss. I watch Ester walk down the hall with Mort flitting alongside. Ester's languorous slither is gone. Now she's walking with a nervous bustle, forearms pumping, off around the corner in a scurry of heels, elbows, and fur.

She came in here thinking she was going to buy me off with a couple of deadbeats and she leaves knowing her job could be on the line. Things change in the good old ad biz faster than the winds on Lake Michigan. One minute, they're all balmy breezes and the next thing you know, you're facing a howling gale.

Go back into my office and shut the door, flip on the radio for cover, and take out my cell phone as I straighten my tie in the small mirror behind my closet door.

"Yo, God, you up there?"

"I need to talk to you. Come in please, come in God." *Maybe He's still in his schnauzer suit.*

"You betcha." *He's here.*

"Hey, thanks for the help with Ester."

"No problem. You handled her just fine."

"How about answering a question for me?" *I'll bet you ten bucks that He'll say, "You betcha."*

"You betcha." *See? I told you. You owe me ten.*

"So who was the creep with the knife?"

"What creep?"

"The guy in my office with the Bears cap. Before Ester came in."

"I didn't see him."

"I thought you said you were omniscient?"

"Sometimes my transponder goes on the fritz when I'm on the other side of the earth."

Wonderful, God's got a broken transponder. What the hell's a transponder anyway?

"I've got to get it fixed, just haven't had time. So—when can I see the ads?" He asks.

When can I see the ads? He's just like all the rest of my clients. Gives out the assignment one day, wants the work the next.

"I need three weeks," I glance at the calendar. "Around the twenty-sixth of March. How's that?"

"Lemme look…hmmm…" He pauses, like he's studying something. *A daily planner? Maybe God's got a Filofax.* "That's going to be cutting it pretty close."

"Close to what?"

"I got meetings."

"For what?"

"Just a check-off, couple people I have to show it to."

"You have to show this advertising? To who?"

"Don't ask."

"But I thought you were God."

"Titles aren't everything," He says. "Okay, I can just make it if you have the ads by the twenty-sixth."

"I promise." Advertising people say "I promise" thirty times a day. The phrase doesn't carry half as much weight as "Check's in the mail."

How am I going to get a fifty million dollar campaign done in three weeks?

"On second thought, make it a hundred, make it a hundred million. I want to make a big splash."

A hundred million bucks! Now He's talking a hundred million! "That's not much time for a campaign of that size. You'll need ten commercials at least, twenty print ads, radio…"

"So you want me to cut it back? You more comfortable with forty million, thirty, twenty?"

Jeez, He's putting the muscle on me worse than the Sirinis. "No, I'll take care of it. The twenty-sixth of March." I circle the date on my calendar.

"You betcha," He says.

"Say, God, could I ask you a question about your funding?" *I'm going to pin him down on this once and for all.*

No answer. I look around. "Yo, God, I need to ask you something."

Still no answer.

"Something important I want to talk to you about."

Shit. He's probably in Sydney by now. So here I am sitting alone in my midget office—*with a hundred-million dollar account. Not a bad day in the old ad biz,* I'm thinking. *I've got Sinkle back on his heels, Ester looking over her shoulder, and in one day I've doubled the size of the account. Ought to go see Sinkle and give him the good news.*

Check my Timex. *Oops, I had a 6:30 dinner with Addy.*

9

This is my favorite restaurant, big barn of a place that used to be an auto body shop, seats over two hundred now. Tall, raftered space with the service bays still visible along the back wall, the bays now bricked-up and hung with modern Italian canvases, Mondrian-looking, bright and graphic. Fifty black halogen spotlights hang from the ceiling, their black cords ending in tiny blazes of blue.

"So, did you have it done here or did you go out of town?" Addy's stroking my cheek with her finger, letting her finger run down the hard angle formed by my chin and jaw.

"Right here in Chicago."

"I can't believe it. You look like you're thirty-five," she says, sitting back and taking a sip of water. "And you remind me of someone, can't think who it is." Addy's puzzling, scrunching up her face trying to figure out who I look like.

"So tell me about your new job," I say to her.

"It's kind of hush-hush so you can't say anything, but I've been named to an interbank task force investigating some irregularities."

"What kind of irregularities?"

Like God snagging ten mil out of the air—that kind of thing? I wonder.

"There's so much drug money running around that we want to make sure banks are not involved in any way, even inadvertently."

Naah, nothing I have to worry about. "I'm delighted about your promotion," I say.

Addy shrugs her shoulders like it's no big deal. First woman at the bank to get an office on the chairman's floor. It looks out over the whole west side and is twice as large as the one I used to have. "It's a necessary step for me," she says. "Takes me out of mainstream for a while and either I'll get shunted aside or I'll bypass a whole bunch of guys." She winks at me like she knows she isn't going to lose this one.

"I've got some news for you, too."

Addy cocks her head. Does it like a chicken, quick, abrupt, like the chicken just saw a fox. Probably because most of the news I've given her is bad. Got demoted, got divorced, lost my vice-presidency, had to sell the house. Getting news from her daddy hasn't exactly been opening Hallmark cards.

"No—good news. About work," I counter.

A waitress swoops down with a margherita pizza and a menu. The pizza is Addy's favorite. Only thing she ever eats that's at all fattening. She sets it down on the centerpiece, two large cans of Italian tomatoes, deftly wheels the cutter back and forth across the pizza, separating it into slices.

Addy narrows her eyes at me. She's skeptical when it comes to good news about BFP&G.

"I just got a big new account," I tell her.

Addy frowns as she lifts a slice of pizza off the tray. More than once, I've told her my career's coming back only to end up peddling noodles and hockey pucks again.

"That's good," she says, patting my hand, "but don't get your hopes up too much."

"I'm serious, it's already in the agency and we're working on it." Addy's still frowning. She takes another piece of pizza, tries to smile. She's remembering fifteen other accounts I thought I had. She's seen me forlorn and disappointed. She's dragged me out of the Flying Schooner late at night. Seen me staring out the window at the backyard on Saturday mornings, so down I couldn't even get up and run the Snapper around the yard. Addy swears she would drive a truck, sell shoes at Payless, join the Bricklayer's Union and become a hod carrier, take a mail route in the slums, anything but go into advertising. At least I brought her up right.

"What kind of account is it?" Addy asks, paying more attention to the menu than me.

Ads for God

"Promise you won't tell?"
She nods.
I look around, lean into her and say, "You won't laugh?"
Addy shakes her head.
I lean across the table, "I'm going to be doing ads..." I point up at the ceiling with my finger and whisper, "...for God."
Addy stops chewing. Tries to follow my finger up into the rafters, she turns her head and squints up into the blazing little lights hanging from the ceiling.
"I know it sounds crazy..."
She looks at me blankly. "For whom?" she asks, as if she doesn't have a clue as to what I'm talking about.
"The big guy upstairs," I explain. *I figure if I can't spill the beans with Addy and Patti Shaw, the two people in all the world I'm closest to, who can I tell?* I stretch a big smile across my face. "I'm going to be doing ads for *God*," I say.
Addy responds with weak smile, "Daddy, I know you've had a hard time at work, but this isn't making any sense."
"I'm serious, Addy. He's hired us to do a campaign and I'm running it. This is big, Addy. He selected me out of all the advertising people in the whole world. And I got my CD job back and a big raise."
Addy has a half-eaten slice of pizza in one hand, a glass of Pellegrino in the other. She looks like she's frozen solid, except her mouth is open slightly.
"God." She says finally. "You're doing ads for God." Addy takes a sip of water, nodding like she's trying to talk herself into it. "What—did He ask you to do some print ads, maybe some commercials, too?" She's trying to hide a smirk behind a pleasant little smile.
"Yes, a whole campaign actually."
"Really, why?" Addy's taking facetiousness to a whole new level, forced smile, phony lilt to her voice.
"His numbers are bad." I look around to make sure no one's listening. Lean in closer to Addy. "This sounds crazy but I get the impression that there are a bunch of gods, you know? And they all compete. Kind of like Procter & Gamble's detergents, Biz, Tide, Cheer, Surf, Oxydol—they all compete with each other even though

they're made by the same company. Or you know, Pontiac, Chevy, Oldsmobile—they're all made by General Motors. And compared to the other guys, 'the other divisions,' He calls them, God's sucking wind. So He hired me to do some advertising for Him..." I sit back and take a piece of pizza. "That's kind of it."

Addy's got that stern look on her face my ex-wife had every time I tried to talk seriously to her. "Have you been having any kind of headaches or black-outs, or seeing things?"

"Nope."

"How much have you been drinking?"

"Nothing to speak of, beer or two once in a while."

"No more vodka?"

"Not a drop."

"Drugs?" I know she's waiting for me to admit some excess that will enable her to explain everything that's happening to her dear old daddy.

I shake my head.

The waitress comes up, then hangs back tentatively. Addy turns to her and hands her the menu. "Nothing more for me, thanks."

"I'll have linguine with white clam sauce," I say. I wait for the waitress to clear the pizza tray and then whisper, "Look Addy, if you're having a hard time with this, think how I felt when I got up this morning and looked in the mirror. I didn't get a face-lift, an abdominal tuck, and twenty years taken off my real age. *He* did it to me. God did. Also gave me this suit, and the tie and the shoes." I extend my leg out from under the table, point at my new Cole-Haans, "Nice, huh?"

Addy looks over the edge of the table at my tasseled loafers. Her face comes back slowly. "God gave you new shoes," she says flatly.

"Yup, and a new car, too. A Range Rover."

"God gave you...a Range Rover?" She says it slowly, like she's convinced I'm crazy.

Oh boy, maybe I shouldn't have gotten into this. Now look at her, she really thinks I've gone over the edge. She's going white, looking down, folding and refolding her napkin. Oh boy, what do I do now? Maybe I'll just shut up. I sit up in the booth, smile. I feel like Forrest Gump. Sitting on the bench waiting for the bus.

Then I get the feeling that my throat is opening, the feeling you first get when you think you're going to throw up, mouth stretching open, but I'm not going to vomit—I try to say "No!" but instead my lips twist out instead and I say in my Tony Bennett voice, "Nobody with sloppy, salt-stained shoes working on my business. No riding around in dirty old cabs for my ad guy, no sirree!"

I look up at Addy. Tears are filling up her eyes. Her face is screwing up, the wrinkles creasing her forehead and cheeks. Her eyes quickly reddening.

Oh, no! Why did You have to go and mouth off? Now she thinks I'm really crazy.

"Your linguine, sir," the waitress says, setting down the bowl of pasta in front of me and trying to ignore Addy who's starting to sob like I just told her I have incurable cancer and will be dead within the month.

I start on my linguine, hoping if I do something normal Addy will calm down. Twisting the noodles around on my fork, I look up at her and say, "That was him, God." I do a little hand motion to refer to the words that came out of my mouth. "I've asked Him not to talk like that but so far that's how we communicate."

"You betcha," He says again. I hold up my hand and do an Atlanta Braves chop, chop, trying to act as pissed as I can. "Stop it," I say. "Look what you're doing to my daughter."

"Aww, c'mon, she'll get used to it," He says.

Addy's got a full-fledged sob going now. She's holding her napkin over her mouth, trying to muffle her blubbering.

Oh boy, this isn't working out the way I wanted. She looks like she's wondering what kind of home she can place me in, remembering that place in Skokie we looked at when we found out Mother had Alzheimer's.

"You can't talk to me like this," I grumble.

"What do you want me to do? Chisel it in stone? Write it on the clouds?" He asks.

I try to brush Him off. "We'll talk about this later."

"*Daddy!*" Addy blurts out, saying "Daddy," like I'm something out of the mental ward at Cook County. I stand up and toss two twenties on the table.

"C'mon, I think we ought to go."

"Be that way if you want," He says. Addy's speechless. The more she looks at me, the harder she cries. I take her arm and start to walk her out. She's still carrying her napkin. People turn and watch us.

"That's enough, all right?" I say to Him.

"You're taking this the wrong way, Addy." I lean close to her as I hustle her out through the tables. One guy's looking at us, giving me a wry smile. I can tell he thinks he's got us figured out: Addy's my mistress and over linguine I've told her that I'm going back to my wife. "I'm okay," I say to her. "I really am. Don't worry about me."

When we get to the coat check, she turns to me and says, "Sure, you're just talking to God, that's all." She zooms her head back. When Addy gets real anxious, she zooms her head back like this and clutches at her throat, a remnant of her mother Reavis.

I hand the coat checks to the girl behind the door. "I know, I have to work something else out."

"You have to what?" Addy's chin goes double with her head zoomed back. Her eyes get squinty and she stitches at her collar with her fingers, gathering it together and then tacking it down.

"Never mind." I take the coats and hand the girl a five. I tip big when I'm in trouble.

"I want you to go back to Dr. Abernethy, starting tomorrow. Tomorrow morning, first thing. You have to." Addy was the one who talked me into seeing Abernethy in the first place. She went to school with his daughter, thinks he's the closet thing to Freud east of the Mississippi.

"Okay, okay, I'll see Abernethy." I help her on with her coat and open the door for her. She goes through it, turning back to me to say, "I want you to see him every day—twice a day if he thinks it will help. And I want you to start tomorrow."

She's still fiddling with the collar of her blouse. It's neurotic, reminds me of Reavis, makes Addy look like a dotty great-aunt who should be filed away in a sunny room somewhere.

"Okay," I say.

"Promise?"

"I promise." I hand the ticket for my car to the attendant. He scampers off down the sidewalk.

"I'll even pay for him if you want," Addy offers. Her hand drops from her collar.

"No, that's okay. Look, I'm sorry to upset you. Can I give you a lift?"

"No, I'm going north and you go south. I'll just grab a cab." Addy sticks her arm up in the air and waves. A cab pulls out of a line across the street and heads toward us just as the attendant wheels up in my gleaming new Range Rover. I dig in my pocket for a dollar. Addy peers at me, then looks over at the car.

I can tell she's thinking, *"That couldn't be the Range Rover my father was talking about...no, it couldn't be."*

The attendant gets out of the car and holds the door for me. "Your car, sir," he says. Addy does a double-take, looking at me, then the Range Rover, then back again.

"Sure I couldn't give you a lift?" I say. Addy shakes her head. She slowly walks in front of my Range Rover toward her cab, giving my new car a little room but still transfixed by the shiny black hood, the high-tech matte-black fog lights. I hand the attendant a dollar and hop in.

"Nice car, huh?" I say to her. She gives me a look. I give it back. Sometimes Addy and I say a lot more to each other when we don't talk.

"You call Dr. Abernethy first thing tomorrow morning," she says, waggling her finger at me as she gets into her cab.

"Yes, dear," I say, waving, watching her cab spin off down the snowy street. I get in my car. The attendant closes the door.

I see Addy turning around to look back at her daddy through the cab's rear window. Looking back at me, a somber and puzzled expression on her face as she tries to figure out how come her down-and-out daddy is now sitting at the wheel of a sixty-five thousand dollar car with a face lift that makes him look like a movie star, a bunch of new suits and shoes, and a big new account that he claims he got from God.

10

The next morning, I'm whipping up Michigan in my Range Rover and I see a familiar figure standing at the curb in front of 850 Michigan. Morris Abernethy, craning his neck looking up the avenue, in his tweed topcoat with the moth-eaten beaver collar.

He's waving at me like I'm a cab, cranking his arm back and forth.

Addy must have called him. Thinks it's serious enough to have my old shrink stand out on Michigan Avenue in the middle of rush hour and flag me down on my way to work. His big face lights up as he sees me pull over. Opens my door and says, "Dinny, Dinny, so good to see you. I tried to call you on the phone, Dinny, but you'd left already."

Morris is the kind of person who has to say your name two times in every sentence otherwise he doesn't think he's making contact. Cars behind me are starting to honk. Morris is leaning over the seat of my Range Rover smiling at me.

"Dinny, you come up and have a cup of coffee with me, Dinny?" Morris raises his eyebrows, turns down the corners of his mouth and opens his hand and holds it out like he's checking for raindrops. It's shrink shorthand, a signal that says, "What's the harm in talking about it?"

"Sure, Morris," I say, figuring it's easier to park and spend a couple minutes than try to talk with him in the middle of Michigan Avenue.

"You come up and lie down. We'll have a little chat, okay?"

"Okay, Morris, you're on," I say. He smiles like I just put a steaming hot plate of potato pancakes down in front of him, shuts the door, and I pull into the lot around the corner.

Ads for God

I used to be a sucker for shrinks. Especially Morris. After four years of lying on his couch, traipsing around in my emotional sandbox, I finally got up the nerve to ask him the one burning question I had about my life. "Morris?" I asked him one morning. "I want your honest opinion on something."

"Dinny, I'll do my best, Dinny," he said.

I turned to him and smiled, trying not to look like the cancer patient asking if the condition is terminal. "Do you think I'm a loser?" I asked.

Morris thought a minute, stuck the tip of his Pentel into his mouth, and then said, "No, you're not a loser, Dinny. You're just a man who's lost a lot. That's all."

Wisdom like that you don't get everyday. That I know. So two months later, I stopped seeing Morris. Figured out that now I knew the difference between being a loser and losing, I could face the world on my own.

His office is in a granite Gothic off Michigan with European elevators, gleaming brass doors, tan marble corridors, and elaborate baroque light fixtures of dark metal and stained glass that make the marble glow burnt umber, like the candlelit nave of a church in Sienna.

Morris meets me in the lobby and punches the button to the elevator, claps me on the back, says, "Dinny, Dinny..." like he knows something's going on. Morris Abernethy has oily white hair curled so tight it looks like it's been marcelled, wears rumpled, threadbare tweed jackets, cheap polyester shirts, and a stretched and stained black silk tie whose knot always works back up around his neck so his collar's a confused jumble. His face looks like the face of the lion I often see sleeping in the sun on a big flat rock at the Lincoln Park Zoo (without the tan hair, of course), but with the same jowls and wrinkles, pinkish and squishy, with soft brown eyes peeking out under his furry brows.

Morris kicks at the pile of mail in front of his office and shoulders his way into the anteroom, waving me toward the couch in his office and mumbling about making coffee. Strange thing about Morris' office is that it always smells like licorice but Morris can't stand the stuff. When I was seeing him, in the long intervals when I was thinking of something meaningful to say, I'd lie there and wonder where the licorice smell came from. I can still smell it as I lie back on the nubby, green-worsted daybed and look up at the ceiling.

Morris has glittered stars in My Little Pony colors, silver-pink, azure blue, and hot rose, pasted to the ceiling. Got them from his granddaughter. The crocheted white antimacassar under my head is the only tidy item in Morris' office. The bookshelves and desk look like DEA agents have recently been in looking for drugs. Drawers are pulled out, books piled in stacks on his desk, papers sticking out everywhere, a couple of Big Gulp containers, and balled-up Quarter Pounder wrappers everywhere. The far wall is covered with Mickey Mantle memorabilia, photos, framed signed bar coasters, baseballs in plastic boxes mounted on the wall, autographs scrawled on programs and popcorn boxes, scraps of paper, a parking ticket—Morris has been a Mantle nut ever since I can remember, even went to his funeral.

I hear Morris grumbling and rattling things in the outer office. "Making coffee in that machine is beyond my current state of technological preparedness," Morris says, walking into the room wiping his hands with a paper towel. "And Zelda isn't coming in today so we'll just have to do without until then."

Zelda hasn't been coming in for as long as I can remember. Addy calls her Morris' absentee receptionist. I only saw her once in the four years I spent with him. Morris sits down beside me with a yellow pad at the ready. "So," he says, sliding his black pen between his lips. "What's up?"

I look up at his kindly face, soft eyes. He's still using the same kind of pen. Felt tip that always leaves black arrows on his lips pointing into his mouth.

I shrug and say, "I guess the most accurate way of describing it is that I'm possessed."

"Possessed," Morris nods, acting like he hears that a couple times a day. "By who?"

I point up at the ceiling.

"Hmm," he says and scribbles something on his notepad.

I love the way Morris scribbles. What would you scribble on your notepad if someone told you he was possessed by God? "Feels he's possessed by God?"

I'd probably scribble, "Fucker's crazy."

"Do you feel possessed at this very moment?"

"Not at this very moment, no."

"I see." Scribble, scribble. "How do you know you're possessed?"

"He talks through me all the time. He gave me a new face, flattened my stomach—what am I supposed to think?"

"How do you know he gave you a new face?" Morris asks questions like this all the time.

"I went to bed looking like I was fifty-five and woke up looking thirty-five. I didn't have any surgery, didn't see a doctor. It was just 'pfffft'!"

"I see, and when you say he talks, he talks *through* you, you said?"

"Yes, He makes my mouth move and He talks."

"I see."

"I sound like Charlton Heston in *The Ten Commandments*."

Scribble, scribble. Puts his pen in his mouth again. I wonder if Morris washes his lips before he goes home. Or if he rides the bus with black arrows all over his lips like he's been snacking on burnt sticks all day.

"Could I have a demonstration?" Morris leans back and looks at me.

I know Morris doesn't believe me. I'm starting to feel crazy again.

"Look, sometimes He talks through me and sometimes He doesn't."

"Dinny, I understand, Dinny. I just thought since you're so specific about his voice and everything, it would be a help to me to experience it. That's all." Pen goes into his mouth.

"Okay," I say. "I'll try but like I told you, it doesn't always happen. I mean sometimes He'll just start talking and other times I won't hear from Him for a couple days."

I wonder if I should get into all that stuff about that transponder thing of His—no, that's too nuts.

Morris looks at me, scratches a few notes on his pad, says, "Hmm."

I feel stupid. The carpet beside the daybed is threadbare from years of patients putting their feet down, not to mention smelling like licorice.

Maybe I should go, I think. *What am I going to do if he doesn't say anything? Morris will think I'm crazy.*

He starts to hum Beethoven's Ninth. Has a habit of humming the Ninth when he's waiting for his patients to say something. Hums deep down in his throat so it sounds like he's snoring. Around about the second verse, I start smelling licorice. Then my lips go into action.

"I'm always here," He says.

"It's Him," I whisper, leaning forward toward Morris. "It's Him." I jab at my mouth with my finger.

"You know that—I'm always everywhere."

"Aha!" Morris says, reaching for the knot of his tie to straighten it. He pulls at it but it's buried too far around the side of his neck. "Aha, aha, aha, aha," he says, giving up going for the tie and starting to scribble like mad on his yellow pad. "How curious, how curious."

"See," I explain. "And it's not me talking, it's him—God—right? God!"

Morris swivels head back and forth like an owl, switching from pad to me, pad to me, flipping the pages on his pad, his eyes widening.

"You betcha."

"See, that's Him, Morris. I told you."

"And your daughter thought you were going crazy," Morris says, throwing back notebook pages and writing furiously.

"I know, I tried to tell her."

Morris quickly scratches some more notes on his pad, then leans in and pokes at my shoulder with his felt-tip. Morris whispers in my ear, "Ask him if he knows Mickey Mantle." I sit up on my elbows. I want to tell Morris that I didn't come in here to lay on his couch and pay him a hundred and twenty-five bucks to talk about baseball.

I mean, I'm the one with the problems.

"Just ask him if he knows Mickey Mantle," he pokes me again with his felt-tip. I decide to do Morris a favor. Addy told me Morris cried for two days when Mantle died.

"Do you know Mickey Mantle?" I ask. Morris cocks his ear and drops his mouth open. He looks like a little kid waiting for Santa to answer.

God says, "The Mick? I was with him yesterday—was it yesterday? Yes, I think it was yesterday. Hit him a couple pop flies."

"Wow!" Morris says, jumping up out of his chair. "Wow, wow, wow, wow! And did he go back with grace, his feet sliding back like this?" Morris has his hands so high up in the air he's almost touching his My Little Pony stars on the ceiling and he's slipping his Earth Shoes back over the carpet like he's Mickey Mantle in Yankee Stadium.

"He goes back like he's gliding on air. The man has such grace, yes, you betcha," God says. And Morris is almost banging into his credenza, he's back so far across his office.

"And the Mick slows down," Morris looks down at his Earth Shoes and stops gliding, then looks up in the air again. "And it's like the ball is on a long wire traveling right into the pocket of his glove and *thunk!* it's there and the Mick takes his hand down like it's nothing, like the ball's come home to Momma, like it *belongs* there."

"You betcha, that's my boy Mickey Mantle."

"Okay, so you see what's going on, huh Morris?" I say, trying to get the conversation focused back on me.

"So what about the Series?" Morris says, striding around his office, completely ignoring me. "Aren't we ever going to see a series in Wrigley Field again?"

"Look, Morris," I say, getting up off the daybed. "I came in here to see you about a problem and you end up monopolizing the conversation—now c'mon."

"The Cubs will rise again," God says.

"Rise again, all right!" Morris exults, extending his arms into the air and striding around his office. "The Cubs will rise again!" He plops himself down on the daybed and takes out his wallet. I lean against the door as he sorts through his cards.

"Okay, here it is!" Morris holds up a small card with the upcoming Cubs season on it. "Now tell me when, because I'd like to get a little money on it, if you know what I mean. So, this year, or next—when?"

"Morris, I'm leaving," I say, starting to open the door.

"Yeah, yeah, yeah, see you later," he waves to me, dismissing me out the door.

"Not next year, pennant maybe, but they don't have the pitchers," God says.

"Pennant, pennant, pennant," Morris says, settling back on the daybed. "Pennant's not bad, but can't you do something about the pitchers?"

"Morris, I'll see you," I say, walking out the door. "You make sure you call Addy and tell her I'm not nuts, okay?" Morris is acting like I don't exist, staring up at the ceiling and God's saying, "I got a couple of Cuban kids I'm working with now. One of them's got an arm like Bobby Feller and the other makes Hercheiser look like he's in Little League. Oh, and sluggers, I got sluggers—got a twelve year-old kid in Ohio who looks like a fireplug, runs like a cheetah, and hits the ball three hundred feet into a good wind!"

As I close the door, the last thing I see is Morris Abernethy, my good friend the psychiatrist, stretched out on his daybed, his Earth Shoes crossed, looking very relaxed, gazing up at the stars on the ceiling, and talking baseball with God.

11

The first thing I do when I get into the office is call Durnberg to see how he's doing with the strategy, the research, and interviews. *God can sit around Morris Abernethy's office and talk baseball all day but I've got ads to do.*

"Good news, Dinny my man. I'll be right down," Panky says over the phone. I gave him the God assignment yesterday and told him I needed a full presentation in less than forty-eight hours. I thought he was going to throw it back in my face, tell me to get lost. Instead, as I told him about the account, he starts thanking me, thanking me so much I start to get embarrassed. Goes from glib to gushy. "You can't believe how much this means to me, Dinny," he says. "I can finally do something worthwhile."

Turns out his parents are Fundamentalists and Panky's been going to Sunday School in tents and speaking in tongues since he was four. As you can imagine, his parents don't exactly approve of him selling Steigerlager and National Distillers. So Panky Durnberg sees the God account as his salvation. "Dinny," he told me. "This is like an advertising assignment from up on high." *Little does he know.*

So he goes on and on and at one point, I'm sure Panky Durnberg has totally lost it. Get this, Panky lets out a wail and drops to his knees, clutches my hand and starts jabbering, looking up at me with his frowzy hair framing his moist little eyes, his Gorbachev mark going bright maroon. "Umphy phan kobba sham," he keeps repeating. "Umphy phan kobba sham" (Or something like that) and I can't for the life of me tell whether he's talking in the tongues he learned in tents or speaking the Sanskrit he learned at UC but he's tugging at my hand like a little kid. The tears are starting to run down his cheeks. I'm thinking he's going to gum my knuckles. "Umphy phan kobba sham," he keeps saying. "Umphy phan kobba sham."

Then he pulled himself together, promised to go out and do six focus groups and a hundred individual interviews, have them tabbed and analyzed overnight. "This is so exciting! I'll stay up all night if I have to!" He kept saying, "Thank you, Dinny, thank you, thank you."

Now Panky's standing in the doorway of my office, leaning against the jamb. There's only a bit of residual motion left in his knees, like the Wailers have taken a break.

"You're going to like what I have to say tomorrow," he tells me. "There's interesting material coming out of the groups." Focus groups tell you what people are thinking, or at least what people want you to think they're thinking. "Hearing these people talk makes me think that we have a rare opportunity with this piece of business," he says, walking into my office.

He looks at the nail on the back of my door, my castoff desk, the file cabinets stacked to the ceiling. "You've got to get yourself a new office, Dinny," he says. "You've got the biggest account in the agency now."

"That's one of the things I've got to take up with Sinkle."

He shuts the door deliberately, looking back over his shoulder at me. "Can we talk?"

He peers around, then speaks in a hush, "This agency's turned into Stalag 17. Sinkle's got the place terrorized. Nobody has the guts to do anything. But you're standing up to him, Dinny, and everyone's rooting for you. You're bringing in this wonderful new piece of business where we can sell hope and joy, goodness, and charity to our fellow man, instead of peddling beer, dog food, and booze."

Panky's hips are rotating now. The Wailers are back on stage. "You can lead us into a new arena, into new horizons of advertising, Dinny. You can take us there."

I'm wondering if he's going to drop to his knees and start *umphy phan kobba shamming* me again. Panky's arms start to lift away from his body, flapping slowly to Bob Marley's music. His voice rises an octave.

Ads for God

"Consider the potential. We work in a business that's under attack from every quarter. We're accused of increasing the prices of the goods we sell, encouraging the development of useless products, for peddling death by advertising cigarettes and alcohol. We get accused of commercializing our culture, destroying the integrity of sports with multi-million dollar endorsements, of turning the Olympics into a three-week Coca-Cola commercial, of corrupting justice when our techniques are used to pick juries and shape lawyer's arguments. They even accuse advertising of debasing the political process!" Panky does a quick turn and a little jump, lands with his feet spread, his hips are swiveling, they remind me of the tub of my mother's washing machine, spinning crazily, full of wet clothes.

"Here's a chance for our business to redeem itself, to regain respect for our profession, and for all of us at BFP&G Advertising to take the credit." He's yelling now, globs of spittle exploding out of the corners of his mouth, I'm wondering if he's going to attract a crowd outside my cubicle. "It's a new dawn for advertising, Dinny. We can finally put our talents and disciplines to bear on something meaningful." The veins are standing out on Panky's neck. His Gorbachev mark is going vermilion.

"We can actually help people. We can sell them religion, bring spirituality into their lives and help make the world a better place, and what's more, thanks to you..." he cocks his hip and shoots his outstretched finger at me. "We can make some money on it, too!" Panky stops, the motion in his body winding down. He closes his eyes momentarily, opens them, shifts around in his suitcoat, straightens his tie, and clears his throat.

"Yes, well, I'm sorry. I got a little out of control there," he says. "I guess it's been a long time since I've felt so inspired." He comes up to me and holds out his hand. "We're all with you, Dinny. Let me know if I can give you anymore help." I shake hands with him. "And thank you, thank you," he adds.

"I appreciate your support, Panky. Thank you." *Panky Durnberg hasn't paid this much attention to me in six years. He wouldn't even look at me when we passed in the halls, and now he's treating me like I'm the salvation of the agency.*

"Guess I should get back to work. I have a lot to do before tomorrow," he says. "And I'm sure you've got your hands full trying to come up with the creative."

I nod. "Look forward to seeing your presentation," I tell him. Panky runs his fingers through his mess of hair, strokes at his Gorbachev mark, which is returning to its normal color, and backs out of my office giving me a wave good-bye.

For an hour, I'm sitting at my desk, thinking. *How do you sell God, anyway?* I look down at my scratch pad. Two dumb ideas for commercials. "Consider a slice-of-life," I've written on the pad. "Not a hokey P & G slice, but a dramatic playlet bringing to life how God can help people..." *Maybe not.* "Think about testimonials, real life experiences of what God has meant to people's lives..."

I don't think so. How am I going to do advertising for God when I can't get a noodle commercial approved? So, what should I do? Try a jingle campaign? Should I put those three new teams to work? Should I try National Geographic tours of churches around the world cut to a great soundtrack, wide angle traveling shots looking up at the architecture of Chartres and the Vatican? Or, maybe I'll do the glories of nature and I'll have those monks singing on the soundtrack—that would be hot. Majestic mountains, fields of flowers, gurgling brooks, and stands of aspens turning gold, yes! The glories of nature, all of God's work brought to life with magnificent footage cut to a great track.

But He said He wanted to increase church attendance. I can't do that with singing monks and pretty pictures. Or, can I? Maybe I need to do something harder hitting, a before-and-after campaign. Show people whose lives have been changed by going to church. Real gut-wrenching stories like you see on Oprah—"I was a drug addict and a bum before I started going to church. Now I have my own business. I just got married and bought a new house. All because of God." Proof that going to church improves your life—maybe not. Maybe these new teams I got will come up with something. Maybe I should just wait until the strategy meeting tomorrow. Or, maybe I should go see Izzy. Aha!

I grab my coat. "I'm going over to Izzy's for a few minutes," I tell the receptionist as I hustle onto the elevator. Izzy is my editor. He edits all my commercials (or he used to back when I was making a lot of commercials). Izzy's a fountain of ideas and he's sort of been my alter ego for years. When you bring your film back to an editor, he sees all your mistakes, everything you've shot wrong, the transitions that don't work, the lines that don't play, and he crafts the commercial, cuts the scenes so they work, stays off the bad actors, mixes, and does special effects so your commercial works, and you look like a genius.

It's freezing on Michigan.

Will spring ever get here? Maybe He cancelled spring and didn't tell anybody. The pavement is streaked with thin peninsulas of ice, the salt melting through the ice to the sidewalk in places, leaving tiny ponds between the peninsulas. I hate having wet shoes and try to stand on the outsides, rocking back on the heels to save the soles. I should have changed into my Bean boots before I left. I feel the moisture seeping into the soles. My sock no longer slides on the wet insole. The fabric sticks. The sock bunches up in damp welts under the soles of my feet. *Damn, winter didn't used to bother me so much.*

No cabs. Plenty of traffic on the avenue but no Yellows. Hear someone clearing their throat, like they're trying to get my attention. Turn around. Guy in a Bears cap, cardboard box under his arm, "Need a cab?" he asks.

It's him again, the guy in my office. What's he doing here? What was his name—Ralph? He's coming too close. I smell garlic. Oh boy, now I'm in trouble. He's going to take out his Daniel Boone knife and poke it through me right on Michigan.

"Yes, I'm just going down the street but I don't want to walk if I can help it..." I say, taking a step away from him, craning my neck to look up and down the avenue for a cab.

"Watch," he says, smiling at me. He holds his fingers up to his lips and lets out a screeching whistle, shrieking and blaring like the air-raid siren back in Stergus, the sound rattling my eardrums. I smell big garlic, hanging in the air around us like a fat balloon. I see a cab cutting across the lanes of traffic toward us. Ralph's wheeling his arm at it. Then a second cab gets the scent of Ralph's whistle and barrels up on the inside, heading in my direction at fifty, working the inside angle. The outside cab cuts hard, dodges inside a panel truck, going pell-mell for the curb, but the inside cab has the advantage, cuts the other one off, and squeals to a stop in front of me. The other cab crunches up against the curb twenty feet ahead. Driver's bellowing, I can see his hand shaking in the air. I duck into the cab quickly. You don't want to be the filling in a cabby sandwich,

"Thanks for the cab," I say to Ralph. Ralph's looking dour, like he wants a tip—or maybe he wanted me to take the other cab. As the cab pulls away, I look back over my shoulder at Ralph walking up to the other cab, getting in. At least the cabby got another fare.

What's with this Ralph guy? Why's he waiting for me outside the building, hailing me a cab? What does he want from me? I turn quickly around in the cab, peering out the windows, trying to find Ralph.

I keep wondering if this has anything to do with the ten million God snagged out of the air. I don't see him. *Naah, it just must be coincidence.* I look at my watch. It's taken me ten minutes to go five blocks. I get out and walk the last block to Izzy's. It's even colder. The wind has knives in it. I lean into the wind and sink my hands into my overcoat pockets. Stomp my feet off when I get into the lobby, soles of my shoes are so wet they make a dull smacking sound on the stone floor. Push the button for the elevator.

Good friends are not supposed to care what happens to you in business. So why don't I have many good friends anymore? With the exception of a few lacrosse buddies who I see once in a while, all my other friends went south when I got demoted. But not Izzy.

"Howya been, Pal?" Izzy asks when he sees me stepping out of the elevator. Izzy's half Hawaiian, half Jewish and has a last name that's almost all vowels, sounds like a mountain on some island out there in the Pacific. Israel Monolookaloo, or something like that. I can never get it straight, much less spell it, so he stays Izzy to me.

Where Izzy got the curly red hair even his mother can't figure out. Used to be a stuntman in Singapore until he busted his pelvis into sixty-five pieces falling from the yardarm of a Chinese junk and got into the safer game of film editing. Throws his meaty arm around me and walks me back to his office keeping up a running monologue on the Bulls, the weather, and what a stinking bitch Ester Platt is. He keeps turning to me and squinting one eye. Like he can't figure out why I look different.

He's really hot about Ester. "The woman, she slices my work to pieces and tells me I can't cut film for shit, makes me try this and try that, and all the while she's got her skirt hiked up to here and her shirt's hanging open giving me a free show and she's acting like I should be enjoying it all, whew! Get me away from that one, the woman's cuckoo."

The corridors are lined with pictures from commercials he's edited, Wheaties, United Airlines, Budweiser, there's even one from my award-winning Steigerlager commercial that I made way back when.

"Dinny, my man, I wish we were back together again just like old times." Izzy looks oafish and ragged around the edges, going bald in places and always needing a shave, but he's got a brilliant mind and an incredible sense of timing.

Whenever I see him, I think of those ratty old bears down at The Museum of Science and Industry, in those big glass cases with their hair falling out. Izzy lumbers, clump, clump, clump (he actually wears huge tan boots flopping open at the tops, the things must weigh ten pounds apiece). His limbs are like hams, shoulders are three feet across.

Today Izzy's wearing a plaid shirt so he looks like Paul Bunyan. And smells like a fragrance factory. Guy goes through a six-pack of Old Spice a week. Which is good for his business, since I'm not sure how often Izzy gets around to showering.

"But I'm hearing good news about you, Dinny," he says, steering me into his office. His office is like a lounge, with overstuffed sofas and chairs all arranged around the monitor. His office is sleek, monochrome, black marble tables, gray upholstery. He sits down at his editing console and lights a cigarette. Izzy used to drink a lot. Now he smokes a lot. Whatever Izzy does, he does a lot.

"It's incredible," I say. "But I think I'm back on top of the pile again." Izzy reaches out and slaps me on the knee.

"I'm proud of you, pal," he says. My knee starts to smart. Izzy's got a big smile on his face.

I always think of a chipmunk when Izzy smiles, even though his head is as big as a basketball. It's the way his cheeks puff out and his eyes go small. A ruddy-faced chipmunk though, for the bar years have given his skin that all-year-long sunburn, smooth and shiny and red as someone who's spent six hours in the sun with no lotion on. "How in the world did you ever pull it off?" he asks.

"It's a long story, but some rich old guy who wants to improve the world picked me out of a hat, I guess."

"Put you on top of the pile, now you're Co-CD and you've got everyone in the agency jumping. I've never seen those people so jazzed, except for Ester. She's not too happy, I'll tell you that. Serves her right. I tell you, I'd turn her work down if I didn't need it to keep the lights on."

"So, I hear this campaign's going to bill something like a hundred million? That's big bucks, pal, bigger than anything you've ever worked on before. You're looking good, too. Lost a bunch of weight, huh?" He slaps me on the other knee. I'm waiting for it to start smarting too.

"Yup," I say.

I know I'm blushing. I've never been good at taking compliments, even from an old buddy like Izzy. "So I'd like to ask you something."

"Shoot, whatcha got?"

"If I wanted to sell God..."

Izzy's face goes suddenly dark. "Sell what?"

Whoops, I'm thinking. *Got to watch that.*

"Not God *per se*—you know, to get people going to church, to increase church attendance, that kind of thing..." Now he's back with me, he starts to nod again, "Would you have any ideas about how to go about it? You have a lot of commercials going through here."

"Increase church attendance—with advertising?" he asks.

He's still having a hard time with it.

"Yes, I mean would you do a visual extravaganza kind of thing with the Grand Tetons and golden fields of hay and deer drinking out of gurgling springs, kind of a glory of nature focus with the Franciscan monks singing over it? I'm just looking for ideas."

"You could, you could. Sure be spectacular, that's for certain. But I'm not sure it would get people going to church, if you know what I mean. I'm not sure the decision to go to church is like picking out a brand of toothpaste or deciding whether you want a Whopper or a Big Mac—but I could be wrong."

"Of course, but if you did the right kind of advertising, don't you think you could get people to be more interested in going to church? Look, Bill Clinton turned the electorate around with advertising in the last election, turned it right around. Got that Morris fellow, they did a bunch of ads and wham, bam! Bill's back in the saddle again for another four years."

"I guess it's possible..."

Izzy's coming around.

"So that's why I'm thinking about some kind of ode to nature thing. Something that would make you feel that the world is so wonderful you just have to go to church and say thanks."

"I don't know if it would work. It might make people feel good, but would it actually get them going to church?"

"That's what I've been concerned about."

"I mean, you could try, I guess." Izzy lights another cigarette. Inhales so deeply he practically smokes a third of the thing in one breath. "How about this?" he says. "What if I get that CD with the monks singing and cut some footage together—see how it looks? Do a little steal-o-matic on it and we'll go from there."

"I'd really appreciate it."

A steal-o-matic, why didn't I think of that? I guess I've been out of the mainstream so long, I've forgotten some of the tricks of the trade. Why not? Steal some footage from other commercials and cut a demo commercial together to the singing monks. See what it looks like.

"No problem. Have it done in a couple of days. Anything else?"

"No, that's it."

Izzy disengages himself from his chair, and we head out of his office. While we're walking down the corridor, I ask, "While we're at, there is something else I need to ask you."

Izzy turns toward me as we walk into his lobby, puts his arm around me. "Sure, pal, anything you want."

I lean toward him and cover my mouth so the receptionist can't hear me. "I'd rather Ester didn't see any of the steal-o-matic, okay? I don't trust her when it comes to this business."

"If she calls, I'm telling the woman I'm busy—okay? You bring me in a hundred million worth of ads, and I'd like nothing better than to tell that witch to take a leap."

"Thanks, Izzy."

"And say hello to that ever-gorgeous Patti Shaw for me, too."

"I sure will. I'm seeing her tonight." I leave Izzy standing in front of the glass doors to his office, head tilted and his eyes squinched up, still trying to figure out why his old friend Dinny Rein looks so different to him.

12

Patti Shaw gets off work at seven tonight. Wheeling around Chicago in my new Range Rover, I pick up Chinese food, then some roses at the little stall on Huron. Patti Shaw's a sucker for roses. Head over toward her place a little after seven.

There was a black Buick Roadmaster parked right behind me at the Golden Wok. Is that the same black Buick behind me now?

I take a right onto Clybourn. Then a left, pull into a space, and stop. Look into the rearview. No black Buick. My father used to have Buicks. I know every Buick back to when they first started making them. Check in the mirror again, No black '94 Roadmaster.

I must have been imagining it.

Patti Shaw's is two blocks ahead. Find a space right in front of her building.

Can't wait to see what she says when she sees me.

Even though her place is in a crappy neighborhood, there's a precinct station right around the corner. No cars even get touched for four blocks around. I take the steps to her apartment in twos. I'm not even breathing hard when I get to her floor.

You can sure get around easier when you drop twenty pounds.

Ring the bell. Patti opens the door. She's wearing red leggings and a tight white sweater, sexy smile on her face, but she takes one look at my brand new face and her eyes roll up into her head. She goes "Unnh" and promptly sinks to the floor, fainting before I can grab her, collapsing right on top of her long silver cigarette holder. It breaks in two so the lit end's melting her hair, making it snap and sizzle so Patti's apartment starts smelling like the experiments I used to do with my chemistry set when I was a kid back in Stergus.

Patti's out cold, eyes flipped up so there's only white showing, lying in the doorway looking like she just died. I have to stamp out her cigarette before I can help her up.

Now I've got Patti Shaw over my knee and I'm fanning her face. Moo shu pork and pink roses all around me. Smoke from her sauteed hair wafting up around us. Does it stink.

She opens her eyes and looks up at me woozily. "You do..." she reaches up to touch my face.

"I do what?"

"You do look like him, that movie star—what's his name?"

"You tell me."

"You look just like that Kevin What's-his-name," she says, poking my cheek. "You look gorgeous! Did it hurt?"

"Nope, they used lasers," I say, helping Patti to her feet. She's wearing black velvet slippers with the toes turned up, little Santa's helpers' slippers.

"You look wonderful. Whoo, did I go out or what?" she says, steadying herself against me.

"Slid right to the floor before I could even get to you."

"I like your new look," she says, slipping her arm around my waist and pushing herself into me. "Umm," she coos as she runs her hand around where my love handles used to be. "Little liposuction too, huh?"

"A little," I say, starting to feel a little perky downstairs, sliding my hands around her backside.

"So Mr. Movie Star." Patti says, pulling away and walking over toward her bar. "What's new at work?"

I know Patti likes to have a drink and chat a little first, but she looks too cute. I peek into her bedroom. The Lava Lamps are going, the lights are low, and the covers are turned back. I just have to be patient.

"I just got promoted, got a huge new account and a big raise."

My words don't register. She's too busy uncorking a bottle of wine. "Those noodle people behaving themselves?" she asks as she pours two glasses of wine out of a skinny green bottle. "You what?" she says as she comes racing over with the wine. "What did you say?"

"I'm a creative director again and I got a big raise. I can afford to send you to school full-time if you want."

"You don't mean it. How?"

"I got this big new account. It bills in the millions, and I just went right in to Sinkle and demanded my old job and a raise. And tomorrow I'm going to get my corner office back."

Patti holds up her glass. "Congratulations, that's wonderful," she says and we clink our glasses. "This is German wine. It's supposed to be good. It's Reisling. They're making it drier now. This is a '95 Trocken Pfalz Ruppertsberger Gaisbohl…"

That's Patti Shaw for you, works in a carwash and pronounces German perfectly. I take a sip.

"What I like is that it's peachy and honeyed with a lingering finish. Taste it?"

"Not bad." *Still a little sweet for me.*

She runs the back of her hand over my cheeks, under my jaw. "I just love the way you look and I'm so proud of you." She turns her hand and combs her fingers through my hair. "So what's your new account?"

I set the glass down, thinking, *I've got to cool it with the God stuff. You'd think I'd learn my lesson after what happened with Addy.* "I'm selling religion," I say. "Trying to get people to go to church."

"Can you make any money doing that?"

"All depends. We make money on how much the client spends. The more cash he lays out, the more we make."

"I like this wine." She gets up and pours herself another glass.

"And I like your outfit," I say to her. Patti comes back over to the couch, blushing and settling in beside me. "Thanks, if I lost ten more pounds I'd be a very happy girl." *Patti, like every other woman I've ever met, thinks she's fat. I prefer to think of her as wonderfully full-bodied.*

"So, Mr. Movie Star, how you going to get people to go to church?" Looks up at me, bats her eyes. "I can't believe how good you look. So how are you going to get them to do what you want, anyway?"

"With TV commercials, magazine ads, I haven't exactly figured it out yet."

"If you can sell dog food that looks like hamburgers but it's really all chemicals, I guess you can sell religion. Maybe you can get Charlton Heston. Didn't he play God in some movie?"

"Moses, I think."

"Close enough. You get Charlton Heston and put him in his robes. I tell you he's one sexy-looking man, remember that chin of his? I used to love that chin. And you have him say your spiel about going to church and I tell you...wait a minute. He's dead, isn't he? Charlton Heston, didn't he die?"

"I don't think so."

"Good, because if he's dead..." Patti shrugs her shoulders. "But if he isn't, you could use him. Couldn't you?"

"Sure I could," I lean in and give her a kiss on the neck. "That's a good idea, Patti Shaw."

Patti pinches my chin between her thumb and finger and leans in like she's going to give me a kiss. Then purses her lips together and suddenly whips away, turns toward the other side of the couch, her back stiffening, as if I'd done something to upset her. *But I didn't do anything.*

"What's the problem, Patti Shaw?"

She scoots around on the sofa to face me, wheeling her hand, like she's trying to get her mouth to say what's on her mind. "You're doing these ads for—for God, aren't you? He's your new client. He's the one who was talking through you the other night and He's the one who got you the raise and the promotion—He is, isn't He?" She peeks over at me quickly and then looks away like she's afraid of what my answer's going to be.

"How did you know?"

It's the only thing I can think of saying to her.

Patti squeezes her eyes shut and nods her head. "I knew it, I knew it."

Once a Baptist, always a Baptist, I'm thinking. *Guess you can't shake that hill country upbringing.* "But it's okay," I say. "He's a good guy, God is. Loose, real relaxed, and friendly. Seems to know what he's doing, I mean, at least so far."

Patti gets up and starts stalking around the sofa. She's shaking her finger back and forth. "That's not the point," she says.

Ads for God

"Patti, it's a hundred million bucks. I can get you a new apartment. You can quit your job." I walk over to the window. "Come over here and look," I say, pulling back the curtain. Patti comes up alongside me and peers out. "That's my new Range Rover. It's a $65,000 car, Patti, and it's mine."

"It needs a wash, any more salt and your paint will start pimpling." is all she says.

"We can take it on trips. It goes anywhere. We can go to the beach, to Wisconsin."

"What's the phrase you use when you give back an account in advertising?"

"'Resign the account?' No, Patti, why?"

"You can't do advertising for God, Dinny, you can't. You can't go turning Him into the Jolly Green Giant—He's God."

"I'm not going to do anything like that. I'm going to do something respectful and inspiring."

'An honest God is the noblest work of man.' Robert Green Ingersoll said that, Dinny, 'the noblest work of man.'"

"All I know is that God calls me on my cell phone and says He wants some ads, okay? He puts some money in an account, and now we're going to do a strategy, make some ads and put them on the air, and hopefully church attendance will go up—it's business, Patti. It's marketing, c'mon."

"'An honest God is the noblest work of man,' and advertising isn't noble. I'm sorry, Dinny, but you know that." She looks up at me for a reaction. I hold up my hands.

What am I supposed to say?

"Can you imagine dealing with a dishonest God, an unscrupulous, deceitful, knavish God? A God who tells lies and dissembles, who cheats and steals? Can you imagine getting down on your knees to pray to God and wondering if He's going to hear your prayers or if He's listening to the guy next to you who put fifty more bucks in the plate? Dinny, when you think about it, an honest God is about the best thing we have going in this world."

"I don't see how doing ads for God is going to turn Him into some kind of shyster. It's just advertising—commercials, print ads. C'mon, Patti."

She's staring at the floor, shaking her head.

Just my luck, I end up with a hundred million dollar account, and Patti has to get a holier-than-thou attitude, decides she has ethics up the ying-yang, and tells me to walk away from a hundred million bucks! Why did I have to get a girlfriend who's so damn principled?

"I'm not sure I can keep seeing you if you go on with this," she says, crossing her arms and turning away to look out the window.

Now I'm in trouble. This is the girl who threatened to sell her stock when Louie wanted her to wear a bikini in the booth for their summer special. And she wanted to sell the stock to a guy named Angelo who just happens to own a clam house in Little Italy. No more bikini talk out of partner Louie.

"Patti, let's have a little talk about this."

She shakes her head, and I'm standing there wondering what I'm going to do when she suddenly starts patting herself, all over her body, slowly at first like she misplaced her wallet, then faster and faster. She lets out a plaintive yelp, then another and heads toward the bathroom, yelping and bent over and heading for the john lickety-split like she's got to throw up. Goes in and slams the door behind her. I'm wondering if she has food poisoning or an ulcer attack and walk over quickly. "Patti, are you okay?" I say, twisting the knob, rattling the door.

No answer. She's got the door locked. "Patti, are you feeling all right?" No answer. I'm leaning into the door, my ear to the wood, listening for puking or crying or something that'll tell me what's the matter with her. Then I start to hear a groan, spooky and rumbling, that turns into a wail and then into a scream and I'm thinking, *she's gone bonkers in there.* Then she starts to giggle and her giggle turns into a laugh and she's locked in the bathroom laughing like she just heard the funniest joke of all time when she screams, "Dinny!"

Then she throws open the door in my face and I stagger back. She's standing there with her arms thrown open wide displaying everything she's got. I almost don't recognize her because now Patti Shaw has the body of a twenty-two-year-old.

13

We have a very nice night, to say the least, and I wake up in the morning to find Patti Shaw standing by the bed inspecting her new body in the full-length mirror on the back of the bathroom door.

Pretty sly work from the Big Guy. He sees Patti's giving me a hard time and he buys her off with a new body. Roses work pretty good on women, furs aren't bad, gave Reavis a mink once and she was civil to me for a month, and everyone knows diamonds have a nice effect. But I tell you, go and give a girl a new body, and you've got a friend for life.

Patti sees that my eyes are open and turns to me. "Dinny, my cellulite's gone, and those spider veins on the back of my knees, Dinny, look..." She's turning and stretching in front of the mirror, running her fingers up and down her body. She's naked except for a little blue pair of lace pants and she's gorgeous. I mean, Patti Shaw was gorgeous before, but now she's got a Venus de Milo body and perfect skin and not a wrinkle anywhere.

What a nice thing to wake up to, I'm thinking, and Patti Shaw jumps on top of me, starts kissing me all over my face and neck, "I'm so excited, how do I thank Him for giving me a new body?"

"Just thank Him, I guess."

Patti Shaw rolls off the bed, kneels down and puts her hands together, bows her head, and shuts her eyes. Could be a scene right out of a Hallmark commercial, except for the fact that Patti Shaw's half-naked and wearing azure underpants. Then she jumps up and prances around the apartment, pirouetting, extending her arms back, and gazing up at the ceiling.

"I can't believe it—I have a new body. A whole new body! Here I am at thirty-nine with a whole new body."

Thirty-nine, that's how old Patti Shaw is—you heard it here first, folks.

"You know—you and me, the two of us—we could go on *Oprah*, write a book like Dennis Rodman. Be on the cover of *The Enquirer*. I could quit the car wash. Make millions. Can't you see the headlines, 'God Gave Them Both New Bodies'," she burbles.

"I don't think so."

"Why not?"

"He's my client."

"So?"

"He wants me to do ads for Him, improve His market share—not go on TV and write books."

"You're right, okay. I got a little carried away. You're kind of like his ad guy, I forgot. You know, I just had a thought about that." Patti turns to me holding up her index finger. "You know how I was talking about using Charlton Heston, in your ads?" she says and shakes her head some more.

"Yes," I answer.

"I don't think you should use him any more."

"Why not?"

"I'd go right for Schwarzenegger. I saw in the *Star* that he's getting thirty million a movie, but since God is your client, I figure He can afford that easy. Imagine this—Arnold Schwarzenegger in nice robes standing on top of a mountain with big clouds all around him. He's holding a big hunk of stone in his arms, his biceps all greasy and bulging, ooooh, I'd like that. Now, I'm not a writer, but what I'd do is have Arnold say, lemme see here, I'd have him point down from the top of the mountain that he's standing on, know what I mean? Like he's pointing at us and then he could say, 'All you humans down there, you get yourselves to church or I'll zap you all with lightning' or something like that, you're the writer—but you see what I mean?"

"Sure do, Patti Shaw."

Patti tosses herself on the bed next to me, turns into me, and gives me a hug. "But, I know you'll come up with the big idea, Dinny. You always do."

14

There's Panky Durnberg walking into the building ahead of me, heading for the 9:30 strategy meeting under the total influence of Marley. This is Panky's meeting, probably the biggest in his career and he's really feeling the Marley. His hips are pulsing under his topcoat, his shoulders shuttling back and forth, and I can almost hear the cowbell downbeat, the electric piano warming through the first four bars, and Bob Marley's voice, clear and cool as a crystal spring bubbling up through the jungle ferns in back country Jamaica.

Panky's got an Egyptian head movement thing going on to the Wailers as he steps onto the elevator. Panky's eyes are closed. He's too deep in the emerald green hills of Jamaica to notice I'm getting on the elevator with him. His chin oozes out with each beat, neck elastic, his whole body an intricate machine, hips opposing pistons, pelvis greasing back and forth, hips out, knees in, elbows gliding forward, and shoulders slipping with the sounds of the steel drums.

His feet are the only part of Panky Durnberg that aren't moving. His desert boots set firmly on the elevator floor, dark around the soles where the slush has soaked in.

Twenty minutes later, carrying a six-inch stack of acetates, Panky's still grooving to Marley as he steps up in front of thirty BFP&G people assembled in the conference room in his wrinkled black suit, tousled hair, and salt-stained shoes. Ester's there, Sinkle too, sitting in the second row with Plevis, the Office Manager, and Murray the CFO. Nobody's missing the first big meeting on the account that's lifted BFP&G to the highest state of yamma-yamma since Benny, Frank, and Gus retired and Sinkle took over the agency.

I'm sitting in the front row, on Sinkle's left side, three feet from Panky Durnberg and his overhead projector that's humming like a light plane circling overhead.

The room is lit like it's high noon in Lauderdale, wall-washers cooking the cream-colored walls, spots blazing down from the ceiling, but the room's as cold as a meat locker. "Makes people think better" is Sinkle's justification for keeping the temperature at sixty-eight degrees.

Panky gives me a formal nod (a week ago, I wouldn't have gotten a perfunctory tilt of the head from him), tucks his green tie into his jacket, slides a sheet of acetate onto the glass, clicks on the overhead projector, looks up, flips his hair up out of the way, clears his throat, and says, "The way I read the data, selling God is a dicey proposition, but if we're thoughtful and precise, the upside is nothing short of astounding." His hips gently rock back and forth to the music as six columns of numbers flash onto the screen.

Panky points to the first column. "Let me show you."

Strategy meetings are like the start of a cattle drive. The cattle are the creative people and the cowboys are management. The idea of the meeting is to corral the creative people so they don't wander all over the place and do all kinds of ads that don't have anything to do with the product; then get everyone's agreement on the right direction so management can drive the entire herd right into Dodge, sell the ads to the client, get them on the air, and start collecting the commission, which is the whole point of the advertising business, at least if you're Steve Sinkle.

Every meeting starts with Panky getting up and defining the target, prime prospect, and his or her attitudes toward the product or service. Usually it's pretty dull and boring, and the creative people are asleep after the first five minutes.

"If the marketing objective is increasing church attendance," Panky says, quickly looking over at me for approval. Nod back at him. *At least I have one ally in the agency.*

"But as you can see from the overlapping influencers, the decision is modal, to say the least." *Modal! Can you believe that? Where does he think he is, Oxford?*

Ads for God

Panky goes on to describe the various family member's roles in deciding to go to church, flipping the acetates, and pointing out the numbers. Father, mother, children, grandparents.

Panky's got red circles and yellow squares with lines running back and forth showing the decision patterns. He's right. This advertising could get complicated.

I hear snoring from the back of the room. I look around. There's Ester surrounded by her group of creative hotshots, eleven or twelve of them, dressed like a rock group from outer space complete with nose rings, (I understand they also have navel rings, but with the weather in Chicago, you don't start seeing midriffs until June), four sets of dreadlocks and one magenta stripe of hair. They wear necklaces made out of the pods I used to see standing in my mother's garden when winter came, Birkenstocks over argyles, hiking boots, red, orange, blue, and yellow fleece vests, and, underneath the fleece, in what looks like a revival of tie-dyeing, color-soaked tee shirts. J. Crew meets the Grateful Dead. Creative is as creative does.

The snoring is coming from an art director named Sticks. Tall, lanky character with an Apache haircut and a beaded buckskin outfit complete with moccasins. Sticks does the college ads for Steigerlager. Sticks' advertising philosophy is "If you can understand the ad, it isn't working." Right now, Sticks' head is hanging over the back of the chair like he's been shot. His Adam's apple is protruding from his neck like a small mound on a bare hillside.

I recognize two people from Media. In contrast to the creative people, the media folks are wide-awake and look like hicks from Kansas in the big city to see a banker about a mortgage. Suits, black shoes, woman with her hair pulled back, man with a thin Desi Arnez moustache that looks like it's been drawn-on with eyeliner.

Media people are essential at a strategy session since they'll be choosing the TV shows and magazines the ads will go in. They need to understand the prospect and the ad strategy in order to make the buys. Just try to sell Depends in *Rolling Stone*.

Two of Sinkle's account flunkies, young Ralph Lauren hit men, sit on either side of Sinkle, lips pursed, looking cool. They are learning the martial arts of the advertising business at the feet of the master: how to intimidate competitors, hoodwink rivals, kiss ass without seeming obvious, and, most important in climbing the corporate ladder—how to convince clients to spend more than they need so the billings will go up and Sinkle will take home a fatter paycheck so he can buy the agency and fire anyone who poses a threat to him.

A skinny copywriter wearing biker's garb wakes up with a start, the chains on his boots and jacket clinking and jingling. Looks around like he doesn't know where he is. Could be Hell for all he knows. Or a strategy meeting at an advertising agency. Probably not too much difference from his point of view.

He blinks. Scratches his nose. Then he recognizes his art-director partner, a sallow-faced character with long stringy hair sitting next to him. Nods and smirks at him. The two of them blew the top off the Steiglager account with an award-winning commercial starring two animated Archaeopteryx sitting on a branch talking about how good things used to be, when beer tasted like beer, and there weren't any of those mean two-legged guys in fur suits skulking around with sticks. The art director smirks back. Creative people like to smirk. Smirking makes them feel more creative, particularly when they don't understand what's going on.

"Now taking this discussion from the theoretical to the practical," Panky continues, holding up a bunch of pictures of movie stars. "We've added the human dimension to enable our creative people to get a grip on the problem."

Panky's used a standard research technique called a card-sort. The research people hold up pictures of celebrities and ask, "If God were human, who would He resemble?"

What Durnberg has discovered from his in-depth interviews and focus groups is that women want God to be part Johnny Depp and part Ronald Reagan, reassuring and inspiring but also alluring and mysterious. Panky holds up the two cards with Depp and Reagan's pictures and calls it the "embodiment of the complex duality of the lover/father."

Men, on the other hand, want God to be macho and invincible, resourceful but with a sense of humor. Over fifty men in Panky's sample picked one card, he points to the column titled "Men—Most Frequently Chosen Card" and holds a picture up in the air. Arnold Schwarzenegger is the celebrity picked by fifty-three men as the person most resembling their idea of God. *Schwarzenegger. See, I told you Patti Shaw is one smart lady!*

Pushing the interviewees further, the research found that men saw God specifically as Schwarzenegger in Terminator 2, with the blazing machine gun on his hip and leather bandoleers crisscrossing his gleaming chest. And when the researchers asked the specific question "If God was going to say anything, what would you imagine him saying?" over 65% of the men responded, "Hasta la vista, baby."

"So we have a complex situation here," Durnberg summarizes. "Almost diametrically-opposed visions of God, romantic father-figure and macho action hero. The situation gets even more complicated when you factor in the children's reaction." Durnberg puts up another chart.

I can hear Sinkle's cell phone cheeping as he punches buttons. Sinkle says into his phone, "Hey, Bert, how about joining me in my box for the Orlando game? Should be a good one the way Pippen is shooting."

Panky explains, "Kids, on the other hand, both boys and girls, fascinated by God's magical properties, see Him as Mighty Morphin Power Rangers first, with Superman and Ninja Turtles not far behind." Panky picks up a grease pencil and draws a tall red triangle on his acetate.

"So we end up with a three-pointed target. Separated by their own perspectives, the three prospects have very little in common."

"Great, Bert," Sinkle says into his phone. "Bring her along. What does she like to drink? Anything special?" Sinkle hikes up his pants leg to show off his cordovan brogues, custom Ralph's, tasseled and perforated and probably worth six-fifty—his shoes alone could cover my rent.

"Did you consider flipping the proposition around, Panky?" I ask. "Asking people how they wanted to be perceived by God?"

Sinkle's still on the phone. "Can't wait to meet her, Bert," he says. Sinkle quickly looks up at Durnberg to gauge his response.

"Very perceptive, Dinny," Panky says and all eyes in the room swivel around to me. Ester sits up in her chair. I used to say brilliant stuff like this all the time, turning a point-of-view over and looking at it from the other side.

Jeez, He's given me my marketing smarts back. I've got the touch, possess the mojo. I'm back in business again!

"That's exactly what I meant when I talked about the incredible upside on this business. Because when we ask people to do what Dinny has suggested, we see a powerful motivator coming into play."

Sinkle flips his cell phone shut. Eyes swing over to me. *Sinkle's not liking what he's hearing. Dinny Rein is making points in a major meeting. He's back from the dead with a hundred-million dollar account and a wicked attitude to go with it.*

Panky draws a circle around his triangle on the blackboard. "When we ask people how they want to be perceived by God, (Panky reaches for a stack of photographs.) they pick out a consistent series of pictures."

Setting the photos up one-by-one on a rail, Panky continues, "The imagery is surprising. People—moms, dads, and kids alike— want to be seen as a healthy, happy unit, each playing their traditional roles in the family. Panky sets up pictures of the Cleaver family, the family from *Little House On The Prairie*, Ozzie and Harriet, David and Ricky. "What we have here is a powerful common need on the part of Americans to be thought of as the idealized family unit. That's a need we can play off in the advertising."

"Sounds a lot like McDonald's advertising to me, Panky," I add. "Mom, Dad, kids, all drawn to burgers and fries with the same broad strategy."

"You must have read my script," Panky smiles at me. "Take a look at this," he says, punching the play button of a VCR. Ester shoots Sinkle a look.

Sinkle quickly sits forward in his chair, like he's taken a 110 volt jolt to the butt. A typical McDonald's commercial starts playing, smiling people, dads and kids and moms, washing cars and romping with puppies, proud parents watching their kids star in the school play, kids in raincoats jumping in puddles, parents tucking kids into bed at night—upbeat, polite rock n' roll with a heavy chorus playing on the soundtrack, except all the product shots, all the hamburgers

Ads for God

and fries have been replaced with scenes of fluffy white clouds floating against a clear blue sky.

"We asked people to take a look at this edited commercial and imagine that the shots of the clouds were representations of God, then to tell us how they felt," Panky says, turning off the VCR.

Ester and Sinkle are scowling at each other. He puts up a new chart, circling numbers at the bottom of columns. He's got reggae fever now, body's squirming and twisting all over the place. "As crude as this commercial is, what we see is over 85% of the people we interviewed find this advertising makes them feel good." Panky's voice is getting shriller. "It makes them want to be better people, and when we asked them whether the ad makes them feel more inclined to want to go to church, 78% said yes!" Panky circles the 78% number with his grease pencil, almost shouting the word "yes."

"What we have here is a powerful motivator to effect a sea change in American culture. We can get American families flocking into church, get them to feel better about themselves, and show them how they can be better, kinder, more loving people—with advertising!" Panky turns to me and beams, juts his chin at me like he's saying, "Way to go, Buddy!"

The yamma-yamma courses around the room, conversation buzzes, and everyone shifts around in their seats. Then one by one, heads slowly rotate around toward Sinkle. Everyone in the room knows it's his turn at bat. Might as well have swung a spotlight onto him.

Sinkle sits back in his chair and turns his shoe so the overhead light gleams off the leather. "I'm glad to see you so enthusiastic, Panky, and you've obviously done a lot of solid work here. But can I ask you a question?"

"Certainly," Panky straightens his stack of acetates.

Sinkle snaps down his trump card. "What about repeat?" he says, in that hard, cold, cynical tone he uses when he wants to poke a hole in a new idea. Asking the question "What about repeat?" is like asking "But will you love me tomorrow?" Sure, the advertising might have a big bang, Sinkle's insinuating, but will it pull over time, stay motivating over the months it runs?

"Exactly where I was going, Steve," Ester chimes in, smiling at him and sitting back in her seat, crossing her legs so the entire room catches a glimpse of thigh. "This feel-good stuff might get you a spike at the beginning, but I'd have real doubts about its pulling power over the long haul."

"Where would you go with this, Ester?" *They're double-teaming Panky, Sinkle's set him up, and now Ester's going in for the kill. I wish I could haul out my cell phone and get some divine guidance right now.*

"I think Panky's walked right past the opportunity." Ester gets up and walks over to Panky. Stands next to him, close, gives him a look like he's got bad BO. Picks up his grease pencil and starts to mark on his acetate.

Panky's gazing over her shoulder like he's the student and she's the teacher. *She's taking over his presentation, one-upping him, using his data and his graphics to make her point.*

"When you have discrete targets like these," she says, circling the three points of the triangle, "and you're looking to build and maintain, promotion is the other way to go." Ester draws arrows inward toward the three points of the triangle. "To me, the advertising approach is problematic at best."

Ester draws a big question mark then squiggles a fat dollar sign in the center of the triangle. "I think the opportunity is here—in customized promotions for each subset with staggered incentives to maintain attendance."

Promotions! I'm thinking. Giveaways, contests, games, incentives—that's Ester Platt for you. The girl's one smart lady. I don't know if you can promote churchgoing with Happy Meals, but it's worth looking at.

"Promotions are where the money is," she says, placing her hands on her hips and looking across the room at Sinkle. "It's a no-brainer to me, Steve, and if I was a smart client, that's the kind of strategy I'd be looking for."

Panky clicks off his overhead. Doesn't want her drawing on his presentation any longer. Then he walks right into Ester's trap. "I'm not sure promotions are appropriate in this situation. I mean, we are talking about God here." Panky says.

What he should have said was "Sure, that's another way of looking at it," but now he's taken sides and right now, Ester will waste him in front of the entire room. Here it comes:

Ester gives him an eye roll and steps away from the overhead. "You want to sell God like hamburgers and french fries. What's the difference? Make ads with clouds in them or give away a few air miles for showing up at church? C'mon, Panky, get real."

She walks back to her chair and sits down. Smug. Two of her writers clap her on the back. *Congratulating her for doing her black widow spider act so well.* Panky shuffles his acetates. *He knows he's finished—mortally wounded from the deadly bite of Ester the Spider Woman.*

Sinkle slips his cell phone into his pocket and stands. "Okay, folks, I think we've got a horse race here. Two valid approaches, each with it's own merits, thanks to Panky here." Sinkle gives Panky a quick jab in the arm then claps him on the back, "Brilliant work as always, Panky. You're a master."

Even though Ester's tire marks are all over him, Panky's doing his lap dog impression, smiling sheepishly, and shucking around under Sinkle's flattery and blandishments. It's amazing what you can get people to do when you pay them enough money.

Time for business. Sinkle aims his finger at me, then at Ester, and says, "You two—you come with me." He strides out of the conference room with Ester and I following. Mort trailing behind. At the door, Ester stands aside, motions me through. I smile, usher her ahead. Nothing doing. She wants me to go first.

I walk through the door, heading down the hall after Sinkle. I don't like having my back to Ester. Turn around. She smiles at me. Mort snarls.

Sinkle in front of me, Ester following. Thug in front of you and an assassin behind. Oh boy, have you got your work cut out for you, Dinny my boy. I catch up with Sinkle. He walks with an athlete's lope, silky and confident. Whenever I walk with Sinkle, I feel like I'm shuffling.

"Let's get a few things clear here so you both know where you stand," Sinkle explains as he leads us into the conference room off his office where his confidential meetings are conducted. Vincent stands guard at the door, grunts at me as I walk past, then says "Good afternoon, Ma'am" to Ester. On top of harvesting his crop of ear-hairs, Vincent also needs etiquette lessons.

Sigourney Weaver turns and looks out the conference room window at the lake, her back turned to me like I don't exist as Sinkle explains. "I want you two to cooperate on this advertising. Ester, you share your people, and, Dinny, you make sure you give Ester access to the client."

He's setting us up to scratch each other's eyes out. It's management la Machiavelli—one of us will knock off the other, and no matter who wins, Sinkle will stay king and the king will have one less noble to worry about.

Ester walks over slowly and leans over Sinkle's conference table. Today she's wearing her standard outfit: short tight skirt, white blouse, flesh-colored high heels with her laptop hanging from her shoulder in a pink silk sling, her thumb hooked in the sling so her blouse stretches across her chest. Ester would wear seamed stockings if it wasn't so obvious.

"Look, you want me to share my job with him—I'll do that, Steve." Ester shoots me a sidelong glance and goes back to leaning over Sinkle's side of the table. "But if the client buys my promotion idea, Dinny Rein is history."

My mouth stretches open. "Don't bet on it," God interrupts.

Holy shit, there He goes again!

Sinkle's chin jumps out. "What?" he asks, his head cocking quizzically, looking at me sideways, trying to figure out where the baritone came from. *Maybe if I take over quickly, He won't say anything else.* I act like nothing happened.

"I'm not sure that's a smart idea, Steve..." I say, noticing that Vincent has put his hand behind his back and is starting to quietly dig at the seat of his striped pants, "...given my relationship with the client." I give him a nod and a sly wink.

You can get away with anything in an advertising agency if you're tight with a client, scamming your expense account, taking five week vacations, getting your ditzqueen girlfriend a cushy job in Media, or arranging week-long brainstorming trips to Bora Bora.

Sinkle doesn't let his eyes drop. He shakes his head and looks Ester right in the eye. "Even if we went with your promotion concept, Dinny would have to remain on the business in an account capacity since he knows the client."

Ester straightens up and walks away from the table. "In an account capacity only, right?" she asks, turning back toward us, hand on her hip, legs crossed, trying to get her job as the sole Creative Director back.

"We'd have to assess that eventuality, Ester."

"C'mon, Steve, if I win, he's out of the CD job."

This woman's really out to get me.

"What are you worried about Ester? You're going be creative director in any case. Now let's start thinking of ourselves as a team."

Whenever someone has to assure you that you still have your job and then tells you to be a team player, you can bet you're soon going to end up holding the short end of the stick.

Ester's eyes flick back and forth. She knows she's surrounded. Sinkle and I are teamed up and she's pinned down with no place to go. "And of course we'll present both campaigns to the client, right Dinny?" Sinkle says condescendingly.

I nod. "Absolutely, the client should see everything we have," I say.

Whoa! Maybe I shouldn't have said that. Now Ester's got a guaranteed way in with her work. But who's going to buy advertising that sells God with giveaway Barbie dolls, Dallas Cowboy caps, and free air miles anyway?

Ester's had enough, pivots on her heel, and walks slowly toward the door. She pauses, turns around, and says to Sinkle, "Is that all?"

Sinkle gives Ester his *"You're deadmeat"* smile, slick and heartless. "For the time being," he says. Ester fires me a look that would burn holes in steel and disappears around the doorway, Mort skittering along behind her at the end of his red leather leash.

"Smart girl," I say, putting my foot up on Sinkle's upholstered chair.

"Right," he says, with about as much conviction as if I'd said it was a nice day.

He blew me away and set Ester up as creative director. Now he's ready to blow her away. People would be safer in the lion cage at the Lincoln Park Zoo than in advertising.

Lorna buzzes and announces that Perry Steiger's on the phone.

"Excuse me," he says, grabbing the receiver. "Perry, how you been?" Sinkle looks up at me like it's time for me to leave, whirls around in his chair, and swings his feet up on his window seat while he talks to Perry Steiger, the Marketing Director of Steigerlager.

I get up and walk slowly around the room, staying in Sinkle's line of sight. Sinkle talks about market share, a fall promotion, and the new can design. He turns and looks at me, scowls, trying to tell me that I'm dismissed, I'm supposed to leave. I'm standing in the middle of his private conference room, right under his Victorian chandelier, like I've scored six goals and I'm waiting for the start of the second half, hand on my hip, other arm held loosely at my side.

Sinkle glares at me again. Clasping my hands behind my back, I act like I'm in an art gallery, walking up and studying the Edwardian lithographs, moving slowly from frame to frame. He's talking to Steiger about the new crop of players the Bears drafted. Swings around in his chair to see if I'm still there. I turn around and wink at him. Sinkle's fuming.

Uh oh, He's going to say something. I swing back around quickly and face the wall when I feel my throat start to open. *C'mon God, please don't queer this thing for me, not right in front of Sinkle. Don't say anything, please.*

I turn toward the far wall. Cough once. "Go for it, Rein," He says. "Waste him. You got him right where you want him. Get your secretary back, get a bigger office, go for it."

Okay, okay, I'll ask him—now go away. Please go away. I cough again. *He'll think I'm a nut case and sic the guys in the white suits on me, c'mon.* Walk to the far wall and pretend like I'm examining an oil painting of Queen Elizabeth.

"Pounce on him right now, Rein. You'll never have a better chance. Go for the jugular. Get everything you can. That's the way you got to be in this business."

"Okay, all right, I hear you!" I blurt out. Silence. Quickly glance over my shoulder at Sinkle. He's staring at me like I farted, head cocked to one side, face all screwed up like he's trying to figure out who I'm talking to. I give him a stupid smile and cough again. Point at my throat. He gets short with Steiger. "Good, Perry, let's have lunch next week. I'll call you." He hangs up. Slowly raises his head, glowering at me.

"What the hell's going on here?" he says, standing and coming around the side of his desk. "Who were you talking to?"

"Just thinking out loud, that's all." He gives me the look he's famous for, halfway between a smirk and a grimace. *He doesn't believe me.*

"Look Rein, you got to introduce me to your client, goddammit, you got to." The blue on his Polo tie blazes like it's battery-powered. "This is no way to do business. Hell, I can provide all sorts of strategic direction to your client, Dinny, and I can help you handle him. Let's just put all that stuff in the past behind us, c'mon."

He puts his arm around my shoulder. Sinkle wears Aramis. "So when do I meet him?"

"After you do a couple of things for me."

Sinkle gives me a sour smile, scowling, knowing he has to put up with me until he can buy out the founders.

"What?" he asks, looking like a seven-year-old kid who has to finish his broccoli in order to get dessert.

"I want my secretary back and I want to hire three teams."

"Okay, your secretary and three teams—so when do I get to meet the client?"

"One more thing..."

"Jesus Christ, c'mon, Rein..."

I look into the dark hole where his incisor used to be. "I'll introduce you, if you give me my corner office back."

Sinkle winces. Walking back around his desk, he shakes his head.

Corner offices confer respect, which is in short supply in the ad biz. People are awed by the windows. They go silent when they walk in, feeling humbled by all the furniture—the mahogany coffee table in front of the chintz-covered sofa, the graceful end tables on either side, the conference table against the windows, the Chippendale chairs grouped around the desk—sensing they are in the presence of someone more powerful, more intelligent, because he has fresh flowers arranged in a fake Ming vase on his credenza every morning, a constantly replenished bowl of apples and kiwi fruits on his conference table, and a barber who comes in once a month, drapes a striped cloth around him, and cuts his hair.

I nod and look Sinkle in the eye. I know he's thinking, *"In six months, I'll own the agency—I'll find some way to get rid of this asshole."*

He pauses a second and then says, "I'll see what I can do."

I smile at Sinkle. A big, wide smile. "You do that," I say. Sinkle doesn't smile back. Leaving his door wide open, I walk out of the conference room into the anteroom. Beethoven's Seventh is playing. I pause and feel my lips go into motion. Time for another divine download.

"Way to go, Rein, you blasted him right out of the sky," He says. "Did you see the look on his face when you asked him for a corner office? He looked like you were asking for the entire agency. What a team we make, huh, Rein? We give them the old one-two punch. You do the ads and I give you the guidance."

Vincent hears me talking and peers into the anteroom, looking around for the person I'm talking to. Time to distract Vincent the butler. I walk up to him and give him a fake jab to the gut. He grabs at his stomach with both hands to protect himself.

"Stay cool, Vincent my man, stay cool," I say, and head out of Sinkle land.

15

Izzy calls the minute I get back to my office, "You got to get over here quick, Rein. You won't believe how this steal-o-matic's working out," he says. "It's goddamn spellbinding, pal. You've got yourself a real winner here."

I'm shrugging on my coat as I'm talking to him on the phone. "Be there in fifteen."

Izzy's never called me about a commercial. He must really have something. I'm out of the office and heading down Michigan before I realize I left my Range Rover in the garage.

Back into the building, I take the stairs down to the basement in twos.

If this steal-o-matic works, I could be out of the woods—way ahead of schedule. Unlock the Range Rover with the zapper from fifteen feet away, run up and jump in. *This car hums. You can hardly tell it's running.* The garage door goes up, and I wheel up the ramp. *Wait a minute,* I see someone standing in the shadows at the top of the ramp. *It's that guy with the blue baseball jacket. He's smiling at me again.* He moves off to the side as I pass. *Or maybe it's just some garage attendant.*

I try to look back over my shoulder but I have to look away as the car bumps up out of the garage. It's dark out, click on the lights, my headlights splash against the steel beams running under Michigan sending pigeons fluttering across the roadway.

I come out of Lower Michigan behind Izzy's building, park in the lot, and click my car locked. Parking lot's small and dark, canyoned in by the surrounding buildings. It's an old loft area. Izzy bought the building for nothing. Head around to the front entrance.

The wind stops me as I come around the corner, blowing hard and flying snow at me.

I didn't think it was supposed to snow. I turn sideways and lean into the weather, slowly making my way along the face of the building until I get close enough to grab the door handle. In Chicago, you have to learn how to walk in the winter or you don't get anywhere. I've seen tourists stuck in the middle of a block, paralyzed by the wind to the point where they have no choice but to get chased back inside.

Izzy's alone in his office. All the other offices are dark. The light from his office floods out into the hall. I can hear the monks singing. I step into the doorway. He's got the commercial running on the big monitor over his head. The sound is in stereo. He's taken footage from everywhere, stock footage of scenery, towering mountains, lush rainforests, helicopter shots down canyons, and flocks of geese against a setting sun.

He's mixed in shots of kids jumping rope, playing baseball, blowing bubbles, and bobbing for apples in the bright sunshine. There are quick cuts from famous movies, Marilyn Monroe's skirt blowing up in the air, Buster Keaton hanging from a clock hand. He's used scenes from sports, the big save in the Olympics to beat the Russians in hockey, Babe Ruth connecting to send one sailing out of the park. I walk into the editing room as the commercial ends, and Izzy swings around in his chair to greet me.

"This is a killer idea, Dinny," he says. "People see this commercial a couple of times, and they'll be flocking to church. Let's take it from the top, okay?"

"Sure," I say, and Izzy clicks in a series of instructions on his keyboard and the steal-o-matic starts running again.

Oh boy, I'm thinking as I watch the kids in the soap box derby, the sunset glowing over the Grand Canyon. *First time I get up to bat and I hit one out of the park. Izzy's right. This advertising has the potential to get millions of people thinking about God again. I don't care what Ester Platt does. This is the big winner. This is the advertising that's going to put Dinny Rein back on the map, lift people's spirits, get them to see the good in life again, and pack churches like there's no tomorrow.*

"So where do you see the campaign going?" Izzy asks when

the commercial fades out. "You're going to need more than one commercial."

"This one will be the flagship. What's this, two minutes long?"

"Just about."

"So we'll spin out all the dimensions of the human experience in the flagship into separate commercials. We'll do one on sports, one on kids, one on love, one on comedians. Hell, we can do anything we want. It's open-ended."

I'm rolling. I'm on a roll with my ideas again. They're flying out of my brain as fast as I can move my mouth. "We can do weddings. We could do a spot with all sunsets. We could do thirty seconds of time-lapse flowers blooming, great moments from the movies, a whole spot on circus clowns—we're selling life, Izzy. We're selling what it feels like to be *alive!*"

Izzy's nodding. "These things will blow the roof off the business. Everyone's going to be talking about them."

"This will be a hundred million bucks of uplift, Izzy. We'll be able to bring some feeling and vitality to people's lives. Get people out of this buy, buy, buy mentality and help them to appreciate the simpler things in life."

Izzy's got his mouth open, eyes wide, marveling at his old friend Dinny Rein who's back in the groove again. *I've got the magic back. My mind's full of ideas, just like the good old days.*

"And we'll get them going to church. We'll pull them in slowly but surely. Maybe I can get a little announcer copy in there to strengthen that communication. I'll work on that."

"Buddy," he says, standing up. "I have to tell you, I thought it was all over for you." Izzy gives me a hug. I can smell Old Spice. "I thought they'd done you in..."

He's clapping me on the back. Now he's got me in a bear hug, lifts me up, and sways me from side to side so the soles of my shoes skim the floor. *There's not much I can do until he puts me down.* My nose itches. "I'm proud of you, pal, real proud of you. And if I was still drinking, we'd go off on one helluva bender right now." Izzy puts me down. I scratch my nose. He hands me a cassette of the commercial.

"Thanks, Izzy," I say, tapping him with the cassette and backing out of his office. "Thanks a lot."

"This is going to be a big one, the biggest thing I've ever worked on. I'll start assembling the footage for the other spots. Get me the announcer tracks as soon as you can." Izzy sticks out his hammy hand, I take it. "Pal," he says. "Pal..."

Shit, I think he's going to cry. I bang him on the shoulder with the palm of my hand and turn and walk out of his office.

Izzy's standing behind the glass door, waving to me as I get on the elevator. I've gone from being the old friend you don't want to talk to for fear he's fallen further to being the hottest thing on Michigan Avenue—the creator of the campaign that's going to have the whole country talking and provide Izzy with a ticket out of Ester Platt land.

My phone starts ringing as soon as I get the Range Rover going.

"Yo, Rein, you sure aced that one. That's a lollapalooza if I've ever seen one. Oh boy, wait until the competition sees this. They won't know what hit them!"

I'm swinging out of the lot and heading for Michigan Avenue. It's starting to snow.

"I knew you could do it, Reinny baby. Way to go."

Reinny, He's calling me Reinny. I haven't been called that since my senior year at Waverly. Back when I was captain of the lacrosse team and highest scorer in the school's history.

"I tell you, the way you captured my magnificence and grace, the majesty of my works—takes me back to the good old days when people used to lie on their backs on scaffolds for months painting pictures of me on the ceiling. When they spent centuries building huge cathedrals. When they composed marvelous hymns and painted whole books by hand with real gold paint. It's an ego thing, you know what I mean? I tell you, Rein, this could be the biggest thing to happen to me since I sent down the kid."

There's no traffic on Michigan, just snowflakes. They seem to bend down and fly into my window as I speed up the avenue.

"Frankly, between you and me and that lamppost over there, I was getting pretty bummed out if you want to know the truth. Jeez, for a couple thousand years now I've been giving the world sunrises sparkling over the blue Caribbean and waving fields of daffodils, glorious calla lilies and endless carpets of phlox, acres of orange nasturtiums that'll poke your eyes out with their beauty. I give them waves and mountains and music and the Grand Canyon. You ever seen the Grand Canyon when the sun is setting?

"I give them Paul Newman's blues and Marilyn's legs, and what do people do? Do people ever say 'thank you'? Do they ever stop in at church and say, 'Hey, God, thanks for the clear blue sky framed by a few puffy clouds you gave us today.'? You know what I gotta do to get a blue sky—you think that's easy? But do I ever hear anyone say, 'Thanks'—just say 'Thanks'? 'Thanks for the Sistine Chapel, thanks for Frank Sinatra's voice'—do they ever do that? No, no, no, all they do is stay home, eat Cheetos, and watch Snoop Doggy Dogg on TV. But you've figured it out, Rein. You unlocked the combination."

"I'm glad, I'm glad, and I've got a lot more work to do on them. If you like them now, wait until you see them when we're finished."

"There're just a couple of things I'd like you to look at, if you don't mind."

Uh oh, here it comes. Pick, pick, pick, the endless comments and asinine critiques—look at this, change that, consider this, try that. Hearing clients pick away at your advertising is like getting pecked to death by ducks.

"Eighty-six the monks, make them go away. They sing nice but after a couple thousand years, you get tired of monks. Need something hip. Get Dave Matthews or Smashing Pumpkins or someone like that."

That's reasonable, I can try other music. "Okay, I'll take a look at that." *What next?*

"And get in some more baseball—I like baseball. Can't play to save my ass, but I love baseball."

"But you're God, can't you do everything?"

"Nope, there's things I can't do."

"Like what?"

"I told you. I have problems relating to large groups and I can't hit for shit. As a matter of fact, I can't even lay down a good bunt."

"Really?"

"Bummer. I got all these great guys to play with and I strike out every time. Very embarrassing when you're playing with Cobb and Ruth and Mantle. Get up there to the plate and fluff three in a row. Feel like a piece of crap. Hell, it's a big deal if I hit a foul ball. They all cheer and clap like I hit one out of the park. Ruthie came up to me once after I hit a long tall ball. Way wide, had to be fifty feet out. The Babe comes up, puts his arm around me, says, 'Two inches to the left kid, and you woulda had one I would have been proud of.' Now that's embarrassing. If I could hit a clean single. That's what I'd wish for—a nice clean single."

"We'll do a whole commercial on baseball if you want."

"Great, I'd like that."

"One more thing I want to do."

"What's that?"

"I want to run the commercial by someone."

"Sure, who?"

"Martha Stewart."

"Who?"

"Martha Stewart, the chef lady on TV, the girl's got a great sense of style."

"Sure, I guess that's okay. Go ahead." I turn off Michigan into the street that runs into Wrigleyville. Snow's starting to build up, blanketing the cars and coating the sidewalks so the pedestrians mince along to keep from slipping, their collars up, heads pulled down into their coats. The streets of Chicago are going from grimy gray to a blue-white, the snow draping over the trees and fuzzing the streetlights with halos.

"She liked it," He says.

"Who?"

"Martha. She loved it."

"You showed it to her that fast?"

"C'mon, I can't play ball but I can still get around pretty quick."

"So, what did she say?"

"I told you, she liked it. She thought it could use some more mushrooms, oh, and one of the rooms needed something on the mantelpiece, a cornucopia or something, but otherwise she loved it. She thinks it'll be a big hit."

Jeez, Martha Stewart saw my commercial—and she loved it!

And God says, He really does, says it to me right over my car phone, "Rein, I got to tell you—when it comes to advertising, you're a genius." That's what He said. God did. To me, Dinny Rein. Right in the middle of a snowy night in the city of Chicago.

16

The creative floor's been in a constant hubbub ever since the strategy meeting. Ester Platt and I have bivouacked our creative troops on opposite sides of the floor, arraying our platoons of writers and art directors up and down the corridors in preparation for the creative presentation on the God account, the hottest account at BFP&G Advertising.

The area outside my office looks like the door to Madonna's dressing room, flocks of writers and art directors hovering around smoking cigarettes and eating Snickers, crowding Evelyn's desk so much she starts to swat at them like flies. "Give me some space!" she barks. "C'mon, scram!" They retreat down the corridor, edging back slowly carrying their Slurpees and Big Macs from the food court downstairs.

Each time I leave my office the writers and art directors clump around me, looking for hints, trying to figure out what I'm looking for, sneaking stuff in front of me to try and get a jump on the competition. They follow me into the men's room and tail me as I head off for Sirini, lobbying me on the sidewalk. "C'mon, Dinny, just take a quick look at this idea and see if I'm on the right track."

"Hey, Dinny, I got to talk to you" I hear as I turn the corner. *It's Scrunch standing in front of my office with a wad of layouts he wants to show me.*

"Not now, Scrunch. Give me a ring later, and we'll take a look," I say as I wave to Evelyn and walk into my office, leaving Scrunch standing in the middle of the corridor with his mouth open. *What nobody knows is I've already got the big idea and sold it through the*

Ads for God

client. But maybe someone will come up with something good. Doesn't hurt to have a backup. And who knows what Ester's going to do?"

"Evelyn, why don't you come in for a minute?" Evelyn's standing in my doorway in two seconds, hands held together over her chest, pleasant smile on her face, ready to do whatever Dinny Rein wants. Evelyn was my secretary for twelve years before Ester banished her. Her desk disappeared one morning when I was out of town. She told me in tears over the phone. A scribbled note on the floor where her desk had been instructed her to go to Personnel. The Personnel assistant told her, "Mr. Rein has a reduced workload and won't be needing you any longer." Not much you can do when you're standing in an airport corridor with your secretary sobbing to you over the phone.

Evelyn was reassigned to the Secretarial Pool, half a floor of typists, noisy Xerox machines, folders and stuffers, and two benches full of slick young messengers in low-riding pants who lope around the agency half-stoned delivering mail.

Evelyn's one of those ladies who's so neat she's almost pretty. Sixty-something and widowed early, her shined shoes, tailored skirts, pressed blouses, carefully-trimmed hair, and eye shadow and makeup modestly but thoughtfully applied, all compensate for her squat figure, pocky skin, and puggish nose.

She lives in a walkup in Rogers Park with her four cats and has a married sister in the western suburbs she sees a lot. She's a bridge freak and has had season tickets for the Bulls ever since they started. She's an active Republican and a fervent believer in her old boss, Mr. Dinsmore P. Rein.

"Sit down, Evelyn," I say. "Tell me how you've been doing." I haven't had much of a chance to talk to her since moving down. Evelyn sits carefully on the edge of my leather armchair like she's not going to stay for long, folds her hands on her knees, and says, "Well..." and I learn all about her new bridge partners, hear about her mother's arthritis. She slips off her blue pump and shows me the corn on the side of her foot she's going to have surgically removed in two weeks, tells me about her two cats that've had urinary problems over the past year and are driving her nuts. "I've had to take my orientals to Mother's and put down cheap carpet from K-Mart until they get over it. But that's enough about me—how've you been, Dinny?" she asks.

"Fine, since I got this new piece of business."

"You look wonderful," she says. I know she's wondering, but she's too respectful to ask how I got to look thirty-five again. "So what's your new client like?" Evelyn arranges her skirt over her knees. "Is he nice?"

"Very nice, nice guy..." I look out at the lake. I can see all the way across the choppy brown surface of the lake, laying out like a piece of nubby worsted from Navy Pier across to Michigan and the funky country towns that line the other shore: Michigan City, New Buffalo, Union Pier, St. Joseph, Benton Harbor. "He's not what you'd expect, for someone with that much money, I mean."

"Really?"

"Kind of unsophisticated, actually, but funny, great sense of humor. Imagine Mike Royko wearing a hard-hat and overalls."

Evelyn beams at me. "I'm very happy for you." She went through all my traumas with Reavis, watched my career spin out of control.

I look out at the lake again and say, "It was about time something good happened."

"You were getting so sour and spiteful."

"Me? Sour and spiteful? Me?" I joke.

Evelyn nods. "It's awful the way this business eats people up." She shakes her head and goes "Tsk, tsk, tsk" and adds, "You were letting it, too."

"I was?"

"You took everything that happened and turned it against yourself—at least, that's how it looked to me."

The shirred surface of the lake reminds me of sitting on Poesemon's metal table how many days ago? Looking out his window and contemplating the diseases I could die from.

"Not any more," I say, standing up. Evelyn knows it's time for her to get back to work but she has more to say.

"Can I tell you something?" She peers out the door, gets up, carefully closes the door, and flips the lock. "You know, I've been good friends with Lorna since we were in Young Republicans together,

Ads for God

oh, twenty years ago. And Lorna (Lorna is Sinkle's secretary in case anyone's forgotten), Lorna told me yesterday that Mr. Sinkle," she whispers, hunching down over the coffee table, looking around as if someone might be listening.

"It's awful what he's saying about you. He says he doesn't think you really have a client. He says you're doing a hostile takeover. He thinks you're trying to take control of the agency and you've gotten the money from somewhere, borrowed it or you're representing some other agency. He isn't sure, I don't think, and..."

"What?"

"Shhh," Evelyn puts her finger up to her mouth. " And he's spreading the rumor that you're..." She looks around again, leans in closer to me so she's almost slipping off the armchair, and makes a circular motion around her temple with her index finger. "He's saying you're *crazy*."

"C'mon."

Evelyn nods. "He's saying you talk to yourself. And I think he's having people follow you, take pictures."

"What? You mean like private eyes?"

Maybe those are the guys in the Buick?

She nods and sits back in the chair, looking around my office. "I think we should be careful what we say, if you know what I mean."

I smile and get up. "Sinkle's the one who's crazy, Evelyn, I can tell you that. And if he's got people following me, that'll prove it." I walk over and open the door.

"I just wanted you to know," Evelyn says, standing and walking past me.

"Thanks, I appreciate it. Let me know if you hear any other gossip."

"I will, Mr. Rein. I will."

Shit, I knew this would happen—this client of mine's becoming a loose cannon. I've got to do something about Him. I shut the door and walk over to my antique RCA radio, turn it on. Old jazz, sounds like Satchmo. Turn the radio up.

"Did you hear that?" I whisper, "Sinkle's starting to figure it out—you got to stop talking out like that, okay?"

No answer.

"You up there? Come in, God." I pull out my cell phone, turn it on, walk around my office, looking up at the ceiling, whispering as loud as I dare. Still no answer.

"Sinkle thinks I'm out to steal the agency, you hear that? That'll get him crazy. He's already spreading rumors that I'm bonkers. He'll have a bunch of guys in white suits chasing me around. You don't know this guy. He's out to get me!"

I'm stomping around the office now, gesticulating wildly, like I'm down in the commodities pits buying corn or soybeans. "He'll have me put away in Sunnydale Acres, he'll throw away the key, and there goes your ad guy, kaput, finished, sayonara, say goodbye to your great campaign. So no more talking through me, okay? No more jokes, no more asides, no wisecracks. You got something to say to me, call, okay? You want to conference, we'll set up a time. So—you got the message? And what's more, you've got to come down here as someone, show up. Even if you have to be Abe Moskowitz. We've got to have a flesh-and-blood client. Otherwise Sinkle's going to get even more suspicious. In the meantime, please keep your trap shut, okay?"

I feel a burp coming up, but it isn't a burp. It's Him saying "You betcha."

17

When the middle of March arrives and the presentation looms, the entire creative floor gears down. People come in early and stay late, cocoon in their offices with the doors closed. The writers stoking up the computer chips, starting to type fragments of ideas, dialogue, then scripts for commercials, acting them out for themselves then trying them out on their art director partners.

I see Rosemary riding through the corridors on her mountain bike wearing gold bicycle shorts and a purple Lurex jog-bra screaming, "Hasn't *anyone* got a fucking idea around here?" People laugh, but the laughter's loud and shrill. Everyone is nervous.

Myself included, since I still can't figure out what to do for a soundtrack.

The writers work until nine or ten or eleven or go home to work all night, bringing ideas in with them in the morning, hoping something—a word, a thought, a cheeky interjection or snappy phrase, smatter of doggerel or retreaded cliché— will spark a response in their partner.

The art directors doodle, waiting for ideas to flow out the ends of their Pentels, ripping off sheets of paper and floating them back over their shoulders, the corridors getting littered with paper, scraps, sheets, pages, color Xeroxes, newspaper clippings. People start looking like basset hounds from lack of sleep, the creative floor stinks of discarded Dominos and Nikes worn too long without socks.

Despite the efforts of Woogie and his cleaning crew, Starbucks coffee cups are scattered everywhere, Domino's boxes jammed into wastebaskets, half-eaten egg foo young molding in sodden containers sitting on conference room credenzas, and empty pop cans and water bottles lie in a scatter around offices. Every evening at nine-fifteen, Woogie's army of dumpy Polish cleaning ladies in powder blue uniforms, all smiles and gold teeth, invade the office. Yet the paper keeps piling up, accumulating in stacks on conference room tables, hanging in sheaves off corkboarded walls, gathering in corners, and stuffed behind doors.

Stalking around in the middle of the night, Woogie keeps muttering at the women, "Is not clean, no? Machingitz ne woseback, machingitz ne woseback," or something like that in Polish as he points out the half-eaten containers of moo shu pork and egg rolls sitting on tables. Always finds time to stick his head into my office, to say "Evening, Mister," and give me a little salute and a big smile that shows off the two huge gold teeth flashing on either side of his mouth.

From what I hear, the guy's a prince, keeps his whole family going over in Poland, plays Santa Claus to the kids over at Cabrini Green every Christmas, and that's on top of being one helluva janitor.

Woogie sniffs out trash like a bloodhound, finds empty Evian bottles stashed behind doors and Styrofoam coffee cups hiding under tables as he shepherds his blue-frocked ladies from one part of the office to the other, sweeping the cleaning ladies down the corridors with his arms like he's herding sheep, exhorting them in Polish. I watch Woogie waving his arms, smiling at his army and think, *He's dutiful, respectful, honest and generous—someday maybe I'll have a client like Woogie.*

The writers start to sell ideas to their partners, scripts get written and rewritten. The art directors start storyboarding, squeaking the action of the commercial out of their colored markers, creating the commercials frame-by-frame. The cardboard flies around the place as they cut and paste, piecing together their storyboards, spray-mounting frames, and applying stickies to carry the dialogue and screen directions under the frames.

An idea for a commercial that reads well from a script on Monday looks lame on a storyboard on Tuesday, so it's back to the computer keyboards, more scripts, the rejected storyboards stacking against the corridor walls, labeled "wryruzic"—Woogie says that's Polish for "trash."

Ads for God

And Woogie must be right since the wryruzic is always gone in the morning.

I hear noise out in the corridor, nervous giggling, lean forward and look out the door of my office. Evelyn's standing in the doorway pointing at her watch.

"It's four o'clock," she says and I look over her shoulder to see a long line of creative people snaking away from my door and down the hall, storyboards under their arms, cassettes, scripts, illustrations, key frames, and videos in their hands. They're punching and joshing each other, fiddling with their hair and hitching up their jeans, acting like teenagers in a junior high school lunch line as they wait to file in and show their work to me. They're nervous, of course. They should be.

This is the God account, this month's superprize in the ad biz, ten or twelve commercials to make, eight million bucks in TV commercial production money available, chance to hit a long ball, make a spot that everyone loves that'll supercharge your career so you can leapfrog your boss or jump to another agency for bigger bucks, more responsibility, and maybe even a corner office and a Ming vase full of flowers every Monday.

Evelyn sends them in two-by-two, in teams, writer and art director. They file in carrying their storyboards, music tracks, and cassettes. Hold their work up tentatively, use the word "like" liberally. "Like, what I want to do is, like, give a feeling of, like,...peace...like, if you know what I mean, like..." one art director explains.

Everything's illustrated with sketchy cartoons or pictures clipped from magazines. A few of the ideas are thoroughly worked-out and storyboarded to a music track or a popular song. One writer even shows me a sixty-second clip of a hit movie to show me what he has in mind. Two teams have rough steal-o-matics.

Nothing close to mine though.

Many of the writers have nothing more than ideas scribbled on bar napkins, or scenes from TV shows or MTV videos that they think might provide inspiration. Some have snatches of song lyrics. Rosemary shows me a visual. This time it's not underpants but the illustration on a religious calendar, Jesus floating in pastel clouds, benign look on his face, coyly holding his robe closed at the knee.

"Imagine it animated," Rosemary says. "Jesus by Disney—pretty rad huh?" Rosemary giggles. "And you know what I thought of for a track, that Doxology thing we used to sing in church—imagine the Stones doing it over this animated Jesus." Rosemary giggles and does a Mick Jagger impression. "Praise God from Whom all blessings flow..." She giggles again and says, "Real rad, huh?"

One of the art directors who looks like Steven Spielberg with a bad case of acne plays a Sting song out of the little speakers of his Walkman and asks me what I think.

"Of what?" I ask.

"Of the idea," he says.

"What, you mean the song?"

"No, man, I mean the *feeling.*"

I tell him it needs more development. He shakes his head—he's thinking, *"What kind of response did I expect from a man as old as my father?"*

One of the teams has a *Field of Dreams* commercial that's interesting. Another has an idea with flowers blooming in slow motion to a Berlioz symphony.

I see the predictable celebrity ideas. Cher in white robes, Clint Eastwood standing out in the desert in animal skins acting like an apostle, clips of George Burns and John Denver. There are ten takeoffs on the latest movies. Two teams are using current hit songs but no one's using reggae yet. *Wait, they will.*

The show takes two and a half hours. We spend most of the time nodding. They tell me how great their campaign will be, and I nod. Then I tell them the modifications I want them to make to their commercials and ideas, kill the ones I think are horrible, like the one with the Flying Nun, and the creative people nod back.

After they've left, I sort through the stack of storyboards the teams have left leaning against the baseboard. Elvis, Beatles, Simon and Garfunkel, Wegman's Weimaraners, animated Tupperware, Fourth of July parades, cotton candy, Michael Jordan dunking, black-and-white movies and old pickup trucks, kids sitting on docks slapping their bare feet on the water, Gene Kelly dancing up walls, clips from the Three Stooges, everything mined from some layer of the American cultural landfill, from movies, music, MTV, the Internet, sometimes from art and infrequently from books, but everything derivative, reprocessed, regurgitated.

I'm wondering if anything's good enough to go to the final presentation. *Wait a minute—what about that Doxology idea of Rosemary's?* "Praise God from Whom all blessings flow..." Maybe that's the answer for the track. "Praise Him all creatures here below..." Yes!

"Evelyn, get me Izzy, will you?" I call out of my office.

My phone buzzes, I grab it. "Izzy, you familiar with the Doxology?" I say. He starts to sing it over the phone. Izzy can't sing, instead he groans in different octaves. "Imagine that as our track," I tell him. "Think of it done by different artists, everyone from Smashing Pumpkins to The Stones. We could cover the musical waterfront—maybe that's the sound we need?"

Izzy answers on the other end, "The words sure are right, 'praise God' will mean 'go to church' to people."

"That's what I'm thinking. It's right on strategy. Maybe I'll get Rosemary to demo up some tracks for us."

"Better do it fast, pal. The presentation's the day after tomorrow, and I've got seven spots to edit."

Tell me about it, I've got to put my entire creative presentation together, not to mention coming up with a client to present it to. As Sinkle said, "We're not going to present this work to the walls, Rein. You better have your client there. No point in presenting ads without a client to buy them."

Ironic, here I have clients pecking me to death for twenty-some years, then I get a big account and I have to invent a client to pick apart the ads. But who am I going to get? Thought of hiring an actor and giving him a backstory, but if Sinkle's got private investigators working on this thing, they'd see through that in a second. I need something brilliantly simple, but so outlandish it's bulletproof at the same time, so show-stopping that no one would ever think of questioning it.

Or maybe I should just walk with the account, take it down the street, set up my own shop? But it would take me two months to get a lease, six months to get a back office working—it'd be a year before I got the ads on the air. Stay where you are, Rein, just get smart about it.

18

Rosemary's up all night doing tracks. She calls me at home from the studio. "This stuff's hot, Dinny. I don't know what you're going to do with it, but I tell you, it's hot. You ought to hear the Stones' version." Studio singers can mimic any musician's style and sound. They are geniuses at ripping artists off.

"When will you have it finished?" I feel like a field marshal running an invasion from my apartment, stealing sleep in between the phone calls.

"Maybe by morning, I've got three studios working. I can't go much faster." Say good-bye and try to go back to sleep. I can hear the wind whistling through Wrigleyville. Sneaking in under my wind stop and rattling the window shade I tacked back up for Patti Shaw's benefit. I flip this way and that in bed. Think of Patti Shaw. Sleep for a few hours. Call the studio.

"Almost finished," she says. "I'll send them over to Izzy's and then I'm going back to my place. I've got to get some sleep."

The tracks are messengered over to Izzy's by the time the sun's up. All his editors are working on the tracks, cutting the new steal-o-matics to them.

I'm on the phone with Izzy every hour. "I think they're going to work, pal," he tells me. "We should have something by tonight." I get dressed and call him from the car on my way to work, Izzy sounds edgy. "Stop bugging me, I'll call you when they're ready," he says.

I walk around the office all day checking the other campaigns. The yamma-yamma around the agency is that Ester's going to walk away with the account. Everybody's asking me if I'm going to show his or her campaigns. They can't imagine I have any of my own. *Why should they? As far as they're concerned, Dinny Rein hasn't had an original idea in as long as they can remember.*

One of the new writers drags me into her office and takes me through her ads, sorting through her storyboards, proudly showing me her spots one by one, and then leans into me and whispers, "This is the only work that stands a chance of beating Ester, Dinny. All the other stuff sucks—if you ask me."

This lady's a carbon copy of someone out of Soho, black on black outfit, face the color of percale. She's supposed to look hip, but all I want to do is ask her to bring me the check. She stands back, crosses her arms and says, "So where's your head at now, Dinny? What are you going to present?"

I check my Timex as I walk out of her office. "Way too early to pick a winner," I say. "We still have a lot of time before the presentation." She looks at me like I've gone daffy, like I'm the only one in the agency who doesn't know that Ester Platt is going to eat Dinny Rein alive.

Izzy finally calls me at seven. "C'mon over and get your socks blown off." I call Rosemary at home and wake her up. "Want to see what we cut to your tracks?"

"I'll be ready in five minutes," she says.

The snow is piled high on the sides of her street. The Range Rover jounces around in the ruts, tossing from side-to-side, the four-wheel drive keeping the tire treads biting. Rosemary's out in front, standing on a snowdrift, waving at me.

She's dressed in white, red cap, carrot sticking out of her mouth. If she weren't so skinny, she'd look like a snowman.

"Nice car," she says as she hops in. She breaks off half her carrot and hands it to me. "Hungry?" she asks. Her glasses are getting steamed up. As we whirl through the snow toward Izzy's, I munch on the carrot and try to find out what she knows about the competition.

"So Ester thinks she's got me beat, huh?"

"She says you don't have squat, Dinny. She's sure she's going to waste you."

"Wait until you see what we've cut, Rosemary. Then tell me what you think."

"Better be good, Dinny. From what I've heard, her stuff is awesome, and she's even lining up some promotional partners, getting ready to put her whole campaign into action."

We'll see about that.

"And you know if Sinkle had anything to say about it, he'd go with Ester's campaign in a second. He doesn't like all the attention you're getting." Rosemary looks out the window at the falling snow. "Have you heard what he's up to?"

"I've heard some rumors."

"He's trying to undermine you by telling everyone you don't even have a client. You've got some rich backer who's supporting you in a bid to take over the agency. He says the account's a big ruse and he's telling people if they side with you, and the agency's taken over, they'll be out of their jobs in six months."

I pull into the parking lot behind Izzy's, park at the entrance since the rest of the lot hasn't been plowed.

"I have a client, and everyone will meet him tomorrow morning," I tell Rosemary as we get out. "In the meantime, let's go take a look at our new ad campaign."

19

The next morning, Conference Room A, the one on the outside wall with the walnut table, is packed and people are so anxious you can hear nerves jangling. Everyone's walking around adjusting everything, window shades, light and sound levels. They're arranging chairs, straightening pads and pencils, emptying the trash. Sinkle's sitting at the head of the table, orchestrating.

The room has one long wall of windows, a long presentation rail on the other. The Levelors on the windows get twisted flat by two account executives who look over at Sinkle for his approval. Too much light, no, he signals, not enough, yes, that's right, leave them there.

Sinkle holds up his hand and gives them a nod, Emperor Augustus of advertising.

Ester's hustling in and out, striding back and forth between the conference room and her people in the hallway.

Sinkle waves at the projectionist, and the halogen wall washers over the presentation rail glow bright, dull down, and get sunny again. Sinkle's secretary delicately straightens the note pads arranged in front of every seat. One of Sinkle's flunkies follows her, carefully paralleling the pencils alongside.

A painter carrying a bucket and brush does a last minute touchup, daubing out nicks in the drywall. Three different people take the same wastebasket out and empty it, three times. An A-V guy checks the sound level. "Testing, one, two, three, four."

I sit across from Sinkle and Ester at the table, watching. Sinkle leans back, puts his shoe up, and buffs the toes of his black wing-tip pumps with a small Dunhill shoe brush, back and forth, back and forth, until the leather sheens like black porcelain.

Ester's painting on a layer of creamy blood-red lipstick with a thin brush, precisely outlining the contours of her mouth in a tiny tortoise shell mirror. She smiles when she sees me watching her. A beatific smile, like she's queen, and I'm lunch meat.

She loaded up her people with assignments so none of them had time to help me. Sounded so apologetic. "We're crunching twenty hours a day, Dinny. I can't give you a single person," she said.

Ester straightens her back and puts on a show for my benefit, her bazooms swelling out against her shirt, her collar unfurling under the pressure, the vee of the blouse starting a quick dive for her waist. "I'm dying to meet your client," she says, blotting her lips against each other.

Ester Platt thinks she's going to pulverize me, steamroller me with an onslaught of fresh, brilliant, and perfectly-executed creative work. A series of promotions designed to send people flocking back to church.

"I bet you are," I say to her. If I didn't have my killer campaign, I'd be worried. Last night at Izzy's, Rosemary said it was the best advertising she'd ever seen. Gave me a big kiss and kept hopping up and down begging to see the spots over and over. "Play them again, Dinny! Run them again!"

Ester swings her eyes away from me and she's up and out of the room to check on her troops in the hallway. I see them as she opens the door. Lined up like they're waiting for a train, the creative people splayed out on long benches with their storyboards, music tracks, and videocassettes arranged in stacks around them.

As a group, her writers and art directors look somewhere between circus performers and street people. Scruffy jeans, tee shirts with Little Bo Peep bending over with her pants down, the Campbell's kids in pornographic poses, looking like they're having a lot more fun than they did selling soup. The creative people's outfits underlining the obvious. In case someone doesn't get it, they are creative—and all the rest of the people in the ad biz are empty suits.

Got that? Good. That's the way they want it.

In the corner with his back to us, Panky sorts through his acetates. His body is activated machinery wrapped in a black suit, armatures and shuttles, flying lifters and pulsing push rods, everything in fierce motion under the fabric.

Sinkle picks up a pencil and raps it on the table. "Okay, Rein, we're ready, where's your client?"

"He'll be here any minute," I say. I fold back my sleeve and check my Timex. Dramatic effect, as if the client is flying in on his own jet. Maybe winging in to Midway any minute.

Rap, rap, rap, from Sinkle's pencil on the tabletop.

Everyone hears the latch click and the door open. Heads turn, and Woogie Strepijichowski shuffles into the conference room, head down, eyes checking for carpet wear. Woogie often walks into important meetings in his blue utility suit—to adjust the heat, lower the air conditioning or change a light bulb.

People are so accustomed to the smell of cooked cabbage and the slight waft of body odor following him around that no one pays any more attention than they would to a busboy clearing plates in a restaurant.

As Woogie rounds the table, I stand, clear my throat and announce, "May I have your attention, please?" Everyone in the room turns. "I'd like to introduce our client, Mr. Woogie Strepijichowski."

You can hear the sound of jaws dropping, everyone gaping at Woogie as he shambles around the table toward me, shiny stains from rousting trash cans greasing the legs of his utility suit. I didn't realize how short and skinny he was, five-five at the most, and if he weighs much over a hundred-and-twenty-five, I'd be surprised. Also could use a shave. *Sure doesn't fit anyone's image of a major advertising client.*

I pull out a chair for him, quickly surveying the group. Normally, ad people are breezy and unflappable, stocked with apt and clever remarks appropriate for every occasion.

But now the group is silent, slack-jawed and round-eyed, except for Sinkle. He's out of his seat and rushing around the table with his hand extended, wearing a face-cracking smile six inches wide. "Mr. Strepijichowski, how good to finally meet you. Welcome to Boston, Frank, Pogue and Gersenweser Advertising."

Sinkle has walked past Woogie every morning for the past fifteen years, has heard him say "Morning, Mister," and has nodded deferentially back at him, but right this minute, Steve Sinkle doesn't recognize the Engineering Superintendent of 621 Michigan Avenue, even though Woogie's wearing the outfit he's worn everyday for the past fifteen years.

The brainstorm came to me in the middle of the night. Sat up in bed and grabbed for my cell phone. Got God on the line, told him about my plan. Thank God, He bought into it. Promised to have Woogie programmed to play him for the 9:30 meeting, straight-up and honest, no more asides from on high or duck-billed platypus mouth movements.

Sometimes, you've just got to talk tough with clients. Now I've got my client right where I want him—on earth, in Chicago, living right in the basement, at my beck and call—who could think of a better arrangement?

"Thank, Mister," Woogie says, pumping Sinkle's hand up and down and smiling, his gold teeth glistening in the halogens. He has a mine full in the back of his mouth, but the two large gold teeth on either side of his upper jaw blaze like high beams when he smiles.

"I work downstair many year. Save money so I be here, yes?" he says, still thrashing Sinkle's hand up and down.

Sinkle's smile is still going strong, but his eyes are narrowing. Maybe he smells cabbage. Looks around at the roomful of stunned and baffled faces. Glances back at Woogie. Sinkle still doesn't recognize him. But from the expressions of the others in the room, he knows something's going on.

His smile tightens, drops his eyes to his hand, like it's time for Woogie to let go.

"Let's get going," I say. "Mr. Strepijichowski is short on time."

"Ja, good," Woogie says, letting go of Sinkle's hand. Sinkle strides quickly back around the table, pauses without sitting down, and looks up at the halogens, eyes squinting, his neck cords going tight. He looks ever so slightly right and left, like he's thinking something's going to hit him.

"What we're going to do here, Mr. Strepijichowski..." I say.

"Ja, ja," he says, the glint off his gold teeth makes me blink.

With the elaborate backstory I've constructed, no one will think Woogie's anything more than a wealthy old coot with a couple of screws loose who made millions in the market while he emptied trash and lived in the basement of the building for thirty years, supporting his relatives in Poland and playing Santa Claus to the kids at Cabrini Green.

"We're going to show you the television and print advertising for the upcoming launch." I turn to Sinkle. "Why don't you have a seat, Steve." Sinkle glances quickly at Woogie again. His head does a little jog forward. He peers at Woogie, then does a double take, like he's finally figured out that his biggest client is the Polish building super who lives in the basement. He sits down. His brow is furrowed deep enough to lose a finger in.

I bet Sinkle's having trouble seeing himself sitting with Woogie Strepijikowski in his skybox at Soldier Field, introducing him to all his golfing buddies at Butler, or having him seated at his private table at the Mid-America Club.

I explain to Woogie that Ester will show her work first, and I'll follow. I ask him to be honest, tell us what he likes and what he doesn't.

"Ja, ja, ja, ja," he says, sounding like a small dog barking.

Woogie Strepijichowski is the perfect person to play God. No one will ever figure it out. I'll be safe from Sinkle and his private eyes and I'll be able to play Woogie Strepijichowski like a damn harp. Boy, are you one smart cookie, Dinny Rein.

I nod at Ester. As she stands, you can almost hear Elmer Bernstein conducting a Hollywood score in the background. Horns and strings, big dramatic music, the violins stinging out vibratos as she slowly sidles out from behind the table.

Woogie's eyes are bulging as Ester slowly rounds the table, swinging her hips, gliding them back and forth, her hair waving gently. She's all radiant smiles and hips and breasts and legs and she comes up in front of him, close, real close, so close their knees are touching and bends over, blouse dropping open, reaching her hand out to Woogie. "So nice to meet you, Mr. Strepijichowski," she says, and before he has a chance to get a good look down her shirt, she swirls around so he gets a tight closeup of her ass and sashays off across the conference room with her buttocks shifting up and down under her tight skirt, her panty hose whispering together.

Woogie's, of course, all scrunched forward on the edge of his chair, eyes swarming out of his head staring at her.

I've got to keep an eye on Ester Platt, make sure Woogie doesn't get too interested in her.

Ester turns and starts her presentation. Does a prologue. Calls in her troops. Introduces them to Woogie and orchestrates their presentation. The creative people straighten their storyboards, then present them, energetically acting out the parts, singing the lyrics.

Woogie's feet are tapping on the carpet. He's smiling and nodding. Her storyboards and print ads are piling up on the presentation rails. The creative people push each commercial down the rail as it's presented to make room for the next.

Ester's got cute jingles for the kids, clever ads for the parents. "The challenge here is to make the whole thing seamless," Ester explains. "So that people won't be able to tell a promotion from a prayer or a slogan from a hymn. They won't stop to think about whether they're going to church to worship or to get air miles, to pray or to get a coupon for a Big Mac. Everything will be so seamlessly integrated, all they'll know is that going to church is fun and exciting. Church attendance will add a vibrant new experience to their lifestyles. Like we say in our slogan, 'It's a fun thing to do.'"

More storyboards, more soundtracks, Ester and her people show one commercial after another. Woogie can't stop saying, "Ja!" The word pours out of him with different colors and inflections, up and down the scales, like notes out of a calliope on the Fourth of July. "Ja, ja, ja, ja, ja, ja, ja, ja."

I can't tell which one of her promotions he likes better. "Ja, ja, ja, ja," he says as more commercials go up on the rail.

She's stair-stepped her promotions—free Barbie Dolls and Power Rangers for the children; air miles on United, free calling time on AT&T, and McDonald's Quarter Pounders for the moms and dads; stepping up to free movie cassettes and Dallas Cowboys stadium seats, camping equipment from Coleman and flashlights from Duracell. The bigger items kicking in after four, eight, and twelve weeks of church attendance.

Her plan is that the kids pull the parents into church initially to get the free Barbie Dolls or the Power Ranger sets, but the parents keep the family coming because they want the free hours of long distance, the five hundred free air miles.

Ester shows families in her commercials as they come out of church, happily toting their Barbies and their camping gear, shining their new flashlights and clutching their McDonald's coupons. They pile into their cars to head for Big Macs at McDonald's or drive out to O'Hare and hop a United flight to Disney World.

Jeez, I'm thinking. She must already have contacted these companies. She's really got this thing worked out. If God is reacting like Woogie Strepijichowski, I could be dead meat.

"And when church leaders see how we're increasing attendance and really start to warm up to our concept, we'll move into Phase Two of the campaign." Ester sits down next to Woogie, turns to him. "One of the problems we've identified with our research, Mr. Strepijichowski," she says, acting ingenuous, stopping just this side of smarmy, "is that the current churchgoing experience isn't competitive with other leisure-time options."

I glance at Sinkle. He smirks back, giving me a smile like he's envisioning a lance sticking straight through my chest. He's got it the way he wants it. Ester looks like she's going to bury me, so he can push me off the stage and into the wings, demote me back into advertising oblivion. Even if I happen to win, he knows he'll be able to complete his buyout, take over the agency, and sooner or later find a way to turn Dinny Rein into a doormat again.

Ester nods at one of her art directors, he puts a large chart up on the rail.

"Here's a list of leisure activities ranked from most to least popular," she says. "And you can see here that going to church is way down on the list of favorite activities." Ester gets up and points at the chart. "Just ahead of washing the car and not that far away from taking out the garbage."

"Is being true?" Woogie asks.

"I'm afraid so."

"Going out with garbage no fun, Woogie knows!"

"No fun at all. You're right, Mr. Strepijichowski, so that's what we want to do for the churchgoing experience, make it fun." Ester nods again, and one of her people peels each of the top cards off ten piles stacked on the presentation rail, revealing pictures of Michael Jordan, Stevie Wonder, Kiss, Michael Jackson, Madonna, singers, actors and sports stars.

"Now imagine Stevie Wonder singing a hymn, Michael Jordan reading the Lord's Prayer, Madonna acting out a parable from the Bible, and imagine piping our guest celebrities into every church in the country so that churchgoers across the nation can enjoy their performances. Just visualize families getting their church bulletins in the mail every week and seeing that Harry Belafonte is going to be singing a hymn or Grant Hill will be leading prayers—I tell you, Mr. Strepijichowski, we'll pack them in like flies.

"And this will kick in the afterburner on our promotion program, attract new sponsors, increase the incentives of our current sponsors, encouraging McDonalds' to step up from a free Big Mac coupon to giving away a whole breakfast. And if they don't, we'll bring in Burger King, or Wendy's, or KFC. We'll have leverage, Mr. Strepijichowski. If Duracell doesn't want to play, we'll sign up EverReady.

"Do you know, Mr. Strepijichowski, that Sunday is one of the slowest retail days of the week? We can ratchet it up, take the thousands of churches in America and turn them into retail outlets, start selling on Sundays, pack the churches, and get a little religion into people's lives. This is a win-win situation right from the get-go. Putting the leading companies of America into partnership with God, that's what marketing can do for you, Mr. Strepijichowski, that's what it can do—if you run our advertising."

Ester walks up to Woogie, says she's finished her presentation, holds out her hand to him, and smiles. "May I call you Woogie?" she asks, batting her eyes faster than a hummingbird's wings.

"Calling me Woogie is fine, is name," he says. Ester's holding his hand. "And I haven't even told you about Phase Three. That's too far down the line but let me just say that if everything goes as predicted, we might be able to make all this promotion activity self-liquidating. What that means, Woogie, is that it won't cost you anything, and it just might pay for itself."

Woogie jumps up and pumps Ester's hand like he's a twelve-year-old boy meeting Marilyn Monroe. "Is very exciting for to spend no money, ja. Very good advertisings. Thanking you."

Ester looks over at me. Smiles like I'm sliced bologna and sits down.

My turn. Sinkle looks at me as if to say "Top that one, buddy boy." I stand up and walk over to the controls on the wall. Ester's

Ads for God

entire group is sneering at me, thirteen sets of arms crossed, thirteen chins in the air. Sinkle's smiling, and Ester's examining her nails.

"Mr. Strepijichowski," I say. "I am going to show you one campaign." Ester's people elbow each other and snicker. From their point of view, the bum of BFP&G Advertising is about to present.

"Ja, ja, good," Woogie says as I darken the room and punch up my video, crank up the soundtrack, and stand off to the side of the conference table so I can gauge the reactions.

Baseball is the first commercial. Then Comedians, then Rock Stars, Nature, Movie Stars, Kids, and the flagship two-minute commercial. The commercials that we've raced to finish over the past three days, edited together with stock footage and stuff we've stolen from other commercials, films, slides from *National Geographic*, anything we could beg, borrow, or steal from anywhere. The soundtrack almost blows out the speakers, the Doxology sung by studio singers imitating the Beatles, the Stones, Eagles, Platters, Simon and Garfunkel, Rosemary's music swelling and roaring while the visuals roll by, light and airy to contrast with the soundtracks.

Bob Hope interrupts the music to deliver a punchline, a six-year-old Little Leaguer hits a homer, then holds up his pants as he scampers around the bases. We see Marilyn Monroe standing over the air grate fighting a losing battle with her blowing dress, a look from Greta Garbo, Babe Ruth hoisting a little kid onto his shoulders, a procession of circus clowns piling out of a small car, kids all covered with cotton candy, two oldsters waltzing, a dog playing Frisbee, a fawn in the woods.

Then a Greek Orthodox funeral for counterpoint, smoking incense and black robes in the rain, a vermilion sunset over San Francisco Bay and a blazing sunrise over the Grand Tetons, Mary Lou Retton sticking it after a triple flip and Jack Benny going deadpan. I even cut in Charlton Heston holding the tablets to make Patti happy.

This is magic, I'm thinking. *They're even giving me chills, and I've seen them twenty times already. Paeans to humanity, odes to life, love, baseball and the movies.* Izzy said this is the best advertising that's ever gone though his editing machine, and he's right.

I look at Sinkle. He's staring straight ahead. Ester's no longer filing her nails. Woogie's got a big smile on his face.

I have a little voice-over toward the end of each commercial, quick takes, all variations on a theme, "If you like what you see around you, stop in at church Sunday and say thanks," or, "When you stop long enough to smell the flowers, they smell pretty good, don't they?" or, "This isn't make-believe, it's life—so live it. And stop in Sunday and give a little praise to the guy who made it all possible."

Each commercial ends with a simple title scripted across the bottom of the screen, "Praise God," in loose, casual type, almost as if a child had scribbled out the words as the Doxology booms along on the soundtrack, "Praise God from whom all blessings flow..." My presentation ends, and I turn on the lights.

Everyone turns to look at Woogie. He's got his handkerchief out, he's dabbing at his eyes.

Woogie's playing it perfectly, squeezing the tears out on cue, acting like he loves the ads.

He stands and takes my hand, "Dis is better. Very better. I like much," he says, winking at me. "Baseball being very favorite of Woogie. How you knowing that?"

I see the blood draining out of Ester's face.

"Thank you, thank you," I say, shaking Woogie's hand. "I think this campaign should do the job for you."

Woogie asks, "How much dollars cost for making?"

"Eight million," I answer. I'm about to explain why the commercials are so expensive, shooting new film, buying the rights to all the footage and signing the celebrities but Woogie interrupts, "What much?"

"Eight million, eight million dollars."

Woogie holds up eight fingers, "Ja?"

"Ja—I mean, yes, here's the estimate." I walk over to him and hand Woogie a sheet of paper and a pen, point to the line where he's supposed to sign. Sinkle knows the commission on production is close to a million-and-a-half, that's why he's smirking.

Ester is not taking it well. She looks like she's near death, face is pasty-white. Staring downward, she slowly rotates a pencil on the table.

Ads for God

"All advertisings eight millions of dollar, no?"

"For the production, yes. We'll be spending a lot more on media, of course," I say, pointing at the line on the estimate. "Sign here, if you will."

Panky Durnberg flicks on his overhead and says, "Now I'd like to give you a topline on our research on this advertising..." Durnberg picks up his pointer and starts to go through his research. "...as you can see..."

Woogie interrupts. "Sorry, Mister, garbage picking up in five minutes. Going is necessary," he says, pointing at his watch.

Did you see the way Woogie blew Panky Durnberg away? Just blew him away, wheeoo! Now that's the kind of client an ad man needs. Woogie scribbles his name on the estimate and starts for the door, shaking hands with Sinkle as he rounds the table.

Panky is standing speechless by his overhead projector. Woogie turns around to face Sinkle. "Good showing—that what say? Good showing, ja?" he asks Sinkle.

Sinkle nods and says, "How about taking in a Bears' game with me some day, Mr. Strepijichowski? We've got a brand new skybox for next season."

Woogie scowls, wagging his finger at Sinkle. "Bears, no—no Bears. Ever since Ditka..." Woogie makes a slicing motion across his throat. "...Bears no good."

Woogie stops by Ester's place at the table. She manages a weak smile. Woogie puts his hand on Ester's shoulder, says, "Too bad, my girlie, too bad for you—but someday me and you go for dancing, no?" He flashes a tooth at her and ambles out of the meeting with Sinkle chasing after him, leaving Panky Durnberg and Ester Platt and her twelve creative people standing speechless in Conference Room A of Boston, Frank, Pogue, and Gersenweser Advertising.

What do I do, say something smart? Just stand here? It's been years since I won a shoot-out. I kind of like it, feels pretty good.

Ester regains her powers of speech quickly, stalks up to me, her dirty little lint ball of a dog snarling down around her ankles. She plants her fists on her hips and huffs, "That stuff of yours isn't advertising, Rein. It's fluff. And when it wears out in a month or so, your client will be begging for my campaign."

"Always good to have a strong backup, Ester," I say, staring into her acetylene eyes.

"If Panky'd had a chance to present his research, *your* campaign would be the backup. Your advertising has no legs. It's got some style but it's really no more than another jingle."

Panky's looking uncomfortable. *Sinkle probably had him bend the research to support her campaign in case mine bombed. Numbers can go any way you want in the good old ad biz.*

Sinkle walks back into the conference room shaking his head. "Where did you find that client, under a rock?"

"In the basement, as a matter of fact."

"I asked him if he had a D & B and you know what he said? He thought I was talking about B & B—the liqueur. He asks me down for a drink, down to the basement. Can you believe that?"

"Cultural differences, Steve," I say.

"Maybe, but there's no way we're going to upfront that TV buy to a janitor who doesn't even know what a D & B is. C'mon, Rein, upfront fifty million to someone who thinks a Dun and Bradstreet is an after-dinner drink?"

I can see a couple of Ester's people snickering.

"Steve, he's good for it."

"For fifty million? Shit, he wears goddamn overalls and has more gold teeth than Oddjob!"

Ester's got her hands folded over her chest. Smug. Delighted to see that I'm running into problems. Her people circle around her, chins lifting, looking defiantly at me.

"How'd Oddjob ever come up with ten million bucks anyway?" Sinkle asks.

"Ever heard of Warren Buffet?" I say. Sinkle gives me an eye-roll. "Mr. Strepijichowski's sister has been cooking for Buffet the past forty years. In 1955, she's serving the flank steak and Buffet tells her, 'Buy IBM, Lottie.' She buys IBM, tells her brother Woogie, 'Buy IBM.' Lottie ladles out some corn chowder back in '61, and Buffet says, 'Buy Merck, Lottie.' Lottie buys Merck, tells her brother, 'Buy Merck.'

"So let's just say that through the years, Mr. Strepijichowski has had the opportunity to do some opportunistic investing."

"Then he should be able to come up with fifty more."

Sinkle's pushing me for proof, pushing me and my new client as far as he can, trying to see if Woogie's really good for fifty million.

"Come on, Steve. We have to buy the time for him. He's our client."

"Not until he puts fifty million on my desk, Rein." Sinkle comes up close to me. Now I know he wears Aramis. See the black hole where his incisor used to be. "Until then, Rein," he says, poking me in the lapel with his finger, "he's your client."

20

I'm heading toward Michigan, taking a walk, trying to think. What do I do now? Tried to get God on the cell phone from my office, no answer. Went down and stood around with the smokers in back of the building, tried him again. No answer. I get my campaign approved and into production, and Sinkle has to go and demand that we upfront the money. If it isn't one damn thing in this business, it's another. So now I've got to get God to round up another bunch of money. That goddamn Sinkle. I'm starting to mutter and curse, kick at slush piles. My neck hunched down deep into my overcoat, I'm grousing out loud, "The son of a bitch has no right to do that! He's never done that with any of our other clients. No one has ever had to pay for television time up front."

I should have known he was going to play hardball. Sinkle's not giving up without a good fight. I might have produced a client and come up with a good backstory but now I've got to get my client to put some real money on the table. And I can't even get God on the phone.

Whoa! What am I talking about? I've got my own God right here on earth. Why am I trying to talk to Him when I should be talking to Woogie.

I double-time back to the building. *Woogie's my man now, he's the guy who'll get me the fifty million.*

I'm through the revolving doors, past the elevators to a door at the back of the lobby. "Basement" the sign reads. I open the door, set of stairs leading down. It's a Mickey Spillane stairway, moody and gray, metal handrail, light pooling out of a shaded overhead. I turn at the landing, go down another flight. Look around, a hand-lettered cardboard sign taped to the wall reads, "Sub-Basmint, W.

Strepijichowski, Super," and an arrow points down the stairs into the dark. I lean around the corner and call down into the pitch-blackness, "You there, Woogie?"

No answer.

"Woogie, you there?"

"Ja, being here. Watch foot coming down," he answers, sounds like he's eating something. My toes tap around for the treads. I'm holding onto the walls. The stairway brightens as I turn a corner. Couple more steps, and I can see down into the sub-basement. It's a used furniture factory. Woogie's got the place decorated in high Salvation Army, a hodgepodge of old furniture grouped around between the boilers and dumpsters, chairs with stuffing exploding out of the seats, end tables with lengths of broomsticks nailed where legs used to be, light bulbs glaring through ripped lampshades and on the floor, a crazy quilt of overlapping rug scraps.

Woogie's sitting in a leather Ralph wingchair, I recognize it as a castoff from Sinkle's office. One of the legs is broken off, the legless corner perched on a concrete block. He's eating an egg salad sandwich in a Subway wrapper, stuffing the escaping strands of lettuce back in with his fingers and wiping his mouth off on the ends of the wrapper.

"Dinny Rein ever having egg salad from Subway?"

"Can't say I ever did."

"Is very good, ja?" Light yellow yoke from the salad clusters between his teeth. "Having seat, ja?" Woogie kicks over a cardboard Tide box for me to sit on.

"So! Advertisings being good, no?"

"I think we've got a great campaign going."

"Ja, ja, ja," he says, continuing to chomp on his sandwich, deftly catching clumps of egg salad and working them back up his lip and into his mouth. "And being good working with you, no?"

I nod my head but I'm thinking, *I guess it's time to talk money. Hate talking money but*—"Say Woogie, there's something I'd like to discuss with you, if you don't mind—"

"Yaa! Shitski," Woogie yells, leaping out of his chair, checking his watch, and heading for the stairs (you've got to see his watch, remind me to tell you about that when I have more time). He chucks his egg salad over his shoulder and starts up toward the landing, doing an eggbeater thing with his arm to speed me up. "It's being going fast to airport at O'Hare, my Dinny friend."

This guy might be sixty, but he takes the basement stairs in twos, and I'm starting to pant as I race across the lobby after him.

We get out onto Michigan and search up and down for a cab. Woogie's looking at his watch, muttering "Shitski, shitski" as I'm hailing for a cab. I look up Michigan, wave down a Yellow coming down the lane closest to me. Cab screeches up in front of us. Door opens. See legs, then fat black glasses. I'd recognize those horn-rims anywhere. Rosemary gets out, plants a fat kiss on my cheek, and gives me a hug. "Dinny, you sold it! You sold your campaign—I can't believe it."

She sees Woogie. "Oh, and this is your client." Rosemary giggles and sticks out her hand. "So nice to meet you, Mr. Woogichowski."

I want to correct her, but we're in a rush, Woogie's checking his watch every five seconds. Rosemary's wearing a Chicago fireman's black and yellow coat and a helmet like the Kaiser's troops wore in World War I. "I'm off for L.A. this afternoon to shoot the commercials."

"In that?" I ask, pointing at her outfit, edging Woogie around her so he can get in the cab.

"No," she says, flinging open her fireman's coat. "In this." I should have known better. Rosemary has on a black bra and gold lamé toreador pants. "Hot, huh Dinny?" she giggles.

"Hot, Rosemary," I say as I maneuver myself around her into the open door. "Thanks for the cab." My loafer squishes into a hillock of slush. I can feel the wet seep into my sock. Rosemary tells me I'm the new hero of Michigan Avenue, gives me another kiss. I wave good-bye and slam the door.

"Airport at O'Hare," Woogie says to the driver. "And stepping hard on it." I shake the slush off my sock. Woogie looks back at Rosemary. "Is pretty tasty cookie, ja?"

"Rosemary's a hotshot, she'll do a great job on the production," I tell him. Woogie checks his watch again.

Ads for God

He has a disturbing habit I never noticed. Hikes his crotch every ten seconds. Cups the crotch of his coveralls and lifts, regular as a metronome. *Must be a nervous tic or something.*

I look around the cab. The driver's eating something. He's from Persia, and the cab smells like he's enjoying a late lunch of marinated goat. Abdul Abdullah chomps on his pita bread as he carries on a running conversation with the eighteen-hundred-and-three other Persian cabbies in Chicagoland over a small CB radio, yammering at his fellow cabbies between the bursts of static in a squeaky, singsong voice that sounds like he's been inhaling helium.

"So what are we going to O'Hare for?" I ask.

"Getting money, no?"

Oh no, I'm thinking to myself. It's snagging money time again. I'm going to be real careful about this.

"Who are we getting the money from?"

The Persian pauses with his goatburger half into his mouth. The mention of money's made him interested. Leans forward, checks around the inside of the cab in his rear view mirror.

"Borrowing from friend, no?"

"Wait a minute," I say. "Wait one cotton-picking minute. What friend is this? What's going on here?"

Woogie turns to me. "Having friend who giving us money for running advertisings, no? Being there in fifteen minutes, getting money, go back and doing advertisings? Is plan, no?"

I look out the window. Abdul's redlining the Yellow, making the motor scream, driving like he's Luke Skywalker corkscrewing his way through the asteroid belt, dodging in and out between cars, sliding the two of us around on the back seat as he weaves across the four lanes of the Kennedy, engine wound out and loose body panels whapping against the frame in the expressway slipstream.

Over the staticky radio, one of the Persian cabbies cracks a joke. Their laughter sounds like a rooster convention.

"I can't believe Sinkle would undermine a hundred million dollar account by asking for the money up front."

"Is not for worrying, my friend Dinny Rein. You needing ten million, you getting ten million. Getting new face and for girl friend new body, no? You saying needing client to come down for working with you, you getting Woogie, no? Now needing fifty million, getting fifty million from friend at O'Hare, ja? Is being easy, no?"

Abdul whips his head around and does a double take when he hears the mention of fifty million dollars.

I'm looking at the smiling, slight and shiny-faced sixty-year-old guy with the thinning hair who's sitting in the back of his cab telling me not to worry about borrowing fifty million from a friend at O'Hare.

Woogie gives me a playful tap on the shoulder, smiles wide so his golds flash. "Like saying in movies, fifty million dollar is 'no problema'."

Abdul opens his mouth so wide I can see goatburger.

"Watch the road, will you?" I shriek as the cab starts heading into the barrier along the expressway. Steering back into the lane, Abdul gives a resigned shrug and continues to weave down the Kennedy at warp speed.

"So, doing advertisings much exciting, ja?" Woogie says, patting me on the knee. "Is business much for excitement, no?"

I nod as I watch the highway signs flash by, thinking, *Life's sure never dull when you've got God as a client.*

Four o'clock and its rush hour mayhem on the downstairs roadway in front of the United terminal. Skycaps buzz around with their hand trucks pyramided with luggage, shouting and waving to clear paths through the teeming travelers; car horns stand your spine straight up as they resonate under the hooded concrete roadway, cabs and limos, buses, stretch Caddys and Lincolns, Hertz and Avis vans weave and jockey, vying for lane position and parking spaces. Businessmen and women scurry back and forth across the concrete. Unlicensed drivers try to hustle passengers, and the overworked airport cops stalk around shouting and blowing whistles.

"Stopping here, stopping here," Woogie says to Abdul, slapping on the seat and poking him in the back with his finger. We screech up at the outside curb in the limo lane.

"Okay dokay, Dinny my boy," Woogie says, putting his arm around my shoulder. "Much listening to Woogie, no? You doing the walking up to cabs, see?" Woogie points at the quarter mile of cabs lined up along the inside roadway. "Then when Woogie tell, you do thing, okay?"

"What thing?"

"Finding friend who borrow money, I show, no worry—so going, going." Woogie pushes me out the door of the cab.

"But how will I hear you?"

"Hearing Woogie fine, no worrying," he says as I walk away from the cab. A sixtyish lady in a plaid suit starts in front of me, grabs the door handle, trying to claim the cab. Abdul barks at her in Persian and chucks his wadded-up goatburger wrapper at her. She shuffles away, snarling something about immigration policy.

I see two businessmen with their bags slung over their shoulders chasing a Hertz bus, running behind the bus shouting and waving their arms. Both are too fat to be running. Smooth wide rolls of oxford-shirted bellies hang over their waists. Candidates for cardiology. An endless line of cabs stretches back along the inside curb.

I walk across the roadway toward the line of cabs, stop halfway across to let a Budget bus blast past. Two hundred travelers wait in line, slowly inching forward as the people in front get into their cabs. Shouting and doors slamming. People sling bags into trunks, jump into cabs, and the cabs swing out of line and head into the city.

"Seeing cab with number 8007?" I hear Woogie's voice running through my brain. "Finding 8007?"

How's he doing that? It's like I have a two-way radio in my head. I search the line of cabs for the number. 5514, 4432, 2348. I see the yellow Caprice. The number 8007. It's three cabs from the front of the line.

"Dinny walking up very slow," Woogie says. I feel like Harrison Ford in *The Fugitive*—at large with everyone on the lookout for me. The back window on my side is open.

I'm five steps away when I see a large man with a dark complexion and sunglasses bend down on the opposite side of the cab and speak to the cabby. Syrian or Egyptian, Mexican maybe, but big enough to play tackle for the Bears. He wears a shiny brown suit with a white banded-collar shirt.

The driver gets out and walks to the back. The businessman slings open the back door and tosses a briefcase onto the seat.

"Crouching down and making small, now walking up to side and do borrow on briefcase," Woogie shouts. "Window open, go quick. No one see, go!"

Wait a minute, I'm not borrowing this—I'm stealing it!

"Going, going quick like bunny, Dinny Rein," Woogie whispers into my brain.

I can see the large man and the cabby hefting baggage into the trunk. I crouch and scramble up to the back door, reach in through the window. My hand closes around the briefcase handle. I look toward the back of the cab. The raised trunk blocks my view.

"Taking briefcase and going very fast away, Dinny. Standing up and going!" Woogie commands.

I pull the briefcase through the window and stand up with my back to the cab, straightening my suitcoat and walking slowly up the line of cabs toward the walkway, melding into the line of businessmen crossing the road toward the limo line on the outer roadway.

My knees feel weak. I shift the briefcase to the other hand, scurrying across the walkway with the crowd. I'm ten feet from Abdul when I start hearing shouts. I duck down and run up to the cab, flinging the door open. The shouting is in Spanish. I look back as I leap in, but a concrete pillar blocks my view of the cab line.

"Driving cab fast, putzball, driving much fast," Woogie's saying, thrusting his hand though the partition and prodding Abdul in the back as I slide into the seat, pulling the briefcase in after me and slamming the door. Abdul wrenches the shift lever down, jams his foot on the accelerator, looks quickly over his shoulder, and pulls out into the traffic.

Glancing into his rear view mirror, I see travelers with their hands over their heads, the large man holding them at gunpoint, a submachine gun leveled at their chests.

"Jeez..." I watch the man smashing briefcases to the concrete, pushing people around. I hear shots, quick pops.

Abdul hunches down behind the wheel. In the mirror, his eyes are as large as Necco wafers.

Woogie's snapping out instructions to me like he just joined the Polish Army. "Big banger in briefcase, got to throw. Got to throw big like baseball," Woogie waves his hands in the air like he's simulating an explosion. "Otherwise balls blow off—boom!"

Woogie wrenches the partition further open, he leans around and talks to Abdul. "Stopping up here, there, there," Woogie points at the breakdown lane. I look down at the briefcase. Harmless-looking. Ordinary brown leather briefcase.

"Stop!" he says. "Here pulling over." Abdul hits the brakes and wheels the cab over into the breakdown lane. What's left of his goatburger slips off the seat into the wheel well.

The ground is covered with gray snow. A guardrail and then a steep slope down to a cornfield.

"Hole in ground?" Woogie says to me, pointing out the window and leaning across me to open my door. "See hole in ground? Throwing case in hole."

"I don't understand." Abdul is turned around in the cab facing us, his eyes darting around. He's cringing down in his seat, I can tell he wants to get out of the cab and start running, not stopping until he gets to the horizon.

I wonder what's in the briefcase. Woogie slides back the two brass buttons, the locks snap open. Woogie upends the case and shakes out packets, packets of money raining out of the case, sheaves of bonds, T-bills, certificates of deposit, all kinds of important-looking pieces of paper tumbling over our legs, some of them have seals and ribbons on them. They're jouncing around the backseat, slipping down onto the floor.

Abdul says something in his screechy-high Persian helium voice when he sees the money.

"Coming to mommy, coming to mommy," Woogie says as the bonds and money and papers bounce over our knees and cascade down into the footwell. Woogie slams the case shut and hands it to me, kicking open my door. I wind up and heave the briefcase over the guardrail.

"Good throwing, Dinny. Now go, now driving!" he shouts at Abdul, punching him in the back through the partition. I see the briefcase sailing up in the air, dropping, disappearing down into the ditch. "Faster than bullet speeding, go!" he yells.

Abdul fishtails out onto the expressway, spinning back gravel as a booming clap of thunder resounds behind us. I look back to see a shower of dirt and grass blowing up out of the ditch.

"That's the last time I'm doing that, okay? The last time," I say, folding my arms tightly across my chest, trying to sound as petulant as I possibly can.

Here I am, I just blew up half of O'Hare and now I'm riding around in a cab up to my knees in someone else's money.

Woogie turns back from looking at the explosion. The packets of bills are piled up to our shins. I remember Scrooge McDuck standing in his money bin. Woogie pats me on the knee. "Easiest money you ever making, no?"

"I can't believe it. We're stealing money!"

"No stealing—borrowing for a couple weeks. Paying interests, is okay, ja?"

"Borrowing—my ass! What about, 'Thou shalt not steal', what about that? Have you ever thought about that?"

Woogie looks out the window. "Rules are for broken."

"Rules are for what?"

"Tsk, tsk, tsk," Woogie says, leaning his head back on the seat of the taxi. I look out the window at the cars whooshing by. Everybody does eighty for as long as they can on the Kennedy. Because they know the traffic will stack up pretty soon and they'll be back to doing ten again.

"You know," I say. "If you're going to act like this, you shouldn't have called them Commandments."

Woogie turns to me, gives me a look like I'm a silly little kid. "What you like better, Dinny Rein, The Ten Guidelines?" Woogie's chuckling, thinks he has a great sense of humor. "Rules for humans, no?" He pokes me in the ribs with his elbow. "We being on special mission, ja?"

Woogie winks at me, big theatrical wink, and slowly raises his index finger into air, pointing straight up at the roof of the cab. "So being okay, ja?" He makes a fist and gives me a soft jab in the biceps. "Now making money neat for bank, ja?" He leans over and starts raking the bonds and bills together on the backseat.

Ads for God

"I can't work like this, I'm sorry." I'm shaking my head. "I can't steal money, even if we're using it for a good cause, I can't."

"Okay dokay," Woogie says, scooping up an armful of money and rolling down the window. "Is being fine with Woogie..."

He's not going to throw the money out the window, is he? He is!

He grabs fistfuls of money, like he's picking up leaves with his fingers, and shakes them out the window into the wind. "So no more needing money, ja?" I see money fluttering back behind the cab, spinning and whirling in the slipstream. "No doing advertisings, ja?"

I'm watching the money spiraling around through the back window and I'm thinking, *There goes the money for your advertising, Rein. There goes your new career. There goes everything.*

Abdul slams on the brakes when he sees hundred dollar bills flying around outside his cab.

"Wait, Woogie!" I quickly reach across him and crank up the window. "Stop!" I say to him as I'm leaning across his lap turning the window crank.

Woogie folds his arms over his chest, looks out the window, "Being not needed, so throwing away, ja?"

I look back at the money scattering through the traffic. A couple of people have pulled off to the side. I can see them running up and down the breakdown lane bending over to pick up the bills.

"Okay—as long as we're just borrowing it," I say.

"Is telling Dinny Rein, is being big borrow from good friend, ja?" Woogie's making piles of the money, carefully placing the packets of bills on top of one another.

Go with the flow, Rein, stop being such a prude. If God's not worried about borrowing fifty million, why should you?

I start helping him pick up the packets of money, one-by-one stacking them on the seat between us. Five million bucks in T-bills, neatly-wrapped stacks of thousand-dollar bills, bearer bonds, commercial paper—all endorsed, all negotiable.

This money's going to get the campaign on the air. It's going to sell God, get people going to church, so get with the program. Stop worrying about the details and go for the big picture. Maybe that's why your career was in the dumper, Rein. You've been pussyfooting around trying to be Mr. Nice Guy, being friendly to everyone, and getting the short end of the stick as a result. Get with the reality, Rein.

Woogie hands me a packet of money, points at Abdul. "Taking care of our nice driving friend here, ja?"

"You betcha," I say, working a couple of bills out of the packet and handing them over the seat. "Here, Abdul, buy yourself some lunch."

21

We buy Abdul's silence for twenty grand and his Raiders gym bag for two, load the money into the bag, and all the way into Chicago we listen to Abdul running at the mouth about the little deli he's going to buy on the South Side with his new-found money. Pita bread, falafel, hummus, and of course, fresh you-know-what.

Woogie tells Abdul to stop at Halstead, grabs the bag, and opens the door.

"Where you going with that?" I ask.

"You carrying fifty million into office? Woogie putting in bank. Give thirty minutes. Then telling Sinkle he rich by fifty million, ja?"

Woogie slams the cab door and saunters off, swinging the bag. I can hear him whistling "When Irish Eyes Are Smiling." The guy can whistle nice.

I'm watching him ambling down the sidewalk, his whistle floating back above the traffic, and I'm thinking, *When you come right down to it, God's really not too bad a guy, particularly when He gets you fifty million bucks.*

I continue on in the cab to the office. Abdul can't stop saying thank you. Gives me the address of his deli as I get out at the office. Makes me promise to stop by for a sandwich. *Oh boy, free goatburgers.*

The sun is shining. The wind no longer has knives in it. I stop on the sidewalk and look down the avenue. In a month or so, the girls will be out. In Chicago, the girls are like flowers. The first warm day in May, they come out in their short skirts and bare midriffs.

I always like to walk on Michigan on that first day in May because I get to feel like I'm nineteen again.

I check my Timex when I get off the elevator. Thirty minutes is almost up, time to see Sinkle.

Vincent tries to stop me as I push past him into Windsor Castle. "Mr. Sinkle's very, very busy," he sputters.

Sinkle's not in the conference room. Down the hall, the door to the boardroom is ajar.

Vincent's doing a bad job of downfield pass-protection, waving his arms at me and tugging at my sleeve as he shambles alongside. He wears out-of-date Aramis, or he's been drinking port, or both. He still has a bad case of the flakes, heavy accumulation of snow on the shoulders today.

I see Sinkle sitting at the head of the boardroom table. The table used to seat the Studebaker board. The founders saved it from a warehouse in South Bend. Queen Anne with fourteen matching chairs upholstered in sapphire-blue velvet arrayed around it. They had to bring the boardroom table in through the window with a construction crane.

Large washed etchings of English country houses line the walls. The walls are covered with repp silk over waist-high wainscoting. Deep purple with thin yellow and blue stripes. Like they stole the tie off a giant banker and glued it around the room. I heard the bill for the walnut wainscoting alone was sixty grand.

Sinkle barely has time to look up before I'm in front of him, saying, "My client just deposited fifty million dollars in the company account." Sinkle thinks I'm bluffing. He smirks and snorts, leans back in his chair, and curls his lip to show me his busted incisor.

"Call the bank if you want," I tell him.

He leans back in his chair. Looks at me. Looks at me some more, then spins around, picks up the phone, and speed dials. "Check the BFP&G account for a new deposit, will you please?" he asks, scowling at me. Pauses. His face goes grim. Says, "Thanks," and hangs up. Swings back around in his chair, starts tapping on his desk with his silver letter opener.

He's dumbfounded, never thought I'd come up with the money. Now he knows I have a real client, a client who can come up with big money in a couple of hours. The commission alone on the media buy for God is enough for Sinkle to take over the agency. I can see him setting aside seven-and-a-half million dollars after I leave, shipping it down to Florida, and getting the papers signed.

"You know, Rein, I underestimated you," he says, looking up slowly.

"How's that?"

Play with him, Rein. String him out.

"A month ago you were barely keeping Sirini and Woof! going and now you've brought sixty million bucks into the agency," Sinkle says.

"In cash," I add.

He nods. "Sit down," he says, motioning to one of the velvet-covered chairs around the conference table. Sinkle settles back in his chair, hands behind his head. He's smiling. "I think you're in line for a new job," he says.

I let him think I've taken the bait. "I think so, too."

"How about Creative Director?"

I shake my head. *Now I've got him off-guard. Keep him there.*

"Chief Creative Officer?"

"Nope."

Stare at him and crack a smile, a little one. Let the corners of your mouth widen, that's it.

Sinkle sits forward, focusing his eyes on me, the beginning of a smirk spreading across his face. *He's starting a stare-off.* "What job did you have in mind?"

There's only one job in this agency that's going to enable me get my ads on the air. Only one way I'm going to protect my campaign from the wolves and vultures around here. Either I walk or I take the top of the hill—here goes: "Your job," I say to him. "President of Boston, Frank, Pogue, & Gersenweser Advertising."

Sinkle smiles and shakes his head, like I'm a little kid asking for an expensive toy.

I stand up. "I'm serious. Otherwise I take my client and his money somewhere else."

"You can't."

I'm hoping he doesn't call my bluff. It would take ten weeks to transition to another agency, and I'd end up with another pyramid of jackals in expensive suits that I'd have to deal with.

"Woogie will go anywhere I say, and a lot of agencies would love to have this account. Call down to the subbasement right now and ask if you don't believe me. He's down there. Go ahead."

Sinkle reaches for the phone. Stops. "Wait," he says. "Okay, okay." His eyes dart around. "But we have to have a board meeting first."

"Have it over the phone—today. I want to read about it in the papers tomorrow."

This campaign is the right way to sell God and it's going on the air, even if it has to be over Sinkle's dead body.

Sinkle gets up. Straightens his suitcoat. Stretches his neck like his collar's too tight. Clears his throat, shoots his cuffs and says, "You understand, don't you, that I will be Chairman?" *He's almost asking me.*

"You can be anything you want—as long as I have a few things."

Sinkle glances at me. *He's off-balance, has no idea of what I'm going to ask for next, now he's the one waiting for the other shoe to drop.*

"Double my salary, give me an unlimited expense account, and I want Ester Platt formally reporting to me. I want you to announce it to her personally. Get her up here right now so there's no question about it."

I'm going to put this witch where she belongs, keep her from ever interfering with my advertising.

I sit down, lean back and lift my feet up onto the boardroom table. I can tell Sinkle doesn't like my feet on his Studebaker table.

But he can't do anything about it. He sneers and puts a call in to Ester. *Here I am in the valley of the shadow of sham and deceit, and Sinkle can't touch me because I've got God on my side and I've got the answer to his advertising problems.*

I look under the table. Sinkle's shoes are gleaming.

Now if I could just figure out how to get my shoes to shine like that. The leather has a burnished mahogany luster with lighter tones on the toes like the leather has dimension, depth, as if you could dip a finger deep into it.

Knock on the door. Vincent sticks his head in. "Ms. Platt, Mr. Sinkle," he says. Sinkle nods, and Vincent swings the door open.

Ester walks into the room cautiously, looking around warily like she's a cavalry scout riding into a box canyon. She sees my loafers perched on the boardroom table.

Sinkle is smiling at her. She knows those are not propitious signs for Ester Platt.

"Sit down," Sinkle motions to a chair. Ester sits down next to me, cautiously, looking at Sinkle but turning her body to me. Ester shifts her butt in the chair, adjusts her skirt. Sea-green skirt, rose-colored shoes. Long legs in glimmering nylon. She crosses her legs. The sea-green skirt hikes up her thigh. She catches me looking at her, leads my eyes down to her lap. Both her hands are there, resting on the insides of her thighs. Her fingers get up and start to slowly walk down toward her knees.

She lifts her eyes to look at me. I sit up, pull my shoes off the table, and clear my throat. Slide my eyes back over to her. She's still looking at me, inviting me to look down at her lap.

Oh boy, this is the way the world works. She senses I'm getting promoted so she's playing to me. Nothing doing, girlie. I've got your number.

"Ester, you've done a great job for us. I want to tell you how much the founders and I appreciate it." Sinkle's got his sincerest smile on. "And because of our confidence in you, we're going to ask you to take on an important new assignment."

Ester shifts her hips so her lap is inclined toward me. I look down. Her fingers are gently carrying her hem higher, one-by-one slowly walking the fabric up her thighs. Now I can see the dark part of her panty hose.

"It's an assignment we wouldn't consider giving to anyone else but you, Ester," Sinkle continues. "And I hope you will be as thrilled with the opportunity as we are in providing it to you."

Ester's smiling at Sinkle like he's telling her he's going to make her Queen of England while underneath the table, I can see halfway up her hip, the insides of her thighs.

She's seducing me while she's getting demoted. It's the food chain according to advertising. Normally, the bigger fish eat the smaller. In advertising, everybody eats everybody. But nobody's having Dinny Rein for lunch any longer.

"I'm going to ask you to take over direct creative supervision of all the accounts in the agency, Ester, including the God account."

"Thank you, Steve. I appreciate the vote of confidence," Ester says, sliding ever so slightly in her chair so she can slant her hips further toward me. "And you know I'll do everything I can to provide the inspiration and leadership you expect of me."

"Good, Ester. That's great. There's just one detail I need to cover with you." Both her hands are under the table now, she's hunching her hips off the seat so she can work her skirt higher.

Ester Platt is offering herself to me in the boardroom, on the sapphire-blue velvet seats of BFP&G's Queen Anne chairs. She's gone from screwing me to seducing me—come to think of it, maybe it's the same thing.

"Yes, Steve."

"We're going to be announcing Dinny Rein's elevation to President of BFP&G Advertising. So you will now be reporting to him."

"No problem," Ester says, turning to smile at me, dipping her eyes under the table. I refuse to follow, fixing my eyes on hers.

"I look forward to working closely with Dinny." She reaches her hand out. I take it. "Congratulations, Dinny," she says, leaning her body toward me.

I know what I'm going to see if I look under the table. Don't do it, Dinny, don't do it. I can feel her hand in mine, warm, softer than I thought, pulling slightly, her eyes dipping down again. *No, I'm not going to look, I'm not—nothing doing Ester. Go peddle your wares somewhere else.*

I pull my hand away. "Thank you, Ester," I say, standing quickly and walking away from the table. When I turn back, she's rearranging her skirt, patting and smoothing it down, crossing her legs, and placing her hands on the table. "I'd like to review that campaign of yours. Give my secretary a call and set up an appointment to see me, would you?"

Ester gives me a nod. That's all, a quick nod. The rest of her is ice. She gets up and strides out of the office without saying anything.

"She's a team player," Sinkle says to me as he watches her walk out of his office. "She'll come around quick. I bet she'll be a big help to you."

You bet, Steve. I've always enjoyed working with man-eating piranhas myself.

"See you later," I say, stooping down and heading out of Sinkledom.

22

"Your daughter called again," Evelyn says, as I head back into my office. "She wants to know if you're free for lunch." I want to hang around the office, watch as the yamma-yamma about the new president of BFP&G Advertising sweeps like wildfire around the office but I can't put Addy off again. Twice I've told her I've been too busy.

Just like in the old days, too involved in the old ad biz to spend any time with your daughter.

I say okay to lunch at Scoozi. "I'll run right over. Meet you there in fifteen minutes," I tell Addy.

Scoozi's packed, as always. The maitre d' points her out to me. Takes me two minutes to get through the crowd.

"Hi, Daddy," she says as I sit down in her favorite booth. She's wearing her banker getup, gray suit and blouse. Sounds tentative, won't look me in the eye.

Probably still wondering if she should be finding a padded room to put me in.

We talk about the weather, the Bulls, I ask her if she's seen Reavis lately, then she stops. Fiddles with her water glass, gives me a gawky smile. Fiddles some more and squinches her eyes together. "So, are you doing any better?" she asks, looking at me sideways.

"Yes, I'm fine, fine." The waiter hands us menus. Addy puts hers on the seat. So it's margherita pizza for Addy again. While I'm studying the menu, I say off-handedly, "As a matter of fact, you're looking at the new president of Boston, Frank, Pogue, & Gersenweser Advertising."

Addy leans back in her chair, like she's been hit with big wind. "You don't mean it? When?" Her face breaks out in a grin, all the laugh lines working together.

"Twenty minutes ago."

She throws up her hands. "How?" she asks.

"You get a big account, you get clout. I've even got Ester Platt reporting to me now."

"You stay away from her." Addy waggles her finger at me.

"Don't worry about that."

"So Morris was a help, you're...fine?"

"Fine, really fine. Just look at me, I'm making big bucks again and I've got the hottest account in the agency."

I give her my Steve Martin smile, all twinkling eyes and sparkling teeth. The waiter reappears. Addy orders her pizza. I have the pasta special, some promise of romano, artichokes, and pine nuts.

When the waiter leaves, Addy says, "You're not still..." and makes a continuing motion with her hand, her fingers looping through the air.

"What?"

"The last time I saw you—just before you went to see Morris—you were talking and acting, you know..."

Okay, Rein, you've got to act real blithe about this... "Oh, you mean that talking to God stuff? No, of course not. I don't know what happened to me. I must have been overtired."

Glad I've got Woogie down here. Don't have to get into all that mess anymore.

"I was very worried. You didn't seem, you know—very *normal* at all."

I put my hand on hers. "Addy, has your daddy ever been normal?"

Addy's shaking her head and rolling her eyes. "Yes, but you were telling me that God gave you new shoes and a Range Rover."

"I guess the business finally got to me."

"So you're okay now?"

"Absolutely," I say, spreading a smile across my face. "Haven't talked to God in at least a week."

"Good, Daddy." Addy hunches forward and gives me a kiss. *She's smiling again. She looks relieved.* "I can't believe you're president! You must be so happy, after all those years of..."

"Didn't look too good for your old daddy for a while there, I admit."

Here comes the food. Artichokes look gray, maybe I should have ordered something else.

"But now I've got my old office back with all my furniture and I got Sinkle to reinstate Evelyn as my secretary, but what's really important is that I've got an ad campaign going for this new client that could take advertising to a whole new level. Make it do some good for a change instead of peddling a bunch of stuff that people don't need."

"It sounds great, I'm delighted everything's going so well for you—you deserve it," she says as she dives into her pizza.

Even though she's a big banker now, she still eats like she's a little kid.

"While I have you here," she folds a slice of pizza and chomps away at it. "I need to ask you something."

"Anything you want, dear."

The pasta's better than I thought, pine nuts keep it from being bitter.

"This project I've been working on at the bank, we're watching the service sector very closely."

"Really?"

"And now that you're president, it's something you might keep an eye on."

"Sure, what's that?"

"We expect illicit money to go to car and boat dealers, when a dealer makes his first million, he always goes out and buys three or four Mercedes and a couple of speedboats. We always see that. And that's the way we've apprehended these people. Now they're starting to get smart and buy businesses with a lot of cash running through them."

What in God's name is she talking about? Illicit money? Businesses with a lot of cash running through them? I can feel my throat tighten up.

Ads for God

Addy goes on, "They've always done stuff like buy laundromats, car washes, movie theaters, that kind of thing. But now we're seeing them buying up small brokerage houses, real estate firms, even a local bank or two. We're trying to keep a step ahead of them and anticipate where they might go next. Now I don't think it would occur to them to buy an ad agency, but who knows? Could be an almost perfect way to scrub a whole bunch of money," Addy looks directly at me. "You people run millions through those places."

This girl's serious. Now I see why they made her a first vice-president. I cough. *Oh boy, am I in trouble.* Cough again. *I think I've got a piece of artichoke caught in my throat.* Grab a napkin. Major cough. *Think I got it.*

"Are you all right?"

I nod. *Yeah, I'm fine, just fine. I've just copped fifty million from some guy's briefcase and put it in our account, and now my daughter tells me that the banking system's almost onto me and that I could be facing forty to life in Leavenworth—it's a wonder I didn't choke to death.*

"No big deal," she says. "Just something for you to keep an eye on."

I try to smile. *Sure, it's no big deal, just a 10x12 cell and a little patch of veggies in the Yard to look after for the next thirty-five years.*

"Are you sure you're okay?"

"I'm fine, I'm fine," I say, *but I'm not. Here I am getting put on notice that I could get forty to life for a fat bunch of felonies, and all of a sudden, oh boy, who am I seeing out of the corner of my eye? Coming toward our table, the last person I'd ever expect to see at Scoozi?*

You guessed it. It's Patti Shaw, heading straight for us, big wide smile on her face. *I guess I'll finally see how my daughter and girlfriend get along.*

She gives me a big kiss, hunches down beside me and bangs her butt into mine to get me to move over. "I was over having lunch with our soap salesman when I saw you—and this must be your daughter."

"Addy, I'd like you to meet Patti Shaw," I say as I scoot over in the booth and introduce the two.

"So I hear you're in banking?" Patti asks.

"Yes, banking," Addy says quickly. "And what do you do?"

"I'm part owner of a carwash over on Elston."

"Not the Starlite?"

Patti nods tentatively, like she's not sure Addy approves.

"I love that carwash. I go in there even if my car's not dirty. I tell you, when I'm bugged with work or something, I just go in there and sit back listen to the music and watch the water fly around and come out feeling like a new person again."

"What kind of a car do you drive?"

"Lexus 400."

"The dark green one?"

"Yup," Addy says proudly. "I've got a platinum Starlite card, free underbody wash every time I go through." Addy points at Patti. "Wait a minute, I didn't recognize you. Aren't you the lady in the booth with the fabulous outfit?"

"That's little old me."

"I love your outfit. I spend all my time with a bunch of boring bankers. I've never met anyone who wears anything exotic like that."

"The outer space theme really is good for the bottom-line. We've put three car washes in the surrounding area out of business."

"Do you ever have guys bothering you?"

"Once in a while, but I just point the nozzle of my high-pressure hose at them and ask them if they'd like to rethink what they've said. Staring through an open car window at an angry woman with a firehose held a foot away usually affects their attitude."

"I wish I had a hose like that at the bank sometimes."

"I almost floated away a bunch of drunk college kids last month. They wouldn't stop with the talk so I wet them down good and then buzzed the crew who wipe down the cars. When those boys saw the size of our guys, they couldn't stop saying how sorry they were."

"I bet," Addy says.

"I made the ringleader write 'I will not sexually objectify women again' a hundred times. I think he got the point."

Addy taps my hand and points at Patti. "You know, I like your friend Patti Shaw."

Ads for God

Patti's blushing. I give her a squeeze and remind her, "Hey—aren't you going to ask about my presentation?"

Patti's hand whips up to her mouth, she gasps, "Oh, I completely forgot, how did it go?"

"He loved my campaign, and Rosemary's off to California to produce the advertising. And you're now looking at the new president of BFP&G Advertising."

"I'm so excited for you!" She gives me a fat smack on the cheek, hugs me, and turns to Addy. "Isn't your daddy just the smartest, most creative person you've ever met? You've got to see his new advertising, Addy. It's so beautifully handled, done with such taste and restraint but it gets to you right here, it just makes your heart go..." Patti pats at her chest with her fingertips. "What did he say about Charlton Heston holding the tablets?"

"Loved it, he loved everything."

She turns to me. "Everything worked?"

"Worked beautifully," I nod and smile. I see the waiter hovering off to the sidelines, holding menus, trying to spur us to order. "Patti, did you want to order?"

"Oh, I'm intruding on your lunch—how rude of me." Patti slides out of the booth saying, "I've got to get back to my soap salesman anyway. So nice to meet you, Addy. You have a wonderful daddy, I just want you to know."

I watch Patti Shaw zigzag back to her table. "She's a lot of fun, Patti is."

Addy's looking down at the table top, softly tapping at it with the pad of her finger, scratching her forehead with her other hand. "I like her, Daddy."

"Patti's a sweetheart. She's smart as a whip too."

"Are you two getting serious?" my daughter asks, looking up at me with eyes that want a positive answer. And I'm thinking, *Oh boy, Dinny Rein, that's one thing you've certainly never thought of. Or have you?*

So I wave at the air and say, "We're just friends." Addy reaches out and taps the top of my hand and says, "Oh, really?" Then she gives me a big smile like she knows better.

23

Rosemary calls me every day from the coast. In between her giggles I hear we've been rained out five days in a row, and the stock footage people are taking us to the cleaners. Rosemary's been fighting with the director, plus she's had a bad case of cramps.

Film production falls somewhere between trench warfare and waiting for paint to dry—wait, wait, and wait some more, and you don't know whether you'll end up getting killed going over the top by a botched commercial or dying of boredom producing it. Except the catered food is good. You can gain twenty pounds if you don't watch out. I hate producing commercials. That's why I'm glad Rosemary's out there.

"We got one great scene today," she says. "And I don't think you'll be able to see the rain at all." She giggles again although I know she's not joking.

"Hang in there," I say. She promises to call tomorrow after the shoot is wrapped. Barring any more rain, we should have the first spots edited in less than a week.

I get up and walk over to the window to look out at the lake, twinkling under puffy clouds and a Crayola-blue sky, like a kid's poster paint picture.

This is what you wanted, Rein. You're on top of the pile now and just think where you were a couple short months ago. Down and out in Wrigleyville, pinching pennies, digging dimes out of the sofa, and stuffing cardboard in your shoes to keep out the wet. Your career was in the pits. You were getting diddled by the Sirinis and snubbed by Woof! while Ester and Sinkle were circling overhead waiting to finish you off. An over-the-hill ad man on his last legs if there ever was one.

Ads for God

Now you look like a million bucks. You've got one of the biggest accounts in town. You're president of the place. You've got killer yamma-yamma. You've stepped over Ester. Sinkle's eating out of your hand. You're getting ready to break a campaign that's going to break new ground in the advertising business, and you've got your marching orders from God who's shoulder to shoulder with you, right by your side. You're running with the big dogs, Rein. So now what?

A cloud drifts over the sun. The lake turns dark, or maybe it was dark and I didn't notice with all the sparkles dancing over it.

Sinkle's got to be waiting in the weeds for me and who knows what Ester's up to? All I have to do is trip once, and they'll be all over me. At least I don't have to worry about my client. All I have to do is get the advertising on the air and watch my ass.

The sun peeks out from behind the cloud and the shimmering starts on the surface again, the sun reflecting off the ripples, millions of miniature mirrors flashing up at me. I remember when I first moved to Chicago, I used to go up to the top of the Hancock on a nice day and stand there for an hour, gazing out at the lake. A carpet of blue, glittering all over. I love looking at the lake when it's like this.

"Mr. Rein, I need to show you something." I hear Evelyn saying in a voice that sounds like she just joined the CIA. I turn around. She's standing in the doorway of my office, beckoning me with her finger. "Don't say anything, just come with me," she whispers.

We hustle down the hallway, get on the elevator and get off at 19. She hurries me back behind the receptionist to the fire stairs, turns around, and puts her finger to her lips as she opens the door and steps into the stairway, looking like a little girl sneaking up on someone.

When we get into the stairway and start climbing, she looks back over her shoulder and says, "I heard that Ester Platt was having a meeting in the screening room and went upstairs to take a peek. You've got to see what's happening in there."

Our feet click on the concrete stairs. Open a door, short hallway to the projection booth. Step up into raised booth, white tiles on the floor, packed with audio and video equipment, long narrow panels of one-way glass looking out on the screening room.

I recognize ten or twelve of the twenty-five or so people sitting in the screening room, men and women, all kingpins of the Midwestern marketing community: McDonald's, Motorola, Quaker Oats, United Airlines, AT&T.

They're listening to Ester Platt as she strides around in the room in her peach skirt, white blouse, and vanilla high heels—perfectly put-together, all business and completely in control. With everyone's eyes on her, as you can imagine. I click on the intercom so we can hear what she's saying.

"Rarely do promotional opportunities, partners of this quality and caliber, come along," Ester's saying. "I'm sure you all realize that. The Olympics is the only one I can think of, but that's only sports. This is religion. An opportunity to partner-up with a philanthropist's effort to integrate churchgoing into American life in a way that's never been done before."

She's pitching her campaign, doing a fifth column thing on me while I'm trying to get my advertising on the air.

"Your products and services can join in that effort. To be able to extend the Friendly Skies, Cap'n Crunch, or the Big Mac experience into the ecclesiastical context, done with taste and respect of course, is a once-in-a-lifetime marketing opportunity. A chance to outflank and outdistance your competition in a way that's never even been contemplated before."

"You've seen the advertising and heard Ester describe what this opportunity can mean to your marketing efforts. Now if I could add a perspective," Sinkle says, standing up and turning to face the audience.

Sinkle's in there too. He is in cahoots with Ester, I knew it. They're getting ready to tube my campaign and put hers on. End run me before my campaign even hits the air. But they'd better watch it, there will be a huge uproar. No one will ever put up with commercializing religion like that. It'll blow up right in their face. Besides, Woogie won't ever stand for it.

Ester backs up, leans against the wall, and lets Sinkle take center stage. Sinkle buttons his suitcoat and stands with his arms

Ads for God

down by his sides, chin raised, like he's out on the Purdue football field with *The Star Spangled Banner* playing over the PA system.

"We have the projections in a handout you can take with you, but the topline is we predict church attendance to go up twenty per cent in six months, forty per cent by the end of the first year. Millions of Americans will be crowding into churches, more and more every Sunday. And these will be people you can own. People who are dedicated to your Mileage Plus Program or your Big Mac promotion.

"Now some of you have already expressed interest, some have already generated your own custom promotions—what we'd like you to do now is commit to us. Sign contracts with us. Get on board before we have to offer this opportunity to your competitors."

Sinkle nods to Ester, and she opens up a large card, 40x60, a huge collage of churches, National Geographic style pictures, white steeples, town greens with red zigzag lines zipping around between the steeples and pictures of celebrities floating above the churches.

The two of them lift it up on the wall rail and Sinkle points to the collage. "This advertising is just the tip of the iceberg in terms of our programs. To give you an idea of where we're going, we're now talking about linking churches electronically to create an Episcopal Network or The Congregational Connection, linked to each other through the Internet and hard-wired through cable so we can develop the critical mass to do in-church programming.

We're talking to world-class celebrities about in-church appearances. As we speak, we've opened conversations with Madonna, Michael Jordan, Sting, Barbra Streisand—those are just some of the many talents we're considering. And we're going with the latest technology, state-of-the-art, big screens, Diamond Vision, and digital surround sound.

We're going to remake the church-going experience in America—remodel religion right before your eyes. Bring it into the mainstream and take it into the twenty-first century. Do for church what Gates did with computer software, and what Stern did for the NBA.

A year from now, I can safely say that you'll walk into a church and you won't even recognize it..." Sinkle lets his voice trail off, continues to walk around the screening room in front of his audience, stops dramatically, looks up at the ceiling, and starts again.

"I think you have to look at what we're offering you this way... If you don't sign up for our program, think of this: you could be giving your fiercest competitor, the guy who keeps you up at night, the guy who makes you miserable, you could be giving that competitor..." Sinkle looks down, takes a dramatic pause, lowers his voice, and says, "…the chance to get in bed with God."

I shake my head. "C'mon, Evelyn, let's go. I've seen enough." *I've got to talk to Woogie about this.*

Evelyn's whispering to me as we walk out of the projection booth. "I'm not sure I want to see Madonna and Michael Jordan in church, you know what I mean? You're not going to let him do all this, are you, Mr. Rein? Your advertising is much better."

"Not if I can help it, Evelyn." I hold the screening room door for her, and we head back down the stairs.

24

I hope Woogie's in, I'm thinking as I open the basement door in the lobby. I hear polka music coming from down below as I take the stairs in twos, grabbing at the handrail to make sure I don't slip.

Sounds like Woogie's giving a party, music getting louder the further down I go. Open the door to the sub-basement stairs, music's so loud my eardrums are warping. As I turn the corner, I look down into the sub-basement. Woogie comes dancing out from behind the furnace, sashaying around, doing the polka with an imaginary partner, bending sideways and shuffling quickly side-to-side through the furniture, an egg salad sandwich in one hand, his stereo clicker in the other. Some of the accordion chords are so loud they make me wince.

Woogie slides around the broken furniture, leaning and dipping with his imaginary partner, smiling like he's dancing with the prettiest girl in the polka contest, and they've just won first place. I see something gold on his wrist.

Wait a minute, two days ago he was wearing a crummy old wristwatch with a cracked crystal and adhesive tape holding the band together, something he found in the dumpster five years ago. Now he's wearing a gold watch, I squint to try and see what kind it is.

The polka music stops. Woogie takes a bow, then a bite of his egg salad.

"Woogie," I say, walking down the last few steps. He whirls around.

"Dinny my friend, Dinny Rein, the man who make advertising magic, ja?" He holds out what's left of his sandwich to me. "Liking egg salad from Subway?"

Look at what's on his wrist! It's a gold Rolex the size of an egg, loaded down with diamonds, *there must be fifty of them. Diamonds! Where's Woogie getting the money to buy gold Rolexes with diamonds? Wait a minute, what a stupid question. I guess if God wants a gold Rolex with diamonds, He can buy himself ten gold Rolexes with diamonds.*

"Nice watch."

"You liking? Woogie get for Dinny also. Have friend down in Loop giving good deal."

"No thanks," I hold up my Timex. "I'm fine with this."

"Have diamonds for showing hours, see?" Woogie holds up the watch. It sparkles in the light from the bare bulb overhead, diamonds in the bezel twinkling, the face bright-white and gleaming.

Not exactly the watch I'd expect God to be wearing, but what can I say? Guess you find out what He likes when you bring the Big Guy down to earth—Rolex watches and egg salad sandwiches from Subway.

"Woogie, can I ask you a question?"

"Is fine."

"It's about Ester."

"Ja, Ester very sad. Too bad she no win, ja?"

"That's not what I mean..." I get up and wander around the basement while Woogie finishes his sandwich. In the corner, I see an old sign. Wood, hand-lettered in pencil. "Boston, Frank, Rein, and Gersenweser Advertising."

Must have been a mockup for the plaque they were going to put on the front of the building, I figure, picking it up and dusting it off. I walk back and sit down in front of Woogie on the Tide box, the sign across my knees.

"I think you should keep an eye on her."

"Not understanding 'keep eye'."

"Watch her."

"Ja, ja, you watching too."

"Why me?"

"Socko boobies, no?"

"No, I don't mean that. I mean I don't trust her."

"Is advertising business, ja Dinny?" Woogie wads up the Subway wrapper and aims at a galvanized trash can. The ball of paper hits the rim and bounces out. "Shitski," Woogie says.

"But I just saw her upstairs selling her campaign to a bunch of clients."

"Ja, ja, ja, I see too, but is Woogie who being client, no? Already tell Ester not buying her advertisings, ja?" He opens a matchbook and uses a corner to clean his teeth.

"I just thought I'd tell you, I get a little worried when..."

"Tsk, tsk, tsk, you have Woogie right here." He's shaking his finger at me. "You have big powers right down in basement and you listening to silly scheming of Ester Platt and Sinkle, ja? Is dumbski, ja Dinny?" Woogie leans forward and pats me on the knee. "Trusting with Woogie. He helping out of everything, ja?"

"So I don't have to worry about Ester?"

"Not being in picture."

"And the fifty million? You're going to pay that back so we don't get in any trouble."

"Was talking at bank today, fifty million paying off tomorrow, with interests, ja? So when we see advertisings from coast?"

"Rosemary says I might be seeing some spots tonight. She says it's really terrific. I can't wait to show it to you."

"Good, ja, ja, I seeing some already. Very good."

How did he see the rough cuts already? They just came back from California.

"You peeked?"

"Ja, ja, you spend eight million of dollar, you peek too, ja?"

I guess it's hard to keep your rough cuts from God. Woogie works a cluster of egg salad out from between his teeth with his fingernail.

"So, for big screening of advertisings, we be doing some scheming, ja?"

"Scheming?"

"Scheming—is what going on in ad business, no? Ester and Sinkle doing scheming, Dinny and Woogie doing scheming too, ja? Figuring Sinkle making changes to your advertisings, no?"

"I wouldn't be surprised. He's done it before."

"So Woogie and Dinny Rein on same team, no?"

Sure is nice to hear this from a client for a change.

"I hope so."

"Then we tell Sinkle go screwing himself with changes, ja? Shaking on it, no?" Woogie sticks out his hand.

"Shaking on it, yes," I say and shake his hand firmly. Woogie gives me a 24 karat smile.

This is the political stuff that used to get me crazy, forming alliances, game-playing, and planning ahead to counter your opponent's moves. Boy, what a smart thing it was for me to bring Him down to Earth as Woogie Strepijichowski. He's going to walk me through this whole political minefield and bring me out safely on the other side.

"You're going to love this advertising, Woogie, and we'll blow them away with it," I say, still shaking his hand.

Sinkle may have Ester on his side, maybe the whole agency for that matter, but who cares? Because I've got Woogie Strepijichowski on mine.

"I'll call you with the exact time for the meeting. It will be tomorrow or the day after." I start up the stairs, looking back toward Woogie and waving good-bye.

"Being looking forward, Dinny. Being very looking forward." I hear Woogie's voice echoing back up the stairs as I open the door and step out into the lobby. Just before the door clicks shut behind me, I hear the polka music starting up again.

Must be close to five o'clock, there's a small stampede going on in the lobby, everybody rushing off the elevators and piling up in front of the revolving doors. A couple people see me as they're getting off the elevator.

"Hi, Mr. Rein!" a secretary says. "Hey, Dinny," Sophie's assistant in accounting calls out. All I have to do is show my face in the agency and people start treating me like I'm a movie star, waving "Hi," rushing up to me, greeting me, shaking my hand, and asking me how the campaign's coming.

I'm beginning to think I have the best yamma-yamma in BFP&G history.

It's a long way from slinking around the BFP&G building, trying to avoid people, skulking around the telephone booths waiting for an empty elevator to ride upstairs, getting in early, and waiting until everyone went home so I wouldn't run into anyone in the halls. Hated the looks I got from people—like they were thinking "Jeez, there's Rein again. I'm surprised Sinkle hasn't fired him yet."

"When are we going to see something, Dinny?" the tall guy who works on Steigerlager (who looks like William F. Buckley, but whose name I can never remember) asks.

"Hopefully we'll be screening the rough cuts for the client tomorrow or the next day," I tell him. "We'll have a premiere for everyone after that." Five or six people are buzzing around me as I walk toward the elevators. Couple of secretaries, the messenger who looks like Roger Rabbitt. I see Sophie from accounting. Sophie's in orange today.

She comes up alongside and says into my ear, "I tell you, it sure is nice to have a buffer between us and you know who..." Sophie points up in the air, towards the executive floor, "...for a change." Sophie'd make a great spokesperson for Tropicana—even her pantyhose are orange.

"Thanks, Sophie."

"And I hear your advertising's going great," she adds. I nod as the elevator doors shut and one of the secretaries leans over and asks me, "Is our client on the God account really the super from downstairs?"

Before I have a chance to answer, the other secretary rolls her eyes and swats her friend on the arm. "C'mon, Cindy, who do you think the client is—God Himself?" We all laugh in that overly jocular way people who work for the same company do when they don't know each other well. Me, the two secretaries, the messenger, and Sophie the Assistant CFO of Boston, Frank, Pogue, & Gersenweser Advertising who's dressed like a piece of citrus on this fine spring day.

Jeez, she's even wearing orange eye-shadow, I notice as she gets off the elevator. *I wonder if she's still importing her yogurt from New York?*

Everyone exits at different floors, the secretaries waving goodbye, backing off the elevator, almost curtsying to me, the messenger who looks like Roger Rabbit telling me to "Be cool, my man," leaving me to travel the last three floors by myself.

I get off the elevator and walk down the hallway toward my office waving to people in their offices, first one side and then the other. They look up as I pass. Wave one way, smile, wave the other way, smiling like I'm the most popular guy at Boston, Frank, Pogue, & Gersenweser Advertising.

"Mr. Rein, Mr. Rein," I hear as I walk around the corner. It's Evelyn, scurrying up the hall as fast as her stubby little legs working back and forth in her tight skirt will take her. She's huffing and puffing as she stops in front of me.

"Rosemary called. She says the roughcuts are all ready and for you to come over right away." Evelyn's beaming up at me like I'm some kind of wonder-worker. "She says they're awesome, Mr. Rein."

25

I gun the Range Rover out of the garage and head for Izzy's. Pitch black under Lower Wacker, someone forgot to turn the lights on. I brake for a Domino's driver coming around the corner on two wheels, red pizza warmers stacked to the ceiling, the pile teetering and swaying in the front seat.

If the spots look as good as Rosemary thinks, we could have the advertising on the air the day after tomorrow. Start blowing out television screens all over the country, pile people into churches, and change the face of advertising forever.

I pull into Izzy's lot. Space at the back against the wall between two trucks.

Television could finally become the positive force for social change that everyone has hoped it would, not through programming—but through advertising!

Get out and click the remote to lock the car. Lights flash and door locks go thunk. The trucks on either side are tall, block out the light.

Panky Durnberg wasn't crazy. He was right. Our advertising will start changing the way people think about life, about the way they act toward one another, what did he call it? A sea change in American culture?

I feel my way down the side of the Range Rover. Something flashes in front of me. I feel my shoulder slumping, knees buckling, then the pain racing down my side like a sharp hot knife, bending me over, and bringing tears to my eyes. I whirl around, see someone in a black cap behind me winding up with a baseball bat. The bat sailing high over his head, lights gleaming off the varnish.

Someone just whanged me in the shoulder with a baseball bat, and they're winding up for a second shot. I spin around and crouch down, scrambling forward to break out of the space between my Rover and the truck.

I'm back at Waverly going low around a defenseman, sliding against the truck next to me, scrambling forward, feet scooting out in front of me. Someone's there all of a sudden, a fist coming up into my stomach, straightening me up, the breath exhausting out of me.

I leap to the right around the back of the truck, springing sideways to get out of the way. I hear the baseball bat crashing against the side of my car, glass shattering, tinkling on the ground, feet stepping on it.

The guy with the bat's chasing me. Crunch, crunch, crunch, my feet are smashing down on the glass.

And I see someone else, dark and moving fast, coming for me from around the side of the truck, bent over and grunting, bent over low so I can't see the face, careening toward me, flying tackle, I see a knife held out, long shiny blade heading towards me.

I whirl left twice, twirling and juking, stutter-stepping left then right, now sprinting forward.

I'm past him. Where's the guy with the bat? He's got to be around here somewhere. I duck again and take off toward the attendant's booth. I'm looking over my shoulder, ripping across the parking lot, my legs pumping like there's no one on the field in front of me, and I'm going for a clear shot at the goal.

Where are they? I can't see anyone. I race past the lighted parking lot booth. No one's in there. *Where'd the attendant go? He was in there when I came in. Fine time to go for coffee.*

I make it around the corner of Izzy's building, galloping like a bandit. The street is brightly-lit. Look behind me, no one's following. Izzy's door is a hundred feet ahead. Slow down to a jogtrot, breathing like I just set a new track record in the 440.

Jesus, was I lucky that guy missed with the bat the first time, I would've been beaten to a bloody pulp by now. My shoulder kills, I reach up and touch it, *ouch!*

As I get off the elevator, I can hear the Simon and Garfunkel Doxology track running, booming down the halls, playing throughout Izzy's office. Now my gut is starting to hurt.

Ads for God

I saw a knife, I wonder if he cut me? I feel around. Nothing, my stomach muscles are sore on one side, that's all.

"Praise God from Whom all blessings flow," I hear, sung in Garfunkel's soft falsetto. "Praise Him all creatures here below..." I walk up to the doorway of Izzy's room. His editing suite is packed with people. Rosemary sidles up to me and puts her arm through mine as I edge into the group of people watching the commercial.

Ouch, I think. *Take it easy. That's the shoulder that just got blasted with a baseball bat.*

"This is life, and you know who made it all possible, so stop in this Sunday and just say thanks," I hear my voice saying at the end of the commercial as a fiery orange sun sinks down into the ocean, a three-year old girl licks an ice cream cone, a grandmother who's a dead ringer for Katherine Hepburn hugs a baby goat, and the words "Praise God" write themselves on the screen.

The commercial ends, the lights come on, and everyone in the room turns toward me and applauds.

It's a love-fest for Dinny Rein. Everybody pawing at me and clapping me on the back. Telling me it's the greatest advertising they've ever seen, how I've made them proud to be in the advertising business again.

Izzy comes up and gives me another hug, lifting me up off the floor. Rosemary's glued to me like I'm the hottest thing to ever hit the advertising business.

Almost makes up for being mugged. Now if I can just figure out how to structure tomorrow's presentation so I can sell my ads to God.

26

I open the door to the screening room. Woogie's coming up in five minutes. Ester and Sinkle are waiting, sitting in the front row. Sinkle's bent over, busy polishing his shoes. He's dressed like a Park Avenue undertaker who has close friends in Hollywood, black suit and gray silk tie, Ralph Lauren goes to Rodeo Drive.

He looks up. "Any reshoots over a hundred grand, Oddjob's buying," he sneers at me, buffing a final highlight onto the toes of his Cole-Haan pumps before tucking his brush back in his pocket.

Hearing "reshoot" from a client is as bad as hearing "carcinoma" from a doctor. Other than losing an account, it's the worst thing that can happen in an ad agency, since the money for the reshoot comes out of the agency's commission. Working for free is no fun—particularly when Steve Sinkle's your boss.

"Who said anything about reshoots?" I ask. Sinkle looks up as the buxom, cherry-cheeked lady from the Polish bakery slumps into the screening room carrying white cardboard boxes of sweetrolls.

"Don't get me wrong, I like the stuff. I really do—it's a little different, but I like it," Sinkle looks over at Ester. "What about you, Ester?"

Ester doesn't do much more than sweep her eyes over me and shrug. But that's all she has to do. As advertising gestures go, a shrug indicates deference, and deference is weakness. Sinkle sees an opening in the secondary and tries a short pass.

"That's what I mean," Sinkle stands. "The stuff's kind of sentimental, but then it jerks you around. You go from a street party to a funeral. I've never seen anything like this before. I tell you, we should be Durnberging this advertising."

Ads for God

I get a quick glance from Ester, might as well be a poison dart, then she says, "Steve, if we tone down some of the music, I bet we can even them out."

Sinkle points at Ester like he's a broker buying a hundred thousand shares of stock on the Big Board, elbow lifted and arm aimed down at her. "Good, Ester, good." He ranges around by the box of sweetrolls, peeks into the white cardboard box, reaches in, and takes one.

"Maybe I should say that to the client up front? I'll just say we want to do a little work on the tracks to even the whole campaign out." He's bending over the box, pretending to pick out a sweet roll. He's doing a stage wait, waiting to see if I'll let him criticize my campaign in front of the client, probing my defense with short passes to see if he can open me up for the long ball.

Pick, pick, pick, he's been doing it for years, criticizing the acting, the dialogue, the pacing, and the photography, getting the client worried, starting to ask for changes here and there, fix this, redo that, change that voiceover, re-edit that commercial, until the campaign starts to lose shape and substance, and he's set the situation up for a sixty-yard pass. If I've seen him do it once, I've seen him do it thirty times.

"If the campaign seems to have this many problems," he'll say after he's torn the advertising apart, then he goes back into the pocket, pump-faking one way then winding up and throwing high and deep, suggesting, "maybe it's time for us to go back to the drawing board."

Then after he's taken the control away from creative director, Sinkle dictates new advertising and becomes savior and star quarterback in the eyes of the client.

"You do that, and I'll walk," I say, evenly and calmly, not even looking at him. "Right out the door. You'll lose half your agency in the time it takes me to get downstairs."

Ester looks at Sinkle. He knows he's going to have to go back to grinding out the yardage on the ground. Takes a bite of the sweetroll. "Uggh," he says, quickly spitting it into a napkin. "What the hell's that?"

"Cream cheese and potato, has some special name in Polish."

"Jeez, I thought it was custard or something. Why didn't you tell me I was eating crap?" Sinkle is trying to wipe the rest of the sweetroll out of his mouth with his handkerchief as Woogie opens the screening room door.

I hardly recognize him. He's wearing a tailored dark-blue suit. His white hair is clipped, blown, and brushed back, face is smooth and berry-brown, like he did some time on a tanning bed. He doesn't look like Guy Lombardo anymore. *Reminds me of someone else—who is it?* I catch his eye. He winks at me and grins. Fiendish grin, eyebrows lifting into two tall arches, eyes sparkling, hint of craziness in there.

Who does he look like? Uh oh, his shirt collar's white but his shirt's blue, dressed to kill. Maybe Sinkle's gotten to him. But how could Sinkle get to God?

He sweeps his wrist up in front of his face so his cuff shoots back and everyone can see his diamond Rolex. "Not being too late, no?"

Hair slicked back, impish grin, eyes flicking around, who does he look like?

"Mr. Strepijichowski!" Sinkle wads the handkerchief into his pocket and grabs Woogie's hand like he's a frat brother he hasn't seen in fifteen years. "What a great-looking suit," he says as he puts his arm around Woogie's shoulder and steers him over to the credenza.

Ester's swinging her hips and tilting her head to the side so her hair falls away from her face, coming across the room toward him, smiling like she's on television. She puts out her hand, takes Woogie's, then darts in and leaves a quick kiss on his cheek. Woogie's eyes dance as Ester steps back.

"How about some coffee and a sweetroll, Mr. Strepijichowski?" Sinkle asks.

"Collachki," Woogie shouts. *(Collachki, that's the word I was trying to think of)* "Being my favorites! Much enjoyments from favorite thing of Woogie." Woogie reaches into the box and hands a sweetroll to Sinkle. "You try, you try."

"No, really, thanks," Sinkle smiles and shakes his head politely.

"Unh, unh, unh," Woogie says, jabbing a finger in Sinkle's face and holding the collachki up under his nose, a sly smile on his face. "Big client say eating. Advertising man must be eating, ja?" Woogie turns to me quickly and winks.

Good, a little signal that Woogie's still on my side.

Sinkle forces a smile. Woogie takes a huge chomp out of his collachki, nods at Sinkle. "Eating, ja?" Sinkle takes a tentative nibble. "No, no, no, big biting like this." Woogie stuffs half the collachki in his mouth.

Opening his mouth wide, Sinkle shuts his eyes, slowly inserts the shiny sweetroll with the congealed center and bites down.

"Good, ja?" Woogie asks. They're chewing in unison, Sinkle forcing a cheery smile as he chomps and grins. "Very good," he says. "Very good," grinning and chewing, "very, very good."

"Eating another," Woogie says, handing Sinkle a second collachki and carrying the box around to us. "Everyone enjoying Polish goodski," he says, passing around the collachkis. Like chewy pancakes with hardened sour cream in the center, there's a hint of rancidity, as if they'd been sitting in a glass case in the sun for a couple of weeks, definitely not Bloomingdale's bake shop quality.

I'm trying to usher Woogie to a chair in the center of the first row so I can sit down next to him and block Sinkle and Ester. Woogie's wearing some kind of Polo aftershave that smells like its part tack room, part orange grove.

Ester's attached herself to his right side and is looking up at Woogie like it's Pageant Night—he's Bert Parks and she's Miss Florida.

I get Woogie to the front row, and we sit down together. Ester quickly sits on his other side, Sinkle in the seat beyond her. Ester does her leg-crossing act, letting her skirt flap open so Woogie gets a good look at her gams, open halfway up her thighs, mocha nylon shapely and shimmering in the overheads.

Woogie's gaping. Ester lets him look. Then gives a mock gasp, giggles at him, and quickly flips the fabric back. Curtain's closed, show's over, but Woogie's leaning into Ester like he's all ready for the second act.

Why's he paying so much attention to Ester? Doesn't seem like a particularly godlike thing to do.

"So, Mr. Strepijichowski," I say quickly. "We have all of your commercials finished and already transferred to the networks. If you give us the go-ahead, they can be on the air tonight."

"Everybody liking advertisings?" Woogie asks, turning to Sinkle and Ester, back to me, eyebrows lifting, a questioning look on his face. Ester shrugs again. I nod.

Sinkle leans over and says to Woogie, "I'll be interested to see how you react, Mr. Strepijichowski."

"Being some problems?" Woogie asks.

"Nothing that isn't easily correctable," Sinkle says.

I glare at him, quickly add, "Let's take a look," and raise my hand to signal the projectionist. The lights subside, leaving two glowing monitors on which the familiar numbers flash, "9", "8", "7", the revolving line wiping each number away to reveal the next. The "2" blinks by, and the commercials begin, the music swelling over the sound system, eight minutes of the most lavishly-produced commercials anyone has ever seen on television.

Hundreds of actors, real people and professionals, costumes, soaring helicopter shots, real people and celebrities spliced together running with the Stones, the Beach Boys, Platters, and Simon and Garfunkel and Patti LaBelle singing the Doxology, Aretha Franklin belting it out as eight million dollars-worth of film extolling art, culture, and humankind runs along in sync. Swooping dips into the Grand Canyon as the sun sets, children romping in fields of blooming flowers, laughter, beauty, quick cuts of jokes from Benny and Sid Caesar, Babe Ruth belting one out of the park, Cary Grant hanging from a cliff, puppies and hugs, everything innocent and lilting, uplifting and glorious, humorous then suddenly somber, with a Greek Orthodox funeral, misty hillside, swaying incense burners, black robes and melodic chanting, John Kennedy saluting his father's caisson, and Martin Luther King's famous speech inserted into some of the commercials for drama and counterpoint.

I look over at Woogie. He's swaying back and forth to the music, tapping the toes of his boots, big smile on his face. Catch Sinkle on the other side of Woogie, he's eyeing Woogie also, checking his reaction.

"Is different, ja?" Woogie asks after the last commercial runs.

Sinkle answers quickly, "Yes, and we were talking before you came in. Some minor adjustments to the music, and we think we can improve the commercials…"

"Ja?"

"Nothing needs to be done to this advertising. It is perfect," I say, getting up quickly and walking in front of the group. Ester is watching carefully.

"Fixing musics, ja?" Woogie asks, turning around to look at Sinkle.

"Yes, attenuate the tracks here and there so it isn't quite so much in your face, know what I mean? Then I think we should Durnberg all of them."

"Ja? What is dis Durnberg?"

"We're not going to Durnberg anything," I interrupt. "And we're not going to fix anything. The advertising is going to stay exactly the way it is."

"I think our client might like a little explanation of the Durnberg process, right, Mr. Strepijichowski?"

"I'll give him a full briefing on Durnberg sometime, but right now, Mr. Strepijichowski, I'd like your okay to put these commercials on the air."

"Ja, we looking again, ja? For eight millions of dollars, Woogie get second looking, ja?" he says to Sinkle, clapping him on the back, smiling with all of his teeth. "Ja, ja, ja, ja, ja," Woogie's chortling.

"Just keep your ear tuned to that music," Sinkle leans in and whispers to Woogie as the commercials start to run again. "And imagine how much we could improve it if we attenuated a few things."

As I sit watching the advertising I've created, I think, *For the first time in my life I'm not peddling some lousy, two-bit product—an overpriced pasta or dog food shaped like hamburgers; dealing with cheapskate, small-minded clients who are always nickel-and-dimeing me and picking over my ads. This is the big time, I've got a hundred million bucks worth of advertising selling nature, family, childhood, innocence, love, joy. I'm selling life. I'm selling religion. I'm selling God—and it works!*

"For a first go-around they're not bad," Sinkle says in a low voice. I watch him leaning into Woogie as the commercials end and the lights come up. "But I say we fix the music and get those funeral shots out of there. What do you think, Mr. Strepijichowski?"

Before Woogie has a chance to answer, I'm up on my feet again in front of the three of them. "Look, this advertising is going to run as it is! Tonight! We can sit here all day and make a million changes." Ester is watching attentively, her eyes going back and forth between Sinkle and me. "But we'll make it better when we shoot the next pool. That's the way we'll improve it, not by picking these spots apart."

"How about getting rid of one funeral scene and doing a quick remix on the music?"

"C'mon, Mr. Strepijichowski," I say, motioning to Woogie with my hand and walking toward the door of the screening room. "We're leaving."

"Wait, wait, wait," Sinkle says, leaping out of his chair, grabbing the box of collachkis and rushing over to block the door. "Let's have another pastry and celebrate. I'll get Vincent to get some champagne, and we'll have a little party out in the lobby. Have everyone in the agency see the advertising and meet Mr. Strepijichowski."

Sinkle stands in front of us holding the open box of collachkis like he's a cigarette girl in a 40's cabaret. "Everybody's dying to meet you," he entreats, eyes wide open, smile stretching across his face.

Within an hour, the lobby is crowded with people drinking champagne and suspiciously eyeing the little squares of Polish sweet rolls Vincent and his hired crew of flunkies from the catering service are passing around on silver trays. I see the silver-blonde in fishnets with the pasteurized skin serving champagne, her skirt still shooting out from her hips. I wonder if she's gotten a job in advertising yet. She winks at me. *I guess not.*

People cluster around the TV monitors watching the advertising. Creative people, Scrunch, Peavis, Sticks in his Indian suit, looking scraggy as ever, Rosemary looking like someone rubbed a lamp—she's got on a casbah outfit complete with the turned-up embroidered slippers, balloon pants hanging off her bare hips, gauzy shirt stopping at her midriff, her hair tucked into a lamé turban. I

Ads for God

see Billy and Roscoe, Sondra in her jumper from Talbot's, media and account people, Murray's bean counters from the seventh floor, messengers in low-riding pants, and secretaries in fuzzy Orlon sweaters as "Praise God from Whom all blessings flow" rings out through the crowd from the monitors set up around the lobby.

I see Sinkle working Woogie's left ear. I hear "all-star game," "Durnberg," "funerals," "music," and "downside"—the man's a fullback pounding away at the same off-tackle slot, trying to poke a hole in the advertising, to show Woogie that there's a problem with it so he can begin to regain control.

The commercials keep running in a continuous loop, Baseball, Comedians, Rock Stars, Nature and the two-minute grab bag of all the scenes edited together to the Stones singing the Doxology. I can hear people in the audience humming along, "...from Whom all blessings flow. Praise Him all creatures here below..."

Sophie the Assistant CFO is still in her citrus mode, except today she's in lime from head-to-toe, her eyeshadow the color of a moray eel's underbelly. "I tell you Dinny," Sophie says. "You're going to put that Doxology tune in the top ten. It's so catchy everyone in the country's going to be singing it!"

I'm standing with Woogie, Steve, and Ester in the center of the crowd, people milling around patting me on the back and shaking my hand, telling me how impressed they are with the work, how much they like my new Italian suit, what I've done for the agency, how proud they are to be a part of God account, and how well the commercials will look on television. Plevis tells me what I'm doing for the agency morale. Murray the CFO tells me what I'm doing for the bottom-line.

"I still want you to look at my book," the lady with the milk-white skin says as I take another glass of champagne off her tray, except now she's got a big-time "come see me sometime" look on her face and she's not calling me "Noodles" any more.

I look around for Woogie. He's with Ester. I can't hear what they're saying but Ester's bending over, laughing at his jokes, and you can guess what Woogie's gazing at.

Watch out Rein. Keep an eye on Woogie. Watch out for Ester. Watch out for Sinkle. Keep an eye on everyone. This is the big balancing act here. I'm back to being the trained seal in the circus the way I was eleven years ago, scrambling my flippers around so I stay on top of the ball. Oh boy, now I know the truth—when you're finally on top, the reality is you've just got further to fall.

Woogie's doing "ja, ja, ja's" to the throng of people who push up to him and pump his hand. "Being much grateful. Thanking, thanking," he keeps saying. "Being much grateful. Thanking, thanking."

A cluster of writers and art directors on the other side of the crowd starts dancing to the music, chanting out the lyrics, "Praise God from Whom all blessings flow..."

Rosemary sidles up and gives me a wet kiss on the cheek. The champagne's been doing its work on her. She blurts at me, "Just wait until this advertising runs. We'll be the hottest shop in the country." Rosemary slinks away, winking, and doing a hula dancer thing with her arms.

I feel someone poking me in the side. It's Sinkle. "Our client has decided to Durnberg the advertising, Dinny," he says.

"Huh?" I say, Sinkle's still poking me with his finger. "Mr. Strepijichowski agrees that there's too much riding on this campaign not to get some feedback on it."

Woogie's been drinking champagne. His tan is going copper. "Ja, feeding back very good," Woogie says. "And my friend Steve here, is going paying for Durnberging, ja?"

"You bet," Sinkle says.

"It's a waste of time and money to Durnberg this campaign," I answer.

Woogie throws his arms around Sinkle and me as if he's The Great Unifier, "Dinny, Dinny, Dinny, in advertising always doing givings and takings, no?" his gleaming face lit up by a two-hundred watt smile and Sinkle on the other side of me nodding and smiling. The two of them over-Poloed in enough Lauren to buy a secondhand Porsche, aftershave so thick my nostrils are getting singed, their hair shined and set, Sinkle's eyebrows shaping over his eyes, forming funnels so his gaze is cold and focused, as if his eyes are saying to me "So long, sucker, your ass is grass."

I'm standing between the two of them getting that sinking

feeling again. That old feeling like I'm being taken to the cleaners, the way I felt when I first sat down with Reavis' lawyer, the way I felt when Sinkle told me he was hiring Ester, when Ester took my title away and cut my salary, all the miserable slights and nasty turns of fate that reduced me to my one-room walkup in Wrigleyville, and turned my career to shit. Just when I think I've got everything going again, just when I've got the rhythm, the pace, and the whole thing figured out, just when I've got my campaign finished and ready to go on the air, here I am standing between Woogie and Sinkle and both nodding at each other like they are in cahoots, and I'm chopped liver, and all of a sudden it comes to me.

Jesus, Rein, you're being set up again. Only this time it's by God.

27

I catch up with Woogie as he steps into the elevator after the party. He's picking lint off the sleeve of his suit. I'm whispering in his ear, "I need to talk to you, right away." Everyone in the elevator is watching us.

"Doing lunching sometime, maybe?" he says, adjusting the knot of his tie, giving me a demonic grin, mouth curling up at the corners. I wait until the BFP&G people get off the elevator.

"Why did you agree to Durnberg the advertising, Woogie? Don't you understand that Sinkle can make those numbers go anyway he wants?"

Who does he look like? It's some movie star? I'm trying to think, who is it? That devilish look, the slicked back hair... Who is it?

"Doing more scheming, ja Dinny? Making other side thinking is winning and letting down guard, ja?"

Yeah, sure, I fell for that one last time.

He adjusts his cuffs. "Liking new suit from Ralph Lauren?"

"Where did you get it?"

I bet Sinkle's buying him the clothes.

"Buying from store I get your suits—is good, ja?"

"Look, I need to talk to you about this research."

Woogie's fiddling with the fabric of his sleeve. "Not being too dark for Woogie, ja? Worrying face is too white so buying sun for face and having nice tanning, no? Is looking better, ja?"

The crowd clears, and Woogie steps off the elevator. I hustle after him through the lobby, scurrying alongside him, trying to keep up.

"You can't take the Durnberg numbers too seriously Woogie. They don't always predict market performance."

"Excusing, Dinny, but having important meeting. Being seeing you soon, ja?" His eyes gleam and his eyebrows wiggle up and down. He's smiling at me like we just heard the same joke.

I wonder what the joke is?

I follow him through the revolving doors. "They'll make these numbers go anyway they want, Woogie. I've seen them do it."

I'm dodging pedestrians, following Woogie. He leans down and gets into a long black car at the curb. I have to pull myself up short to keep from crashing into a little man in a black suit who's holding the door open for Woogie. Man's holding a sandwich. It's from Subway, I can tell by the wrapper. Car's a Mercedes, some kind of stretch limo about a half-block long.

As he gets in, Woogie turns back and flashes me a smile. Takes the sandwich.

I know who he looks like! Chauffeur shuts the door. Car's gleaming in the noontime sunshine.

I watch the Mercedes pull out into the Michigan Avenue traffic. I'm hearing Janis Joplin singing about God buying her a Mercedes Benz, while through the rear window, I'm watching Woogie pulling away in one, eating his egg salad from Subway, giving me a leer through the window, eyes twinkling devilishly, and his mouth twisted into a prankish grin so he looks like—*that's who he looks like! Woogie looks just like Jack Nicholson! Wonderful, God's wearing a diamond Rolex and riding around in a stretch Mercedes looking just like Jack Nicholson, acting like he's got more important things to do than listen to me, Dinny Rein, the person who's supposed to be his ad guy.*

I turn and walk back into the building. Past the brass plaque reading, "Boston, Frank, Pogue, and Gersenweser Advertising." It needs polishing. Chalky-green paste building up around the base of the letters, black outline on the granite almost worn away. The plaque on the wall leading to the elevators is going green also, needs Brasso badly.

I guess when Woogie's busy being God, you don't get your plaques polished.

I walk around my office for an hour picking up things and putting them down. Got the heebie-jeebies bad. Evelyn leaves me alone. I give Patti Shaw a call. "She's gone to class," Louie tells me.

Everyone in the office sticks their heads into my office as they head out the door, everyone tells me how great my ads are, and that they can't wait to see them on TV tonight. I say "Thanks" eighty-five times, then put in a call to Izzy.

"Why don't you come over and watch your ads break?" he says. I tell him I have problems.

Izzy clears his throat and says, "Come on, Rein, don't we all?"

We've roadblocked the evening news on all three networks and Fox, CNN, and The Weather Channel, so no one can miss the campaign, the whole world will be seeing my ads. Izzy zaps back and forth between channels on his big screen TV. We see Comedians on ABC and the flagship on CNN. We see Nature and Baseball. They look better on TV than they did at the agency.

For an hour, we watch the advertising. Then Izzy turns off the TV and asks me what's wrong. I ask him if he's got a couple hours. He says sure. So I tell him the entire story. From the cell phone call at the Marriott to the stretch Mercedes I saw Woogie getting into this afternoon. He sits with his arms resting on his knees, listening patiently. It takes over an hour. He gets up slowly and takes a long look at me. I can't tell whether he wants to hug me because he thinks I'm daft or hit me because he thinks I'm lying. Then he leaves the room and comes back with a Budweiser. *Guess I've driven him to drink again.*

"Okay," he says as he glugs down half the can. "Let's see if I got this straight. God wants you to do advertising for him because His market share is off."

"That's what he came down here for, yes."

"And Woogie What-Ever-His-Name-Is is God's stand-in."

"Right," I say. Izzy shakes his head and finishes his Budweiser.

"Okay, and now you say Woogie's looking like Jack Nicholson, wears diamond Rolexes, and fancy suits from Polo." Izzy ticks off the points with his fingers.

"And he's riding around in a stretch Mercedes."

"And that's what's got you worried."

"There's something wrong. I can feel everything unraveling. Woogie's staring at Ester's legs. He's avoiding me. He's wearing the same suits as Sinkle. Things just don't feel right."

"And the other night you got mugged, and you're wondering if it has anything to do with your ripping off fifty million from some big guy at O'Hare?"

"Not to mention the ten million I got earlier from God."

Izzy points at me with his finger. "Right, the ten million you got earlier from God."

"Plus I feel like I'm being followed all the time. There's some guy who wears a Bears hat, looks like he used to be a prizefighter..."

Izzy's nodding, striding around the editing suite. He chucks his beer can into the trash and walks out of his office again. He comes back with a six-pack. Hands me two cans.

"God gave you the suits and shoes and the Range Rover too, huh?"

"Right, and the new body and a new body for Patti Shaw, too."

"Yes, and the new body for Patti Shaw."

Izzy polishes off his Bud and cracks another. He stands up and arcs the empty can into the trash,

"And you've seen a shrink about all this. You're sure you're not..." Izzy circles his finger around his temple. "You know?"

"I told you, I go see my shrink, and he ends up hogging the whole session talking baseball with God." The beer tastes good. I slosh the suds around in the bottom of the can.

"God plays ball?"

I nod and open another beer. "He plays with Ruth and Mantle all the time."

"And he comes down to earth and funds a multimillion-dollar advertising campaign. You do the ads, they're going to be a big hit. So everything's okay up to today, right?"

"You got it."

"But now you think God's turning on you because He's agreed with Sinkle to Durnberg the advertising."

"And he's wearing Polo and riding around in a stretch Mercedes. Plus he won't talk to me."

Izzy lets his head hang down between his knees, shakes it slowly, looks up at me wags his head back and forth again, and says, "I tell you, pal, this advertising really is one crazy business."

28

Izzy and I drank beer until two in the morning, I think it was two. I can't remember what we decided I should do. All I know is that I have a tremendous headache when I wake up and my clock radio reads 9:15. I reach for the phone, call Evelyn. She asks if I'm sick. *The lady knows me better than my own mother.* Then she tells me to turn on *The Today Show* quick. I feel around for the clicker. *Where is that damn thing? Here it is.*

Holy shit! I sit up in bed. *They've got my advertising running on The Today Show.* They're doing a whole feature on it. On the reclusive Chicago philanthropist who made a fortune in the market and who lives in the basement of a Michigan Avenue building...*Look, there's a shot of Woogie coming out of the building and getting into his Mercedes! There's a shot of the plaque on the front of the building. Boston, Frank, Pogue, and Gersenweser Advertising. There's a picture of me! Dinny Rein! Me, on TV!* And Matt Lauer is saying how critics are raving about the advertising, and Katie What's-Her-Name (the pixieish lady with the short hair who on some days looks like Tinkerbell) is interviewing some lady on the street who's saying, "I think it's the most wonderful thing..."

And I'm standing up on my bed in my underpants punching the air and cheering her on as the lady says, "Finally, there's something inspiring on TV, something that just makes you feel thankful to be alive!"

"Take that, Sinkle," I'm yelling and bouncing up and down on the bed. Katie What's-Her-*Name (Couric, yes, that's her name)*, Katie Couric interviews another person and asks, "The aim of this advertising is supposed to be to get people to go to church. Do you think after seeing this advertising that you'll be going to church more often?" The woman pauses, nods, says, "Oh, yes, definitely. It made me aware of how much we have to be thankful for."

"Yes!" I yell. "Did you hear that, Woogie? Did you hear that, God? The woman's aware of how much she has to be thankful for! I'm right, I was right all the time! So take your Durnberg results, take Ester's campaign, take all the Happy Meals and free air miles, take all that and stuff it, okay? Because my advertising is working! It's working, damn it all. It's working just the way I said it would. I told you! I told you it would!"

I gobble three aspirins, take a shower fast, put on my best Perry Ellis, and I'm out the door heading for the lot where I park my car. Then I remember, car's down at the dealer getting the window fixed. So I decide to walk, start down the street, and what do I do?

I walk straight into springtime in Chicago. I feel new air, suddenly warm on my face, soft and gentle with a touch of moisture in it. I stop, look up and see the leaves starting to unfurl on the trees, hear birds chirping. Winter hits Chicago swiftly and suddenly like an all-out howitzer attack, but spring sneaks up on the city so stealthily you hardly notice its arrival.

I look around, see the girls walking up and down Michigan in brightly-colored cotton skirts, sleeveless blouses, bare midriffs, see college kids playing Frisbee on the sidewalk in front of Brookstone's, daffodils poking up out of the planters at Saks, and the crisp blue sky up above crowned with towers of nimbocumuli.

The sun is shining on my side of the street. Now I've got kind of a jaunty little walk going with the *Zippidy Doo Dah* song going through my head, my new shoes with the spongy rubber soles springing off the sidewalk as I enjoy the first day of spring and my new found notoriety.

My ads are on the front page of the paper, passing newspaper boxes I see the story all over the *Tribune* and the *Sun-Times*. I stop and buy a paper. One night on TV and the advertising's a national sensation. Everyone's picked up the story of the reclusive building super who's spending a hundred million dollars encouraging people to appreciate life and go to church.

Ads for God

The article in the *Tribune* is headlined, "Super-Billionaire Encourages People To Stop And Smell The Flowers With Campaign Of Expensive New Commercials." Woogie's picture is on the front, the story inside. The story of Woogie Strepijichowski, the Polish immigrant who made a fortune in the stock market through his connections to Warren Buffet. Thanks to my own clever little backstory.

We all should have clever little backstories like that, I'm thinking. *It would make life so much easier.*

My photo's at the top of Lazarus' story inside. George Lazarus, Chicago's ace advertising reporter, credits me with the advertising, talks about my ascendancy to the presidency of the agency. I'm noticing some of the people I pass smiling and nodding at me.

I'm feeling like the hometown hero, the ad guy who makes good.

It's getting warm, no more walking, I want to look crisp when I get to the office. I look around for a cab. There's a cab at the curb up ahead, sitting in a pool of sunlight. *What luck!* I walk up to it and open the door. Get in. Push a cardboard box across the seat and pull the door shut behind me. "550 North Michigan, please," I say to the cabby. No answer. The cab pulls out and heads down Michigan. I look down at the box, blue lettering reads "Sunbeam Automatic Toaster." Picking up the box, I hold it up to the partition so the driver can see it. "Someone left a toaster back here. Did you know that?" I ask.

Driver pays no attention. Instead, a head slowly rises from behind the front seat, like it's coming up out of the water. I see a blue-and-orange Bears cap first. *It's that guy from my office with the Bears cap and the box.* Big smile on his face, *it's Ralph, and that's his cardboard box!* Ralph jumps out at a light.

No thanks, I don't think I want any of this. I lift the door handle and open the door. *I'm getting out of here, I don't care if we're in the middle of traffic.* Ralph starts to get in my side, shoves me back into the seat. I push against him. He pulls something out of his coat, stubby Army-green plastic, holds it up against me. My body stiffens, I turn into a board, ears ring, I see bright lights, jaw's locked, I can't think. Brain's blinking back and forth between pitch black and a blinding bright light.

Wake up and I don't know where I am or what happened. Look around. I'm in the same cab, the guy with the Bears cap sitting next to me, he's got a green plastic thing in his hand, like a fat handle to something. Two points with a wire between them.

Maybe it's some kind of stun gun. What did he do, zap me with it? I feel woozy. Then I feel myself sliding across the seat. The cab's almost up on two wheels, the driver's a maniac, taking a corner at thirty-five, weaving in and out between cars as he speeds up the street.

Ralph turns to me, big smiling face, staring at me, switches the stun gun to his left hand and holds out his right to me. "Ralph, remember?" I shake his hand. He holds up the stun gun, looks at it like it's a rare treasure, turns to me and says, "Stun gun, one-hundred twenty-thousand volts." He waves it in front of me. "I hold it on your chest and I turn your heart to Jell-O." He does that high horse-whinny laugh that shows too many dark teeth.

Jesus, put a red suit and a long tail on this guy, and he could easily audition for the Devil. A car swerves into our lane just ahead of us. The cabby gives the car a long blast of his horn, then screams out the window, "Fuck your mother!"

He guns the engine and now he's speeding up some street I don't recognize, spinning the steering wheel like he's driving bumper cars, honking and careening back and forth down the avenue. The driver takes a wide turn onto a side street, tires squealing, turns around to me, screws up his face into a grimace, and says, "I hate city driving."

These guys are nuts and they're kidnapping me.

Ralph gives the cardboard box a thump. "This's a toaster," he says, pointing at it. "Wife, she goes through a toaster every six months."

I nod, peering out the window, trying to figure out where the cab is heading. I don't recognize the neighborhood.

We're going west, maybe?

"You know something about toasters?" he asks, reaching into his pocket.

"Some," I say.

"Is Sunbeam a good brand? I mean, they all toast. What's there to it? Burning bread, know what I mean? But after the toasting, how's the reliability?" He's shaking out a bandana, Bulls bandana, red, white and black.

"I'd say Sunbeam's reliability is pretty good," I say, wondering what he's going to do with the bandana.

C'mon, God, c'mon Woogie, one of you please rescue me. What? Is your transponder on the fritz again? Where are you? Get me out of here, okay? He's either going to blow his nose or blindfold me. *Good, he's blowing his nose.* He explodes a rattling honker into the Bulls bandana that sends the tails flying out. Swipes at his nose. Sticks the bandana into his nostrils and scours, one by one. Shakes out the bandana again and turns to me.

"That's good, that's good. Cause I been buying Toastmasters, and they don't last, you know? Marie goes through two a year. Holds that bar thing down so it never gets to pop. And, as a matter of fact, if you're a toaster and you never get a chance to pop, your insides melt—that's what happens—your insides melt like butter and start to smoke, okay? So me? I hear screaming, come into the kitchen smelling something burning, and the toaster's sitting there on the counter smoking like Marie's set off a bomb. And she's standing there with her hands on her hips, looking at me like it's all my fault. So here I am with a new toaster, second one of the year, and it's not April yet."

The driver turns at Milwaukee. I watch the street sign whiz by. Ralph turns to me and motions, like he wants me to come closer.

"What?" I ask.

"Come here," he shakes out the bandana, grabs me by the hair and pulls me to him. Got a fat clump of my hair, scalp's burning.

"What are you doing?" Man is strong. I push against him. He's got me in a lock. He swings the bandana around my head, grabs the other end and pulls it tight. The lights go out.

"So it's good you say Sunbeam's got the reliability," he says, tightening the bandana, knotting it in the back. He adjusts the fabric around my eyes, snapping it down over my nose. "Maybe Marie'll get a year out of the Sunbeam. You can't see nothing, right?"

I nod. *I can't see nothing. He's right about that.* "You know, I think you guys have got the wrong person."

No answer. I can hear honking, like we're in a traffic jam then a screech of brakes and I hear the driver scream, "Your ass!"

I try another tack. "What would you want with me?" I say. "I'm in advertising."

"That's why I asked you about reliability." I hear Ralph say. Then his voice gets edgy, he says, "What you think I am, stupid?" I feel something hard against my leg and *zap!* he stings me again with the stun gun and my muscles lock and my brain blinks on and off and now my hand's banging against the door, *whap! whap! whap!* like it's gone spastic on me. I'm struggling to stay conscious, blinking and shaking my head. I feel wet on my lip. Reach up and touch it. Warm—I taste blood. I must have bitten my tongue. I hold my sleeve up against the tip of my tongue.

Jesus, what are they going to do with me?

"Look, my name's Dinsmore Rein," I say. "I live in Wrigleyville."

I feel Ralph groping for my hand. He takes it and shakes it. "Ralph Krimski," he says. "Nice to meet you again. And up front driving, you got Vinnie. Right Vinnie?"

"Nice to meet you," I hear from the driver's seat.

These guys are psychotics. What are they going to do? Take me to a vacant lot and beat me silly with something, zap me with the stun gun until my heart turns to aspic?

"Can you please tell me where we're going?"

No answer. I can smell rubber. There's a tire factory west on North Avenue somewhere. *Maybe that's where we are. I can't see a thing. He's got the blindfold on so tight it's cutting into the skin around my eyes. My body aches all over. Tongue's still bleeding, I can feel the wet on my suit sleeve.*

We go for five, maybe ten minutes without talking. *I can't tell, I can't see anything. All I can hear is traffic and the whining of the cab's motor.* Then Ralph, *I think it's Ralph*, says, "Marie lost a baby last year."

"Ralphie, the guy doesn't want to hear about your personal life, okay?" I hear from the front seat.

"Went six months, got that far, she got to six months. Then she lost it, lost it just like that." I hear him click his fingers.

Ads for God

I nod, hardly feeling any sympathy for someone who's been zapping me with his personal-sized cattle prod.

"Lost it," I can hear Ralph clicking his tongue. "Sometimes I wonder about that Marie—can't keep a kid or a toaster."

"Ralphie, talk about baseball or something, will you?"

How did I end up in a car with two goons like this, and where are they taking me?

"You like peppers?" the guy up front asks.

"I want you to drop me off back at the agency, or just let me out anywhere."

I wonder whether Ralph's going to hit me with the stun gun again.

"We got Diane making peppers, that's the reason I ask. All colors, red, green, yellow. You like 'em hot though?"

"I don't need lunch. I want you to let me out, okay?"

No answer. Where are we going?

The radio clicks on, Richie Valens singing, *La Bamba*, loud, then the Platters, twenty minutes of oldies. The Four Tops, The Shirelles, Freddie and the Dreamers, whoever it was that sang that song about the party lights, *Patsy Cline, maybe?*

I hear the tires whirring along the roadway, screeching once in a while as the cab wheels around a corner.

We're going fast—must be in Elmhurst by now. C'mon God, c'mon Woogie, come on you guys, come and save me from these maniacs. You made me look thirty-five again, helped me get Sinkle and Ester on the run and got us sixty million bucks, now get me out of here fast, c'mon, work your magic and do an Abe Moskowitz on me. Get me out of here right this minute.

I can feel us turning off onto a bumpy road. Hear gravel skittering out from beneath the tires. Pull to a stop, door opens, hand goes under my armpit, pulls me out. I can feel Ralph and Vinnie on either side of me.

I can't see shit. I'm stumbling around like a blind man. I tilt my head back, see if I can see out of the bottom of my blindfold. *Yes!* I can see brown grass covered with patches of ice, small concrete statue of a deer. Still has Christmas lights wound around its antlers. They're holding me up so I don't stumble, up stone stairs. Someone's holding a door open for us, I can hear the hinges squeaking. My feet feel carpeting.

People start to speak in Italian, or maybe its Albanian or Yugoslavian, Greek even. Guide me into a room, everybody's talking at once, sounds like the lobby of the UN Building. I feel a hand on my neck. Someone bends me down hard, doubling me over. I'm stumbling. My legs start to cramp. I have to hold my arms out to keep my balance. I hear rattling. They turn me around and fold me back onto something low, stool or shelf. Door shuts, metal rattling again.

Where in the shit am I? I tilt my head back to peek out of the blindfold, hit my head. *Ouch!* I reach out, feel metal squares, cool and slippery. *Am I in some kind of a cage or something? Dog cage maybe.* Stomp my feet. Metal rings out a racket.

Somebody screams out something that sounds like "Megotzaphaa!" and pounds my cage so hard I duck reflexively, like they whomped the top with a baseball bat or something. Cage is still ringing.

Maybe I won't stomp my feet again. C'mon, Woogie, c'mon God, get that transponder fixed and come spring me from this place.

I hear sizzling, smell food, hear talking, plates clattering, the place sounds like a busy diner during the lunch rush. Door to my cage rattles, opens, I feel something pressed into my hands. Feels round like a plate, it's warm.

"Eat, it's peppers," woman's voice says. I run my hand around the outside of the plate, find a fork, or maybe it's a spoon. Pick it up, start to push the peppers around the plate.

It's a bitch eating when you're blindfolded. Get something into my mouth, crunchy, taste oil and garlic, *wow, jeez, that's hot!*

Hear my cage open again. Hands moving around my head. Blindfold's coming off, woman quickly backs out of my cage carrying the bandana that was wrapped around my head. She's in her fifties, portly-stout, flowered dress and lots of gold teeth. She locks the door, steps back fast like she's afraid I might bite her.

I look around. Big room, living room in a suburban tract house, no furniture except for a long table filled with people eating peppers, salad, drinking wine. Fifteen or more, mostly men, couple women. They look Ukrainian or Greek, have that Eastern European-look, dark, burly. But I can't tell for sure. See Ralph and the cab driver. I'm scrunched down, back bent, sitting on a small, three-legged stool, a baseball bat leaning against the outside wall of my cage. The cage is less than four feet tall, short and narrow.

"Yo! Advertising man, you like the peppers?" a thick-faced guy with fuzzy hair sitting at the head of the table calls to me. He's turned around in his chair, looking into my cage.

"Very good. But can you tell me why I'm here?"

The man at the head of the table starts to laugh. He must be the ringleader, or the head guy, because everyone else starts to laugh along with him. The ringleader gets up from the table and comes over to my cage carrying his napkin, still chuckling.

"See, we're dealers. Art dealers," he says, crouching down next to my cage. "Paintings, etchings, sculpture, that kind of thing." I look around the room. Paintings hung on the walls. Black velvet, sofa-sized kind. Beach scenes and sunsets, mountain ranges.

Art dealers—I bet, I'm thinking. "And we get paid good. Been working a long, long time, the family has. We make good money. So that's where you come in. You like more peppers?"

"No thanks, I'd like to know where I come in."

He stands up, hitches himself in the crotch, shakes out a leg, "Ah, see, we lost some money. Big money. Ten million dollars, and we trace it to you. Got your name on a piece of paper, Dinsmore Rein, no?"

I knew it, I knew it all along, God didn't snag the ten million out of the air, He stole it and pinned it on me!

He turns and calls over his shoulder, "Where's the paper, Krimski?" Ralph, the toaster guy, gets up from the table and hands the ringleader a piece of paper. He unfolds it and holds it up to my cage.

It's the same sheet of paper Sophie showed me. Jesus Christ, He steals the money and I get screwed for it. What kind of lousy damn deal is this?

"Let me explain," I say, looking up at him through the metal cage. *I need to do some fast talking here.*

"You got our money."

"No, it wasn't me. Someone else took it."

"And who's that going to be?" He's got his head tilted to the side, friendly smile. Looks like the actor with the fuzzy hair who used to be in the Tostitos commercials—Avery Schreiber maybe?

"You're not going to believe this."

"Try me, okay?" He reaches for the baseball bat.

"God."

He screams that word again and beats on the top of my cage with the baseball bat.

Oh boy, that didn't work too well. I duck so fast I fall off my stool. He's bashing in the top of the cage with the bat, leaving deep dents in it. *Whang! Whang! Whang!* My ears are ringing. I'm looking up seeing the bat crash into the top. *Whang!* Four, five, six hits. Then he stops, tosses the bat across the room, it goes rattling across the floor. "Vinnie," he shouts. "Gimme the hand thing."

C'mon, I've had enough of these lunatics, whoever they are. Will you come and get me out of here, please God or Woogie or whoever You are—right now! It's your damn problem. You stole their money. I didn't have anything to do with it.

I crawl back up and sit on the stool. Feel my cell phone sticking into my stomach.

Maybe I could call 911. But everyone's watching me, I'm their dinner show. Pull the phone out, and they'd be after me in a second with that baseball bat. People are still eating peppers, passing the platters around, having a grand old time eating and drinking wine. Watch as Vinnie the cab driver comes around the table carrying something. I see one of the women at the table cover her eyes.

What is it? What are they going to do to me?

Hands it to the guy with the fuzzy hair. Some kind of homemade metal contraption shaped like a hand, or half a hand, like a steel golf glove except it's got thumb screws all around the outside and a wide lip where the wrist would be. Opens a small door in the front of the cage, he's attaching it to the outside of the cage, clamping the lip to the cage so it's like half a hand extending out from the side of the cage.

Ads for God

C'mon, God, get me out of here, please. I just want to go back and make some ads, c'mon God!

The fuzzy-haired guy is on his knees now working with the contraption, undoing the thumb screws so the metal hand opens in two parts, a top and a bottom.

"You putting your hand into here," he says to me. I look at him and shake my head.

It's some kind of torture device. They're going to do something to my hand.

"No, please, I don't want to. Honest, I told you God stole the money from you. Come on, I'm only an ad guy."

Fuzzy-hair is shaking his head. "Vinnie, I need some help here," he calls.

What's Vinnie carrying? Oh shit, it's an electrical cord. He's got an extension cord, wires are bare at the ends, crouches down by my cage and carefully twists each end of the wire around the metal bars.

They're going to fry me in here, fricassee me to a tee. Stands and walks backward with the cord playing through his hand. I crouch down and lift my feet up off the floor of the cage.

I'll have to hold this position or I'll get fried, my back broiled and my feet sautéed. I look at fuzzy-hair. Back at Vinnie. *I couldn't hold my feet up like this for more than two minutes.* Vinnie stoops down and holds the plug of the cord up to an electrical outlet.

They wouldn't dare do this to me. I see the woman who was shielding her eyes get up from the table quickly. She's shaking her head. She runs out of the room like she doesn't want to see what's going to happen.

"Those bugs in the summer, get cooked on the wire things?" Fuzzy Hair yells at me. "Go ssst! ssst! ssst? Know them? So you want to be cooked like a bug, ssst! ssst! ssst? Or you want to put your hand in here?"

He looks up at Vinnie. "Plug in, Vinnie, go ahead." The woman who gave me the plate of peppers wails, jumps up and hustles out of the room. The other women are staring down at their plates, won't look up at me.

These guys are serious.

"I'll put my hand in," I say, quickly stuffing my hand into the metal glove.

C'mon, God, come on, don't let him do this to me. He's tightening up the thumbscrews, quickly, going from one to the other so my hand is locked in, tips of my fingers sticking out the ends.

What are they going to do to me? Crush my hand with the bat? Cut my fingers off one by one?

"Can I finish my peppers, Ivan?" Vinnie asks.

Ivan, Krimski, who are these guys? Russian gangsters, Greek smugglers maybe?

"Sure, finish your peppers. I finished my peppers. You finish your peppers," Ivan says. Vinnie drops the electrical cord on the floor and goes back to the table.

"Okay, now here we go," Ivan says, reaching around behind his back. "Now you be telling Ivan how we get our money back." He reaches behind his back, shows me a pair of electrician's pliers, chrome with bright red plastic handles, opens them, slides the jaws around the nail of my index finger and clamps down. I can feel the pliers pulling my nail up, the soft flesh stinging, "One by one, we pulling out from the fingers. Very hurting, I tell you. Nobody goes through more than three, hurt too good, okay? So you say where is money before I pulling."

What am I supposed to tell him? That God's got the money, and He's going to be using it to do an advertising campaign? He works the pliers closer to get a better bite, pushing the skin back from my nail. I can feel the tug of the teeth.

"Look, God's got your money, and He's using it to fund an advertising campaign we're doing at my agency—He's got a proxy named Woogie. He's the building super but he's really God. You have to believe me. I've got an in with Him—I'll help you get the money back. All you need to do is talk to Woogie—I promise."

Ivan shakes his head and spits on the floor, puts both hands around the pliers, bears down on the handles, hunches up his shoulders and gets ready to pull. I close my eyes and get ready to scream. Everybody at the table has stopped eating. They've turned to look at me. The women have their hands over their eyes. One of them starts to sob. "Somebody stop him," I yell.

Ads for God

Why did this have to happen to me? I was just an over-the-hill ad guy trying to hold my life together. Now I'm locked in a cage about to have my fingernails ripped out. I'm waiting for the pain. I imagine it will be hot and searing, flaming up my arm and burning throughout my body.

Then I hear a low groan, deep, heavy moan, and a loud thump and open my eyes to see Ivan lying beside my cage on his side, his mouth open, eyes wide and glazing over. Screams from the people at the table, the women rushing up to Ivan, throwing themselves on him. Eyes look like the ones you see on flounder lying on ice in the freezer case, going glassy fast, his skin is white. Ivan needs 911 quick. The women are crying and pounding on him. If he isn't dead already, they'll do him in with their fists.

I hear someone at the table shouting, "Fucking peppers killed Ivan, fucking peppers!"

Pandemonium goes on around me like this for five minutes, the women wailing in Greek or whatever, men lurching around over Ivan, pounding their fists on the table, screaming and whacking at my cage with the bat like I had something to do with what happened.

Ivan's skin's starting to go gray fast, funny stuff foaming out of the corner of his mouth, pink and frothy. The men are pushing and shoving at each other, yelling in Russian or some Slavic language.

Ivan's paying no attention. He's lying ten inches away from the front of my cage. The phrase "stone-cold dead" comes to mind.

Ralph, my friend from the cab, seems to be the new Ivan. He stalks over, the others behind him, stands over Ivan, and shouts. His buddies take Ivan by the feet and drag him away. I watch his head thump across the floor, jumping as it hits a sill, his eyes still open, the left one open wide and locked on me.

Ralph picks up the pliers and crouches down. He looks pissed. He thumps himself on the side of the head like he's got water in his ears, says something in Greek, snaps the pliers open and shut.

Oh no, it's pliers time again. Here it comes again. They're going to get me good now. I try to pull my hand out of the clamp, squirm it back and forth trying to loosen it, but it's stuck hard, tightly held in the steel glove. Ralph works the nose of the pliers around the end of my nail.

Just as he starts to squeeze the pliers together, he stops. I'm figuring he's summoning up his strength to pull my nail out in one fell swoop, but instead he gasps for air, clutches at his chest with both hands, and tumbles backward. I see Ralph's eyes fixing on me, going wide as saucers like he's just seen the devil. Then he topples back and crashes to the floor, twitching mightily, his feet kicking out at my cage, *slam! slam!*

Jeez, maybe I'm getting some Divine Intervention here, finally! The women are screaming bloody-murder. The place is up for grabs, everyone rushing around shouting and yelling.

Then He goes into action, my friend from upstairs, doing a Universal Studios number on the house, bringing special effects to the suburbs, shaking the house like the whole place is on springs, *bangity, bangity, bangity, bang, bang!*

Rocking it back and forth and up and down on its foundation, sending plates flying and furniture crashing down. It's a scene right out of an earthquake movie. Somehow he gets a wind whipping though the place as if someone opened the door during a hurricane. It blows the art off the walls, and there's yellow, red and green pieces of peppers whirling around and napkins and tablecloths and forks and spoons all banging and whomping up and down in the air making a helluva racket. I watch as the place empties out in a flash, people piling through the doors, yelling in Russian or Greek, ducking glassware and peppers, flying spoons and black-velvet paintings, people pushing each other out of the way in a mad scramble to get outside, looking back over their shoulders in horror at the guy in the suit bent-over and locked inside the steel dog cage, the guy who's killed off two of their men and set the house to shaking off the Richter scale.

Me, Dinsmore P. Rein, ad guy for God.

Of course, you can imagine what happens now that the Holy Ghost is on the scene, he gets even more show-offy, trying to impress me by doing Hollywood stuff like spinning the thumbscrews on my metal glove so they drop right out and popping the door and the top off my cage.

It's the damn least He can do. I'm feeling really pissed off as I climb out and stretch and shake out my hands, pick a piece of red pepper off my shoulder.

Then I whip out my cell phone, wrench up the antenna, look up at the ceiling, point my finger, and shout at the top of my lungs, "I quit! I fucking quit—okay God? You hear that? I resign the account."

No answer. "Take this job and shove it. Do you hear me? I'm sick of this!"

No answer. I hear knocking, tapping, metal on glass. Look up.

It's Woogie outside the window holding up some kind of contraption and smiling at me. He's pointing at the machine, grinning.

"What are you doing out there?" I'm yelling through the window. "Get your ass in here. I quit!" He gives me a cute little wave and walks away from the window.

This is out of control. I can't have some building super with some gismo from Star-Trek ruining my life like this.

"Sorry for being late," he says, walking in the front door holding his contraption. "Is transponder not working so good." Woogie whacks at the machine he's holding with the heel of his hand. He slams it again. The machine buzzes and beeps, a yellow light starts to blink. It's the size of a loaf of bread, looks like Army surplus, camo green but with so many buttons, dials and lights it looks bogus, right out of some sci-fi show on TV.

"Is on fritz, ja? You having screwdriver?" Woogie starts opening drawers.

"To hell with you and your rinky-dink machine, I quit!" I hear noise from outside, push back the curtain and peek out the window. See the Greeks or Russians or whoever they are piling into the cars and trucks parked in the driveway. One of the cars backs up onto the street with its doors swinging open, people trying to scramble in, frantic pushing and shoving, Keystone Cops in the suburbs.

Woogie comes up behind me, looks out the window. "Is scared good, ja? Never coming back for bothering Dinny. How you like wind from machine, is good, ja? Liking way machine giving heart attacks? Is good, ja?" He's adjusting the transponder with a butter knife he picked up off the floor, turning screws, tightening wires.

What a bizarre looking contraption.

"Nothing about this was good! Nothing! First I get kidnapped, then they put me in a cage, whack it with a baseball bat, then they almost pull my damn fingernails out." The last car screeches out of the driveway, veering from one side of the road to the other, doing a mad weave down the street.

"But no do, ja? Because at last second, transponder come off fritz, work fine, ja?" Woogie appreciatively pats the machine.

"Look, I appreciate it, don't get me wrong. But you cut it a little close, okay?" I hear a buzz from the transponder, a long, steady drone increasing in intensity.

Woogie says "Shitski!" and frantically fiddles with the thing. He's got it perched on his knee, spinning buttons and twirling dials. The drone turns into a rattling buzz that jangles the window panes and makes me hold my hands over my ears. Woogie's pounding at the side of the machine with his hand. Lights are flashing, the thing's making all sorts of grating and gnashing sounds like something's really screwed up inside. Then it lets out a wailing siren that quickly fades and blue smoke streams out of the sides like it's given up the ghost.

Woogie stalks over to the table and slams it down. "Shitski, is busted for good now." The machine whirrs, thrashes around on the table a couple times, lets out a final puff of blue smoke, and goes silent.

"Okay, that's it," I say. *I've had enough of this hocus-pocus. Rube Goldberg machines and getting kidnapped.* "Get the big guy back, Woogie. I want to talk to him. I want to talk to God!"

Woogie turns to me, hands held out and turned up in the air. "But Woogie being God, ja?"

"Not the God who hired me in the first place. I want to talk to the guy with the big baritone, the guy who talked me into all this. I've had enough of this crazy bullshit. You tell him that Dinny Rein wants to talk to him—now!"

Woogie's looking down at the floor, "But Woogie doing good, ja? Getting fifty million, buying advertisings, doing good scheming with Dinny Rein, ja?" Woogie picks up the transponder, holds it up. "I get machine fix quick. Is needing new motherboard is all, ja? One week at shop and is all fix." He gives me a shrug, a hopeful little smile.

I'm shaking my head, thinking. *How did I end up out in the middle of the sticks with the Polish building super and a busted miracle machine?* I pick a painting up off the floor. Black velvet painting of a naked girl sitting on a rock in the jungle with baby deer grouped around, the White Rock Girl on location in Borneo. I turn the painting over. Baggies of white powder taped to the backside. *Okay, that's it, I've had it!*

"Look at this, Woogie. Art dealers, my ass," I say, chucking the painting back on the floor. "These are damn drug dealers. You stole drug money. You lied to me, Woogie, got me mugged, kidnapped, almost tortured."

He doesn't answer. He's staring down at the floor, sheepishly shaking his head.

"Get me God this very minute, Woogie!" I yell at him. "I've had it!"

Woogie won't look up at me, says, "Suiting yourself," and slowly swings around, pulls his transponder off the table, turns, and shambles out the open door. I watch him, stepping out the doorway, going down the stairs, head down, and walking like a funeral dirge is playing.

Jeez, now what have I done? Told my biggest client to go get fucked, that's what. Maybe that wasn't so smart. I run to the door, look outside. *At least I can apologize. I mean, what if God doesn't show up? What if He doesn't call? Then where would I be?*

I look to the left and to the right. The cab we came out in is parked on the grass. No sign of Woogie. I sit down on the steps. Look out at the landscape. Bunch of stubby houses built too tall for the flat farmland. Sore thumbs sticking up out of the prairie. Get up and walk around the back of the house. No Woogie Strepijichowski. The grass around the house shoots up in clumps, like someone gave it a bad haircut.

I take out my cell phone, stare at it. *Come on, God, give me a ring. Maybe I should head back into town, what ever way that is.* I check the cab, keys are still in the ignition, toaster on the backseat, *I'll buzz back into the office and see if I can find Woogie, give him a piece of my mind.*

231

Then my cell phone rings. *Okay! Maybe it's the big guy!* Pull up the antenna and lean against the cab. *It better be Him.* "Hello?" I say.

"I'm sorry, Rein."

"Sorry's not good enough—I almost got my fingernails ripped out."

"You didn't have to treat Woogie like that. He's trying to do the best he can."

"Woogie—What about me? I get followed, I get mugged, I get kidnapped, almost tortured—and what? You expect me to walk around singing a lullabye? C'mon!"

I walk back into the house. *I'm thirsty.* Walk over to the dining table. "I've had it with all this craziness!" There's a plastic bottle of water on the table. I look around for a glass. Pick one up off the floor. Pour myself a glass of water, squeezing the phone between my neck and shoulder.

"Look, I'm only human," I hear Him say.

God sounds like an old man, His voice is scratchy and reedy. He's losing the booming Tony Bennett baritone.

"You're what?"

"I slipped up. I should have destroyed the deposit slip in the first place. Then they couldn't have gotten to you. But we kept them away from you a bunch of times, remember the parking lot? There were other times, too. We're trying to do the best we can for you down there. But I don't have the resources I used to. Frankly, I'm a little short-handed…"

He sounds so apologetic—He should be after what He put me through!

"I don't care about your problems up there—you shouldn't have stolen the damn money in the first place! What about the Ten Commandments. What about 'Thou shalt not steal'? What about that?" A plate of peppers is overturned on the table, I turn it over, taste a yellow pepper.

"Everything's relative."

"Oh c'mon, not you, too?" Peppers are good, I take another.

"Things have changed. I tell you, things aren't the same."

"But you're supposed to be God. You're supposed to be perfect."

No answer, silence. Finally, He says, "I was. I mean, I used to be. It's a long story." He sighs.

"I got time," I say, picking at the platter of peppers. "C'mon, out with it."

"You got to promise not to tell anyone. I don't want any of this getting out. It wouldn't look good. Could wreck my reputation."

"I promise."

He sighs again and says, "Where do I start?"

"How about the beginning?"

"That's as good as any. Okay, so Man was created in the image of God, right?"

"Right."

"Well, here's the big news. It goes both ways."

"What do you mean, 'goes both ways'?"

"The image of man reflects back—what you do reflects back on us. It's the bounce-back effect. What you do boomerangs back at us big-time."

"I don't get it."

"We didn't either, but it stands to reason, doesn't it? Especially that capitalism stuff. We'd seen all the rest, wars and inquisitions, pogroms and crusades—all that was old hat. We expected that from you guys. But we'd never seen the likes of capitalism. Especially in the last fifty years. That damn invisible hand was what did it. Beckoning to us, inviting us to take a look.

"We look down and see you guys amassing capital, buying businesses, building factories, making money, wearing big fur coats and driving sleek cars, drinking champagne and doing the Charleston, constructing the Empire State Building and inventing television. Then you start going into space and getting fancy, building Disney World and the Space Needle, and then we're seeing Hollywood movies and Las Vegas gambling, franchising, derivatives and Elvis Presley.

"We're seeing personal computers, Burger King and Wet 'n Wild, hearing Bing Crosby and Englebert Humperdinck, John Denver and Madonna. We're seeing you buy Puff-A-Lumps and Air

Jordans, eating Nacho Fast's, Krispy Kreme's and Chips Ahoy. Well, one long look was all it took and zingo!

"Before we knew it, that invisible hand is up our backs, manipulating us like a bunch of dummies, and, before we know it, we're all wearing Girbaud jeans and Gucci watches, drinking single malt scotches and staring at our laptop screens to make sure the other gods aren't stealing share from us. That damn capitalism snuck up and bit us all on the ass big time. Never even saw it coming."

"Capitalism?"

"Yeah, capitalism—individual initiative, individual ownership, the profit motive, market share, power, ego, money—the whole enchilada. It's like oobleck. Rein, you know what oobleck is?"

I shake my head, munch on another pepper, while He explains "It's in one of Dr. Seuss' books. It's slimy green gook that sticks to anything. Get it on one hand and try and pick it off with the other and the oobleck sticks to that one. Put your foot up to separate your hands, oobleck gets on your foot. Get the other foot in there, oobleck's on it too. Pretty soon, you're all oobleck. Oobleck's everywhere. Everything's ooblecked.

"That's what happened with capitalism, changed us from a bunch of nice old guys who used to sit around smoking stogies, strumming our lyres, and talking peace and love into a bunch of power-hungry scoundrels scrambling all over each for a bigger piece of the pie. Now we've got a corporate structure worse than General Motors, and it's sell, sell, sell from morning to night. Hell, we've even got brand managers."

"Brand managers in heaven?"

"You betcha, category managers even. Get this, 'managing religious equities' is their new buzzword. I must hear it five times a day. The place is crawling with the creeps. We got brand managers, consultants, agents, promoters, and meetings up the ass. That's why I was late. I was in another damn meeting. And now everybody's getting loosey-goosey with principles. Everything's done for the sake of expediency and the almighty buck—and the Ten Commandments?—they go right out the window."

"You're kidding."

"I wish I was. Heaven used to be one helluva fine place. Now it's a total rat race. And you know what they say about the rat race..."

"Even if you win, you're still a rat."

"You betcha. Lily Tomlin said that."

"I know. She's one funny lady."

"Funny lady, you betcha. I gave Tomlin her sense of humor, as a matter of fact."

"No kidding."

"You betcha, back in the good old days I used to do a lot of fun stuff like that. Robin Williams, I did him too. Kid didn't have a funny bone in his body until I got to him. I used to love doing that kind of stuff."

I nod, look around the place. Godawful mess, looks like a frat house after a big party. Broken glassware, overturned plates, busted black velvet paintings in sloppy piles. God's quiet, not saying anything.

I'm feeling kind of sorry for the old coot. He's facing the make-your-numbers gun like everyone else.

"So, I guess that's why you needed a killer ad campaign from me, huh? We've gone and made heaven just like earth, so you've got to advertise to keep your share otherwise the competition eats your lunch."

"You betcha. Not that anyone blames you. We all thought we were safe up there, then bingo! Now we're worse than a bunch of free agent football players. Greedy, venal, selfish, sneaking around stealing share from one another. And here I am down here getting my hands dirty, hustling ads, ripping off Russian drug smugglers to pay for the air time. When I should be sitting up on a cloud somewhere, thinking divine thoughts and watching the angels romp around. What a bummer!"

"So tell me, how's everyone liking the campaign up there?"

"That's the good news—everyone loves it. Everyone's falling all over each other trying to find their own Dinny Rein to do the same thing for them. Your ads are the talk of the town."

"So maybe you can get an advertising budget now. Stop funding your ads by snagging money from people, getting me kidnapped and mugged in parking lots?"

"You betcha, don't worry about that anymore."

"Otherwise, I'm out of here. Okay?"

"I hear you," He says.

"Good." I open the front door. There's a shoe sitting on the driveway. Cab I came out in is parked on the grass next to the concrete deer. Something green is tumbling around on the gravel. A wool scarf being tousled by the wind. "I'm heading back into town, but there's a few more things I need to talk to you about."

"Make it fast. I've got another meeting coming up."

I get in the cab, still on my cell phone. *I bet those smugglers are still hightailing it toward the horizon, wondering what the hell happened to them.*

I pull out of the driveway, head out of this subdivision. Endless rows of ticky-tackys plunked down on the prairie. *This must have been all farmland up until recently. Should have left it that way.*

"So I can trust this Woogie guy, he's okay?"

"He's Me on earth—what do you want? He's a little rough around the edges but he's the best I can do down there. Unless you want Lucinda."

"Lucinda?"

"The black lady on the bus."

"No thanks, what about Abe Moskowitz?"

"Abe's no longer with you."

"So what about all this stuff with Ester's campaign? Don't I have to worry about Sinkle pulling a fast one on me?"

"Let them play their games. Woogie'll watch out for you. He's my boy."

"What about his transponder? He said it will take a week to get it fixed. What if the Russians come around again?"

"It just came out of the shop, got the thing fixed in a jiffy, whole new motherboard. It's ready for anything. Can tell you President Clinton's temperature within a tenth of a degree, the exact dewpoint on the other side of the earth, even what kind of pasta the Pope's having for breakfast. The thing can see backward or forward four thousand years, ten thousand years if you want. Nothing will come near you."

"What about the people we lifted the fifty million from?"

"I said, nothing will come near you." *Now He's got the baritone back, sounds pissed.*

"You'll still be around if I need you?"

"You betcha, but we got meetings off site for the next ten days so Woogie's your man. He'll take good care of you—right now I got to run. See you later." My phone goes dead. Muzak starts playing. A voice says, "The person you were talking with has temporarily left the area..."

I head back into town on the expressway, Ralph's toaster bouncing around on the seat behind me.

I'm thinking about God and the mess He's got up there. I used to think God was God. Now I realize He's like any other client with people breathing down his neck, being pushed this way and that, always having to keep an eye on his competition, worrying about whether someone's stealing share from Him, trying to keep his agency on track, having to go to a million meetings—and I thought I had problems.

Cell phone rings. "Mr. Rein, are you all right?" *It's Evelyn,* I look at my Timex. It's 1:30. *She must have thought I'd been kidnapped or something.* "I've been trying to get you for the last four and a half hours—I've been worried sick about you."

She's been worried sick—she doesn't know from sick. "I'm fine, Evelyn. I had a few things to do and I guess I left my phone off."

"Your picture is in the paper, and everyone's talking about your advertising. Lorna even said that one of Oprah's people called. Everyone thinks your advertising is wonderful, Mr. Rein."

"That's very nice to hear, Evelyn."

Then Evelyn says, "I almost forgot, Mr. Rein, your daughter needs to talk to you. She says it's important."

"I'll call her."

"Right away, Mr. Rein, she's called three times."

For some reason, Addy won't talk to me on cellular, makes me find a pay phone. Pull into an Amoco on the expressway. Buy a Wing-Ding for lunch and dial her number at the bank. "What's up, Addy?" I ask her as I munch on my Wing-Ding.

"Are you sure no one's listening?"

"Maybe some crows. I'm outside a C-store in the cornfields somewhere."

Boy, it's flat out here. On a good day I bet you could see Mexico. Wing-Ding tastes good, haven't had anything except a few hot peppers.

"What are you doing out there?"

"It's a long story." *If only she knew.*

"Congratulations on your advertising. It's a big hit. Everyone's talking about it. It's all over the papers. Did you see your picture?" We talk about the campaign for a couple of minutes, then I ask her why she's been calling me.

"This will probably turn out to be nothing, but it's about this client of yours, Mr. Strepijichowski..."

Oh shit, here we go again...

"What about him, Addy?" I feel the sleeve of my suit. The fabric of my sleeve is hard where the blood dried on it. *So far, this has been a wild day—why shouldn't it get a little wilder?*

"Is he really on the up-and-up?"

"As far as I know, why?—*Sure, Rein, lie to your daughter. This is just wonderful. But what am I supposed to do? Tell her he's a stand-in for God and he's gone around ripping off the money from drug dealers to run the advertising?*

"It's just with his name all over the papers, some of the people here are starting to poke around and ask questions. People get curious when someone pops up with so much money like that. And what's so odd is there doesn't seem to be any financial history for him. There are no records of any trades he's made, any record of cash inflow or outflow. He's got a lot of money, that's for sure, but we can't figure out where it came from. It could easily be some kind of complicated trust arrangement, but before the FBI gets involved and it gets turned into a big witch hunt, I thought I'd ask you."

FBI, witch hunt—wonderful. That's just what I need. "As far as I know, it's all from investing in the market. He said he's close to Buffet, the big investor who's made billions buying and selling stock. That's all I know."

I should have thought of that. I've got to get to Woogie and get him to invent some records or something. He'll know what to do. Won't he?

"I'm sure if he's a client of yours, he's on the up-and-up. I bet we'll find something soon."

"I'm sure you will, dear," I say.

29

"Woogie!" I'm yelling as I take the basement stairs in twos. "Woogie, you there?"

"Jeez Louise," I say out loud as I see what he's done to the basement. Place has gone from a used furniture mart to Sofa City. Couches, divans, ottomans and sofa sleepers are crammed into the basement, end tables, coffee tables, lamps, and throw pillows all over the place. Some of the furniture is grouped in arrangements, much of it's hodge podge, fabrics and colors clashing, the sofas stuffed together, end tables piled on top of one another, as if he'd ordered twice as much furniture as the basement could hold, and the deliverymen had jammed it all in willy-nilly.

"Liking decorating?" I hear from the other side of the basement. It's Woogie, standing in his underwear grilling a hotdog over a Bunsen burner, muscle-T stretched down and tucked into black Jockeys, patches of curly gray hairs on his arms and chest, "Dinny staying for lunching?" he calls to me. "Having many kielbasa, ja." He's waving a package of hotdogs at me.

"No, thanks, I need to talk to you about something." He's wearing black thigh-highs, imitation leather sandals. Woogie's got a little belly, drooping pudge suspended above the elastic of his Jockeys. He's holding the kielbasa on the end of a fork. It's getting burnt to a crisp, popping and sizzling in the short blue flame.

Maybe I should say something about what happened out there, try to apologize.

"Look, I'm sorry about what I said about you out there in the suburbs…"

Ads for God

"Woogie try do best he can, ja? Machine go on fritz. Is hard doing all kind of tricks, ja?"

"I was pretty upset. I hope you don't take it personally."

"Is being okay, Dinny Rein. Is being okay." He doesn't look up at me, keeps turning the kielbasa in the flame.

I wonder if I've hurt the old guy's feelings?

"So advertisings doing good, ja?"

"Everybody loves it—but we've got some problems."

"What is problems?"

"With the money, Woogie. We need a paper trail fast."

"What is this trail of paper. Explaining to Woogie."

"Records, financial records, evidence of where the money came from. Oherwise they'll start thinking you stole it."

"Me no stealing, Dinny Rein do it." An impish grin wipes across his face.

I sure hope he's kidding. "What do you mean?"

Woogie whacks me on the back. "Just doing big joke on friend Dinny. Not for worrying. Woogie get bank to making many records for money. Be all fix in..." he checks his Rolex, "two hour, ja?"

"Can I ask how you're going to do that?"

Woogie throws his arm around me, pulls me to him, "Dinny, my friend, you being saved from gangsters, ja? Getting big money for advertisings and for you and for girlfriend Patti Shaw is new body, all very hard tricks for Woogie, ja? So why you being wondering if Woogie can get records from bank? Is piece of cake, ja?"

I sure hope so, otherwise we're going to have the FBI swarming all over this place.

"Is something Woogie must be telling Dinny Rein," Woogie says as he squirts French's over his kielbasa, drenching the dog with generous spurts of the yellow goo.

He looks so serious. What's he going to lay on me now? Woogie picks up the kielbasa in his fingers and maneuvers it into his mouth. "Is about testing campaign of Ester's in market to see if having upside, ja? Is good idea?" Woogie hikes at his crotch with one hand, leaves a smear of French's on his Jockeys.

"Wait a minute, you told me her campaign was dead." The French's is going all over the place. He's wiping it on his muscle-T. It's on his cheek, on his chin.

"Keeping open options, Dinny—is what saying, ja? Not for worrying. Everyone much liking advertisings of Dinny Rein."

"But going into a test market, there's no need to do that."

"Ja, for no money get good learnings, Sinkle say."

"Sinkle's behind this? He's been talking to you?" *Maybe I did piss Woogie off.*

"Is not for Dinny being worried. Is only talking testing in Peoria, ja? Little town down in sticks, ja? And advertising of Dinny Rein is running over all states, no?"

"And that's the way it's going to stay. We're not doing any test in Peoria."

"Better talking to Sinkle. He talking testing in Peoria, ja?"

"We'll see about that," I say, heading for the stairs.

"If getting hungry much later, coming back down for kielbasa, ja?" I hear Woogie saying as I open the door to the basement. "Maybe later, Woogie." *Right now I've got a little matter I have to get cleared up with Steve Sinkle.*

I duck my head down and head through the tunnel into Sinkle's office at a good clip. Burst in to find Plevis and Murray the CFO sitting around Sinkle's desk, reading glasses down their noses, spreadsheets draped over the desk like bedsheets. It's money counting time.

Counting all the damn money I've made for them.

"Out," I say to them, cocking my thumb back over my shoulder like I'm hitchhiking.

"We're having a meeting," Sinkle says, his expression inviting me out.

"You *were* having a meeting. We need to talk. Now you guys get out, go." Plevis and Murray scramble around the desk, gathering up the sheets of paper. I sit down on the window seat, turn, and look out at the lake while Murray and Plevis shuffle the spreadsheets together and jam them into folders. The lake is bright blue and sparkling, haze settled over the far shore.

"Call us, Steve, when you want to get together again," I hear Plevis saying as they leave.

I turn to Sinkle. He's swinging around in his chair.

"You were supposed to stay on the sidelines," I say, pointing at him. "Then I see you in the screening room selling Ester's campaign in front of all the marketing honchos in the Midwest, and now Woogie's telling me you're talking about doing a test market."

Sinkle nods. I walk past his desk, turn around, and face him. "I tell you, Steve, I'll walk with this account. I'll walk right out of here. Neither me or my client needs BFP&G Advertising any longer."

Sinkle doesn't smile. His voice goes quiet. "Look, Rein," he says. "We're talking about running one dinky market test, that's all. All these companies are scared shitless of taking their marketing campaigns into churches."

"They should be. It'll blow up right in their faces."

"That's why we're going to run a two-week test in Peoria, sixty or eighty thousand bucks. It's tiddlywinks. C'mon, Rein. One peep of protest out of Peoria, and say sayonara to Ester's promotion campaign. Your advertising is our mainline campaign. Everyone loves it, and everyone in the agency's one-hundred percent behind you."

Of course they're all behind me—holding a big gun to my back.

"Sure, even Ester?"

"Ester Platt works for us. She's a team player."

You bet, some player—some team!

"I think we owe it to the business and to your client to fully evaluate the promotion dimension. It's good business to take a look at it, in case we ever need a backup. But between you and me, I don't ever see it going anywhere."

Is he lying, waiting for the opportunity to sell Ester's advertising, undermine my position, get my campaign off the air, bring in fifteen new clients, and get total control of the agency again? Of course he is.

I lean over his desk, narrow my eyes, and lower my voice. "No way, Sinkle, you start that test in Peoria, and I'll pull the God account, you understand?"

Sinkle clasps his hands behind his head, leans back. Looks at me. *He's going back into the huddle, going to call a new play, end-around, no more up the middle. Here it comes...*

"I just got a topline from Panky on the research. Did you hear?"

Watch it Rein, he's suckering you into something.

"I'll get him up here. You can hear it for yourself." Sinkle jabs at his intercom. "Lorna, tell Durnberg that Dinny Rein and I want to see his toplines on the advertising. As soon as he can, please?"

Sinkle gets up from his desk and picks up a tennis racket. Metal, with a fat head. Walks past me into the center of his office, stops and turns, and takes a slow swing at an imaginary ball. "Your campaign even seems to be motivating. That's the thing that surprised me." Sinkle sets up in a stance, hunched over, racquet held across his chest, bouncing slightly on the balls of his feet. "I knew it would be high in the Like Factor. I never expected it would get people thinking about going to church." Sinkle stands and takes a long, slow swing. "But it seems to have the potential to pack them in." He looks over at me as he finishes his swing. "Just like you said, Dinny."

Is he setting me up? Or is he playing it straight. What's going on here? I'm sick of all this political crap, everybody hiding in the weeds.

Durnberg has to crouch to get through Sinkle's tunnel. He comes into Sinkle's office hunched over, like he's got a back problem. Stands up straight when he gets in. He's carrying a folder full of papers.

"Show Dinny what you've found." Sinkle throws an imaginary ball up in the air and reaches high for it, arching the racquet in a long, slow-motion serve. Durnberg sets the folder down on Sinkle's desk, opens it, and hands me a sheet of paper.

"As you can see, the toplines are terrific." I look over the scores.

These are some of the highest Durnbergs I've seen. Ester's advertising would never be able to beat this.

"Very high on the Like Factor, almost off the chart," Panky continues. "But I've never seen Intent To Change Behavior this high either, and the Recall numbers are strong. People are really remembering these ads." Panky's coming across the room with his hand outstretched. Sinkle's racing back into the corner, looking over his shoulder at some imaginary ball, his racquet at the ready.

"Congratulations, Dinny," Panky says, pumping my hand up and down. "From these numbers, I think you're about to make some advertising history."

Sinkle takes a slow, powerful swing. Then trots over with his racquet and throws his arm over my shoulder. Somehow I get the feeling that I'm his tennis opponent, and he just whipped me in straight sets.

But he's giving me an earnest expression and saying, "Good work, Rein. I had my reservations about this advertising but not after scores like this. Good going." Sinkle puts out his hand. I shake it.

Maybe he's shooting straight. No phony smiles, no flashing teeth, no black hole. Maybe I shouldn't be so damn paranoid. My ads are all over the tube, everybody's loving them, and with these Durnbergs, that test market in Peoria will be dead as a doornail.

30

I head back to my office feeling like I've scored a hat trick in the biggest game of the season, three goals against a team we weren't supposed to beat. Nobody's ever seen Durnberg scores like that, off the charts, totally unassailable.

Busted the First National Bank of Durnberg, I did. Sinkle's got no way to get to me now—as long as I keep Woogie on my side. That campaign of Ester's is going to be relegated to the sidelines forever. Wheeoo!

Evelyn gives me an odd look as I head into my office, like she had something for lunch she didn't like. "Two gentlemen are in your office, Mr. Rein," she says and shrugs like she couldn't do anything about it.

Two pasty-faced guys in gray suits, crew cuts, sideburns lifted to the tops of their ears, skin scrubbed so clean they look like they just got out of the spa after extensive exfoliation, are standing in my office at parade rest, legs spread, arms behind their backs. They look like Army CPA's but I quickly find out they're FBI as they simultaneously flip open leather cases and shine their badges at me, flicking them so the lights sparkle off the chrome.

"Mr. Rein, FBI, we'd like to ask you a few questions, if you don't mind," the skinnier one says. His ears stick out like Tommy Smothers'. They introduce themselves. Both of them abbreviate their first names. G. Frommer and L. Stephens.

I hope that's not what their mothers named them. They tell me what they're doing. *It's all government-speak, but it sounds like they could be on that task force of Addy's.* I offer them seats. *I sure hope Woogie's getting his numbers together.*

Ads for God

I guess I should be worried that two FBI guys are in my office quizzing me but all I can think of is how they keep their skin so white. The color of mushrooms comes to mind. Maybe the FBI mandates that agents apply a double coat of sunblock every day and must always stay in the shade. The skinny one, Agent Frommer, notices a display of Woof!Burger packages on the shelf behind my desk. "You do those ads for Woof!Burger?" he asks, pointing up at the packages.

"Sure do," I answer. *Everybody's a sucker for talking dogs, even pasty-faced FBI agents.*

"If you don't mind me asking, how'd you get that German shepherd to do the samba?" Frommer says.

"Trick photography, mostly, special effects."

He clicks his fingers together. "You know, that's what I've been telling my wife. She swears it's trained to do the samba, but I told her that's ridiculous. German shepherds can't dance. I know, I grew up with one."

He looks over at his partner. "I can't wait to tell Doris," he says. His partner nods. Agent Frommer looks very smug.

Time to get down to business. The other agent takes out a steno pad, says, "You have a client named Mr. Strepijichowski?"

"Yes, I do." He jots down something.

"What do you know about his financial history?"

C'mon, Woogie, get your numbers together. I check my Timex. *It's been at least two hours since I saw Woogie. I'll give him a few more minutes, and then we'll find out how well his transponder's working.*

"My client is a very modest person, almost to the point of being shy, I'd have to say. So other than what you've read in the papers, I honestly don't know much about that side of him."

The agents glance at each other.

I just flummoxed them. It's the ad guy in me. Able to explain anything with something. Reality la carte.

"Is there some reason you ask that question? I mean, do you suspect him of something?"

"Just routine questions, Mr. Rein. No reason in particular."

I look at my watch. "I'd start by talking to his bank, if I were you."

"We've been to his bank. That's one of the reasons we're here."

"Have you talked to them recently?"

"A few days ago."

"Give them a call now, Mr. Strepijichowski mentioned just this morning that he'd given the bank more leeway in discussing his financial situation. He understands now that he's in the spotlight, he has to operate a little differently."

Boy, are you good, Rein. You're almost ready to go to work in the White House. "So you might want to check..." I say as I hand my cell phone across the desk to G. Frommer. *If G. Frommer did something about his ears, it would help his career immensely.*

As Agent Frommer's talking to the bank, I reach back and haul down a package of Woof!Burger. Take a Magic Marker, write, "To Doris, Glad you liked my commercial, Regards, Dinny Rein."

Frommer hangs up, snaps my cell phone shut. "You've been very helpful, Mr. Rein. Apparently the bank now has all the information we need, and we won't have to bother you anymore." The agents leap to their feet like a drill sergeant just barked an order.

As I shake hands with Frommer, I hand him the box of Woof!Burgers. "I wrote a little note for your wife, with my compliments, Agent Frommer."

Frommer takes the box like I just handed him the keys to the city of Chicago, smiling so wide I can see most of his teeth. They're so white they look like a row of Chiclets. *How do these FBI guys stay so clean?*

31

As I head out of the office that evening, I stop as I get off the elevator.

Wait a minute, that's Ester Platt coming out of the door to the basement. I walk up to her as the door clicks shut. *I've caught her red-handed, trying to get to Woogie behind my back.*

"Down in the basement checking out the air conditioning system, Ester?" I say to her. "Or were you down there trying to peddle your campaign to my client again?" *She's carrying a folder. Wonder what she's got in there?*

"I don't understand why you're so paranoid about doing one little market test, Rein," she says. "Your attendance figures aren't that great. Did you see the numbers from St. Louis?" She holds up the folder.

Something looks different about her...her hair is mussed up, her lipstick is smeared. No—it's not possible. "Spokane's no great shakes either. You'd be smart to have a backup in case your numbers keep going south like this." She sees me looking at her hair, tries to push it back into place.

She's been up to something down there with Woogie, and I bet it's more than going over market share numbers.

"Ester, you keep away from my client. The next time I find you trying to get to him, I'm taking you to Sinkle, and that'll be the end of your career at this agency. You hear me?"

Ester gives me one of her practiced sneers. "Have a nice evening, Dinny," she says, tosses her hair, and clicks off across the lobby.

I head down the stairs quietly, figure I'll sneak up on Woogie. *See if anything's amiss.* I hear Woogie whistling. It sounds like "When the red, red robin comes bob, bob, bobbing along..." Turn the corner, peek around, he's sitting on one of his sofas, his transponder in his lap, twiddling with the dials and whistling away. But the sub-basement's been completely redone.

Where have all the sofas gone? There's a grand piano, top propped up, then I see a plastic basketball hoop. *There's a pool table over there. What happened down here?* Woogie's wearing a silk dressing robe, Chinese dragons curling around it, same sandals and thigh-highs on his feet. *In that robe he looks like Liberace. One minute, he's Nicholson, the next he's Liberace.* I see something moving on the sofa beside him. A large freezer stands against the far wall, huge microwave, big screen TV turned to the Shopping Channel. The sound is off, some lady's trying to sell birthstone rings. *Where did all this stuff come from?*

"I just saw Ester leaving," I say, trying to act casual.

"Ja, ja, Dinny liking new decorating? Like some shooting hoops with Woogie?" Woogie lifts a basketball off the floor, tosses it to me. "Is having signature of Shaq, ja?"

I catch the ball, turn it. "See, it say to Woogie Strepijichowski from Shaq, ja?" *How'd he get Shaq's autograph?*

"What was Ester doing down here?"

"Ester bringing down feedbacks from all over country. She showing to Woogie. Is good knowing how advertising working." Woogie puts the transponder on the seat next to him, throws his arm over the sofa.

"Just as long as you don't pay too much attention to a bunch of numbers."

"Is not good for St. Louis, ja? Go down big in south part of Illinois and St. Louis, ja? So why not seeing ads of Ester in Peoria, ja Dinny? Maybe do big upside, have two advertisings—is better, ja?"

I'm standing on the good old slippery slope of the ad biz again. Before my campaign's even settled in, the client's wanting to test another. It's the good old CYA game, got to have a backup. See any softness anywhere and you call for a backup so no one can blame you for anything. Then get in there and fiddle and fix, fine-tune and adjust so much you muck up the mainline campaign so it doesn't work anymore then shift to the backup and order the agency to do more work. Why not? They're on commission anyway.

"I don't have anything wrong with a test market, Woogie. My problem is with Ester's campaign. It's pulling people into church for giveaways, for free stuff, for toys and air miles, not to worship God. And isn't that what we were trying to do in the first place? Don't you want people to come to church to pray instead of coming for free floor mats, coupons for chicken tenders, and boomboxes?"

Woogie gets up from the sofa, pulls his robe together. Walks over to the freezer, opens the doors, and stands staring into it. He's nodding, deep in thought.

Maybe I really made an impression on him. Maybe I've got this campaign of Ester's shut down once and for all.

Woogie pulls out two freezer bags, slams the doors, and comes back toward me.

I can tell he's going to make a major pronouncement, tell me that I'm right, and Ester's campaign is out of the running. Tell me that he understands the difference between selling God with an exquisitely-crafted emotional appeal and peddling Him with coupons, air miles, and giveaways.

"Is good thinking from Dinny Rein." Then Woogie holds up the two bags, looks at the one in his right hand and asks, "So now Dinny liking Totino's Pepperoni Pizza Rolls with big pizza taste in bite-sized snack from Pillsbury Company?" Then he holds up the other bag and says, "Or Dinny wanting other favorite of Woogie, "Ore Ida Bite-Sized Tater Tots with fantastic french fry taste?"

32

You don't know what it feels like to have the most talked-about campaign on television. Advertising is like Reddi-Whip, and when an ad campaign makes a big splash, everyone wants to stick their fingers in and get a taste. So you do an eye-catching campaign and you get to be king of the cultural hill for a couple of days. I'm on *Oprah*. I do *The Today Show*. I'm in *The New York Times* and I do a segment on *NPR* with Woogie. Woogie sings a Polish folk song off-key and insists on saying hello to all his relatives back in Poland. "Allo Mankewicz, allo Grimski, allo Mirisov..." going on and on until the interviewer has to cut him off.

Everyone's talking about the artistry of my advertising. How the campaign adroitly sells God without commercializing religion, how it's uplifting and inspiring while subtly encouraging people to attend church. I'm sitting on her couch while Oprah gushes, "It could have been so awful, but you made it wonderful." She puts it in her top-ten all-time great advertising campaigns along with Apple's *1984* commercial, Coke's Mean Joe Green ad and Gatorade's *Be Like Mike*. She calls it "the triumph of the soft sell," and runs the commercials twice on her show. I get a standing ovation from Oprah's studio audience.

I'm in *USA Today* and *Time*, do *Rosie O'Donnell*, and *Regis and Kathie Lee*. Margaret Sirini calls to congratulate me. Doesn't even drop one barb into the conversation. Says everyone in her congregation loves the advertising and attendance at her church is up by something like 15%. Rodriguez knocks on my door and asks me to sign his crutch. Abdul Abdullah sends me over a complimentary quart of hummus. Delbert gives me a free tune-up on my Range

Rover. When I walk down Michigan Avenue, people nod and wave at me like I'm a celebrity.

Patti Shaw loves to take walks with me. She waves back at people like she's the celebrity, cranking her hand back and forth at the wrist like Queen Elizabeth. We stop in front of Tiffany's one afternoon. Patti stares at a rock in the window and gives me this goony-eyed look. The diamond's the size of my thumb. I tell her I'm in advertising, not oil, and gently steer her away from the window. She's looking back at the ring for a half a block, then quotes someone I've never heard of. "The diamond is the crystalline revelator of the achromatic white light of heaven," she sing-songs.

She's crammed full of stuff like that from these courses I talked her into taking. Now she drops a new pearl every two minutes and gives me random lectures on stirring topics like tectonic plates and the shell method for determining volume.

Izzy says I should ask her to marry me. Izzy's two ex-wives ahead of me, so I figure listening to Izzy on marriage is akin to taking the Reverend Jim Jones' advice on what's the most refreshing soft drink.

One Sunday, I take Patti Shaw up to the church I used to go to in Evanston, back when I was married to Reavis. Just out of curiosity, to see if my advertising's having any effect. Patti Shaw's perched high up in the Range Rover, looking down at all the blooming daffodils as we speed up Sheridan, ogling the flowering crabapples and cherry trees.

There are so many cars at the church, I have to park three blocks away and sit a row behind Patti Shaw since the church is packed. Used to be the place was always close to empty, but now these ushers in dark suits walk slowly up and down the aisles quietly asking people to bunch together so they can squeeze a few more people in.

The minister even refers to my advertising in his opening remarks, cracks a little joke. "I'm delighted to see our church full of people on this beautiful spring day. You know," he says, "I used to think watching television was a waste of time, and in particular, the commercials. But I might be changing my point of view a little bit on the commercials." Everybody in church gets a chuckle out of that.

Patti Shaw turns around and gives me a smile. *Who would have ever thought, back when I was peddling orzo and red dye #3, that I'd be sitting here getting credit for filling up churches with my advertising?* I'm looking around at all the earnest faces, the awkward pre-pubescent boys with their shirt tails out, ties askew, the bent-over grannies, gray-haired and lace-collared, holding their hymnals up to their faces, straining to look through their glasses so they can read the words, the moms and dads beaming at each other as the candy-apple red and honey-yellow light filters in through the stained glass, the music from the organ streaming around the church, the voices swelling as they sing the hymn, Patti smiling back at me again. I start to wonder, *Maybe, in an odd sort of way, this was what I was meant to do all along. Maybe that was my mission, to do ads to get people thinking the right way, stop being so material, start being more spiritual, stop some of the feedback.*

Then I sit up in my seat and say to myself, *C'mon, Rein, cut the prophet stuff—you're just an ad guy, Rein, not some apostle,* but then everyone starts singing the Doxology, "Praise God from Whom all blessings flow..." and they seem to be singing it with more energy than I remember. "Praise Him all creatures here below...", and Patti Shaw turns and looks back at me. *Damn, she's crying, smiling but tears are running down her cheeks, and I can tell she's so damn proud of me.* Then the service ends and we're walking out of the church with Patti holding my hand. We step out into this blinding, bright-white sunshine. I look around at all the people standing in clutches around the church on the shiny green grass, robins hopping all around, a light wind feeling its way through the new leaves, families, kids, oldsters, and the minister at the entrance shaking hands. It's a damn Normal Rockwell painting come to life, and I think, *Whatever it all adds up to, Rein, at least you did do one helluva fine ad campaign.*

And we're riding back into Chicago after the service, and neither one of us says much of anything serious except we talk about the flowers lining the sides of Sheridan Road and how nice the lake looks with the puffed-up clouds arranged above it like some Impressionist painting, chalk-white over the royal blue of the lake. Patti puts her hand on my knee. I look over at her, and she quietly says, "I was wrong about your advertising. You know when I said you shouldn't do it? I was wrong and I want you to know that."

Ads for God

"Thanks," I say, and when I look into Patti Shaw's eyes I see something that I haven't seen before. *Or maybe I have,* I think, *and I just never noticed it.*

"You're doing what you believe in for the first time in your life, and I like that," she says, pointing her finger at me, and I feel like she wants to say something else but she stops, looks out her window and we go back to saying nothing, speeding back into Chicago under the sparkling blue sky and the billowing cumuli.

After a couple weeks, the fever pitch of the campaign introduction dwindles, and it's back to business as usual around the office. Forbes Sirini and the president of Woof!Burger both call, quickly congratulate me on the campaign, then go on to bitch and moan about their businesses for at least a half hour.

"Glad to see you're doing such a good job for God, Rein," the King of Hockey Pucks says. "But Woof!Burger sales are circling the drain." And Forbes tells me he's sick of seeing my face on TV. "How about showing your mug in my conference room for a change?" Clients are like kids, do a favor for one, and the others feel cheated.

Sinkle's thrown me the Steigerlager account and made me point man for new business, so I've got to go out and do a dog and pony for the beer guys next week and answer a whole stack of new business calls, half-inch pile of pink "While You Were Out" slips on my desk.

I sort through the top few. Guy from Frito-Lay thinks Cheeto's could benefit from the same kind of campaign I did for God. "Please call back at your earliest convenience" is the message he's left. The Director of Marketing for Merrill Lynch wants to fly me to New York to talk to their team of brand managers. She wants to talk about tie-ins, says it's a natural for two category leaders like God and Merrill Lynch to get together.

Shit, I'm thinking. *I'm back to peddling products. Here I was promoting peace, love and happiness, trying to make some difference in the world, adding some joy to people's lives, and now I'm hawking noodles and dog food again.*

Plus, people aren't paying attention to me the way they used to. Everyone's trajectories used to intersect in front of Evelyn's desk.

People stood out in the hall begging her to make a space for them on my Daily Planner. They were always piled up waiting to see me. They'd sneak past my door taking peeks to see if they could duck in and catch a quick meeting with me, even intercepted me on the way to the men's room. My phone was constantly ringing off the hook with requests like "Come look at this rough cut, Dinny," or "We have to get your opinion on this in the next ten minutes." Now I'm sitting alone in my office staring at a two-inch thick document on the new dental plan and a stack of messages from people who want to ripoff my campaign for God.

Guess that's what happens when you do great ads, you get kicked upstairs, and everyone else has all the fun. But that's the way it goes, Peter Principle I guess, get people inspired, point out the creative direction, give them their marching orders and get the hell out of the way. After all, I can't be involved in every little decision. But compared to how I used to feel, now I might as well be sitting on the sidelines watching while the game goes on without me.

I'm about to call the Queen of Financial Products in New York when I see Addy's face smiling in my doorway. "Can I bother you for a minute?" she asks, striding in and right off the bat, starting to *ooh* and *ahh* about Patti Shaw. Addy goes on and on about how wonderful she is, turns out they've gone out to lunch together a couple of times.

"Speaking of her, Daddy, you need to pay more attention to her."

"Excuse me?" *What is she talking about?*

"She gave you a hint."

"A hint?" I ask, still in the dark.

"In front of a certain jewelry store on Michigan Avenue?" *Now I think I understand.*

I nod. "I was a little non-plussed, I guess." *"Non-plussed" is adspeak for "scared shitless."*

"Want to know what Patti Shaw said?"

Oh boy, I can guess.

Addy imitates Patti with her shoulder thrust out, chin high, and arms cocked. "Patti Shaw put her hands on her hips like this, and she said, 'If a man can't take a hint like that, either he's plumb dumb or plain chicken—and in either case, I'm not interested.'"

Ads for God

Oh jeez, guess I've got to step up to this one. I riffle through the pages of the dental plan, say in a scratchy voice, "I hear you."

"The girl's got gumption, Daddy. She could easily take a walk, and you'd never see her again."

I nod. Addy nods back and we both know it's time to talk about something else. "I can't believe your office, your new campaign, so much has changed." She goes on to say she thought I was really losing it. And when I started talking about God giving me new shoes, she was sure.

"I got to thinking I should have you locked up, Daddy. It was that bad. Then you do this total turnaround and now look at you! You're president of the agency, the whole world's talking about your ads, and I bet you're making a million bucks."

I watch as Addy gets up and walks around picking up my old knickknacks, my lacrosse stick, the gold statue I got for a Steigerlager commercial, holding them for a while, acting like she's doing a stroll down Memory Lane. She remembers my office from the good old days when I used to bring her into the agency on Sundays, and she'd sit on the floor and draw with Magic Markers for hours while I thought up noodle commercials. Addy picks up the Gold Lion I won at Cannes for my first Woof!Burger commercial, small gold statue in a green leather box with tiny doors.

"I remember when you won this, Daddy. You called us on the phone and I'd just been to the Lincoln Park Zoo. The lion roared at me, and I ran out of the lion house crying, so I told you to please leave your lion in France, remember?"

"Yup, told you I'd bring it back in a cage." Addy sits down with the Gold Lion, opening and closing the doors.

"And I said, 'Okay, but still keep it at the office.' That lion sure scared the pants off of me." We nod and laugh and sit there for a few seconds. Addy carefully shuts the doors on the Gold Lion.

Then out of the blue, she puts down the award and says, "Oh, by the way, you know that conversation we had about your client?"

For weeks I've wanted to ask her what's up with the FBI, but I figured no news is good news.

"It's all turned out to be nothing," she goes on to say. "One tax thing the IRS is still checking out, but it doesn't have anything to do with you or your client. You know those IRS people, got to turn over every rock and look at every little thing," she says, giving them a dismissive wave.

We chat for a few more minutes, then I walk Addy to the elevator and give her a kiss goodbye.

When I get back to my office, I call Tiffany and ask about the ring in the window. Guy sounds like Delbert Peabody's older brother. He gives me the grade, cut, clarity and color, and puts a "sir" at the end of every sentence. I bet he's wearing a dark gray suit and a midnight-blue silk tie and has a perfect complexion for a fifty-year-old. I don't dare ask him for the price. We make an appointment. His name is Reginald Foster. I know I'll never get to call him Reggie.

I put in a call to Woogie, but he's not there. I try to stay as close to him as I can but I hardly get to see him since it's baseball season, and he spends most of his time in Sinkle's box at Wrigley Field watching the Cubs play his favorite game.

There's big action around the sub-basement though. Someone's always delivering stuff. Every day there are five or six boxes sitting outside the door to the basement, often some UPS guy standing around in shorts punching data into his clipboard. One day it's four cases of Fruit Rollups. Another day, I see five cases of Lucky Charms, couple of Cocoa Puffs, then there's Coke and kielbasa and Slim Jims and Jiffy Pop, Krispy Saltines and Log Cabin Syrup, Eggo waffles and Old El Paso One Skillet Mexican.

Go down to see him one day. He isn't there, probably at the double-header at Wrigley. Sub-basement looks like a cross between the A&P loading dock and a sports bar. Cases of groceries and pinball machines, pachinko, ping-pong and Peter Pan peanut butter, slots and Mrs. Paul's Fish Sticks, Foosball and Ore-Ida French Fries. There's a blackjack table piled high with Snack-Wells Devil's Food cookies, some boxes open, some empty and tossed on the floor.

Where does all this stuff come from and what does he do with it? I'm thinking as I stand there surveying the sub-basement.

Go to a Cubs' game with him. Meet him in front of the park since my apartment is three blocks away. He pulls up in a white stretch limo. He's got some Polish cookie in a short skirt with him. He's duded up in a dark green leisure suit and white patent leather shoes. They're both eating Baked Lays from giant bags and munching on Haagen-Daaz ice cream bars at the same time. Woogie's packing two Pepsi Big Gulps in each pocket—some picture.

We go into the park, and he eats five hotdogs before the first inning's over.

How does he eat so much without gaining weight? Does look a little fleshier around the jowls.

I tell him about the new pool of commercials, ask him if he wants to take a look. "Just happens I have a set right here," I say, pulling a bunch of the storyboards out of my coat pocket. Show him a Little League baseball commercial which he loves, plus one on flowers Rosemary did.

"Whoops," his guest says as she spills the sauerkraut off her hotdog onto one of my storyboards. Much dabbing at the laser print with napkins. Most of the color runs off.

"Have to be buying that one now," Woogie jokes. I leave at the end of the fifth, Cubs are ahead, and Woogie's chickie is getting sloppy on beer. Woogie gives me a hug when I leave. Everything seems hunky-dory.

That evening I'm lying in bed with Patti Shaw watching *The Tonight Show*. Jay Leno's cracking jokes about Clinton. The one about the party at Greg Norman's is pretty funny. I want to tell her about the major mineral deposit in the Tiffany's window that I just wrote a whopper of a check for, but I've got to wait until it's sized before I give it to her.

Buzzer downstairs sounds, *bzzz, bzzz, bzzz.*

"Who the hell's ringing me at eleven at night?" Get up and look out the window. Can't see anyone. Lean way out against the glass. See a stretch limo.

I'm not supposed to be going to L.A. for a couple days. Pull on a robe, slap down the stairs in my barefeet. Get to the lobby, peer around the corner. *It's Woogie at the front door. What the hell does he want?* Open the door.

"Needing having conferencing with good friend Dinny Rein, ja?" Woogie says. He's wearing a cream-colored shirt, open to the waist, blousy sleeves, like something you'd see Tom Jones sporting on stage. Chest is bronze, he smells like Aramis. I'm waiting for him to break into *It's Not Unusual* at any minute.

Instead, he looks up the stairwell and asks, "Is all right coming upstairs to apartment of Dinny Rein for conferencing?"

"Sure, c'mon up," I say. From the click of his footsteps on the metal stairs, sounds like Woogie's wearing taps. Wonder if he's taking lessons.

Wonder what goodie he's about to lay on me. Stop in front of my apartment door.

"Patti, throw something on. We've got a guest," I say to her through the door. Patti opens the door a couple seconds later wearing my old bathrobe.

Woogie hems and haws, makes small talk with Patti Shaw, then he throws the curve ball. Sits down on the bed and starts shaking his head. At first, I think he's going to fire me.

When clients start shaking their heads, ad guys start worrying.
He tells me I shouldn't be worried.

Now I'm really getting worried. He tells me it doesn't mean anything, tells me I shouldn't think a thing about it, tells me it won't make any difference, tells me he won't pay any attention to it, tells me it's only a drop in the bucket, tells me he approved it to get Sinkle off his back, and says, "It for keeping peace in big advertising family of Woogie Strepijichowski."

Then he tells me the test market's been running in Peoria for two weeks. Says he hasn't wanted to upset me. Then he puts a big smile on his face, digs around in his pocket, offers me a Pepperoni Slim Jim, shakes my hand, and says, "Hoping Dinny Rein understanding only for getting off Sinkle from back of Woogie Strepijichowski."

I sit in my bathrobe munching on the Slim Jim, thinking, *I've never had one of these before, not bad at all.* Then I stand up, hold up my arms like I'm surrendering and got into my aggrieved ad guy act. "If that's what you want, Woogie, it's fine with me. It's your money."

Patti's swinging her head back and forth between me and Woogie.

"Ja, ja, but not for changing campaigns, ja? Campaign of Dinny get big numbers with Episcopals in Kansas. Dinny see?"

"I did. The campaign's doing well all over."

"Is what Woogie say, everything good with advertising of Dinny Rein. Not for worrying."

"Run the test market as long as you want, Woogie. Just don't let Sinkle start fiddling with my ads, okay? That's the only thing I ask."

"Being fine and dandy with Woogie, ja?" He curls back his cuff to check his Rolex. "Big floor show at club on south side in thirty minute. Dinny and Patti Shaw liking coming along with Woogie? Having big car downstair."

Watching a floor show at two in the morning is not my idea of a good time, even if it's with my biggest client, so I say goodnight to Woogie and watch as he walks out my door and down the stairs.

Patti and I stand at the window as Woogie ducks into his car, his chauffeur shutting the door behind him. "Kind of hard to think that we're watching God getting into a stretch limo to go to a floor show on the south side, isn't it?"

"Naah," I say, "in the ad biz you get used to everything."

33

I propose to Patti one evening at my favorite restaurant. And when I haul out the blue box and set it down in front of her, she melts faster than the mozzarella on her margherita. I wasn't able to speak when Reginald told me the price. He said it without looking up. He said, "Eighteen thousand dollars, sir," like I'd just asked him what day of the week it was.

At Tiffany, they must give lessons on how to pronounce prices. Bill Murray would have stepped back and screamed, "Eighteen thousand bucks?" But all I could do was nod at him until my voice came back.

Eighteen grand for a rock, Rein. You must have some loose screws up there I'm thinking, until I see Patti's face when she opens the box, goes white, goes pink, eyes explode with tears. She shrieks like a rat just ran over her feet, jumps across the table, and plants a fat one on my lips. She's got tears running down her face and she's all choked-up saying, "No one ever did anything like this ever before for me, Dinny, no one ever did..."

She slips the ring on her finger and holds my hands in hers and tells me how wonderful I am and that she'll quit the Starlite Drive-Thru and go to school full-time and she doesn't care what happens to me, I can get fired by God and go back to working for the Sirinis, and we can both lose our looks but it won't bother her.

The only thing I feel queasy about is when Patti Shaw looks out over the restaurant and says almost to herself, "Momma will finally be so proud of me," like her mother never thought she'd land me, and I'm thinking that maybe I got set up again.

So what? I say to myself. *Being set up never felt so good.* And we hold hands and gush over each other like a couple of teenage lovebirds and push the pizza aside and order fancy French champagne and caviar from the Caspian.

And I'm real glad that Patti Shaw feels so good about our future together, because the next day I'm sauntering up Michigan on one of those showcase early summer days with the bright blue skies and warm wind flowing in off the lake. I'm thinking about Patti Shaw and my head's not hurting at all from the champagne we drank the night before. I stop since I feel my cell phone ringing in my pocket, rattling against my spleen, intruding on my walk up the avenue, and I'm getting the feeling it can't be good news. For some crazy reason, I'm getting this eerie feeling and thinking, *This is the cell call that's finally going to get me fired.*

Take the phone out, flip it open.

"Rein, where are you?"

It's Sinkle, and he's got that glint to his voice.

"Walking up Michigan."

"Come right up to my office. I just talked to Strepijichowski. We got problems."

"What kind of problems?"

"With the ads, get your butt up here."

"Everyone loves the advertising. I was with Woogie the other day at Wrigley Field. He just bought a new pool of commercials. And I saw him the other night, and he said the advertising was fine."

"That was yesterday, and this is today. Get your ass in here, and we'll talk about it."

When I walk into his office, Sinkle's got his feet up on the desk, hands clasped behind his head, his eyes following me carefully. The vamps of his shoes are covered by kilties, the flanks of the pumps gleaming amber in the light from the window.

He smiles at me and says, "All he wants is for you to take out the funeral scenes and put in some shots of people walking into church, Rein. I don't think that's a big deal."

"I'm not going to change the commercials," I tell him. "I don't care what he says." I'm trying to act cool. But Sinkle's the one who's looking cool wearing a blue seersucker suit and yellow knit tie, so cool he should be selling ice cream.

"Why didn't Woogie tell me to my face?"

"He knows how much you care about the advertising."

Sinkle's trying to wear me down, acting like he's speaking for Woogie.

"There's no reason to make those changes, Steve."

"The client has asked for the changes. That's enough."

"I'll talk to him."

I'm sure Woogie's not behind this, after all, he promised.

"If I were you, I'd make the changes right now, particularly with what's happening in the test market."

"What's going on?"

"The numbers are amazing. Church attendance up fifty percent in just a couple weeks. Pepsi's with us big-time now, Betty Crocker's come on board, AT&T's just signed up, and United is going to let us know tomorrow. This thing is really catching on. Hell, for the past two days I've been on the phone with the marketing people from Coca-Cola. They've been begging us to give them a five year exclusive on the Lord's Prayer."

"C'mon, Sinkle, you can't sell the Lord's Prayer."

"That's what I said."

"Good."

"I told them no way, not the Lord's Prayer."

"Some things are sacred."

"Damn right, can't have our valuable equities locked up like that. I don't care if Coke offers ten million, we'll only give them the Lord's Prayer for a year. That's it. Hell, next year Pepsi could call and offer us twenty million."

This is nuts. "You can't sell the Lord's Prayer."

"I'm not selling it. I'm offering sponsorship. That's all. Come on, Rein, this is business."

"There are some parts of the human experience that can't be peddled. Church isn't a retail outlet."

"That's not what the numbers are telling us, Rein. So far people love it, no negatives, nothing. Panky's starting to think we should be taking it regional right away."

"But what about the Durnberg numbers on my campaign?"

"They're in the bank, Rein. Now let's see how much better

we can do. Take the learning from the test market and use it to strengthen your advertising."

"The learning from the test market is people will go to church to get free stuff, that's all. We're getting them to go for the right reason, to worship God—not for free Barbie Dolls."

Sinkle stretches out his leg so the tip of his shoe catches the light. "So if we get them in with Barbie Dolls instead, that's some big problem?" Sinkle starts one of his silent smiles. The grin creeps across his face, lip curling up to show teeth,

I can see his incisors. There's the black hole. Don't get rattled, Dinny. Stay cool. He's just looking at you. That's all.

"Play it out, Rein. Ride with it a little. We're not taking your ads off the air. All I'm saying is that in view of what's happening in the test market, it makes sense to strengthen the 'go to church' communication in your commercials. Take out those downer funeral scenes and put in a sequence of some smiling people walking into church. Just a few scenes, that's all we're asking for."

We, who's "we"? He's trying to act like everyone wants the changes, so I'll water down my advertising, and then he can take potshots at it, tear it apart then take it off the air for some minor surgery, and my campaign will damn well die right there on the table.

"Nothing doing. I'm going to talk to Woogie." I start back through the tunnel.

Sinkle calls, "If you're heading downstairs, you won't find him there."

"Where is he?" I stop and look back at him.

"Out on church checks."

"What?"

"Visiting churches in the test market. He heard about the numbers and wanted to get a feeling for what's happening."

I'm going to get to the bottom of this. "I'm going down there."

Sinkle swings his feet off the desk, picks up his tennis racket and says, "Good idea, Rein. See for yourself."

34

All the way down in my Range Rover, I'm thinking, *Peoria's the quintessential heartland small town, cozy and conservative, full of straight-arrow, hard-working people who love to bowl and play Parcheesi, watch Little League games, eat pot-luck suppers and all fall asleep before Leno comes on. Selling God with promotions and giveaways will never play in Peoria. It's the place where my campaign will reign. If they loved it in Evanston, they'll love it even more down here.*

But as I get into town I'm seeing groups of people milling around in front of churches. *J. Beresford Tipton must be in Peoria handing out money,* I'm thinking. *There are so many people standing around. And on a Wednesday evening. I guess people don't have that much to do down here.*

I find Ester first. At the last church on the list.

How did she get down here? Where's Woogie? She's wearing slacks, standing in front of the church talking with the minister and some guy wearing striped Nikes and a Dallas Cowboys warmup suit, powder blue and white, with a Cowboys baseball cap.

Pull my car up to the curb and park. Ester's talking to the Dallas fan and a minister. *Wonder where Mort is?* I get out of the car and walk toward them. They don't see me, too busy talking. The minister motions. They turn and walk back into the church. Stone church, small and settled into the ground, ivy growing over it. Episcopal, I think, has that quiet money look that the Episcopal churches around Stergus did. Solid and stable—not showy or grandiose.

Ads for God

I wait for a group of churchgoers to come out of the entrance. A couple are carrying small tote bags, logos on the sides. Hormel chili, Betty Crocker frosting. Walk past them, go inside.

My pupils iris wider to accommodate for the lack of light. Tall stained glass windows line the walls. The setting sun throws jellybean colors across the pews and the stone floor. Dark wood altar at the back. Rows of heraldic flags hanging from the rafters. Looks like King Henry the Eighth's refectory.

I see Ester talking to the minister. Portly man in a dark suit, clerical collar, typical white hair and ruddy face. They're standing in front of a display, some kind of a cardboard construction set up under one of the stained-glass windows. I pick a program off a stack sitting on a table and head down the aisle toward them. Notice a colorful round splotch about the size of a shirt button at the top of the program.

Damned if it isn't the Pepsi logo. *Pretty clever,* I'm thinking to myself. *Getting Pepsi to pop for the programs.* I walk around a stone column to see what Ester and the minister are looking at.

It's Woogie. He's the guy in the Cowboys outfit! All dressed up to go to Texas Stadium for a big game. He's got his hands behind his back. He's leaning forward like he's in an art museum, studying the display. Where did he ever get that outfit? Looks like he could easily have a handful of gold chains around his neck.

The display is a diorama, three-dimensional, featuring a big plane, jumbo jet, with United Airlines logos all over it, hovering over a construction of Jerusalem done from an overhead perspective. I can see the curvy streets, the small squares.

Somebody put some money into that. I bet if I was closer I could see the Wailing Wall.

I walk up to Ester and Woogie. "Dinny, my friend," Woogie says. Ester gives me a sneer, then deigns to introduce me to the minister. Doesn't say hello, doesn't tell him I'm president, just says, "This is Mr. Dinny Rein from our agency." We shake hands, exchange comments about the weather, my drive down and other small talk. Then the minister goes on to say how excited he is about our program.

"Minister telling he have twice people from last week, no?" Woogie's grinning and nodding. I'm looking around, above the jumbo jet, two poles extend up from Jerusalem holding a banner that reads "Win A Trip To The Holy Land."

"We didn't have half the displays we have now but our Sunday attendance was double what we did the previous week," Reginald the minister says, as excited as a little kid with a new train set. "It's truly wonderful what your program is doing for us," he says to me.

Ester gives me a snide look as he continues, "We're seeing people in church we normally only see on holidays, even some new faces. Come and look at our newest displays. They just set them up yesterday."

The side aisle of the church is crowded with cardboard, enormous displays like you find in movie lobbies, with fold-outs and three-dimensional depth, executed in full-color, some twelve feet long, some five feet high.

We squeeze through the aisle past Disney's huge illustrated diorama pushing what I guess is their new animated Christmas release. It's titled "The Greatest Story." The diorama shows a moonlight scene of a desert valley seen over the shoulders of the Wise Men as they gaze down from a hill upon a small straw-roofed farmhouse, light streaming from its windows, a small crowd of people clustering around the open doorway.

"The logistics are complicated but we're getting the hang of it," the minister says as we walk past the Mattel display. "We've learned we have to verify attendance as people come in. It's too complicated once we start distributing the items. Gets to be a bit of a madhouse."

"I bet," I say, as we pass a toy display. Mattel is introducing a new line of dolls. "Disciple Dolls" they're named. Colored plush with little plastic sandals and simulated-wood shepherds' crooks. A tie-in with the Disney movie. *Disciple Dolls—give me a break.* They're shown seated behind a long table, in the same arrangement as in the famous painting. To me, it looks more like Kermit the Frog and his friends at the Last Supper.

"They've promised us the dolls in six weeks, so far they're one of our hottest items. Mattel's practically giving them away they're doing so well on volume."

McDonald's has a diorama promoting their All-American Choir, Big Macs and large fries dangling over the photograph of the singers, their eyes all up in their heads ogling the food. "Of course, the McDonald's coupons are a hit with nearly everyone. Who doesn't enjoy a Big Mac and fries?" the minister adds. Ester's taking notes, managing to shoot a scornful sneer at me every couple of minutes.

"Is very amazing, no Dinny?" Woogie asks.

"Amazing," I say. *They've taken a nice church and turned it into a damn supermarket.* Near the altar, I can see a cardboard life-size Betty Crocker dressed in an angel suit hovering over an angel food cake, serving a slice to show off the fluffy texture, her angel wings fluttering to keep her aloft over the top of the frosting, her halo jauntily cocked over one eye.

"Everything's in such restraint, such wonderful taste, don't you think?" the minister asks.

"Ja, ja, ja, ja," Woogie answers, walking past the displays, smiling and nodding at Ester.

Woogie seems like he's really bought into this thing. Or maybe those corporations bought him off with all that free stuff they packed into his sub-basement.

"Let me show you one of the things I'm proudest of. It just came in." The minister strides past the Betty Crocker display, up the stairs to the altar, picks up a silver chalice, and turns to face us. "We used to have the shabbiest vessels. I was almost embarrassed to use them, all dented and scratched. But look at this." He holds up the chalice for us. Shiny silver pitcher, embossed with all kinds of scrollwork and engraved doodads, ebony handles. "Isn't it beautiful?" He turns the pitcher in his hands. "And I think the logo is so nicely understated, don't you?" he says, pointing at the small enamel Gallo crest on the side of the chalice. "If we meet our numbers, we'll be eligible for a full set. That's what's so wonderful about your program, Mr. Rein. It could have been so tacky but everything is so appropriate."

Yes, I always did want to stare at a nicely-photographed Big Mac and a large fries when I was sitting in church, get served communion from a chalice with a tasteful E & J Gallo logo, get nicely-designed coupons for cake mix and have a chance to win a free first class trip to the Holy Land.

I hear hammering from behind the altar, someone calling, "Raise it up two more inches!" I lean over the choir pews, look up past the altar. Two carpenters are on a scaffold, high up above the altar. They look like they're attaching a framework, some kind of steel support. The minister sees me looking up at the workmen and explains, "That's where the big screen is going to go. We're getting a whole new sound system along with it, stereo and digital sound, state of the art. We'll be the first church in Peoria to have it. The congregation's very excited."

"And it's all underwritten by the local Sony distributor," Ester adds. "Doesn't cost the people of St. Michael's a penny."

By the time they get finished, I'm thinking, *this church will look like the inside of a K-Mart, big screen TV's and end-aisle displays, coupon promotions and shelf danglers looping from the pews. And they're going to corrupt every church in the country the same way, put in big screens so Madonna can sing "Rock Of Ages" to everyone in stereo and surround sound while nationally-coordinated campaigns put a coupon for twenty cents off a Nestle's Whatchamacallit in every churchgoer's hand and McDonald's does a blitz of all twelve thousand churches in America to sell their newest sandwich and the hymnals are stuffed with flyers from Paramount for their latest movie. There'll be free key chains from the local car dealer in the collection plates. American will double Advantage miles for church attendance during the holidays. Ben & Jerry's will book the lobby to sample their new Kiwi Garcia flavor. Countrytime will have a stand outside in the summer with cups of lemonade and people will get five minutes of free MCI time so they can call Grandma right after church and tell her about all the good stuff they got. The churches of America will turn into one enormous Disney World—chock-full of promotion and advertising, all of it cleverly-themed and expensively-executed, peddling everything from God to Feen-A-Mint.*

"No one in your congregation is bothered by the commercial tie-ins?" I ask ruddy-faced Reginald.

"Oh, they're always the nay-sayers and stick-in-the-muds. You've got those in every crowd," he says. "But in general, I think everyone feels it's high time for religion to get a little razzmatazz."

You betcha, a little razzmatazz for religion—just what it's always needed.

Ads for God

I stand off to the side as Woogie and Ester follow the minister around the church, checking out the new displays, talking about how they're going to accommodate the increasing numbers of worshippers. Woogie's "ja, ja-ing" and Ester's being the marketing guru, quizzing the minister, making notes, and jotting down new ideas for tie-ins and promotions.

I head outside, through the dark lobby, past the tall stone pillars into the sunlight. The lawn in front of the church is turning green. There are pansies in the planters. I look back at the church. I see the words "Erected 1885" carved into the arch over the entrance.

This church has been here over a hundred years as a house of worship and we're turning it into a Wal-Mart. And I used to worry about the morality of selling dog food shaped like hamburgers.

Just imagine where they can take this. First they'll go regional, attract more sponsors, make more money, the media will pick it up and they'll spin the thing faster and take it national. Then developers will pick up the scent of money and religion will be opened up for retail.

They'll start building megachurches with huge auditoriums that seat seven thousand at a service. They'll be anchor tenants of enormous new malls, the right side of the church opening right into Sears, the left onto a thirty-thousand square foot food court, a twelve-screen theater just off the lobby and an entrance to Six Flags just around the altar. So you can pray and then have pancakes at Shoney's, get your tires rotated while your kid's being christened, have Happy Meals after Communion or put grandma in the ground then lighten things up by taking the family next door for a fun-filled afternoon at Wet N' Wild. Sinkle was right. Church will never be the same again.

I've got to stop this. I'll talk to Woogie. Get him to see the light. He'll listen to me.

"Religion has been taking a backseat in American life for too long, and you folks are finally doing something about it," I hear the minister saying as they come out of the church.

"If this is the front seat, it belongs in the back seat," I mutter. No one pays any attention.

"I think what you're seeing here is just the tip of the iceberg in terms of the ideas we'll be implementing," Ester says. "Just wait until we get that big screen up and operating. I bet you'll be renting trailers and doing an outside feed to accommodate the crowds."

I walk up to Woogie, hook my arm though his, and lean into his ear, "Let's take a little walk, here, Woogie. We need to talk." Ester gives me a cutting glance. She's about to object, but I steer Woogie away quickly. We head down the sidewalk away from the church. Birds are flitting around. The new leaves on the trees shade the sidewalk. A fat jay tugs a worm out of the grass. I hear the *ringle, ringle, ringle* of a Good Humor truck. We cross the street, head into a small park surrounded with a wrought-iron fence.

"Woogie, look, this promotion thing is not right. Stick with our advertising, it might build a little more slowly, but people will be there for the right reasons. I went to a church in Evanston a few weeks ago. It was packed. And people were there for the right reason. They're there to worship, not to get hamburgers and fries and free tickets to Disney World."

I shake my head. Woogie motions back toward the church. "I'm seeing fulled-up churches, Dinny Rein. Wednesday night is full with people. Woogie seeing people who walking into churches again. Warming heart of Woogie big-time."

"But they're coming in for hamburgers and free angel food cake, Woogie. They aren't here for the religion."

"Dinny splitting hair, ja?"

"I'm not splitting hairs, Woogie. Look what happened to heaven!"

Woogie puts his arm over my shoulder. He's short so he makes me stoop to one side. I have to be careful of the cracks in the sidewalk. The setting sun slants through the trees and birds are racing around making nests before the sun goes down. There's a Civil War memorial in the middle of the park. The grass is turning emerald. We lope along for a minute or two then Woogie stops, turns to me, rests his hand on my shoulder, and sighs.

"We talking, ja?" His face is droopy, eyes look tired.

"Beg your pardon?" I ask.

"Us being honest with other?"

"Of course."

"Letting in on secret, my friend Dinny Rein. Is not Woogie in driving seat, ja? Not show of Woogie no more. See, hundred year ago, Woogie get big kick upstair. Bring in new guy with sharp pencil.

Boss, he count paper clip, big on bottom line, make life no good for Woogie."

"You've got a boss?"

"Isn't everyone having boss? And boss, he no care if people coming for hamburger or praying, ja? He see number up two thousand in Peoria. He giving pat on back, say 'good going Woogie'. After hundred year of frying butt of Woogie, Boss saying 'good going.' You seeing now, Dinny Rein?"

"So it's like some kind of corporate setup you've got up there."

"Big office, big, big. At least Dinny having corner office. Woogie having sit in hall. Secretary no more, one line on phone." Woogie's shaking his head. He wipes at a corner of his eye with the tip of his finger. "Is new game now, is all numbers. What I say? Is way is, ja?"

"Is way is?" I ask. *Jeez, it's really come to this, has it?*

"Is way is. Ja, Dinny Rein, is way is. And get worse yesterday. Boss call me in, say he want Woogie be figurehead. I say what is figurehead? And he say figurehead like Colonel Sanders, figurehead like Dave Thomas. I say, 'But Woogie is God!' And you know what he saying? He saying he no care. Taking it or leaving it, that what he saying."

"I'm sorry, Woogie."

"Ja, ja." He's sniffling, dabbing at his eyes with his finger.

"Can I ask you a question?" He nods, squeezes his eyes together. I see tears.

"In terms of the advertising, I mean, you'll keep running my advertising, won't you?"

"Ja, like advertisings, upstairs like advertisings too. Boss having cassette, singing along all the time. Never liking Doxology too much before, now loving it. Tapping his foot, big singing, ja?"

"So I don't have to change it, do I? Put all those church shots in?"

Woogie shrugs. "Being up to you, Dinny Rein. You being big ad guy, you figuring out." Woogie gives me a tap on the shoulder with his fist, face brightens into a smile, "Liking doing ads with Dinny Rein, liking very much."

"Me too, Woogie."

"So, going back now..." Woogie starts down the sidewalk toward the church.

"Where? Back to the basement?"

Woogie shakes his head, waves again, then walks away, down the street, disappears behind a tree and never appears on the other side. I'm left standing alone under the elms on a street in Peoria, wondering, *Jeez, God got demoted. How do you like that? Maybe God'll get canned. Maybe they'll bring a new guy in. Can't ever tell in these corporate setups. Anything can happen. They could go with my campaign, Ester's—they could fire us all. You can say the same thing about advertising that people say about Chicago weather, if you don't like it now, don't worry—it'll change.*

35

I don't see Woogie Strepijichowski for five days. Not that I don't want to. He's not there. I go down to the basement twice a day, sometimes three. "Woogie, you there?" I lean down the stairway and call.

Walk down into the basement, poke around. Nothing but empty boxes of Ralph Lauren and wadded-up Subway wrappers with dried bits of egg salad on them.

Woogie isn't there on Thursday or Friday. I even check over the weekend. Not there on Saturday or Sunday either. "Yo, Woogie, you down there?" Hear a noise. Walk down the stairs. Nothing. Place is empty. Just a tan high heel lying on the floor next to the Tide box. Pick it up.

It couldn't be...naaah, she's not even in town.

Another week goes by. I try to get God on my cell phone, try three times a day. Stand in my office, look up at the ceiling, say, "Yo, God, c'mon in, I need to talk to you." Just the way I used to. No answer. I try standing in the places where I did my duck-billed platypus act with him. I stand in my bathroom at home and speak to the ceiling. I talk to the acoustic tiles in my office. No answer.

I even take a ride on the 309 bus to see if I can find the buggy lady who tried to beat me to death with the newspaper. Nothing—I guess you only meet crazoids when you don't want to.

Meanwhile, the whole week Sinkle's bugging me to make the changes in my advertising. In between talking to Ester on the phone while she's running around the country putting her promotion campaign together. Even drafted some of my people to go to the coast to help her with the production. So when I walk down the hall on Monday morning, many of the offices are empty. Place feels dead, like it does on a weekend. There's a note taped to my door. I tear it off and open it. "Your secretary called in sick," it says.

I walk in and sit down behind my desk. Look out at the lake. Flat calm and gray-blue from the overcast sky. A sailboat sits a mile or so out, not going anywhere. I pick up the printout from the Media Dept. on the corner of my desk. Memo from Sinkle on the top. "Note continuing success in Peoria." Red line drawn to the bottom of a column of figures. The word "Up" is written alongside the number "125%".

If anything ever played in Peoria, it's this campaign, I'm thinking. *How am I going to keep my advertising running in the face of this? Have to rely on Woogie, I guess—if I can find him.*

"Can you sign something for me?" I hear. Look up to see someone standing in the doorway. It's Rosemary. I've seen some outfits on Rosemary but this one takes the cake. She's wearing a white tutu over a green nylon bathing suit. She'd look like a forest fairy except she's wearing orange and yellow harlequin tights and black hightop Converse, with her hair teased out in spikes, like a blown-apart Brillo pad.

She giggles. Some people giggle when they're nervous, Rosemary giggles all the time. "Got to go out to the coast, produce some spots for Ester," she says, giggling her way in. "I need you to sign this travel thing." She comes over to my desk, drops the paper in front of me. "You don't mind, do you?" She's chewing gum, standing with her arms back, winding up like she's fixing to leap a stream. Giggles again. *Rosemary's one strange girl.*

"No, not at all." I open my desk drawer to get a pen.

She's leaning her head against her shoulder, looking at me wistfully, chomping away on her gum. *The gum's purple.* "You don't mind that I'm working for Ester, I mean," she says.

"It's all for the good of the agency." *That's the way it is in the agency biz. People go where the action is.*

"Yes, but your campaign is so much better."

"Thanks, it just isn't packing the churches as fast as hers."

"Give it a chance, it will. It's just the novelty of getting free stuff at church that's working for her now, but that will wear off—everything does." Rosemary cocks a hip, crosses her legs. "I hear you can get a hundred-dollar Coleman bug zapper at the Congregational churches this Sunday for fifty points and $19.95."

"Really?"

"And I have a friend in Peoria who needs two more Sundays and she gets free airfare to Vegas and a hotel for three nights. Never thought that's what you're supposed to be going to church for—but anyway, your ads are still running, right?"

"So far."

"And you've got an in with the client, so you can do what you want, right?" Rosemary gives me a tap on the arm. Giggles again.

"You bet."

Sure I have an in with the client, I just can't find him.

"So I'm sure everything will work out all right. It sure was fun working with you." Rosemary half-skips, half-pirouettes out of my office, spinning out the doorway and down the hall, purple gum, harlequin tights and all. I'm thinking, *Now I've got to find Woogie—get this straightened out. How am I going to find him? I've looked everywhere—wait a minute.*

I remember that Ester's secretary keeps Mort in a crate when she's away from the office. Otherwise he pisses all over the carpet. I check my Timex. It's lunchtime. Maybe her secretary will be away from her desk. I can sneak in and try to have a little heart-to-heart with Mort.

I've tried everything else. Maybe God will come back as the schnauzer, the way He did before, I'm thinking as I head down the hall to Ester's office. *Maybe I should give him a dog biscuit. See if I can loosen him up first.* Stop at the candy machine off the lobby. Buy a package of fig newtons. Mort won't be able to tell the difference. He can't see anything through that hunk of hair hanging off his forehead.

I'm in luck, no secretary. Open the door to Ester's office, Mort's cage is on the credenza. Sucker's sleeping. I unwrap the fig newtons and walk up to the cage. I think I see one eye opening.

"Mort, I brought you a peace offering, nice dog bone," I say as I hold the cookie up to the cage. Mort sniffs, sits up. I squeeze the handle on the side of the cage. The door pops open and Mort jumps out. He lands on the floor, shakes himself off, and yawns. I lean down and hold out the fig newton.

"God," I ask, "You in there?"

Mort sniffs the fig newton, growls.

"Okay, it isn't a bone. It's a cookie. So what?" I crouch down, hold the fig newton out to him. *C'mon, Mort, take the damn thing.* He sniffs it, takes a tentative bite.

This is a good sign.

"So look, God," I say as I watch him gnawing on the cookie. I let go of it. Mort folds down on his haunches, the fig newton held between his paws. I drop down on all fours, kind of tilt my head so I can look under the hair into his eyes, "I'm looking for a little guidance here. Everything feels like it's going south on me. Got any ideas about what I can do?"

Mort's gnawing on the fig newton. Cocks his head.

It's God and He's going to talk to me! He's looking straight at me with his hairy little eyes. *He's going to give me the answer on why my campaign's going down the tubes and what I should do about it.* "C'mon, God, say something!" He stops chewing on the fig newton, shifts his head to the other side, as if he thought of something.

"I've been a good guy, God. I've done everything you've said. Did the ads the way you wanted them, got people flocking into church. Now give me some guidance, God." Mort lets out a little whine, plaintive, like he feels sorry for me.

He's going to give me the word, show me how to get out of this mess. He finishes off the fig newton, looks up.

"Tell me what I should do!" I say as he gets up off his haunches, licks his lips. "Speak to me, God, speak to me!" I'm staring into his beady little brown eyes, looking for an answer when all of a sudden, I hear water. *Oh no...*I hear it splattering...*it can't be.* I look up over Mort's back. *It is.* His back leg is cocked up in the air.

I stand up. Mort shakes his butt off and goes over and sits down behind a chair, his back to me, leaving behind a puddle the size of a salad plate soaking into the rug. I walk out of Ester's office, thinking. *Guess God's not coming back down as a dog. Not even for a fig newton.*

I'm like this for a day and a half, rattling around the office, trying to get God on my cell phone. Evelyn's been out with some flu from Taiwan. My campaign's still running but I can't find Woogie. Izzy says I shouldn't worry. Patti says I shouldn't worry. What do they know?

Then the phone rings. Surprises me. I jump out of my chair. Because Evelyn normally gets it. I pick it up. It's Lorna, Sinkle's secretary. She's acquiring an English accent from hanging around with Vincent, talking through her nose like she's inviting me to tea. "Mr. Rein," she says. "Mr. Sinkle would like you to come up here and see him as soon as possible."

"Let me talk to him."

Not going to have Sinkle summoning me with his damn secretary.

"I'm sorry, Mr. Rein," Lorna says. "He's on the phone with Mr. Strepijichowski right now."

I'm in Sinkle's office in two minutes flat, just as he's hanging up the phone. Bangs his hand flat on his desk and jumps out of his chair, looks like he just won the Big Ten Championship. "We're going regional with Ester's campaign, West Coast feed, one-third of the damn country, Rein." He grabs my hand and pumps it up and down, like he's drawing water from a well. Mile-wide smile, Sinkle's all teeth. "Another thirty million bucks, Rein," he says.

I want to sock him in the nose.

"Congratulations, this is the biggest thing that's ever happened to this agency and you deserve a lot of the credit." Sinkle's off on an exultant stroll around his office, taking big sliding steps like he's skating, twirling this way and that, his hands in his pockets, head tilted up at the Queen Victoria chandelier, "We'll be one of the biggest agencies in town. We'll have all these huge accounts doing promotions with us. Hell, if we could pick off a United Airlines or a chunk of McDonald's, we could be billing half a billion. Half a billion, Rein! And that's just for starters."

"You're going to keep my campaign running over the promotions, right?" Sinkle stops, looks out at the lake. Picks up his binoculars, raises them and focuses on a sailboat a long way out.

"For a couple more weeks, sure."

"What the hell's that mean?"

"At least until we get the promotions geared up."

"Over my dead body. My campaign's staying on the air."

"Look, Rein, you're missing the point." Sinkle walks behind his desk, opens his palm toward the chair in front of his desk. "Sit down," he says. I pull the brass-studded leather chair away from the desk, lower myself into it. "Let me let you in on a little secret." Sinkle lifts up an art card, six inches high, a yard long, a series of illustrations on it. "You know what these are?"

"Look like crosses to me," I say. Sinkle lowers his head so his chin's almost resting on the card, smiles down at it like it's his newborn baby.

Ten or fifteen different art treatments of the cross, one drawn in perspective, one cross done in Art Deco, one in a puffy cartoon style, one with a smiling face and little feet. There are crosses drawn in 3-D, some streaking cosmic dust, some striped, multi-hued, polka-dotted—I can see the art director who designed them saying, "I want to update the cross while keeping it user-friendly at the same time."

"One of these will be the most important marketing force of the twenty-first century, if we manage it right." Sinkle gets up and perches himself on the corner of his desk, art card across his lap, "I'm leaning toward this one here at the moment," he says, pointing to a cross with speed marks flying back from its edges. "But we'll Durnberg them all and see where we come out. "

Sinkle pulls an easel loaded with a stack of cards around in front of me. "Rein, what we're about to do here is lay the foundation for the biggest entertainment, communications, and licensing conglomerate the world has ever seen." He reveals the first card, pictures of different churches grouped inside a circle. "What we'll do is amalgamate all the denominations, pull them together into a co-op. We're turning the churches into distribution centers already. When we get the broadcasting going, we'll have a damn network. And we're just scratching the surface of what we can do with the churches of America."

"So we consolidate congregations, get the cable hookups working, put the whole thing together so we've got a hundred and fifty million people pulling on the same oar. It's happening right now. Hell, no one wants to get left out of this thing. It's the power of the almighty dollar. The only holdouts are the Seventh Day Adventists and they'll be jumping on the bandwagon any minute now. Anyway, so we put all these churches together under this logo. Then we begin."

Ads for God

Sinkle shows me a card with the cross logo printed on a pack of Wrigley's Spearmint. "Okay, so think of our logo like the Good Housekeeping Seal on products. You don't think marketers would be scrambling all over each other to get our cross on their cough medicine or shaving cream?"

Sinkle starts flipping through the cards, flinging them across the room as he displays them. "They'll pay through the nose to get the cross on their potato chips or life-care centers, on toothpaste and toasters, automobiles, bank cards, and bubble gum."

He's sailing cards across the room showing the cross on tubes of Crest toothpaste, tucked in beside the Ford logo, on boxes of cough medicine, and bags of potato chips. "But we don't stop with endorsements."

He points to a card with the cross standing leaning against a stylized TV camera. "We're already doing our own programming so we'll broadcast it, then move into our own cable channel, develop our own talk show. We'll make those Pat Robertson people look like pikers. We'll be producing our own films. We'll be in movies and cable and publishing and recording." He's showing me cards with the cross on a TV screen, on the cover of a book, on a CD, a movie cassette. "From endorsements, we'll move into manufacturing, toys and apparel, jeans and athletic shoes. Then we'll move into foods—we'll have our own lines of snacks, beverages, entrees and desserts. We'll go into theme parks, perfume, travel, lodging, gaming, real estate—we'll be everywhere."

Sinkle's put the cross on game boards and on the backs of jeans, on airplanes, hotel marquees, bottles of perfume, road signs. "When we're finished, we're going to make everything Eisner's done with Disney look Mickey Mouse," Sinkle chuckles. "And I'm not kidding, because we're talking about the most potent logo in the history of marketing. This goes way beyond religion, Rein, way beyond. This is the power of a simple logo made into the most pervasive and powerful marketing force the world has ever seen."

This man's a maniac. He's off his rocker, I'm thinking, scowling at him and shaking my head. *He'll never pull this off.*

"And if you think I've got a screw loose, Rein, just take a look at this..." Sinkle pulls the cross logo off the board, reveals a card with the Coca-Cola wave, the Nike swoosh, the Ford oval, and the Levi's leather label. "Four of the most powerful logos in the world and this logo already has the same power..."

Sinkle slaps the cross up next to the Coke logo, "...the same recognition, the cross just hasn't been marketed, Rein. It hasn't been marketed! And we're the ones who are going to do it." Sinkle stops, sets the easel back against the wall, shoots his cuffs, and sits down. He leans across his desk.

"And you, Dinny Rein, you can have anything you want. So make your call. Do you want to run entertainment or publishing or food or what? Take your pick of any division. Woogie likes you so you can have anything you want."

"Woogie likes me?" *Why's he saying Woogie likes me?*

"He talks about you all the time." *Is that where Woogie's been? Hanging around with Sinkle?*

"I want my campaign on the air. That's what I want, Steve." *He's not getting me to back down.*

"C'mon, Dinny, where's your vision? I always thought you were an imaginative guy. Leave the advertising behind. It's chump change. Go for records or publishing. Hell, toys alone could make you a multi-millionaire in a couple years. We're going to be taking a ride on a tidal wave here."

"You can take your tidal wave and stuff it, Steve. I want my campaign on the air. You saw the Durnbergs, some of the highest we've ever seen. It just needs a chance to settle in. It's not the kind of campaign that works overnight. This is the campaign that gets people into church for the right reasons."

Sinkle's shaking his head slowly, looking down at his desk.

"Who cares what gets them into church? Hamburgers, bug-zappers, love of God, faith—who cares?—as long as they spin those turnstiles. We're talking about leveraging religion into a multi-billion dollar business."

"Steve, I've put my heart and soul into this advertising."

Sinkle stretches out his fingers, forms them into a tent, swings his chair around to look at the lake. Sinkle's silent treatment. He swings back, curls his lip, and says, "You don't realize that no one gives a shit about your heart or soul. That's the problem with all you

Ads for God

creative people. You always think your ideas are so precious. C'mon, Rein, who the hell cares?"

"Woogie Strepijichowski does."

He looks at me and laughs. "You're naive, Rein, naive and self-righteous. Two qualities that in this business add up to stupid." Sinkle turns and picks up the binoculars. Lifts them up to look out at the lake.

"I don't care what you think, just keep my campaign on the air."

"We can't afford to run two national campaigns," he says.

"Who says?"

Sinkle lowers the binoculars, looks at my suit, turns back to the binoculars. "Your client," he says.

"Woogie would never say that."

Sinkle smiles. I see black hole. He chuckles, snorts, and shakes his head. "Don't bet on it, Rein," he says and we sit there in a stare-off.

Sinkle's bluffing. Woogie would never agree to take my ads off the air. It's another one of Sinkle's attempts to end-run me, that's all.

Sinkle's intercom rings, Sinkle grunts, and Lorna interrupts, "Mr. Strepijichowski is on his way in to see you."

Sinkle gets up, straightens his tie. "Now you'll have a chance to ask your client, Rein," he says with a smirk. I look toward the door. I can hear Woogie's voice outside. I hear Ester laughing. Sinkle sits down, swings his feet up on his desk, and turns to look back out at the lake with his binoculars.

The door flings open and Woogie strides in carrying a bunch of shopping bags, Bloomingdale's, Tiffany's. He's wearing a green silk shirt open halfway down his chest, big gold cross hanging from a heavy chain, something the Sheriff of Nottingham would have worn. Dark sunglasses, hair slicked back, and with the big Cheshire Cat grin on his face. Now he looks like Jack Nicholson again but on his way back from Vegas with Ester Platt following him.

She looks like she's been spending time at Bergdorf's, silk pantsuit, gold jewelry, flashing diamond studs in her ears. She's got bags from Hermes and Lord & Taylor. They both have that "bringing home the bacon" look that my mother used to have when she came back from shopping at the A & P.

Woogie's smile fades when he sees me. Looks at Sinkle, back at me. Sinkle lowers his binoculars. Woogie slowly walks up and sticks out his hand. "Long time no seeing Dinny Rein, ja?" I shake Woogie's hand. He steps back. He's wearing pleated serge pants, seven-hundred dollar shoes. He looks down at the floor.

Whoa! Something crazy's going on here, I'm thinking, as I watch Ester take out a large manila envelope and set it down on Sinkle's desk.

"Here's the thirty million. Now let's go for it, Steve, make the buys," she says, standing back as he opens the envelope.

Ester and Woogie got the money by themselves. They're going to run her campaign on the West Coast, kill mine, and use the money to take Ester's national. Woogie's getting money for someone else, that means I'm finished unless I can turn him around.

"Woogie, I need to talk to you." Woogie gives me a frown, fiddles with his gold chain, coughs, stares at the carpet.

"Come on, Rein, don't make this any more difficult on our client than it already is," Sinkle says as he pulls a stack of certificates out of the envelope. They look official, stock certificates, bonds, T-bills.

"What happened, Woogie?"

Ester's got her arms crossed. She's standing over Sinkle as he counts the certificates, smirking at me.

Woogie turns toward Sinkle. "You giving Dinny pick of jobs?"

"I went through the whole thing with him, offered him anything he wants."

"No choosing good job, Dinny?"

"We had a deal, Woogie."

"Dinny not liking doing line of ready-to-wear for God, ja? Maybe doing sports, ja?"

"Woogie, we're doing a great advertising campaign. That's what we're doing."

Sinkle swings his feet up on his desk, takes the stack of certificates, and fans himself with them. "Woogie and his board made a decision based upon market performance, Rein. It's business, Rein, pure and simple."

Ads for God

"But what about the Durnberg scores. How do you know my campaign isn't the one that's really packing them in?"

"Can't you smell the coffee, Rein? It's final." Sinkle chucks the certificates back on his desk. Leans back, clasps his hands behind his head.

Okay, that's it, I've had it. Gloves off, here we go! "You think you're so smart, don't you Sinkle? But you don't even know who you're dealing with here, do you? Do you have any idea who Woogie Strepijichowski is? And what this thing is all about?"

Sinkle looks tired. Gazes up at the ceiling. I point at Woogie. I'm yelling, "Well, I'll tell you! Woogie Strepijichowski is God. That's who he is. He's God!" I turn to Ester. "That's who you've been shopping with—God! And he doesn't have a board of directors, that's bullshit. He's just one lousy God—there's a whole mess of them up there and a big boss God that they all report to. How do you like that? Some huge conglomerate of Gods up there with offices and a big building and telephones, right, Woogie?"

Woogie and Sinkle are shaking their heads, rolling their eyes at each other. "Tell him, Woogie," I say, swinging my arm from him to Sinkle. "Tell him."

"And you talk to these Gods all the time, right?" Sinkle snickers, as he slides opens a desk drawer.

"Yes, I do—or I used to before Woogie became God."

Oh no, I'm starting to sound like I'm bonkers.

"And these are pictures of you talking to God, right?" Sinkle hands me a sheaf of glossy black-and-white photos. I see myself in my office, lip stretched out. Walking down the street, talking to God, looking like I'm certifiable. He's got pictures of me at home and at Patti Shaw's.

How did he get all these pictures? Those guys in the Buick must have been following me the whole time taking pictures.

Sinkle walks up to Woogie, puts his arm around him, and nods at me. "I told you we should have had him committed. Didn't I, Woogie?"

"Ja, is too bad for Dinny Rein."

"He's God, I'm telling you." I'm shouting now. "All that stuff about Warren Buffet is bullshit. I made it up. He's God. He disappears into nowhere. He intercepts wire transfers—okay, okay, I'll prove it to you."

I walk over to Sinkle's desk, take the certificates off the desk, hold them up in the air. "Where's this money from? Huh? Where did it come from? Tell me! Did you get it from a drug courier at O'Hare, snag it out of the air, knock over a Wells Fargo truck?"

Ester walks over and puts her arm through Woogie's. "We got it out of Woogie's safety deposit box at the bank. Didn't we Woogie? And there's a lot more where that came from, right, dear? I saw it."

Dear? She's calling him 'dear' and look at the way she's looking at him. Like he's her sugar daddy or something!

"This is all bullshit. He's God, I tell you. He's God! Okay, check out the Warren Buffet thing. Call him in Omaha, right now. I made that whole thing up."

Sinkle's tapping his desk with his silver letter opener. "We did. Buffet says Lottie Strepijichowski is one of his most trusted and loyal people and that he enjoyed meeting Woogie last year in Omaha. The three of them went to the movies together."

"Ja, see *Toy Story,* is good movie."

Holy shit, I've been set up big time. "Woogie, tell them you're God. C'mon, Woogie, you got to tell them!"

"Very sorry for you, my friend Dinny," Woogie says.

When God won't admit He's God, you know you're in deep shit.

Sinkle pulls out his shoe phone and starts to dial. "I can call the hospital right now. They can have people here in five minutes." The three of them, Woogie, Sinkle, and Ester, are staring at me, looking at me like I'm a freak.

"Woogie, we had a deal. The scheming, the big guy upstairs who liked my campaign, you said he sang along with it. C'mon, Woogie."

"Ja, better calling hospital, ja," Woogie says, shaking his head. Sinkle hits the SEND button on his phone. I step back. They're looking at me like I've lost it.

This is the end of my campaign, the end of my career. Sinkle puts his arm over my shoulders, takes me by an arm, nods at Woogie and Ester and starts to steer me toward a chair. "Why don't you just have a seat, Dinny."

Ads for God

Uh, uh, sorry, no thanks—I'm out of here. I slide my shoulder hard into Sinkle and pivot around into Woogie, pushing through them like they're a couple of D's and I'm going for the goal back at Waverly. Sinkle's still got my arm but I twist away, turning and swirling, my feet spiraling me over the floor. *I'd feel better if I had my lacrosse stick, but here I go anyway.*

Turn, duck a shoulder, I'm heading for the door, juking and twisting, Sinkle lunging after me, slotback from Purdue against an ace attackman from Waverly. "Lock the door!" he shouts at Ester as he grabs at my coat tail.

I spin again, coming back the other way, tearing my coat tail out of his hand, and stiff-arming Ester as she comes up to me, sending her crashing back onto Sinkle's desk. I'm up and out through the passageway, ducking down and sprinting like a madman, Sinkle right behind me, Ester shrieking and Woogie shouting in Polish, "Machingitz ne woseback, machingitz ne woseback!" I'm past Lorna, galloping down the hallway, right onto the open elevator, slam the button, doors close, keep my finger on the down button, 20, 19, 18...then the freefall down to the first floor. Walk through the lobby quickly.

I hear a siren *oogah, oogahing* up Michigan. I duck around the corner of the building, take the stairs in twos down to the lower level, the roadway under Wacker. I can hear the sirens screaming overhead.

They're probably running into the building with the straitjackets and syringes full of sleep juice right now, looking for the flipped-out ad guy who talks to God.

I head for the lake, Olive Park. They'll never find me there. Sewage treatment plant for the city, it sticks out into the lake, has lots of big trees. Slow down to a jog as I come out from Lower Wacker into the sunlight. Sprinting guys in suits tend to attract attention.

Start walking. Get to the end of Ohio, just on the edge of Olive Park. Phone rings. Take it out, it's Addy. Her voice sounds edgy. "Daddy, are you at work?" she asks me.

"Not exactly," I tell her.

"Good, I'd stay away from there if I were you. The FBI's going to shut down the place in an hour or so. It doesn't have anything to do with you. But stay away from there just the same. It's going to get messy."

"What's going on?" I ask her.

"Tax evasion, they've really nailed that Sinkle character. He's been tucking millions away. I think some other people are involved also, the CFO and the office manager. What's his name?"

Sinkle got greedy and they caught him.

"You mean Plevis, and Murray the CFO." *I hope Sophie wasn't involved.*

The wind is picking up, waving the trees back and forth. No one's in the park. It's dreary and somber except for the whipping of the wind and the noise of the lake. I can see the lake at the far end, brown and frothy, tan waves with mocha crests surging up over the concrete seawall, hanging in the air at the height of the handrail, their tips frothing and bubbling until they lose momentum and lie back down.

Must be some kind of storm kicking up.

"They tripped over it when they were poking around the agency. Your client's money was clean, but what Sinkle was doing with it wasn't. So the agency will be locked down for a couple of months while they audit."

"Who cares? I don't work there anymore."

"What happened?"

"I just got fired."

"But what about your client and your campaign? It was doing so well."

"That's the advertising business for you, Addy."

"What are you going to do now?"

"Get another job, I guess—don't know."

I walk through the park quickly, lean over the handrail, and watch the waves. Addy tells me she's worried about me, wants to have dinner. I tell her I'll call her later.

As soon as I hit the END button, my cell phone's ringing again.

"Yo, Rein, how'd you like that ending?"

It's Him.

"What do you mean, how did I like it? You trashed my career. You set me up. You lied to me."

"Hey, but we had some fun along the way, right Rein?"

"Fun? You call that fun? That Woogie guy ruined me. His damn egg salad sandwiches, his gold Rolexes, the guy screwed me."

"He was your idea. You asked for him."

"He let Sinkle get to him. He set me up."

"Nasty business, that advertising."

"Hell, the way Ester's hanging on him, he's probably screwing her too."

"Shit happens."

"I can't believe you killed my advertising."

"It was out of my hands, Rein. There was nothing I could do, got out-voted all the way around."

I stand with my arms resting on the rail, the lake doing a slow-motion roll in front of me, the waves rolling now, bulging and smoothing out with pockets of foam working up the inclines then spinning down the slopes, whirling and twisting. I can hear the wind starting to howl in, having worked up a head of steam rolling its way down the lake.

This sure is some storm for the summertime.

"How'd you like the way I took care of Sinkle, though? The IRS'll put him away for at least ten, and when he gets out, those drug guys will hunt him down and cut him up in little pieces. Took care of those other two slimeballs, Murray and Plevis too."

"What about Ester?"

"Got her too, but they'll let her go after a couple days. She'll do okay for a while. She'll open her own agency, manage the campaign until the people up here get tired of it. She might last a year, year-and-a-half. Then we'll fire her, get someone else in there. That's the way it goes in advertising, right?"

"If you wanted her campaign, why didn't you just pick Ester Platt in the first place? Why did you put me through all this?"

"I like you, Rein. I wanted you to win. It just didn't work out that way."

"I'd hate to see what you do to your enemies."

"You betcha. But we all have to have some fun sometimes."

"You took me for a big damn ride. That's what you did."

"Kind of what life is, huh, Rein, a big damn ride? So, Rein, we'll see you around, huh?"

"That's it? After all this?"

"That's all, Rein. As Woogie says, 'Is way is, ja?'"

Click, and He's gone. I fold up my cell phone. Stare at it a minute.

This is where it all started, on a damn cell phone, and this is where it's going to end. God sold me and my advertising down the river— tried to buy me off with a line of religious ready-to-wear. To hell with him!

I flip the phone shut and heave it over the railing into the lake and sit there watching the water fuming and spuming, the waves sloshing up over the seawall, thinking about my cell phone scraping and scratching over the sandy bottom somewhere down there.

To hell with you God. To hell with you and your whole damn organization up there. I give you a great ad campaign and you trash it for a quick fix so you can make your numbers and impress your boss. You're no more than a sleazy hustler, a peddler at the level of Willie Loman, a hawker of Happy Meals, Barbie Dolls, whatever it takes to make 'em smile and spike that share, pack those pews, bingo-bango, slam-bam, thank you Ma'am for the few share points and hope to see you next Sunday, same place, same time except we'll have Celine Dion in person singing the Doxology and a preview of the Mt. Sinai edition of the new Dodge Durango up on our giant Diamond Vision screen.

You're no better than the marketing director of Woof!Burger peddling his rhinestone leash promotion or the Wolfgang Puck gourmet version of his lousy red-dye laced dog food. Sell, sell, sell the sizzle and who gives a shit what happens to the steak as long as the numbers are going up—to hell with the spiritual health of America, to hell with convincing people to come to church for the right reasons, to hell with life, liberty or the pursuit of happiness—it's two share points, free air miles, and a couple lousy plastic dolls that we're falling all over ourselves for. Dammit all to hell!

I stand up and kick the rail so hard I start to think I've broken my toe.

And we came so close. I'm limping, left shoulder slumping down when I walk, my toe killing me with every step, slowly making my way out of Olive Park.

Ads for God

We came so close. I'm remembering all those bright-faced people at that church in Evanston, holding hands and smiling at each other, candy-colored light streaming through the stained glass, Patti Shaw smiling back at me, people reveling in the fact that they're alive, not buying or selling or thinking about making their next buck, but just alive! That's what it could have been each and every Sunday all over America.

But no! Now we're going to peddle the cross, slap it on everything from chewing gum to jet airplanes, cover every inch of the world with asphalt, make it safe for shopping centers, then develop the piss out of it so the only scenery we see is cellular towers and strip malls, the only language we have is commerce, the only art we have is advertising, and the only music we hear is the sound of funds zinging back and forth through the air—shit!

The wind has died down. The leaves in the trees have stopped their mad rustling. Sun's trying to shine.

So what the hell do I do now? At least I've saved a few thousand bucks, I've still got my Range Rover, and I've still got Patti Shaw. I should call her. Ooops, I threw my phone away. I'll call her from the car.

I catch a cab outside of Olive Park, gently lifting my damaged foot in. The cab driver's an octogenarian, drives slower than mud oozes. He crawls up to the pedestrian entrance of my garage. I hop out, slam the cab door, go inside. Walk down the first row of cars, *Where did I leave it?* I peer around the concrete pillar. *There it is!* Over in the corner, all black and shiny under the overheads. Hit the clicker and hop in. Push the POWER button on the car phone. Start the car and head up the ramp onto Michigan. Dial her number.

"Starlite Drive-Thru Clean Car Experience," Patti answers.

"Let's go for a ride."

"I get off in an hour."

"I need to talk to you."

"Can't it wait an hour?"

"I just got fired."

"You're kidding! Oh, jeez, after you did that great advertising?"

"No gratitude in this business."

"But you worked so hard at it."

"I'll be okay."

"Just don't get down about it. You tried hard to make it work."

"I know."

"Any ideas on what you're going to do?"

"Pick you up in ten minutes."

"I'd like that. I'll be waiting in the booth. Give you a free wash. It'll make you feel better. So God fired you, huh? I can't believe it."

"Bing, bang, just like that."

"Jeez, and I thought you guys were getting along great. So maybe we'll grow old together real fast, huh? That was a little joke."

"It was funny."

"Don't say goodbye, Dinny. Just come and pick me up quick."

"You betcha," I say and hit the END button as I cruise on up Michigan Avenue thinking, *Thank the Lord for Patti Shaw.*

The traffic is light for a weekday. Starts to pile up as I get to Ontario, cops everywhere. I see squad cars in front of the agency, squadrols and unmarked cars, Chicago police, gumball machines blinking like crazy, cars pulled up every which way on the sidewalk, people from the agency clustered around. The light in front of me goes red and I stop and watch as a bunch of plainclothes cops come swarming out of the agency, pushing their way through the BFP&G employees crowding the sidewalk. I can see a bunch of secretaries that I recognize. *There's Durnberg and there's Rosemary. The cops are escorting someone. Who is it?*

The place is crawling with cameras and news crews. Flashes going off all over the place. I sit up in my seat to see better. Everyone's up on their tiptoes, craning their necks to see who the cops have. The cops are manhandling them through the crowd, two guys.

It's Murray and Plevis. They arrested them. There's someone else coming out. The cops push the crowd back. *I think it's Sinkle!* I hear the crowd roar. People are jeering and whistling. Now I can see it's Sinkle. They've got him in handcuffs, his hands are held together in front, head down, and he's taking mincing steps. Through the mass of cops I can see a wire running down to his ankles. *They've got him in leg restraints, holy shit.* They're taking him away. All of a sudden, Sinkle lifts his head and turns toward my car. Catching his eye, I laugh at him and when I do, the light goes out in his expression and he ages twenty years in a heartbeat.

And there's Ester coming right behind him. Doesn't look too sexy all tied up, walking like she's got to take a leak. *Wonder what they got her for? Accessory or something? Who cares? How she's going to feel when they ink her and roll the pads of her fingers over the paper, make her bend over naked, toss her orange overalls, usher her into a cell and clang the door shut?*

Ha! Ha! I think as I hit the steering wheel with the heel of my hand. *There is some justice in this world. Maybe I lost my job and my campaign, but they're ending up in the clink!*

I watch as a cop puts his hand on top of Ester's head and shoves her into the backseat of a squad. Sinkle's bent down into another one. Sirens start. The cop cars slowly surge through the crowd. The BFP&G people are pounding on the roofs, bending down to yell at Sinkle. I see a secretary screaming at him.

What are all these people going to do for the next two months with the agency shut down? These people have families to feed and mortgage payments to meet. No wonder they're yelling at Sinkle—he's lucky he's going to jail.

The cop cars make their way through the crowd, bump down off the sidewalk and head up Michigan. Ten or fifteen of them, lights flashing, sirens wailing like Clinton's in town. The lights go green. The cops urge the traffic up the avenue. I drive past the entrance to the agency. Yellow tape all around the front door. Plaques still tarnished.

I wonder where Woogie went?

I pull up to another light, sit back, and look up through the moonroof at the clearing sky, robin's egg blue in places, promise of a great afternoon.

I'll find something to do. My skills are still marketable, particularly after the great campaign I just did.

Just as the light goes green, the car phone rings. *Must be Patti again.* Hit the SEND button. "Hello?" I say. Silence on the other end of the line.

"Hello?"

"Excuse please, may have talk with you?" a voice asks, in a singsong almost falsetto tone.

"Who's this?" I ask.

"Mr. Gautama..." *Gautama? Where have I heard that name before?* "...pardon undue curiosity," he goes on. "But would appreciate opportunity to discuss with you."

Whoever this is, he sounds exactly like Charlie Chan.

"No problem, but can you fill me in on who you are? I can't place your name right at the moment."

"Familiar with big copper statues in jungle with legs folded and face in repose?"

Big copper statues...big copper statues with legs folded—of course! I remember from doing crossword puzzles with Reavis—Gautama is Buddha! That was Buddha's name when he was born back in Nepal. Damn, it's Buddha I'm talking to. He must have heard about my campaign.

"Have something very important. Would like your able assistance."

"Shoot, Mr. Gautama, go right ahead."

"Would be so kind to consider taking advertising account of Mr. Gautama?"

Would I be so kind? This could be huge. Huge! With China opening up and everything? Hundreds of millions of people. We're talking big here.

"Entirely possible, Mr. Gautama. There's just a few things we'd have to work out like compensation, strategy—that kind of thing, but I'm sure that won't be a problem."

"Answers very simple, just avoid picking and choosing."

I like that in a client, single-mindedness, decisiveness. "So what kind of communication are you looking for, Mr. Gautama?"

"Maybe find clue in statement, 'Enlightenment is seeing Buddha nature within own eye?'"

"Sure, I see where you're going. Interesting. I think we can work with that."

Kind of a mystical thing, I can visualize it right now! Helicopter shot over the jungle, tropical birds cawing, hearing that plunky, plunky Japanese music on the soundtrack and then we zoom into the Big Guy sitting in a clearing...

"You paint branch well and you hear wind."

He's poetic. Yes! Haiku! We'll have haikus seeded through the soundtrack.

"Good idea, Mr. Gautama. Yes, that's where I'm going with it too. Powerful visuals combined with poetry..."

"Letting mind free to be itself. Not looking to others for own hands and feet."

"I'm tracking with you, Mr. Gautama. I'm right with you!"

"Rain hears itself falling and makes it's own silence."

"Good, good."

I wish I could write some of these things down.

"What I tell is not secret. Secret is within you."

I like a client who respects his agency—I think we can get along fine.

"Pardon intrusion, but may ask question?"

"You bet."

"Small point of information, but having international capability? Most interested in test market in Shanghai. See how best penetrate China, re-establish Buddhism?"

As I hear him ask the question, I'm thinking. *There are two hundred BFP&G people standing out on Michigan Avenue right now with no place to go, nothing to do—I can hire them, take over a couple floors in the Marriott, have an operating ad agency by this afternoon.*

"No problem, Mr. Gautama..." *I can start my own agency with the Buddha business, sell God the right way. Maybe make Panky president, the guy's brilliant, make Rosemary the creative director—she's someone I could have fun with. We'll open offices all over the place, do marvelous ads full of poetry and flowers, get Buddhism really cranking in China again,* "...no problem at all, Shanghai, Peking, Canton, we can run a test market anywhere you want."

"Have old saying: 'On whose door does moonlight not shine?'"

"Precisely, Mr. Gautama. It's a very, very small world these days." *We can go international, convert millions of Chinese from Communism, attract clients based on the work we do for Buddha, sell stock in the agency, improve the quality of life all over the world with advertising. Then go public and make millions while we make the world a better place and Patti Shaw and I will be set for life. Wheeoo!*

"Yes, now pardon please," he says. "So sorry but have to return to happy family. May call tomorrow for further discussion?"

I'm turning off onto Elston and I see Patti Shaw waving at me from her glass booth. I say into the phone, "You bet, Mr. Gautama. Talk to you tomorrow. Call anytime. I'll be here."

"May leave with one thought, please?"

"Shoot, sure, go ahead, Mr. Gautama." Patti's waving me into the open bay of the car wash. She's got me set up for the Supreme Cosmic Treatment, full underbody wash, triple bug pass, hot carnuba double-baked wax finish, and clean water rinse.

"Needn't seek wonders," Mr. Gautama says. "Wonders come of themselves."

"Well put, Mr. Gautama, very well put—talk to you tomorrow..." and as Patti Shaw hops into the front seat looking delectably pert in a tight top and short skirt, I hang up the phone. Patti Shaw gives me a wet smeary kiss on the cheek and we're off into the prerinse of the Starlite Drive-Thru Clean Car Experience, water swooshing all around the car, *Top Gun* music pounding through the windows, and strobes firing wildly all around us as Louie lets loose ten pounds of twinkly glitter. There's a million watery stars catching the light and bouncing it back at Patti Shaw and me and I'm thinking, *Damn, Rein, I guess there is a God after all.*

At least, that's the way I see it.

THE END

Made in the USA
San Bernardino, CA
05 February 2016